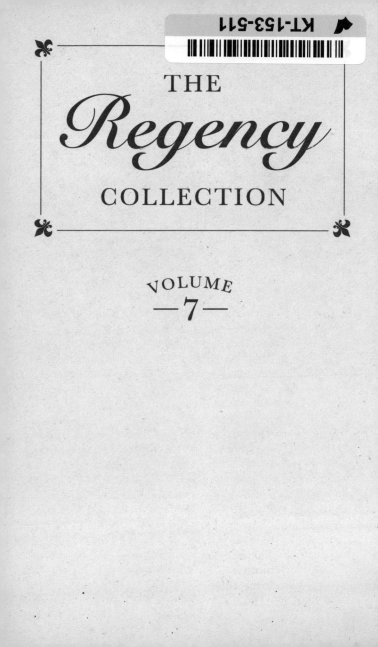

THE

Regency

COLLECTION

VOLUME
—7—

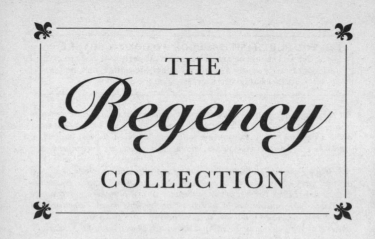

THE
Regency
COLLECTION

VOLUME
—7—

The Cyprian's Sister
by
Paula Marshall

A Compromised Lady
by
Francesca Shaw

DID YOU PURCHASE THIS BOOK WITHOUT A COVER?
If you did, you should be aware it is **stolen property** as it was reported
unsold and destroyed by a retailer. Neither the author nor the publisher has received any payment for this book.

*All the characters in this book have no existence outside the imagination
of the author, and have no relation whatsoever to anyone bearing the same
name or names. They are not even distantly inspired by any individual
known or unknown to the author, and all the incidents are pure invention.*

*All Rights Reserved including the right of reproduction in whole or in part
in any form. This edition is published by arrangement with Harlequin
Enterprises II B.V. The text of this publication or any part thereof may not be
reproduced or transmitted in any form or by any means, electronic or
mechanical, including photocopying, recording, storage in an information
retrieval system, or otherwise, without the written permission of the publisher.*

*This book is sold subject to the condition that it shall not, by way of trade
or otherwise, be lent, resold, hired out or otherwise circulated without the
prior consent of the publisher in any form of binding or cover other than
that in which it is published and without a similar condition including this
condition being imposed on the subsequent purchaser.*

*MILLS & BOON and MILLS & BOON with the Rose Device
are registered trademarks of the publisher.*

*First published in Great Britain 1999 by
Harlequin Mills & Boon Limited,
Eton House, 18–24 Paradise Road,
Richmond, Surrey, TW9 1SR.*

The Regency Collection © by Harlequin Enterprises II B.V. 1999

The publisher acknowledges the copyright holders of the
individual work as follows:

The Cyprian's Sister © Paula Marshall 1993
A Compromised Lady © Francesca Shaw 1995

ISBN 0 263 82351 2
106-9911

*Printed and bound in Spain
by Litografia Rosés S.A., Barcelona*

THE CYPRIAN'S SISTER

by

Paula Marshall

Dear Reader

When I began to write historical romances for Mills & Boon®, I chose the Regency period for several reasons. I had always enjoyed Georgette Heyer's novels—still among the best—and had spent part of my youth working at Newstead Abbey, the home of Lord Byron, one of the Regency's most colourful characters. It involved me in reading many of the original letters and papers of a dynamic era in English history.

Later on when I researched even further into the period I discovered that nothing I could invent was more exciting—or outrageous—than what had actually happened! What more natural, then, than to write a Regency romance and send it to Mills & Boon—who accepted it and started me on a new career.

Like Georgette Heyer I try to create fiction out of and around fact for the enjoyment and entertainment of myself and my readers. It is often forgotten that the Regency men had equally powerful wives, mothers and sisters—even if they had no public role—so I make my heroines able to match my heroes in their wit and courage.

Paula Marshall

Paula Marshall, married with three children, has had a varied and interesting life. She began her career in a large library and ended it as a senior academic in charge of history teaching in a polytechnic. She has travelled widely, has been a swimming coach, embroiders, paints pictures and has appeared on *University Challenge* and *Mastermind*. She has always wanted to write, and likes her novels to be full of adventure and humour.

Other titles by the same author:

* linked
** Schuyler Family saga

+ linked
++ linked

CHAPTER ONE

BEL PASSMORE was sorting papers in her late sister's pretty study, a thoughtful expression on her face. She had just read a letter written only three weeks ago, dated May 21st 1818, a letter which bore out what the great banker Mr Thomas Coutts had told her yesterday afternoon. The letter was still in her hand when there was a knock on the door, and she lifted her head to call, 'A moment, Mrs Hatch, and I will be with you.'

The house she was in, also her late sister's, was a little jewel box, perfectly appointed, filled with treasures. Above the hearth a portrait by Thomas Phillips of that same sister, Mrs Marianne St George, apparently known in London as Marina, presided over the room. Marianne—no, Marina—looked enchanting, a remote, cool goddess; Pallas Athene, goddess of wisdom, rather than Venus, goddess of love, which Bel had just discovered that she had actually been.

Phillips had painted her at night in a grove of trees, a sickle moon showing through them—perhaps, improbably, he had seen her as a chaste Diana, because the Grecian robe she had worn, the jewel in the shape of a half-moon in her hair, and the tiny bow she was holding in one charming little hand, reinforced the notion of a chaste huntress.

Chaste! Bel gave a sharp laugh, and returned to her task, a task which she was determined to finish as soon as possible so that she might return to her own life, after deciding what she was to do with the remarkable fortune which Marianne's lawyers had told her that she had inherited, and which her visits to Thomas Coutts, of Coutts Bank, had confirmed in all its majestic details.

Three short weeks had been sufficient to change her life completely. Impossible to think that it was less than a month since she was living in the pretty village of Brangton in Lincolnshire, a parson's daughter, ignorant of anything but the banal round of pleasures and duties associated with a young and orphaned gentlewoman in the country.

Her life there with an elderly aunt in modest circumstances was made more easy because of the small income regularly sent to her by her widowed sister, living in London, who was happy to help out by remitting to Bel and Aunt Kaye a few modest pennies, as she had put it, when her husband had died, leaving her, she had said, everything.

Bel remembered Marianne's visits—she had to think of her as Marianne; Marina was someone whom Bel had never known. She had arrived, modestly dressed in her decent black, handkerchief to her eyes every time she had mentioned the late Henry St George's name; later, still modest, clothing good, but inexpensive, eyes downcast, visiting old friends, saying that she could not return to Brangton, all her social life was now centred in London.

Aunt Kaye had suggested to Marianne recently when Bel was reaching the age of eighteen that Marianne might like to take Bel back to London with her, introduce her to Marianne's wide circle of friends, perhaps find her a husband with a modest if useful income, since there were few for Bel to marry in Brangton.

Marianne had looked at Bel, charming in a white muslin dress that was dated by London standards, wearing a straw hat with a wide brim, a sash of pale green silk wound round the crown, enhancing the combination of red-gold hair, ivory complexion and brilliant green eyes, with dark arching brows, which were beginning to make Bel a beauty after whom every eye would turn to look—especially as the face was matched with a figure of stunning perfection and grace.

But it was the look of perfect innocence, of candid, unaware charm which gave Bel her greatest distinction and which had made Marianne draw in her breath a little. 'Oh, no,' she had said vaguely, 'I think that Bel is formed for country living—her very name, the one we use, fits her so much more than a Londonised Anne Isabella would. She must marry some good little country gentleman, not some bored townee. Besides, town would ruin those delicate looks.'

Aunt Kaye, Bel thought, remembering this conversation, not many months old, was no fool, even if innocent of the great world.

'But you do not object to living among bored townees, Marianne,' she had said. 'Indeed, your own looks have improved since you left Brangton, not deteriorated.'

'Ah, but I am not Bel,' Marianne had replied incontrovertibly, 'and I can best help Bel by providing her with a good dowry to take with her to her husband, and by your letting it be known that I intend to do so—*that* should serve to encourage gentlemen to come calling, who might be deterred by thinking that Bel is nothing but a poor parson's undowered daughter.'

'Oh,' Bel had said, 'do I really want to marry someone who might not offer for me if he thought that I had only a little to bring him?'

'You have virtually nothing to bring to him without my help, so we must use our common sense and my money,' Marianne had replied, she who usually behaved as though common sense were a virtue she might have heard of, but rarely practised, so airily unworldly had she seemed, 'when it comes to marriage and the setting up of establishments. Even the most virtuous and loving of men would expect his wife to bring something with her to their wedding- day; such a consideration would do him no discredit—quite the reverse. No, Bel must marry here, I insist.'

Well, Bel thought grimly, consigning yet another document to the fire, I now know why Marianne did not wish me to join her in London, and where all the money came from for the last ten years, to keep me in modest comfort, her in luxury, and enable her to leave me a fortune on her untimely death—and what am I to do about the fortune? For after all I am a parson's daughter, and a virtuous one.

But Marianne was a parson's daughter, too, said a tiny voice in her head, and that did not stop her from following the way of life which has enabled us all to live in luxury, instead of being little better than paupers since Papa died six years ago.

'I must think,' she said aloud, on her knees on the hearthrug, then thought, When Marianne visited us, she was so vague and gentle, almost other-wordly, so very much the parson's elder daughter that we assumed that she led a quiet life in London, full of good works and virtue; we were perhaps a little surprised that she did not remarry, to have someone to shelter her from the harsh realities of life.

The harsh realities of life! And what a joke that was. She remembered the letter arriving from the lawyers, to tell her that Marianne was dead, had died of a fulminating illness of the stomach, quite suddenly, after being in perfect health, and that Bel was her sole heir, and it was to be expected that she would visit London to settle 'your sister's considerable estate'.

That had been the first puzzle, 'considerable estate'. Marianne had always said that her fortune, which her husband had left her, was modest, had sighed that she could only dower Bel with a few thousands, and the papers for that, which had not been completed before her death, were waiting for her, Bel had learned when she reached London, her signature not now needed, since she had inherited all.

Bel had gone to London, leaving Aunt Kaye behind—that lady's rheumatics were troubling her more than usual—taking with her only her elderly maid, Lottie, as a dragon to repel boarders, as Marianne had said of her guardianship of Bel on her last visit—a piece of London slang, not too polite, she had added on Aunt Kaye raising her eyebrows a little.

The first surprise had been Marianne's home, in Stanhope Street, near the Park, now named after the Prince Regent. Bel had expected something small and modest, not the splendour of the house in a row which was obviously occupied by upper gentry, if not to say minor members of the nobility—a house near by, she discovered, had been occupied by Viscount Granville and his family.

The next surprise was the luxury of the furnishings, more splendid than anything Bel had ever seen before, paintings, tapestries, china, silver, bibelots, the three bedrooms also perfectly appointed, the small study so elegant, with its break-front bookcases, Buhl desk, cabinets of cameos and porcelains; the whole place reeked of wealth.

The two servants left—the rest had been discharged after Marianne's death—were a housekeeper and a maid of all work. The housekeeper was as close-mouthed as Lottie, and the little servant girl was the same—even Lottie complained that their conversation with her was limited to yes, no, and perhaps.

At first, nothing seemed untoward, except that, on seeing her immediate neighbours when leaving the house to visit the solicitors, Bel had bowed to them, a man and a woman, and they had both turned their backs on her. Perhaps, she thought, that was London manners, and then she remembered that when she had visited the church on the following Sunday, and those same neighbours had been there, the whole congregation had stared at her when she entered, and again when she left, and although the parson had greeted her his reception of her had been cool, and the whole thing had left an odd taste in her mouth.

And then the solicitors, Fancourt and Hirst. *That* had been most disturbing. On giving her name to a man in a kind of sentry box at a very grand office in Lincoln's Inn, he had stared at her in the most frank manner, almost insolent, waved her in with a quill, and, although she could not fault the grave gentlemen who had interviewed her and had informed her of the stunning size of her sister's bequest, there had been something distinctly odd about their manner.

Finally, all the papers signed and she having been given the address of Coutts Bank which she needed to visit to sign still further papers to take possession of her sister's account there, one of the two men, the younger one, had leaned forward and asked her, almost a grin on his face, 'I must enquire, madam, do you intend to keep on the business?'

'The business?' she had faltered, her wits, she thought afterwards, a little addled by the shock of her sister's sudden death, and the magnitude of what she had inherited. 'Pray, what business is that?' For she had not seen any evidence of a business in Stanhope Street, was only aware that Marianne had lived on what her wealthy husband had left her.

'Oh, come. . .' began Mr Hirst, to have a detaining hand put on his arm by the older man, Mr Fancourt, who said, very courteously,

'We must leave Miss Passmore to her grief, my dear Hirst. Time enough for her to think of other matters later,' and he bowed her out, both of them going through the polite rituals demanded in such circumstances.

Other matters? What could he mean? Bel thought. Happily her meeting with Mr Thomas Coutts was not so mysterious, that gentleman being a model of polite regret for her grief and congratulation on her great good fortune.

But even he looked at her keenly, enquired after her country circumstances, and then said, quietly, 'I expect that you will be going through your sister's papers when you return to Stanhope Street. It is of all things essential that you do so speedily. If. . .' and he hesitated '. . .if, after doing so, you feel that you require. . . assistance. . .pray do not hesitate to call on me.'

Bel took the puzzle home with her, for it to be resolved when she opened Marianne's desk, and began to look through her papers. Mr Coutts had given her a letter from Marianne, which she read before she did so. The letter was also baffling, and she read it twice, in some wonder.

Dear Bel

If you are reading this, I shall have died suddenly, without ever having told you my true circumstances which have enabled me to leave you what I hope is a more than modest competency. You will find some of the answers in the letters and papers in my desk, but the real meat of the matter is to be found in a secret cupboard behind the books on the second shelf in the right-hand hearth alcove in my study. It is for you to do what you wish with what you find. The cupboard is well hidden, but if you place a firm finger on the exact middle of the central panel, and push, it will open and you will find there—what you will find.

It was obvious to Bel that Marianne did not wish to put anything on paper, even in a letter reposing in Coutts Bank!

Having opened the desk, to find pigeon-holes stuffed

with letters and papers, most of them apparently innocuous, if a little cryptic, she moved to the alcove,
removed the books on the second shelf and did as her
sister bid—to discover a cupboard, crammed with documents, two ledgers, plus a small cedarwood box.

Bel removed everything from the cupboard, and
began to read through it, with mounting incredulity
and a face which flushed hotter and hotter with every
passing word.

Brutally and briefly she learned that her apparently
modest sister had been a courtesan, a Cyprian, of the
first stare. Far from having married the man whom she
had met when a companion in London, Henry St
George, she had been seduced by him, and then
deserted, but left with a small apartment and a lump
sum, both parting presents, his letter said, 'to one who
has pleased me, but from whom my marriage now
debars me.'

Bel read the first page of Marianne's ledger.

I was not deterred by this betrayal—seeing that it
was the second which I suffered—his refusal to
marry me after ruining me being the first. For I
decided that with the money I had saved, and what
he gave me on parting, I would set myself up as a
Cyprian of the first water, my talents seeming to lie
that way, and offering me a better living than being
a governess or companion ever could. From then on,
I concentrated on milking men of their money, as
they have milked me of virtue and reputation.
Marina St George, I called myself—the second name
to punish *him*, and the first because it carried no
taint for the family I felt compelled to support. If
you ever read this, dear Bel, forgive me.

The ledgers and the letters proved that Marianne
had carried out her intent by virtue of her sexual
accomplishment and her business brain—for not only

had she charged high rates and accepted magnificent presents from a select band of wealthy and titled lovers, but she had also lent money at extortionate rates of interest to those less wealthy, and furthermore, to Bel's fascinated horror, she had blackmailed many of the great men who had enjoyed her favours secretly while preserving their reputation to the world, by threatening to expose them, if not further recompensed.

Although they had not known the full extent of Marianne's career, her neighbours had certainly known that she was a courtesan, thus explaining their behaviour to Bel and that of her lawyers, as well as Mr Coutts's offer of help should she feel that she needed it. He had rightly seen Bel as the chaste and innocent girl she was—so like Marianne as she had been before she left to become the companion to a lady of wealthy family in Bruton Street.

The cedarwood box contained love-letters from a person of such high standing that Bel consigned them to the fire without reading other than the first—but it was apparent that Marianne had also acquired a fair fortune from him—and he had commissioned the Phillips portrait and presented it to her.

Oh, yes, Marianne's fortune was fully explained.

The other ledger detailed her income and its sources, and the documents consisted of the incriminating letters of her powerful lovers, who seemed impelled, thought Bell critically, to immortalise their folly on paper, unaware that each was only one of many whom Marianne was remorselessly persecuting.

What now exercised Bel was whether she should accept a fortune made by such methods at all. Was it right, was it proper, that she, a virtuous young person of good family, the daughter of a parson, the great-granddaughter, through her mother, of an Earl, should live on such ill-gotten gains, not only the fruits of vice, but of blackmail and usury? Would it not, perhaps, be better to give the whole lot to a home for fallen women, leaving herself and Aunt Kaye a pittance to live on? Would such an act be quixotic, rather than virtuous? She could not tell. Oh, dear, she thought, can Marianne's dreadful example be infecting me?

She had taken the puzzle to Mr Coutts, confirmed from him that Marianne had indeed been a notorious courtesan—the most famous in London when she had so unfortunately died, he said, who was able to pick and choose her lovers. He was not at all surprised by the fortune which she had amassed.

'Your sister's understanding was excellent,' he had said. 'Unlike many young women in her condition, she did not waste the—er—fruits of her labour. She consulted me frequently on financial matters, made many wise investments, and I see no reason why you should refuse your unexpected good fortune.'

Well, that was as may be, Bel had thought, but she had listened to him carefully when he had told her that if she proposed to retire to the country again, as she had informed him she would, then it might be advisable to go through Marianne's papers and dispose of most of them.

It was this advice that she was busy carrying out when she heard a violent knocking at the door. The letter which she was examining was from a young man infatuated with Marianne, to whom she had lent several thousand pounds at an extortionate rate of interest, and he was begging further time to pay, having already paid over a sum in interest larger than the principal! It was apparent that Marianne had been a skilful usurer as well as a whore. Bel felt quite faint at the thought, remembering her sister's delicate charm and apparent innocence.

She kept the housekeeper waiting while she bundled the ledgers and most of the documents back into the cupboard, rapidly replacing the books, finally calling, 'Come in,' to repeated impatient bangings.

Mrs Hatch, the grim-faced woman whom Bel suspected of being Marianne's watchdog, said, 'Lord Francis Carey to see you, madam, if you are At Home.'

And who the devil was Lord Francis Carey? thought Bel rapidly, seeing that his name had not been on any of the documents she had read, nor was he listed in Marianne's business ledger, so crammed with the names of the rich and the powerful; but, before she could ask, Mrs Hatch was brushed to one side and a large gentleman entered, saying impatiently, 'I have no time to waste, madam, even though I am sure that your day is free for all the folly you may care to carry out,' and, pushing Mrs Hatch, protesting, through the door and out of the room, he shut it behind him, and turned to Bel, to say grimly, 'And now, madam, let us come to terms, and quickly. From what I have heard of you, you are not backward in demanding your pound of flesh, so let us get down to it, at once, and no skimble-skamble, if you please, for I know exactly what you are, and am not to be bought off by anything you can offer—either your person, or your promises!'

CHAPTER TWO

WHAT Bel saw at first glance was the hardest, haughtiest man's face which she had ever encountered. A pair of grey eyes, as cold as a wintry sea, were set beneath thin arched eyebrows in a face as imperious as an eagle's. The mouth was as firm and cruel as a mantrap's jaws, and his blue-black hair was cut fashionably short, adding to an almost imperial presence.

He was slightly over six feet tall, his body was beautifully proportioned, and he held himself as though he knew it. He possessed broad shoulders, a deep chest, a narrow waist and hips, with long legs ending in the inevitably perfect boots of a youngish gentleman of high fashion. She judged him to be in his early thirties.

He moved towards her with a superb arrogance, the habit of command so strong in him that it seemed as though everyone else was put on earth to be his servant and to carry out his orders.

Bel hated him on sight. His face, his body and his clothes were all anathema to her. And to address her as he did! He deserved, and would get, no quarter.

'To what,' she enquired, her voice poisonously sweet, 'do I owe the honour of your visit, sir?'

'No honour is intended, madam,' he replied, and his voice was acid, corrosive, vitriol to shrivel her and all that she stood for. 'I can assure you of that.'

'Oh, then,' said Bel, her voice still so sweet it was nauseating, cloying, 'to what do I owe the pleasure?' She would not be put down by insult, not at all. It was plain to her that he had mistaken her for Marianne, and she did not intend to enlighten him—yet.

'No pleasure either, madam,' he said grimly. 'I must insist that I take no pleasure in consorting with such a one as you. Only the direst necessity would bring me to this—house,' and the look he cast on the pretty room would have had it bursting into flames, so fierce was it.

'Oh, that is of all things the most convenient,' responded Bel, who was discovering in herself a fund of nastiness which she had not been aware that she possessed, but by all the gods of legend he deserved every unpleasant word which she flung back at him, 'seeing that I feel the same about you, sir, which makes us quits.'

The fine eyebrows drew together and rose alarmingly; the mouth thinned even further. 'I have no wish to be quits with you, madam, no wish to know you at all.. .other than for a quite obvious and brief purpose. . .'

'Nor I to honour or to. . .pleasure, you, sir,' Bel threw at him when he paused a little for breath, 'and it would satisfy me greatly if you quit my house on the instant. My only regret is that I possess no footmen to drive you from my presence. Pray leave at once!'

He made no effort to leave, merely said, through his excellent teeth, 'I had not heard that you were impudent, madam; on the contrary, I was told that you dripped honey. I see that, as usual, rumour lied.'

Bel might remain outwardly cool, but she was seething inside. How dared he? Oh, how dared he? To say that he wanted her only for one purpose, and that briefly—in direst necessity, indeed! For Bel was not so innocent that she had not caught the insult.

'Come to the point, sir, I beg of you. Philosophic discussion on the nature or otherwise of my conversational powers is a digression I do not wish to encourage—unless, of course, we move on to the nature of *your* manners towards a lady—or rather the lack of them!'

'Lady, Mrs Marina St George? Lady? What lady seduces a very young man, and then gets him into her financial toils—with blackmail threatened? A whore, madam, a very whore. By God, were I not a man of some honour I would take you on the instant, unrecompensed, as your payment for criminal conduct. Be grateful that I neither do that, nor send for the Runners.'

'All this puffery, sir,' riposted Bel contemptuously, 'directed towards the wrong quarter. I fear you are a little behindhand. I am not Mrs St George. You may observe—it cannot have escaped your notice, so eagle-eyed as you are—that I am wearing black. I am, sir, her younger sister, up from the country.'

Lord Francis stared at her contemptuously, took in the whole enchanting picture—the ivory skin, green eyes, red-gold curls, enhanced, not diminished by the depth of her mourning black.

'Oh, madam, I thought by the colour and cut that it had been one of Marina's conceits! Up from the country, you say? I assume that you have been practising there the profession which your sister so successfully followed in the town! No matter, I will deal with you instead. By the state of this room you are settling your sister's affairs. You may settle this one—with me.'

'I will settle with my principal, sir, since I gather that you are not he,' Bel flung at him, white to the lips, the temper, signalled by her red hair, so strong in her that she wished that she were a man, to call him out, or 'plant a facer on him', as Garth, the vicar's son with whom she had played as a child, had gravely informed her, when he had been wild with a schoolboy's ambition to be a bruiser of quality.

'Indeed you will not. The young fool could not protect himself against your late sister, and since you seem, by your tongue, to be an even greater scorpion than she was, it is my duty, if not my pleasure, to see you off.'

See her off! By God—for Bel's internal language was growing more unladylike by the minute—she would see *him* off, if it were the last thing she did.

Tactics! Tactics! What served her on the chessboard might, inexperienced as she was, serve her in life.

She sank down into her chair, clasped her forehead with her left hand, picked up her quill with her right, spoke in faltering accents, quite unlike her recent fiery speech.

'Forgive me, sir,' she achieved. 'I am quite overset; my sister's sudden death, the long journey here, the lawyers, and now. . .this. . .' And she heaved a dramatic sigh.

Lord Francis, a man not to be easily caught by anyone, as all London could have informed Bel, stared suspiciously at this transformation, not softened at all by the tear-drenched green eyes which were now raised towards him.

'Oh, we are singing a different tune now, madam, are we? What brought this about—the threat of the Runners, or a sudden access of common sense?'

'Neither, sir. The knowledge that. . .shouting at each other will not bring us to a conclusion, and I am anxious that this transaction of which you speak should be concluded. If you will please give me the name of the young man of whom you speak, and explain your relationship to him.'

Francis Carey, a man who temporised with nobody, was certainly not prepared to be temporised with by a whore on the make, as he judged Bel to be, but he decided that if madam's opposition had collapsed so dramatically she was either engaged in tricking him, or had given way before his own intransigence. That being

so, he decided to finish by being as brutally frank as he
had begun.

'My nephew, madam, Mark—Marcus—Carey,
Viscount Tawstock, who, I admit, is the veriest fool,
having been over-indulged by a stupid mother——' *Did
Lord Francis Carey like nobody?* was Bel's immediate
and uncharitable thought, masked by a heaving bosom,
showing for the first time a maidenly distress which she
did not actually feel '—came upon the Town last year,
and among other follies became embroiled with your
sister——' he almost spat the word at her '—conceived
that he was passionately in love with her, proposed to
make her Viscountess Tawstock, save the mark, and
was foolish enough not only to write her a proposal of
marriage but to borrow money from her, having
thrown away his allowance on the gaming tables.'

He paused for breath, and about time too, thought
Bel, busy deciding what to do next—for the letter
relating to the money borrowed by Marcus Carey was
the one which she had been reading when his uncle
arrived, and somewhere in Marianne's secret store she
was sure his letter of proposal—useless now—existed.

No matter; Lord Francis had obviously come here,
not knowing of Marianne's death—and where had he
been, not to know that?—to frighten Marianne away,
and was still, not knowing that she, Bel, was no threat,
trying to warn Bel off, presumably frightened that she
would continue with Lord Tawstock what Marianne
had begun.

For one delirious moment she contemplated 'going
into the business', and doing so. Her own strong sense
of rectitude, her revulsion for the life which poor
Marianne had apparently perforce chosen stifled the
unworthy thought at birth. But this arrogant monster
deserved to be taught a lesson, and somehow she
would teach him one.

She fumbled among the papers on the desk, although

well aware that the relevant letter was placed immediately before her. No matter; let him think her disorganised, scatter-brained. She appeared to find it at last, waved it distractedly at him. 'Forgive me, sir, I am not *au fait* with such matters. I am not sure whether in inheriting my sister's estate I have inherited the right to the monies owing to her—but whether that be so or not,' she added hastily, seeing him about to open his mouth, 'I am sure that you would not wish to see these papers, or the love-letters and proposal which he made to my sister, published to the world as an example of his folly.' And that, your haughty lordship, is a pretty threat to make, is it not? She continued rapidly again, 'That being so, I am prepared to return all the papers to you in return for some service which *you* might do *me*—but I am a little exercised as to the nature of the payment.'

She stopped, smiling sweetly at him through her tears, aware that for the first time she had wrong-footed him.

'You are?' he said glacially, but against his will suddenly fascinated by the sheer impudence of the young woman opposite him.

'Yes,' replied Bel, outwardly appearing to recover from her recent distress, and inwardly beginning to enjoy herself. Where, she thought, was all this coming from? From what hidden depths was this dreadfully devious behaviour emerging?

'You see, reading over Marina's papers, and being aware, by hearsay, of course, that to be a... Cyprian of the very first stare is different from offering such a ...service in the countryside, I need a little advice if I am to carry on poor Marina's...business...success-fully. Who better than to perform such a service for me, by tutoring me, as it were, than such a one as you, so obviously *au fait* with everything as you are? And then you could have your nephew's...indiscretions back, and we shall all be happy, not least yourself, having performed such a pleasant and trifling service to gain your ends. Your patronage would help to ensure my success.' And she fluttered her eyelashes at him, quaking inside at her wicked daring, for his face had grown still, and slightly flushed as he took in what she was saying.

'By God, madam, are you proposing that I should be your pander?'

'No, indeed, not at all,' replied Bel, obviously prettily agitated at the very thought. 'Just the one service, small indeed, which you might. . .perform for me. And after all, you cannot pretend that gentlemen hesitate to recommend pleasing. . .ladybirds. . .to their friends. I have been instructed quite otherwise. That is all that is necessary for you to gain what you want. Our intercourse would then be at an end. . .unless, of course, you wished to be a regular client. I might allow a discount for *that*.'

Bel had the delight of seeing him rendered almost tongue-tied by her insolence. What she did not understand was that a pair of green eyes, red hair and a superb figure, allied to a ready wit, were beginning to work their magic on even such a hardened specimen as Francis Carey, who had long told himself that women, virtuous or loose, played no part in his life.

Desire roared through him, so suddenly and unexpectedly that he almost gasped. This. . .lightskirt, so fresh and seemingly virginal, had roused in him passions he had long thought extinct.

If he were honest, from the moment he had first seen her, so unlike the brass-faced creature of his imaginings, she had aroused the strangest stirrings in him. As a result of the effect the lovely eyes, the smiling mouth, the air of virtue—denied to some extent by her ready repartee with its hint of forbidden knowledge—had had on him he had become immensely

taken with her, which to some extent explained the
coarse cynicism with which he had spoken to her, in an
attempt to deny her attractions.

Oh, no, he had no wish to be tempted by a woman
again, particularly by a deceptive little bit of muslin
working her practised tricks on him!

But tempted he was. His hands curled by his sides; if
he had answered her immediately his voice would have
been thick with long-suppressed desire—no, lust, it
must be simple lust which gripped him, the result of
long continence. And now that continence was at risk,
and he had the most overpowering wish to take her
into his arms, to make love to her until that charming
face was soft with fulfilled passion beneath him... He
must be going mad to think such thoughts, but yes,
improbably, he was going to consent to what she had
suggested.

He told himself sternly that he was merely doing so
to dig young Marcus out of the pit into which he had
been pushed by that hellcat her sister—but that was
not the truth—he knew better than that, and, worst of
all, he was so roused that he wanted her now, this very
minute, on the carpet even, no time to wait. He savagely bit the inside of his mouth, to feel it fill with
blood, anything to assuage the actual physical pain he
was feeling. And now she was speaking again, mocking
him.

'Silent, sir? You were voluble enough a moment
ago.'

'Your impudence serves to silence me, madam, and
I also need to consider your proposition.'

'Do not take too long,' Bel could not resist taunting
him, her tone a trifle pert, but none the worse for that,
she thought. 'The post awaits. Mr Leigh Hunt might
like this prime piece of scandal for his news-sheet—
another member of the aristocracy to expose.'

Francis Carey did not know which he wanted to do

more—strike her, or push her against the wall to take his pleasure. His normally restrained behaviour, so long practised that it had become a habit, saved him.

She was speaking again. 'I own that I am not too sure how exactly to converse with those of the first flight. By your own grasp of language you seem to be well enough informed to instruct me in that a little, too.'

Francis found his voice at last. 'Conversation, madam? You wish me to instruct you in conversation also?'

'By all means. I understand that these days lively repartee, as well as. . .expertise. . .elsewhere, is much in demand among the gentlemen who will be my. . . clients. I know I can supply the main part of the business, but conversation. . .of *that* I am not so sure.'

Francis succeeded in curling his lip, and achieving normal-sounding speech, something of a feat in the state to which he had been reduced. 'Oh, I would not have thought, madam, that you would have any difficulty in that department, on the evidence of our *conversazione* so far,' and then before she could answer him, 'As to your proposition, madam, yes, I find it. . .agreeable to me. I am willing to. . .tutor you. At once would be. . .most pleasing to me. Fortunately I am at a loose end at the moment—I am usually a busy man. I take it that the house is in readiness for . . .visitors; we could set to straight away.'

This was not at all to Bel's taste. She had no intention of allowing this arrogant brute to as much as touch her, and in her inexperience did not know the degree to which she had stirred him—almost dangerously.

'Oh, no,' she said sadly, bringing a fine lace handkerchief into play, 'not so near in time to my discovery of my sister's death. It would be improper, as you would surely agree——'

Not so improper, thought Francis, savagely, as leaving me in the state to which you have reduced me, but compelled to nod, since speech seemed suddenly beyond him again, as the houri's luminous green eyes did their work on him.

'No, you must allow me a week to recover. I need at least that...to do myself justice.'

You need nothing, was his unspoken reply, for I am the one to do myself justice, and that I could do on the instant, but decency...yet where was decency in all this? For she had bought him, not he her, by the promise of Marcus's incriminating papers in exchange for his body—for that was what their bargain amounted to.

Bel peeped at him over her handkerchief, and was not too innocent to understand that Lord Francis was in a fine pelter over something—surely the man could wait a week to sample her? No, she decided, ten days, time for her to arrange to get clear away, for she had no intention of keeping any bargain which she might make with him. He, and every other fine gentleman who had enjoyed her sister, and the other unfortunate women who sold their bodies for money, could pay for his lust. That she wronged Lord Francis a little she was not to know, and in the mood she was in the knowledge would have made no difference to her.

'Ten days,' she said, and then dropped her face into her handkerchief, sobbing, and the sobs were not all counterfeit, for she found that she was suddenly weeping for the lost sister whom she had never really known. 'Ten days; you can give me that, surely.'

Francis wanted to give her nothing, but the thought of the double gain—Marcus's papers, and the enjoyment of the woman before him—spurred him on. He nodded, reluctantly.

'Ah,' breathed Bel, putting down the handkerchief and picking up the quill pen again, 'we have a bargain, I see. Your nephew's papers in exchange for my...

instruction at your hands,' and she began to write, affecting a die-away air that had him all the more hot for her, every expression on her vital face beginning to affect him strangely.

'Allow me to make a note.' And she continued to write nonsense on the paper before her, anything to keep him hanging on in suspense, since it was plain that he had changed dramatically from the violently aggressive man who had forced his way into Marina's study.

Common sense suddenly hit Francis hard over the head, stifling the demanding pangs of desire which he suddenly understood had been rendering him foolish. Why he did not know, but something in her posture, some hint of mockery affected him. With one bound he was over by the desk, and had wrenched the paper on which she was writing from her.

He read it, stared at it, then, 'Three blind mice,' he read, 'written in a fine scholarly hand—an educated whore, by God.' Rage mixed with lust, a totally delightful but potent sensation, had him in its thrall. 'Why, you bitch, what games are you playing with me?'

His aspect was suddenly so frightening that Bel quailed. She realised that she was going too far, did not want to be raped in Marianne's study, for now she could see what the poet called 'the lineaments of desire' plainly written on his face. Half of her was triumphant at the sight—oh, yes, he wanted Bel Passmore, did he not, but he would never get her, that was for sure—and the other half was fearful at what she might have provoked.

'No games,' she said. 'I was merely writing to. . .keep myself steady.'

'And if I take you at your word, madam, then you will not cheat me?'

'No,' replied Bel, and this was not, she told herself, truly a lie, for, although she had no intention of keeping any rendezvous with him, neither did she ever intend to use Marcus Carey's indiscretions on paper, or his borrowing of money from Marianne, against him or his uncle.

'So,' said Francis, much against his will, though his will, for once, was weak, 'I shall be here on the first of June at three o'clock of the afternoon, at your wish, madam, and afterwards you will give me everything on paper pertaining to Marcus Carey, Viscount Tawstock, and his debts will be cancelled.'

Bel crossed her fingers under the desk, met his eyes with her own, greenly limpid, and thinking, God forgive me, said, 'Yes, a bargain.'

'Good.' He turned on his heel, gave her one last searing look, threw at her, '*Auf Wiedersehen*, madam, until we meet again,' and was gone through the door, leaving Bel to fall forward, drained, across the desk — only for her, a moment later, to sit up smartly again.

Well, one thing was sure. There was no question of her giving up Marianne's wealth now; she would live on it in comfort if only to put out her tongue at every member of the male sex who saw fit to exploit women, and damn them all, and that self-righteous monster Lord Francis Carey the most of all. Self-righteous! Why, the brute could hardly wait to get his hands on her. Another hypocrite unveiled.

What a pity she could not see his face when he arrived to find her gone!

Francis Carey, that man of discretion, probity and, as Bel Passmore had immediately seen, damned arrogance, arrived back at Hathersage House just off the Strand, where his older half-brother, Jack, paralysed and dumb these last three years since a riding accident, still lived, leaving his unsatisfactory wife Louisa to try to check the unwelcome excesses of her son Marcus, who had gone to the dogs the moment he had achieved

the age of twenty-one and been relieved of his uncle's
guardianship.

The Carey family, or rather the senior members of
it, comprising the paralysed Marquis of Hathersage, his
wife and only child, were as poor as church mice;
ironically, the only wealthy member of the family was
Francis himself, the late Marquis's child by his third
wife, whose vast estates had been settled at the time of
her marriage on any male child she might bear.

This unusual turn of circumstances was fortunate,
for the Marquis, almost in his dotage, had been so set
on marrying her that he had agreed to these unequal
terms, with the result that Francis's inheritance had not
been swallowed up on the gaming tables where his
father had spent the last years of his life disposing of
his once great wealth—which he had wrongly assumed
to be bottomless.

To Marcus's resentment of his uncle as guardian was
added his further resentment of his uncle as the
wealthy man which he was not.

He was in the big shabby drawing-room, standing
over his weeping mother, when Francis came in to tell
her that she need not worry overmuch, he had come to
an agreement with Marina St George's sister and heiress, and Marcus's name was saved.

Marcus was not grateful. 'What the devil's all this,
sir?' he exclaimed rudely. 'Who gave you leave to deal
with my debts? The whore is dead, and can persecute
me no longer, nor her doxy of a sister either.'

Francis winced: when another used the language
with which he had recently abused the St George's
sister, he disliked the ugly sound of it.

'You are mistaken, sir,' he replied stiffly. 'The
woman was in a position to do you a mischief. You
were not to be found, and your mother was agitated
on your behalf, so I attempted to bring the sister off. I

think that I have succeeded, but of course I do not expect gratitude.'

'No, indeed,' said Marcus unpleasantly. 'Interfering again, I see. What was the sister like?' he enquired eagerly, more concerned with that than with his new safety from scandal and ridicule, his uncle noted with disgust.

'What you might expect,' said Francis, lying through his teeth. He had, unexpectedly, no wish for his nephew to be chasing Miss... He suddenly realised that, for all his cleverness, he had no idea of the name of Marina St George's sister!

Marcus flung away. For all that he was not so many years younger than his uncle, who was the child of his grandfather's old age, he seemed a boy beside him, his mother thought dismally, remembering what Francis had been at Marcus's age. But then Francis had probably been born old and steady and high-handed, although his high-handedness had usefully saved Mark from more than one scrape. She always called him Mark, so much warmer than cold, classical Marcus, she thought.

Francis was a little worried that the name of the houri whom he was to bed in ten days' time was unknown to him. But what of that? Meanwhile Louisa moaned and sighed at him, bade Mark thank his uncle, advised him to be more like Francis, at which Marcus glowered at his uncle and flung out of the room—to the devil, his uncle supposed wryly, unaware that that same monster of truth and probity whose praises his mother was singing was glumly contemplating the acres of time which would have to pass before he saw the St George's sister again!

As in the pretty study where he had met her, he thought once more that he was taking leave of his senses. He was in England for only a few weeks, having come over from the Paris Embassy, where he was stationed as an attaché, for some instructions relating to the parlous state of Europe in the aftermath of the Napoleonic wars.

Everything seemed to be going wrong at once, he decided, both publicly and privately. How could he be in such a damned taking over a pretty little Cyprian who would always sell herself to the highest bidder; and why could he not work this unwonted state of passionate arousal off on any piece of muslin in a nighthouse, or in a private love-nest?

But he knew that he couldn't. Fastidious to a degree, he was only too well aware that after years of Puritanical abstinence the lure of a green-eyed, red-haired witch with a provoking smile and tongue had been too much for him. Oh, well, he would probably feel better in the morning, would have returned to his senses, be his usual self, might even reconsider the bargain, except that in some strange way honour seemed to be involved in that, too.

Not only could he not let Marcus down, but he had pledged his word to her, and what a joke that was— honour to a courtesan!

But he felt no better in the morning, nor the following morning, or any other morning afterwards, and while he was sitting in committee-rooms, talking with grave, black-coated gentlemen about what was happening in Spain, Italy, passing on his unsatisfactory master's messages, being deferred to by some, given orders by others, a pair of bewitching green eyes haunted him.

And on the final day, a sunny one, June the first, 'the Glorious First of June,' that great sea battle, he remembered—naturally so, because he had been an officer in the navy in the late wars—he dressed himself as carefully as a green boy going to meet his love, instead of a seasoned man preparing to bed a damned cheating whore, a phrase he used to mock at his own unlikely passion.

Driving to Stanhope Street, he doffed his hat at passers-by whom he knew, mentally rehearsed what he would say and do when he was with her, burning to see her, to hold her in his arms, to…do all the unspeakable things with her which he had not done to a woman for years, and finally drove down the street in a swelter of desire to the St Georges' house—to stare at drawn blinds, shuttered windows, and a board outside, advertising that the house was for sale!

He threw the reins to his tiger, Cassius, a nickname given to him in jest because of his lean and hungry look, like Shakespeare's murderer of the same name in *Julius Caesar*, and half ran to the front door, to bang the knocker on the door in a tattoo sufficient to wake the dead.

A well-dressed fellow emerged from the next house to stare at him, since no one answered, and a strange slow rage, quite unlike any he had ever experienced before, began to consume him.

He hailed the fellow imperiously, to receive an equally imperious stare in return. 'I see that the house is for sale,' he managed, with reasonable equanimity. 'Do I infer from that that the occupants have left?'

The fellow's stare grew lubricious. 'Why, sir,' he began, 'if you have business with the new doxy, you will be disappointed, I fear,' and then stopped dead in gasping fright as Francis leaned over the railings to seize him by his stock with such force that he was half strangled.

'And damn you, sir,' said Francis in a deadly whisper, 'give me a straight answer, a yes or no; I want no damned moral sermons from strangers who do not know my business.' And he released the man just enough to allow him to croak from his half-ruined throat.

'Pardon me, sir, but they all departed forty-eight hours agone, in a hired coach, and the furniture went after them, but where they went I have no knowledge, nor any wish to know. Too happy to see them go, and their gentlemen friends with them.'

Gone! Francis suddenly had total recall of that mocking, mischievous face, and knew that she, who-ever she was, had never had the slightest intention of honouring the unlovely bargain which she had made with him.

The rage which swept over him, as he stood there, frustrated, was of an order which he had never experi-enced before. He loosened his grip on the man, said savagely, 'Stay a moment, until I give you leave to go,' and stared at the blank windows. He did not even know her name, nor where she came from, nor how to find her. Her lawyers, her bankers, the real name of Marina St George—he was sure that it was a pseudo-nym—were alike unknown to him.

He only knew that in his baffled desire he felt murderous enough to kill her for the trick she had played on him, and that if he ever met her again he would make madam pay for what she had done after a fashion she would never forget.

Hell knew no fury like a woman scorned, said the old proverb, but what of the scorned man? What pity did that man stand in? What flames of frustration consumed him? And why should he feel such insensate anger towards a woman with whom he had only spoken for a few short minutes?

He turned towards the man he had cowed with his ferocity. 'Do you know by what name the woman who came to live here after Mrs St George's death passed?'

The man was pleased to thwart him. 'Indeed no, sir,' he smirked. 'I am happy to inform you that I have, and had, no wish to have truck with any such creatures!'

'Then damn you for a mealy-mouthed, canting swine, who probably takes his pleasure in alleys,' replied Francis savagely, nothing gentlemanly left in his make-up, he thought dismally when he finally returned to Hathersage House. He seemed lost to decency and proper conduct, he who was usually known for the correctitude of his behaviour and his keen sense of honour. The red-headed witch had deprived him of both.

But she had forgotten something in her desire to humiliate Francis Carey, to leave him in a cold stew of frustrated lust. The bill of sale on the house gave him the name of the agent who was selling it, and who would be aware of the owner's identity, and he drove there at speed to trace the bitch who had cheated him so vilely.

To find a dead end; for the house had been placed on the market in the name of Coutts, the banker, and Francis knew full well that were he to visit Thomas Coutts, whom he knew quite well, indeed banked with, that gentleman would tell him nothing, if such were the instructions of his client.

And so it proved. Mr Coutts welcomed Lord Francis, served him sherry and biscuits, asked after his career, but on Francis's enquiring about the property in Stanhope Street which the banking house had placed on the market Mr Coutts had regretfully shaken his head, and told him that his client had demanded strict confidentiality. He could tell my lord nothing. Another dead end: the witch had disappeared into the obscurity from whence she had emerged.

Of course, if he had ever met Marina St George, so that he had known at once that it was not her to whom he was talking when he had thrust his way into the study, then things might, just might, have been different.

He told Marcus later that he was probably safe, and would hear nothing more of his letters or his debts, for he judged, correctly, that the vanishing lightskirt had been so careful of her name and her circumstances because she wished to disappear completely, probably to set herself up elsewhere, trap fools, and laugh at them behind her hand when she had succeeded in duping and frustrating them.

But oh, my dear madam, he promised her that night as he made ready for bed, his whole body one mass of frustrated and unfulfillable desire, if ever I meet you again, then beware, for revenge is sweet, and it shall be as slow and long as I can contrive to make it!

CHAPTER THREE

'Now, my dear Bel,' said Lady Almeria Harley to her best friend, Mrs Bel Merrick, that charming red-headed widow whom every eligible male who lived in or visited Lulsgate Spa had tried to woo or win at some time or other in the two years which she had lived there, 'you are not to make faces at me. It is time that you were married again. A pretty woman needs her own establishment, a kind husband, and a brood of handsome children. If Henry Venn is not good enough for you, then there are half a dozen delightful fellows who would be only too happy to take you in matrimony.'

'No doubt,' retorted Bel, smiling and holding up the pretty little baby's gown she was busy sewing, 'but I dare swear that when you came to marry it was not one of a half-dozen or so delightful fellows, but your own dear Philip Harley whom you chose to accept. I promise you that when I find someone who means to me what Philip so obviously does to you I will snap him up on the instant, but until then I shall remain a widow. After all, I am still not yet twenty-one, and would like to enjoy my single state a little longer, seeing——' crossing her fingers surreptitiously as she spoke '—that I enjoyed it for so short a time before I was married.'

Bel marvelled once again at her own powers of deceit. Sometimes her own duplicity, her powers of invention, frightened her, but she always felt the need to protect herself. After she had fled London, leaving behind, with the help of Thomas Coutts, no clue to her identity, she had returned briefly to Brangton with a faithful and silent Lottie, having pensioned off Mrs

Hatch and given the little maid enough for a dowry, to find Aunt Kaye rapidly failing.

She never told her of what Marianne had become, and had sworn Lottie to secrecy, so that Aunt Kaye had died happy to the knowledge that dear sweet Marianne had left Bel enough to set her up for life. Bel had then decided that that life was not to be passed in Brangton—where she might be traced—but that she would retire to Lulsgate Spa in Leicestershire, where she knew that a varied and rich society obtained, where she might find a new and happy circle of friends, and a place of her own.

Being a supposed widow conferred respectability, and Lottie was sworn to secrecy over that; she was a hard-headed, silent woman who needed no telling why. After she had arrived in Lulsgate Bel had hired a companion, Mrs Broughton, to give her respectability, a quiet, vague, rather silly woman, if kind, who accepted that Bel had been married off young to a rich old man, who had soon died, and that Bel, having no relatives, had chosen to settle at Lulsgate in search of company, and—who knew?—a second husband, Bel had said to anyone who cared to listen, smiling sweetly as she spoke.

Lady Almeria Harley was the wife of the vicar of St Helen's church, set in the centre of Lulsgate, its beautiful vicarage beside it, so that Bel, looking out of the drawing-room window, could see the church's thirteenth-century spire, with its truncated top, known as the Little Stump to the locals, because it was not so impressive as the Stump at Boston in Lincolnshire.

Opposite to the church were the Baths, which Bel could not quite see, although they were visible from the small house which she had bought, The Willows. Small was perhaps the wrong word for it, it being so much larger than anything Bel had ever lived in before she had inherited Marianne's fortune.

'I am quite serious,' said Lady Almeria suddenly, after fifteen minutes' companionable silence, removing a row of pins from her mouth in order to speak without swallowing them. 'I do admit that there is no one whom I could wholeheartedly recommend to you, but I am sure that one day soon I shall be able to match-make with a good heart—seeing that you will not wear Henry Venn.'

The look she gave Bel on saying this was for some reason vaguely conspiratorial, as though she had something up her sleeve, Bel thought, and then forgot her thought.

The Reverend Mr Henry Venn was the curate of St Helen's, who looked after the Lady Chapel at Morewood. He was moderately wealthy in his own right. 'I own,' said Bel serious now, 'that I am quite attracted to Henry, in a lukewarm way, you understand, but if I take Henry then I have to take his mama, and *that* thought I cannot stomach. Besides, his sense of humour is deficient, and I should be sure to say so many things at which they would both look sideways!'

Almeria's charming laugh rang out. Bel's ever-ready sense of humour was one of the things Almeria liked about Bel, coupled with Bel's good heart and industry. She had recently been made, despite her youth, the leader and the organiser of the church's sewing circle, 'So reliable, Bel,' being the usual comment, so that when old Mrs Harper went to her last rest no one, not even the old tabbies, as Almeria irreverently called them, who were the church's mainstay, had objected to Bel's replacing her.

Tact as well as charm and humour typified Bel, Almeria thought once more, watching her friend, and she thought that she knew a man who might appreciate her, and she hoped to introduce Bel to him one day soon, but until that day arrived she would continue to tease Bel about suitors, for she knew that despite her charm Bel was sufficiently hard-headed not to accept anyone for the sake of it.

'The town is filling up with visitors,' commented Almeria, watching the procession of fashionably dressed people walk by the vicarage windows. 'August usually brings the most, the London season being almost over. Philip says that although he prefers Lulsgate empty they bring much needed money into the town and give occupation to many. How many shops would Lulsgate support if there were no visitors? he says. Think of the sempstresses and milliners who would have no work without them, to say nothing of the lodging-house keepers, and those who rent their homes out for the summer, to pay for their few weeks at Brighton, or in London in June.'

Both women were silent. For all the wealth which Lulsgate contained, they were well aware of the poverty which the ending of the wars had brought, and that Morewood, once a pretty agricultural village, was now a small town of frameworker knitters, made desperately poor by the depression and the coming of the new machines, which produced more cloth but needed so many fewer workers to manage them.

It was those thrown out of work for whom Almeria and Bel were making baby clothes, and there were times when Bel, visiting Morewood, thought, And what should I be doing, with Aunt Kaye's small annuity disappearing with her death, and a pittance of my own, if Marianne's wealth had not saved me from penury?

In an effort to banish sad recollections she said, determinedly bright, 'And last night I finished *The Nun of Torelli*; are not you going to ask me what I thought of it?' and the face she showed Almeria was full of amusement, none of her true thoughts visible.

'Well, since you ask,' began Almeria, her own lively

face responding to Bel's promptings, 'yes, what did you make of it?'

'Such a strange nun.' Bel held the little garment, now finished, up again to admire it as she spoke. 'Not that I know any nuns, you understand, but I should be astonished to discover that they passed their time running around underground crypts, spending the night alone with handsome young mercenary captains, and being rescued from pirates at sea; all that was missing was a burning windmill, a beggar who turned out to be a prince—oh, and a little common sense on everyone's part, in which case, of course, there would have been no story!'

'Of course.' Almeria was delighted to have Bel's wit in full flow again; she had sensed a quietness, almost a reserve lately in Bel's manner. She was not to know that Bel had recently been having second thoughts about her many deceptions because, since the flowering of her friendship with Almeria, she had come to hate deceiving her.

'What Bel needs,' she said later to her husband after dinner, Bel having left earlier in the afternoon, 'is a husband, someone to love her, to do for her what you do for me.'

Philip Harley poured himself a glass of wine. He was an orthodox churchman, not by any means an Evangelical, and did not see the need to deny himself the small luxuries of life, a little wine being one of them.

'I'm sure she has had, and will have, offers,' he said gently. Sometimes, he thought, his Almeria was a little impetuous and needed guidance—discreet, of course.

'Oh, offers,' said Almeria; 'there is no one in Lulsgate good enough for her. No, I was thinking of someone else.'

The telepathy of happily married couples informed Philip of her meaning. He put his wine glass down carefully, said slowly, 'No, Almeria, better not try to interfere if it is Francis whom you are thinking of, if you have invited him here to throw Bel at him, or him at Bel. He is not a man to play with.'

Almeria rose, put her arms around his neck. 'Now, Philip, you are not to scold me, but they are made for each other. He ought to marry again, and a woman with Bel's wit and fire, to say nothing of her looks, would be ideal for him. No milk-and-water miss would do for Francis; *he* would not want her, and *she* would not stand up to him.'

Philip disengaged himself gently and gave her a loving kiss. 'I don't like matchmaking at the best of times, and I don't think you really know your half-brother. He is not to be manipulated; nor, I think, is Bel.'

'Oh,' said Almeria sorrowfully, 'now you wrong me. I have no intention of manipulating them. I merely intend to have him here, introduce them, give them the opportunity to see how well they suit. Beneath all that severity Francis is, I am sure, a man who needs the softer passions, however much he tries to deny it. He is at a loose end at the moment since being seconded from the Paris Embassy to work at the Foreign Office. I have not told Bel that he is coming, nor him that I have a pretty widow waiting for him. Give me credit for some delicacy of thought. I simply hope that they will find one another.'

Philip thought of Lord Francis Carey, that rather grim man, sighed, and wondered. He did not doubt Almeria's delicacy, but she was planning to throw two people together, and experience—for he was rather older than his wife—had told him how little that sometimes answered; but he decided to say nothing further—better so.

Bel knew that Almeria's half-brother was coming to stay in Lulsgate. Almeria had let it slip one afternoon

at the subscription library, or rather, she had overheard
Almeria telling Mrs Phipps so. She had expected
Almeria to say something to her of the visit, they were
so close, but no, and Bel, who was not over-curious
about other people's lives and doings, because she had
no wish for them to be over-curious about hers, had
forgotten the matter completely until she had met
Almeria in the milliner's that morning.

She was trying on an enchanting poke bonnet, but
did not like the gaudy red flowers decorating it, and
was discussing having them replaced by blue cornflowers with Mrs Thwaites, who made and sold them, when
Almeria came rushing in, all aglow.

'Oh, Bel, there you are. I just missed catching you
before you left home. Mrs Broughton told me that you
were coming here—I haven't a moment to breathe, my
brother arrived late last night, earlier than expected,
and I am giving a little supper party this evening for
my most intimate friends to meet him. Do say you will
come, I beg of you.'

'Of course.' Almeria's impulsiveness amused Bel as
it did Almeria's husband, being so unlike the calm face
which Bel had presented to the world since Marianne's
death. 'I shall be delighted. Do I dress?'

'Indeed,' said Almeria, and, remembering Philip's
injunctions against matchmaking, added, 'I shall expect
all my friends to be looking their best. Wear your
delightful bluey-green gauze,' she could not help adding;
'it goes so well with your eyes and hair—and now forgive
me, I must rush. Between being a parson's wife and a
great hostess, no time to breathe,' and she was gone.

Typical of Almeria not to inform me of her brother's
name, thought Bel, amused. She knew from something once said that Almeria's maiden name had been
Freville, and assumed that her brother was the Hon
something Freville, Almeria's father having been an
earl.

What she did not know was that Almeria's father had died young, Almeria's mother had married again, and was the Marquis of Hathersage's second wife, but had died in childbirth nine months after the wedding, and that Almeria's brother was a half-brother with a different name. Had she known the brother's name, she would have run screaming from the milliner's, but, happy in her apparently secure world, she ordered the cornflowers for her bonnet, walked on to the mercer's where she bought some book muslin for a dinner dress, and went happily home to care for her garden, talk to Mrs Broughton, enjoy a light nuncheon, and play the pianoforte while Mrs Broughton did her canvas work, to such a complacent Eden had she finally come.

'Now, Francis,' said his half-sister severely, much as she had done to Bel Merrick a few days earlier, 'you are not to make faces. Quite proper for you to do the pretty to all my friends immediately and at one go. No time wasted, and you will be at ins with everyone, and have time to decide who will do, and who will not do.'

'Useless to argue with you, I know, my dear Almy,' said Francis lazily; he was draped over an armchair too small for him. 'You are the most managing creature I know, beneath all the piff-paff. I wonder how you stand it, Philip. No, on second thoughts I do not; such wonderful powers of execution must make for a well-run establishment, if nothing else. You are putting on weight, I see, and do not look like a managed man.'

'Oh, we manage one another,' said Philip truthfully, 'and there is a lot in what Almeria says.'

'And do I dress?' enquired Francis, still lazy, unconsciously echoing Bel Merrick.

'Of course,' said Almeria affectionately. 'Everyone will expect you to be the epitome of London polish, seeing that you are who and what you are.'

Francis laughed. He was always at ease with

Almeria, and if he could find a woman like her, he decided, he might change his mind and marry again. He looked merrily across at his brother-in-law, raised one eyebrow at him. 'Now why,' he drawled, 'do I gain the impression that Almy has some ulterior motive in inviting me here? That she is determined that I shall find a Lady Francis in one of the pretty young heiresses or buxom widows who frequent Lulsgate in its high season?'

'Oh, come, little brother,' riposted Almeria, not a whit put out that, as usual, Francis had caught her at her games, 'you flatter yourself——' to have him riposte,

'Not at all, and "little brother"? Why, you are not so many years older than I am, and half my size. Do you wish me to dish the English language altogether by calling you big sister?'

'You may call me what you like,' said Almeria, leaning over and kissing his cheek, 'provided only that you stay as easy as you are with all my friends when they arrive tonight, and do not come the high-handed grandee with them!'

'Agreed,' he said, catching at her hand and pressing it, 'and tell me also, Philip, why you should be so lucky as to catch one of the few truly agreeable females in the world for a wife!'

Dressing for Lady Almeria's little supper, which would probably not be little at all, Bel found herself wondering what the brother would be like. Like Almeria, she hoped, brown and jolly, of amiable appearance; or would he possess wintry grey eyes, a hard face and a superb body?

She blinked with annoyance as Lottie eased the sea-green gown over her head. Would she never get that monster Lord Francis Carey out of her head? How was it that, whenever she read of a man in a novel, or thought of one whom she might like to come calling, he always seemed to look exactly like the brute who had insulted her so?

Why, even the mercenary captain in that ridiculous farrago *The Nun of Torelli* had in her imagination taken on the appearance of the noble ruffian whom she had cheated so neatly. She could forget him for weeks and then he would start walking through her dreams again. Damn the man, and damn the circumstances in which she had met him. Well, she was unlikely ever to meet him again, and perhaps she ought to start thinking of Henry Venn as a possible husband—and why should the odious Francis Carey make her think of marriage, for goodness' sake? *He* certainly had not seemed to be a marrying man—far from it!

She set in her hair the half-moon jewel which Marianne had been wearing in the Phillips portrait, and placed a small pearl necklace round her neck, pearl drops in her ears, and a pearl ring on her finger. They were all that she had kept of Marianne's jewellery; the rest had, with the help of Mr Thomas Coutts, been sold, and the proceeds wisely invested.

Kid slippers on her feet, a cobweb of a shawl and a tiny fan of chicken feather, dyed sea-green, completed her toilette. There, that should please Almeria, convince her that Bel Merrick just might be husband-hunting. Mrs Broughton had cried off, so Lottie would escort her there, and would take her home—she was to help in the kitchens, having begun her career in them, and was not too proud to revive it occasionally, for the Harleys' cook-housekeeper was her best friend, and the two old women helped one another out when Bel or Almeria entertained.

The company was almost completely assembled in Almeria's drawing-room when she arrived, to be smothered in an embrace before Almeria held her off to examine her. 'Oh, famous, my dear. You should be gracing Town with your looks and presence. You know everyone here, I think, except of course, the guest of honour.'

She led Bel across the room, bowing and acknowledging her many Lulsgate friends, towards the hearth, where a group of people stood talking together. Philip was standing before the empty fire-grate, speaking to a tall dark-haired man who had his back to the room, and was bending to listen to what Mrs Robey was saying. Mrs Robey was a lady on the make with a daughter to marry off and the daughter was standing shy and embarrassed before the London polish of Almeria's brother, Bel supposed.

'Oh, do forgive me for interrupting,' said Almeria gaily, tapping the tall dark-haired man on his arm, 'but, Francis, I do so wish you to meet my dear young friend, Mrs Bel Merrick, who as I have already informed you quite brightens all my days for me.'

With a muttered, 'Pray excuse me,' to Philip and to Mrs Robey the tall man turned to give Bel his full attention, and, his having done so, they stood staring at one another.

Oh, dear God, thought Bel frantically, how can you play such a dreadful trick on me? For the face of Almeria's brother was that of Lord Francis Carey, and she saw his expression change immediately from one of polite amiability to one of an almost unholy glee as he, too, recognised the lady to whom Almeria had so blithely introduced him!

CHAPTER FOUR

His face changed again, so quickly that the stunned Bel almost thought that she had imagined what she had seen, and he was bowing over the hand she was offering to him.

'Delighted to meet you, madam,' he said smoothly, straightening up, so that she could see the mockery in his hard grey eyes, 'absolutely delighted,' and the ring of sincerity in his voice also delighted Almeria, who was innocently unaware of how two-edged, if not to say two-faced, his declaration was. 'My sister has been telling me that she has many charming friends in Lulsgate, and from the manner in which she has introduced us it is plain that you are one of the most favoured. You will not take it amiss if I inform you that I am determined to know more, much more of you—will seek by every means to improve our acquaintance.' And his eyes were devouring her, taking in every line of her body, even more curved and desirable, he noted, than it had been two years ago. How wrong he had been to delay coming to Lulsgate Spa!

Bel had thought that she would not be able to speak, had feared that he might unmask her immediately, like a villain in a melodrama, and declare, Ho, there, this woman is a fraud, a Cyprian like her late notorious sister of whom you have all heard.

But no such thing, and she had no time to think, simply to murmur graciously, and her cool tones astonished her, 'I am always pleased, sir, to meet a valued relative of my dear friend, Lady Almeria Harley. I hope you will enjoy your stay in Lulsgate, Lord Francis.'

Bel was trying to take her hand back, but he would not let go of it, raised it to kiss it again, said, his eyes hard on her, 'Now that I have met you, my dear Mrs Merrick, I know that I shall enjoy my stay immensely. You cannot conceive of the pleasure it affords me to meet such a charming person as yourself. And now, forgive me, I must tear myself away, return to Mrs Robey. I was informing her of the delights of the London season just passed, and of the coming trial of Queen Caroline; such a pity that virtue and beauty are not always allied, don't you think? Yes, I see that you agree with me. Let us speak again soon.'

Oh, she would die, thought Bel, as each sentence he uttered carried a double meaning to taunt her, causing one vast blush to overcome her whole body, so that she thought that everyone in the room must be staring at her.

But no such thing to that, either. Even Almeria, who had been half listening to what had passed, seemed to have seen or heard nothing untoward; was pleased, indeed, that on the face of it Francis seemed to have been attracted to her dearest friend and protégée.

'What a splendid fellow he is,' she said fondly to Bel, when Francis had returned to the group by the fire. 'I knew he would like you, and I was not wrong; he seemed quite struck. And he has a genius for saying and doing the right thing; I had no fear that you would not like him.' She seemed oblivious of Bel's unnatural silence, so pleased was she that her innocent little plot seemed to be working.

'I have placed him next to you at supper,' she murmured, 'so that you may further your acquaintanceship with him. I am determined that my best friend and my dear brother shall also be friends. He has been a lonely man recently, and I am trying to repair that—where better than Lulsgate Spa for him to recover his old spirits?'

Where, indeed? thought Bel sardonically. I am sure
that he will recover his spirits completely in returning
the disfavour I did him, with interest, if I read that
haughty face aright, but aloud she said, 'Oh, he seems
quite charming, if a little too polished for Lulsgate.
London polish, I presume.'

'Oh, and Paris, too,' said Almeria enthusiastically,
'and Bright really must announce supper now. The
party is all assembled, and food is the cement of
conviviality, Philip always says—to say nothing of drink
for the gentlemen.'

So there was Francis Carey taking her into supper,
whom she had last thought of as standing on the
pavement at Stanhope Street, staring at the empty
house and the 'For Sale' notice, knowing that his prey
had escaped him—only to find her, by fortunate accident, two years later, enthroned in respectability in
Lulsgate Spa.

He was, she now had time to notice, magnificently
turned out in the almost black that fine gentlemen
were now wont to wear. Only his waistcoat, embroid-
ered with yellow roses, spoilt the chaste perfection of
his *tout ensemble*. He was a dandy almost, his stock a
work of art, like the rest of him.

How could she have dreamed of him, seen him as
the hero of *The Nun of Torelli* or any other piece of
nonsense? And how could she ever have thought that
she would be walking in to supper with him, her hand
on his arm, feeling the living, breathing man, warm
beside her, so very much in the flesh—making her
uncomfortably aware of her own flesh, feeling naked
almost, although she was wearing a considerably more
chaste turn-out than most women had chosen to appear
in?

So why, she thought crossly, did she have the
impression, once he had touched her, that all her
clothes had fallen off? Neither Mr Henry Venn's nor

any other gentleman's touch had ever had such an effect on her before.

Did he know? She had the uncomfortable impression that he did, and once they were at table he turned to her with the utmost solicitude to ask her whether she was comfortable, and whether she needed water immediately. 'You appear a touch pale, madam. Are you sure that you are feeling quite well? Is there anything I might be permitted to do for you, any trifling service you would care for me to perform?'

'Not at all,' retorted Bel, almost shrewishly, she feared. 'I am in the first stare of health,' thinking, Oh, how dare he? Someone would surely notice; such two-edged comments could hardly escape detection.

But no, Almeria, not far from them, leaned forward to say, 'Commendable of you, Francis, to care for Bel's welfare.'

'Bel,' he murmured, before he turned to speak to Mrs Robey on his right. 'Charming, quite charming, nearly as much so as. . .Marina. And Mrs. Do I take it, dear Mrs Merrick, that you are a widow, so young as you are?'

She must say something, she who was usually so charmingly free with her opinions, was noted for her repartee, her acute wit.

'Indeed, sir. I was married young to a much older gentleman, who unfortunately died soon after our marriage.'

He leaned forward to say, very softly, so that no one could hear him, 'Oh, indeed, I understand you completely. Of his exertions, I suppose.'

Bel was in agony. Not only from embarrassment as to what he might say next, but quite dreadfully his last comment had made her want to laugh. She was trapped, but would not be put down, said loudly, 'No, you mistake quite. Of putrid water, which brought on palpitations, other more dreadful symptoms, and death. Oh, my poor Augustus! Yes, now I do feel overset.'

There: if that did not hold him, nothing would. 'Forgive me,' he said to Mrs Robey, who might think him unmannerly if he attended to Mrs Merrick too constantly, 'but I fear that Mrs Merrick is not after all on her highest ropes,' and he called to Bright for a little brandy, to add to Mrs Merrick's water glass, as a restorative, he announced gravely.

Bel found everyone looking at her, with varying degrees of sympathy. Henry Venn, who was temperance-minded, said a little reprovingly, 'Are you sure, Lord Francis, that it is wise to ply Mrs Merrick with drink?' to which Francis, busy pouring Bel an extremely liberal dose of brandy from the bottle which he had firmly taken from Bright's hands, replied,

'I am persuaded that brandy, and brandy alone, will restore Mrs Merrick to the charming state which she was in on her arrival here. I do hope, Mrs Merrick,' he said as he handed her her glass, 'that nothing that I have said or done has brought on this fit of... discomfiture.'

'Not at all,' said Bel, drinking her brandy and water, and aware of every guest's eye on her. 'May I assure you that nothing you could say or do would ever overset me—quite the contrary.'

His pleasant smile at this was one of genuine admiration, and he chose to favour Mrs Robey with his conversation, after Bel had assured Almería that her malaise was passing.

'It was only that I thought suddenly of my poor late husband Augustus,' she explained shyly to Almería and the table, 'and I was distressed all over again. He loved such occasions as these.'

'And bravo to you, my dear Mrs Merrick,' she heard Francis murmur in her ear when the third covers arrived. 'Such *savoir-faire*, in one so young, but then, I forgot, so. . .experienced, too.'

'Thank you,' was Bel's response to that. 'I know exactly the value to place on any praise which I receive from you.'

Francis could not help but admire her. A houri, a lightskirt, passing as virtuous, deceiving his sister and the polite world she might be — but what spirit, what sheer cold-blooded courage, to defy him so coolly when he was doing everything to provoke her into indiscretion.

Oh, she was going to pay for her cavalier treatment of him two years ago, but before he enjoyed her in bed, where she belonged, he was going to enjoy her everywhere else, too, with the world watching. What a pity virtue had not been included in her many attributes!

'And was there a Mr Merrick?' he enquired again in a tone so low that no one else could hear.

'How can you doubt it, sir?' was all she chose to say.

'Oh, easily, easily. You have packed a great deal of living into a short time, my dear Mrs Merrick, since Lady Almeria informed me, just before I escorted you into supper, that you have been living in Lulsgate for almost exactly two years. I calculate on that basis that after your London adventure you must have met, married and buried your late husband in less than six weeks.'

'You forget, I might have met and married him before——' Bel paused. She did not wish to say anything incriminating, even in the low tones of the supper table, with everyone else conversing freely with their neighbours. Fortunately for her, young Amabel Robey had Henry Venn fully occupied.

'Before? Before what, madam? I am agog.'

'Which is what Mrs Robey will be if you do not attend to her a little more,' responded Bel smartly. 'I am not obliged to tell you the story of my life over the supper plates.'

'A great pity, that,' he said lazily, 'since I am sure it would be of the utmost interest. Another time perhaps.'

Oh, damn him, thought Bel, he has the most dreadful effect on my internal language, and he is as light-footed as a. . .as a. . . She could not think what he was as light-footed as, resolved to turn her attention to Henry, who was worriedly asking her whether she felt any effects from the brandy, all of which she had drunk without even noticing that she had done so!

'None at all,' she said severely, thinking how soft Henry looked after she had been inspecting Francis Carey's hard face. Was he soft all over? Was Francis Carey hard all over?

Oh, dear, it must be the brandy causing all these improper thoughts, and she tried to concentrate on Henry's tedious conversation about the next bazaar which was being held in the vicarage grounds, weather permitting, to raise money for the fallen women of Morewood, there being presumably none in Lulsgate, since the fallen women there plied a good trade among the summer visitors and did not need financial help.

If it were not the brandy which was upsetting her, thought Bel, it must be the frightful effect of sitting next to Francis Carey, who now turned his attentions to her again, and was asking her solemnly where she lived, for he would like to pay a call on her on the morrow to ascertain whether her malaise was chronic, or merely passing.

'Merely passing,' said Bel firmly. 'Not worthy of a call.'

'You must allow me to be the best judge of that,' announced Francis soulfully, his eyes wicked. 'Besides, think how pleased Almeria would be if we enlarged our acquaintanceship. Oh, yes, I do wish to enlarge my acquaintanceship with you, dear Mrs Merrick. I wish to see so much more of you; you cannot imagine how much more I wish to see of you.'

Bel could not help it. Wrong and wicked it might be of her, and oh, how she disliked him, saying all these dreadful things to her, but his appalling jokes were too good not to laugh at. She could really be no lady, she decided, between a bout of frantic giggles and her efforts with a handkerchief to pass it off as a mere consequence of eating something which disagreed with her a little.

Scarlet in the face, she allowed Francis to pat her on the back, heard Henry say, 'Most unlike you, dear Mrs Merrick, to be so distressed, and twice in a night, too.' The tactless fool, she thought indignantly, and, fortunately for Bel and everyone, Lady Almeria rose to her feet and led the ladies out of the room to leave the gentlemen to drink their port, while the ladies sat over the tea-board, settling Bel in a chair and anxiously asking her whether she was quite recovered.

'Oh, indeed,' responded Bel, giving for her what was almost a simper, 'I believe it was the August heat which affected me.'

'How unfortunate for you,' said Mrs Robey, ever one to improve the shining hour. 'Now my dear Amabel is never affected by the heat, are you, my love?'

'No, Mama,' replied that young lady meekly, but before her mama could gather any congratulatory smiles on her hardihood she added, unluckily, 'You know it is the cold which oversets me. Why, do you not remember, Mama, only last winter...?'

'And that will be quite enough of that,' announced her dominant mama. 'May I say what a fine finished gentleman your good brother seems to be, Lady Almeria? One is astonished that he is not married yet. Where are all the ladies' eyes? I ask myself.'

One would be astonished if such a haughty creature were to have been snared and married, thought Bel naughtily, and surprising for dear kind Almeria to have such a brother as he is. And then she recollected: half-brother only, of course. That must explain all.

Almeria poured Bel more tea and said warmly, 'You and Francis appeared to be getting on famously. I am so pleased; I felt sure that you would be kindred spirits. He has such a taste for reading as you do, and his wit would sort with yours.'

Bel nearly choked over her tea on thinking of the conversation in which she and Francis Carey had indulged over supper, so different as it was from Almeria's kind imaginings.

Mrs Venn, who considered that Mrs Bel Merrick usually had far too much attention paid to her—enough to turn such a young person's head, and she didn't want dear Henry marrying her, by no means—said loudly, 'My dear Henry has a pretty wit too, but then he does not possess a title and ten thousand a year, so admiration for *his* wit goes abegging. I consider Lulsgate has as much to offer in *that* line as any London salon.'

Bel winced over her tea at this none too veiled insult aimed at Francis and Almeria, and thought again that so long as his mama would be part of his future household there was no question of her accepting poor Henry.

Lady Almeria, though, treated Mrs Venn as though she were some gnat buzzing about—making somewhat of a noise, but not really doing any harm—her bite lacking even the gnat's venom.

'Oh, Francis rarely puts on airs,' she said cheerfully, 'and as for wit, one can hardly claim that Lulsgate is awash with it, dear Mrs Venn, though it does you credit to think so. Local patriotism is always a virtue, I think.'

Dear, good Almeria, thought Bel with a rush of affection, so perfectly formed to be a satisfactory parson's wife, quite unlike myself with my dreadful wish not to be put down, and my equally dreadful ability both to catch *double entendres* as well as to create them. What sort of man am I fit to be the wife of? I wonder. Francis Carey, I suppose, since he seems to be as disgracefully improper in his conduct and speech as I am in mine.

This untoward thought shocked her so dreadfully that she sat there with her mouth open. How could she even think such a thing? Why, she hated the monster, did she not? He thought her a lightskirt and worse, showed her no respect—no, not a whit—might be going to tell Almeria at any moment that she was not fit for decent society—indeed, she could not imagine why he had not had a private word to that effect with her already...and here she was, mooning about being his *wife*. Not only light in the head, but fit for Bedlam.

She had just consigned herself to a dank cell, and a bed of straw, with Almeria visiting her once a sennight, when her fevered imagination was soothed a little by the entry of the gentlemen, which if it did nothing else would put a stop to the inane conversation to which Lulsgate ladies, left on their own, were prone.

Bel had been brought up by an eccentric papa who had educated her as though she were a boy, and Aunt Kaye had been such a learned lady that she even knew Greek—which was the reason, she had once said sadly, that she had never married—and in her long-ago youth had been a pet of the great Dr Johnson himself, so that gushings about sweetly pretty bonnets and the unsatisfactory nature of servants had not come Bel's way until she had been settled in Lulsgate, and part of her attraction to Lady Almeria, and Almeria's to her, was because they were both rather out of the common run of women in their interests.

The gentlemen were all a little flushed, except for the two men of cloth, Philip and Henry, and the look on Lord Francis's face, Bel saw with a sinking heart, was even more devilish than the one he had worn at dinner. He was making straight for her, too, and she could feel Mrs Robey, and all the other women with pretty young daughters, bridling at his partiality for a widow, as he finally arrived by her side, said softly, 'You will allow, Mrs Merrick,' and pulled up a chair to sit by her, 'and perhaps you could persuade Almeria that a fresh pot of tea would serve to satisfy your humble servant's thirst.'

Your humble servant, indeed, thought Bel—what next? But she did as she was so politely bid. Almeria rang for more tea, and while he waited for it Francis Carey proceeded to tease Mrs Bel Merrick under the guise of paying her the most servile court.

Oh, if she had known she was going to pay for it in this coin, was Bel's inward response, she would have turned him out of Marianne's home without a thought, not tried to punish him for his insolence to her.

'You have relations in Lulsgate, I collect, Mrs Merrick, to cause you to settle here?'

'No, sir, not at all,' was her stiff reply. 'I have, unfortunately, virtually no close relatives since my aunt died.'

'No? Your husband had relatives here, then?'

Bel had always understood that it was grossly impolite to quiz people so closely on such matters, but perhaps, like many grandees, Lord Francis made his own manners.

'My husband had few relatives, sir, and none in Lulsgate. The reputation of the place attracted me.'

'Now there you do surprise me,' he said, bending forward confidentially, and fixing her with his hard grey eyes. 'I would have thought Lulsgate far too dull a town to attract such a high-stepper as yourself, and as to having no, or few, relations, I can hardly tell whether that would be a convenience or an inconvenience. It would depend on the relatives, one supposes. Some, as I am sure you are aware, might even be grossly inconvenient.'

'Since I have so few,' she parried spiritedly, 'it is difficult for me to tell. Now I do believe that you have a few inconvenient relatives yourself, or so I had heard, given to making unfortunate acquaintances, with unfortunate results.'

Lord Francis, accepting a cup of tea from his sister, who was up in the boughs with delight at the apparent sight of Bel and Francis on such splendid terms, chuckled drily at this, took a sip of his tea, shuddered, 'Too hot,' put it down, leaned forward again, and said, most intimately, 'Are you threatening me, Mrs Merrick? Most unwise.' And from the killing look he fixed on Bel Almeria was certain that her dream of wedding bells might yet come about.

'Threaten you?' said Bel innocently. 'Now how should I do that?'

She had no idea how the wicked spirit which was beginning to inform all her conversation with him had begun to alter her whole appearance. The slight flush on her ivory face, the sparkle in her eye, the charmingly satiric twist to her mouth were beginning to affect the man opposite to her in the most untoward fashion.

Francis Carey had begun his campaign against her with the decision that he would harden his heart against the harpy he judged her to be. He would desire her, lustfully, would feel nothing for her, but see her as a body to be won.

Alas, with every word which passed between them, his desire for her as a woman, rather than as an object to satisfy him sexually, grew the more.

Oh, he wanted the revenge he had promised himself if he were ever fortunate enough to find her again, but

more and more that revenge was beginning to take a
different form from the one he had first contemplated.
For he wanted her to respond to him in every way—
yes, every way. He had for a moment considered
exposing her to his sister once her supper guests had
gone, but now he had decided that he would enjoy
himself more in this dull backwater by taking on this
mermaid at her own game, and beating her.

He had, after losing her, enquired of Marina St
George and her reputation, but this woman was St
George's best, he was sure. He had not heard that the
great Marina was remarkably witty, but her sister
certainly was. And clever enough to pass as an innocent, for he was quite sure from what Philip Harley
had told him of her, in answer to his apparently idle
questions, that she was not plying her trade in Lulsgate.

Presumably with what she had earned herself, and
had inherited from her sister, she had acquired a
fortune of a size large enough to keep her in comfort,
for the time being, at least. He was also certain that
the late Mr Merrick was a convenient invention, to
confer an aura of respectability on her which she might
not otherwise have possessed. Oh, he was going to
enjoy himself in Lulsgate, that was for sure!

Bel could almost feel his thoughts, apparently
respectful though his face was, for she read his body—
and his eyes—and both were disrespectful after the
subtlest fashion. How do I know such things? she
thought, a little shocked at herself, for this was not the
first occasion on which she had read men and women
correctly, divining their real thoughts rather than their
spoken ones. Had Marianne been able to do it? Was
that why she had been such a great courtesan?

She avoided pursuing the matter further, and said
swiftly to him, 'If you continue to direct your whole
attention to me, sir, you may create criticism of yourself as well as of me, and I am sure that you do not

wish that to occur, for Almeria's and Philip's sake, if not your own.'

Francis almost whistled. By God, she was shrewd as well, and recalled him to the proprieties. He rose, said to her, 'Oh, madam, you presume to teach me manners, such a highly qualified dominie as you are, but you are right. Provincial life is different from London life, and I must remember that. I will call on you tomorrow, madam, and we shall carry our acquaintanceship further; you may depend on that.'

It was a threat, Bel knew, but she had driven him from her successfully, and could breathe again. If that were so, however, why did she feel so desolate at the monster's going?

She watched him walk away, tall, with an air of such consequence and purpose that he dimmed every other man in the room. She was not yet aware that she performed the same disservice for all the women in the room—but Francis knew, as he knew of his own talents—and he looked forward to the future.

CHAPTER FIVE

BEL waited for Lord Francis Carey to call on her with a flutter of excitement gripping her in the oddest fashion. It seemed to be centred at the base of her stomach, and yet be able to spread at times to other, more embarrassing parts of her body. Mixed with this was a combination of fear and exhilaration. She feared to see him—but panted to see him.

The pleasantly dull tenor of her life in Lulsgate Spa, a dullness which had wrapped her round and comforted her since Marianne's death, had disappeared, presumably for as long as Francis Carey made his home with his sister. What surprised her most of all was that the fear that she might encounter him again, now that she had encountered him, had turned into something quite different, and infinitely complex.

She looked around her pleasant drawing-room, that haven of quiet which she had built for herself over two years. The little desk in the corner had come from Marianne's study, as had a large armchair; the rest was the pleasantly shabby furniture from her father's home at Brangton, even down to some of the religious tomes which sat in an alcove of bookshelves by the hearth, mixed in with more frivolous works like *The Spectre of Castle Ashdown* and *Emily Wray: A Sad History*—the last so unintentionally amusing that Almeria and she had laughed themselves into crying when reading it, so unlikely was Emily with her fictional trials.

Well, she was not Emily, whose one response to trouble was to faint upon the spot—Francis Carey would soon find *that* out; but all the same unease became the most powerful of her feelings as the day crawled by without him appearing. Oh, drat the man, why could he not get it over with?

For his part, Francis was in no hurry. Let the bitch wait; do her good to suffer, was his savagely uncharitable thought as he made a slow toilette and ate a late breakfast in his sister's breakfast-room, as pleasantly shabby in its own way as Bel's home.

Then he read a two-day-old *Times*, savouring the thought of Mrs Bel Merrick—he still did not know what her maiden name was. . .maiden name, a good joke that, he thought sardonically—waiting anxiously for him, perhaps even shedding a few tears. He laughed at himself and put down *The Times*. Bel Merrick, shed tears? Another joke, remembering the proudly defiant face which she had worn two years ago, and again last night when he had confronted her and mocked her during supper and after.

Like Bel, he had the feeling that life was going to be far from dull before he had madam beneath him, and it was certainly not going to be dull then, not at all. Strange that for the first time in years he was hot for a woman, and that woman a. . .Cyprian, a creature he had always avoided in the past. Well, he thought sardonically, Shakespeare was right again. 'We know what we are, but we know not what we may be.'

He pulled out his watch as Almeria came in, a child clutching at her skirts, watching him around them: his nephew, Frank, named after him.

'Hello, old fellow,' he said gently, putting out a hand so that Almeria might set the shy child on his knee, where he played happily with his uncle's watch. 'I thought,' he offered Almeria casually over the top of Frank's head, 'that I might pay your pretty little widow a visit.'

He was interested to see how Almeria brightened on hearing Bel spoken of. She had sunk into a chair opposite to him. She was wearing an apron, he noted, and was a far cry from the somewhat empty-headed but perfectly dressed beauty who had taken the London season by storm before accepting Philip Harley, the poorest of her many suitors, whom she had married against everyone's wishes and forebodings that it would not last.

They had not known how strong-minded and loving Almeria was. 'I am jam-making later on,' she said. 'Cook is getting old, needs a helping hand and I do not like being idle while others work. Oh, Francis, I should not say so—Philip would say that I was interfering—but I am so happy that you and Bel appear to be at ins. She is the dearest friend I have ever had, despite the difference in our ages. Her mind is so good. You will ask her to join us on our trip to Beacon Hill tomorrow, will you not? She would enjoy a jaunt there in your curricle, always providing the weather is fine.'

Francis had the grace to feel a little ashamed, would have liked to say, perhaps, Her mind is the only *good* thing about her, but refrained, showing Frank how the watch opened, and even revealing its workings. Frank loved the little wheels he saw, and said so.

'I remember,' said Francis, amused at the small boy's solemn scrutiny, 'how when I was Frank's age poor Jack showed me his watch, and how it delighted me,' which was a way of avoiding discussion of Bel Merrick, he knew, and served to divert Almeria.

'Jack grows no better, then,' she said quietly.

'Not at all, and never will.' Francis was short. 'And more's the pity. He is a good fellow, and both his wife and son needed the guiding hand he would be giving them—particularly Marcus, who is more outrageous than ever. When he heard I was to visit you, he talked a little wildly of coming here himself—with some of his more disreputable friends, I suppose. Said he would not put you to the trouble of giving him a room, would go to the White Peacock.'

'Nice to see him at all,' said Almeria, who loved Marcus for all his harum-scarum ways, she not knowing the worst of him.

'And now I must be going.' Francis retrieved his watch from his nephew, put him gently down. He was so surprisingly good and patient with children, thought Almeria regretfully, he really ought to have some of his own. All his haughty pride disappeared when he was with them.

Francis was not thinking of children as he strolled through Lulsgate Spa, noting the Baths, the Assembly Rooms, a small classically fronted building with a vague stone god standing in front of it. Vague, because no one knew who the god was supposed to be. The less reputable but still charming house, where a private club in which one might game was established—public gaming houses being forbidden by law—also interested him, and he promised himself a visit—in the intervals between persecuting Mrs Merrick, that was.

Her own house, built early in the eighteenth century, was small by the standards of the vicarage and some others, he noted, but obviously perfectly kept, which was not surprising, as she was so perfectly kept herself, he thought with a somewhat savage grin at the pun. He knew that his savagery, if contained, was never far from the surface, and he thought—nay, hoped—that the hint of it, plus a hint of wildness which he thought he detected in the St George's sister, would give salt to their encounters. To his horror he found his breath shortening at the very thought. No, he must at all times be in control; one slip and the tigress would have him, and not the other way about.

The conceit amused him. Two tigers prowling, the one around the other. His fists clenched a little. How had the tigress convinced Almeria that she was only a pussycat?

No matter; he stared at the knocker in the shape of

a grinning imp before rattling it sharply, and then standing back, to be admired in all his London finery by a passing group, who rightly identified him as a gentleman of consequence, come to grace Lulsgate Spa.

Bel was in a fine old taking when she heard the knocker go. She was stitching at her canvas work, a charming design of yellow roses, to be a cushion cover to enhance her battered old sofa. It had been Mrs Broughton's turn to read aloud, and she was sitting in front of the garden window, reading not an improving work—Mrs Broughton had no mind for improving works, nor talent for reading them aloud—but a charming piece of froth entitled *Lady Caroline's Secret*.

Mrs Broughton, who was a woman of sound common sense when not reading sentimental novels, was so distressed by Lady Caroline's ridiculous secret, and the absurd lengths to which she went to keep it, that she could barely restrain her sobs as she read of them. Bel could hardly restrain her laughter. Having a few real secrets of her own, she could not take Lady Caroline seriously, but could scarcely inform Mrs Broughton of that interesting fact.

The sound of the knocker, while distressing her in one way, saved her face in another. She really must pass poor Caroline on to Almeria—she would enjoy her for sure—but in the meantime here undoubtedly was the monster come to attack her.

She compelled herself to sit still, to yawn a little even, one graceful hand before her mouth as the maid of all work came in.

'Gemmun to see you, mum. Are you in?' A pair of phrases which it had taken Lottie a week to teach her, so shy was she.

'Indeed, pray admit him. He did not give his name?'

'It was Lord Francis something, I think, mum.'

'Oh, how too delightful!' exclaimed Mrs Broughton, who was always impressed by a lord. 'So flattering of him to visit us so soon!' She put down *Lady Caroline's Secret*. Real life suddenly attracted her more.

Both women rose to meet him. He was as splendid as ever, Bel noted, his tailcoat today a deep charcoal and his trousers charcoal also, but of a lighter hue. By his expression, one of power contained, he was out for blood, and, if so, she was ready to meet him, supported as she was by the presence of Mrs Broughton.

'Charge, Chester, charge! On, Stanley, on,' she thought in the words of Sir Walter Scott, only to remember the next bit of the quotation, 'Were the last words of Marmion.' Well, they were not going to be *her* last words, by no means, and the small defiant smile which her face bore as she thought this was noted by her enemy.

So, madam was prepared to fight, was she? Good!

'Ladies,' he said, bowing, 'pray be seated. I am come to renew a friendship, newly made. Delighted to see you both again. In good health—industrious too, I see.' His sardonic gaze encompassed Bel's tapestry.

Bel and Mrs Broughton made suitable noises in answer to this, his splendour and address, Bel noticed wryly, quite overcoming Mrs Broughton: she obviously thought him one of the Minerva Press's heroes come to life.

'I am not always the industrious one,' she answered, happy to find something innocuous of which to speak. 'Today it is Mrs Broughton's turn to read to me. We were just palpitating together over the happy accident that the hooded stranger Lady Caroline met on a glacier high in the Swiss Alps turned out to be her true father, whom she had never before met. You may imagine the affecting scenes which followed, almost melting the snow and ice in which they were set!'

If Bel could not prevent her wicked spirit from

displaying itself, even to this odious nobleman whom she had decided she could not abide, then Francis Carey could not help giving a delighted crack of laughter at this piece of satire.

'Oh, now I see how you won Almeria over!' he exclaimed. 'By sharing her delight in reading such novels, but equally her appreciation of their many absurdities.'

Won Almeria over! He made her sound a worse plotter than dastardly Guido Frontini, Lady Caroline's villainous pursuer; but her reply to him was gentle.

'Quite so, and you, I had not thought you to be a devotee of the Gothic novel, Lord Francis. Blue books and red boxes are more in your line, surely?'

Better and better, thought Francis. It will be a pleasure to overcome such a learned doxy. Madam has received a good education, somehow, somewhere. It will be an equal pleasure, perhaps, to discover how.

Aloud he said smoothly, 'Blue books and red boxes are sometimes so exquisitely boring, Mrs Merrick, that relaxation is required—and then I was wont to raid Almeria's bookshelves, and the habit still endures. One cannot be constantly austere in one's reading. Even the great Dr Johnson once wrote a novel.'

'Oh, *Rasselas*,' said Bel carelessly, as much to inform Mrs Broughton, who looked a little surprised at this news, as to display her own learning, although the delightfully sardonic quirk of Lord Francis's right eyebrow served to inform her that he was perfectly aware of that learning. 'But hardly in the line of the Minerva Press. Where are the Italian Alps, the ruined castles . . .the heroine disputing with the climate in quite the wrong turn-out?'

Mrs Broughton was vaguely distressed. 'I thought,' she trembled, 'that you enjoyed what I was reading to you, dear Bel. Perhaps you would prefer something a little more serious in the future,' and she looked with regret at poor Lady Caroline, now face-down on an occasional table.

Bel's, 'Not at all, I find them most enjoyable,' was followed by Francis's comment, meant particularly for her,

'Better she disputed with the climate, madam, than with the hero. Heroes and heroines should never be at odds. Unlike their real-life counterparts, where odds are more common than evens—as you, I know, are well aware.'

Oh, dear, he is at it again, was Bel's inward comment to that. Not only will it be difficult for me to keep a straight face if he goes on, but I shall find myself responding to him in the same coin, and perhaps even Mrs Broughton will notice what we are doing.

'Oh, real life and novels are always different, Lord Francis,' she explained, as one to an idiot, 'since in them everything is resolved at the end, and that is rarely true in life, there being no end there, except the obvious one which we shall not mention.'

'No, indeed,' he replied instantly. 'Happy to learn that you understand that. It will make matters between us so much easier if we know where we stand. You agree to that, I hope?'

'In that, if nothing else, we are in agreement,' she answered smartly. 'Plain speaking is always better. A little more of it and Lady Caroline would not be in such a pelter.'

'You really wish it?' he said, eyes wicked. 'Plain speaking? Would you wish some informed plain speaking from me, Mrs Merrick? That would remove misunderstanding, I am sure, but would it be wise?'

Oh, damn him, damn him. She knew now why he was a diplomat, so rapid in his responses, so pointed in them, but the poison disguised so neatly beneath the sugar.

Fortunately for Bel, Mrs Broughton was as charmingly and blindly amiable as she was kind and useful as a companion and watchdog, literal-minded to a fault, and she saw nothing untoward in the veiled exchanges going on between her mistress and her visitor. On the contrary, she thought how splendidly well they were doing together, and after a few more exchanges of a like nature she thought to further Bel's interests by saying eagerly, 'You are interested in gardens, Lord Francis? I saw your eyes wander to the view outside. Perhaps you would like dear Bel to show you around hers; it is a little gem, and all due to her exertions. She makes a delightful sight, potting plants, I do assure you.'

'Oh, you need not assure me, Mrs Broughton. I can quite imagine it—seeing that Mrs Merrick is a delightful sight at all times, and all...places.' And his dreadful eyes caressed her. 'I should be delighted to have such an...experienced guide to lay the delights of her... garden before me.'

Bel privately damned Mrs Broughton. She had absolutely no wish to be alone with Lord Francis, either in a garden or anywhere else, where his conversation would, no doubt, become even more pointed; but there was, in politeness, nothing for it.

She rose, said, resignedly, 'If you really wish to study the delights of nature, Lord Francis, then I will be your guide,' and led the way through the open doors—to Purgatory, doubtless—where else?

Bel's garden was large enough to have pleasant flower-beds in the new informal style which was becoming popular, a small glass-house and, through an archway, a kitchen garden with a south-facing wall. James, her gardener, who came in several days a week—she shared him with other like-minded ladies—provided salad stuffs, vegetables, and fruit from the cordons on the warm wall.

They strolled at first among the flowers in full view

of a beaming Mrs Broughton who could already hear wedding bells as she watched them engaged in apparently amiable conversation. Had she been nearer, she would have retreated in shocked dismay.

At first, all was proper, Lord Francis saying nothing but um and ah, as Bel gave him a short lecture on her plants, showering him with Latin names and erudite horticultural information. If his expression was even more sardonic than usual, his haughtiness a little more in evidence, they were shielded from Mrs Broughton by the fact that his head was bent to gaze, apparently admiringly, at Bel.

He had to confess that she made the most charming picture. She was clad in a simple cream dress of fine muslin with a faint amber stripe running through it. The collar was chastely high; in fact the whole of Bel's turn-out apparently sought to convince the beholder of its wearer's extreme sense of virtue. Even the red-gold curls, which he remembered as riotous in London, had been carefully confined, and the luminous green eyes were modestly veiled, and did not flash fire until he became too provoking.

Francis decided to be provoking.

He was admiring a small goldfish pond, and Bel had begun a short lecture on the care and feeding of fish, designed less to inform him than to keep him from speaking, when he leaned forward, took her by the arm, and said gently, 'You make a most damnably desirable spectacle, my dear Mrs Merrick; allow me to desire it in a little more privacy,' and he led her firmly towards the archway into the kitchen garden, away from Mrs Broughton's interested eyes, where they would be quite alone.

'So,' said Bel, who had been hoping that he might have changed his mind about her after seeing her with his sister and in the chaste confines of her home, 'by

your language—for you would not speak so to a lady—
you still consider me a. . .lightskirt.'

'Oh, come,' he mocked. 'Plain speaking, you said;
we both know exactly what you are, and for the
moment it is our little secret.' He was still walking her
towards the kitchen garden, adding, 'I must confess
that if it gives me greater access to you I prefer early
plums and late lettuces to goldfish—though had you a
mermaid in your pond I would have admired that. But
the only mermaid in Lulsgate Spa at the moment is
your good self, whose company I propose to enjoy
until the weather changes.'

He released her, but not before he had turned her
towards him, 'To enjoy the view more easily,' he
informed her with lazy hauteur.

Bel stepped even further away from him; to her
horror she found that his lightest touch had the most
disastrous effect on her, and the sight of him so near
to her was even worse. She supposed that it was fear
which was causing her to tremble and her whole body
to ache, not yet knowing that quite another emotion
was affecting her.

He smiled and narrowed the distance between them
again, his grey eyes glittering. Bel's breathing shortened still more, but she could not retreat further; she
would end up inside the row of lettuces if she did.

'Why are you here?' she enquired hoarsely. 'What is
the true purpose of your visit?'

'Ah, so we arrive at the meat of the matter, madam,
no prevarications. It may have escaped your memory,
but we had a bargain, my dear Mrs Merrick.'

'A bargain?' Bel kept her voice steady with
difficulty.

'Yes, my dear houri. A bargain, freely offered by
you, not by me. I was to. . .instruct you, you remember,
in exchange for certain papers. I am here to. . .fulfil
that bargain.'

'I did not mean——' she began, heart thudding, fear of him, she was beginning to realise, mixed with a most dreadful desire, so that she was almost mesmerised by the sound of his voice, a beautiful one, exquisitely modulated, used to command and also to enchant, although Bel was not aware that he had done little enchanting with it of recent years.

'You "did not mean"? of course you *meant*. You meant to make a fool of me, leaving me staring at a deserted house like gaby. No, I will teach you, slowly, not to make bargains which you do not intend to keep, and I hope to enjoy that charming body, usually reserved for those who pay you well—without paying you anything.'

Bel licked her lips, tried to pull her wits into some sort of order, for this was worse than she had feared, and said, as the thought struck her, 'You could gain your revenge so easily. Why have you not informed your sister—oh, not of the truth, but what you mistakenly think is the truth?'

'Tell her who and what you are, you mean? The courtesan with a blackmailer and usurer for a sister, she using her charms in bed to cheat and deceive as you used them out of bed to cheat me, with promises you never intended to keep?'

His lip curled; he was enjoying the distress he could tell she was suffering beneath her brave front.

'Yes,' said Bel, suddenly fierce, showing spirit. 'One sentence is all that is needed; why not say it?'

'Because I wish to enjoy myself...and you. You humiliated me, madam, and I have carried the memory around with me for the last two years. Oh, sometimes I forgot, and then at the most inopportune moment I would remember; see you again, mocking me. Oh, you roused me, dear Mrs Merrick, as you well know, held me off with promises, sobbing about your sister's death. I should have remembered how truly hard-hearted courtesans are. Now I shall make promises to you which *I* intend to keep. When I think fit I shall tell my sister exactly what I have discovered you are, a lightskirt who plies for hire most viciously; but when and where I choose to do that, and how long I shall take, I shall not tell you. . .you must live in delightful anticipation. . .as I did.'

'And which of us is the more vicious, sir, tell me that?' And then, 'No, you cannot do this. You do not know. . .you are cruel, so cruel.'

'Yes, I am cruel, rightly so.' And he laughed grimly. 'And what is it that I do not know? Pray tell me. I need to know everything about you, as I intend to make you keep the bargain you made with me—eventually—lest you betray poor Marcus, as your sister did.'

'I am not what you think.' Bel offered this sturdily, not apologetically. 'I am quite innocent, not a Cyprian at all.'

Lord Francis looked her up and down, and she followed suit by so scanning him. He was delighted at the sight, for winning a spiritless whore would have been no pleasure. The cool perfection of that lovely face, framed in its light curls—some of which had escaped from the severe style in which she had bound her hair—the careful and tasteful toilette—all presented to the world a model of apparent virtue.

'Oh, you are exactly what I think you are——' and his lip curled '—a whited sepulchre, a worm on the rose of this small town, not because you are a whore, no, not at all, but because you pretend to be what you are not. You are dishonest, madam.'

'And you are vile,' retorted Bel, 'to conduct a. . .' and she remembered, such a strange memory, *The Nun of Torelli* '. . . vendetta. Yes, you are vile even were I the creature you think I am, doubly vile because I am innocent. Oh, you are like all men, to despise what all men use and pay for. You flaunt yourself as virtuous, walk where you please, remain respected, while condemning those with whom you take your pleasure to be unconsidered outcasts.'

'I repeat: your trade is not what I protest, but the dishonesty with which you plied it—and your pretence of virtue.'

'No pretence,' flashed Bel, and suddenly was steady, a rock, her own fists clenched as she had seen his were—and why was that? 'I will not consent to this. It is war, sir, war, with no quarter. I will give you nothing.'

'On the contrary, by the time that all is over you will give me everything, beg me to take it, and I will debate whether I wish to do so.'

Oh, but she was gallant, and his fists were clenched because were he to do what he so desperately wished he would be upon her, to compel her at once to give him what he so dearly wanted. He must make her beg, if only to stop himself from doing so!

'Come,' he said—he could not prevent himself, 'a foretaste,' and before she could stop him she was in his arms and he was kissing her, and she was responding, madly, wildly, against all sense, all reason, until, remembering where they were, with Mrs Broughton perhaps beginning to wonder what they were doing, he pushed her away.

'No dishonesty there on my part. You know why I want you—and you, were you practising your usual arts—or were you being honest too?'

He held out his arm, and perforce she took it, so that when they came into view again he was passing on to her his sister's invitation to the picnic on Beacon Hill, 'and Mrs Broughton, of course,' he finished, giving that lady a gallant bow which had her admiring him all over again. 'I look forward to seeing you both; I shall call for you at eleven of the clock.' For he had told Bel he would brook no denial, and she dared not offend him, lest he tell Almeria her secret straight away.

'So charming, so gracious,' gushed Mrs Broughton when he had taken his leave. 'If only all fine gentlemen were like him!'

And thank God that they are not, was Bel's response to that, but so steady was she, so much herself, that nothing of her distress showed.

One art she was rapidly learning was that of consummate self-control, and she thanked Lord Francis for that, if nothing else.

CHAPTER SIX

As HE walked back to the vicarage, Francis Carey's thoughts were a strange mixture of an almost savage pleasure, frustrated desire and, astonishingly enough for such an arrogant, self-assured man, a feeling which was almost shame.

Nonsense, he told himself firmly, she deserves all that I care to hand out to her; but he was almost relieved when he reached the Harleys' to discover such a brouhaha that it was enough to drive Bel Merrick temporarily out of his head.

Little Frank ran to meet him, pulling at his hand, three-year-old Caroline toddling behind. Frank was holding a miniature wooden horse, and Caroline was dragging a new rag doll behind her. 'Oh, Uncle Francis!' exclaimed his nephew. 'Ain't it jolly, Cousin Mark has come, with presents; now we shall have some famous times!' for heedless Cousin Mark was quite naturally a roaring favourite with equally heedless small fry.

Francis lifted little Frank up, walked into the drawing-room to discover Marcus sitting there, as carelessly turned out as ever, hair and stock awry, drinking port while Philip Harley drank water, and Almeria was exclaiming, 'No, really!' and, 'Never say so, Mark!' at every other sentence.

'Oh, there you are, Uncle,' cried Marcus, as though the last time the two had met they had parted as bosom bows, and not, as usual, at daggers drawn over Marcus's ever-growing debts. 'I'm sure that you'll be pleased to hear that I have decided to come and retrench in the countryside, leaving Town to improve my financial situation as well as my health. I am at the White Peacock with a couple of friends, have no mind to add to poor Almeria's expenses,' ignoring the fact that he had already added to them, since Almeria had just asked him to bring his friends along to dinner.

'I have been asking whether there are any pretty young girls here, with good competences,' he rattled on gaily. 'The pretty part is essential, the competence would be an added virtue. Almeria informs me that, while there is no one here to rival Miss Coutts in terms of the available tin, there are some quite decent belles, including of all things a pretty young widow with more than a competence, but she's saying hands off to that — reserved for you, I gather.'

Now why should that careless reference to Bel Merrick make Francis clench his fists and want to strike his inoffensive nephew? For it was Bel whom he did not want to be exploited, he oddly discovered, not Marcus whom he felt should need protection!

He stared coldly at his nephew. Did this idle lounger really resemble himself? He supposed he did. They both possessed the same grey eyes, dark hair, and somewhat straight mouth. But where Francis was severe, Marcus was slack; where Francis looked like a grave Roman senator of the old school on a coin, Marcus rather resembled a dissolute young Roman emperor in the last days of that Empire's decline. Not that Marcus was vicious, Francis decided wearily, simply idle and stupid, the spoiled son of a silly mother.

'And who are these friends you are inflicting on us?' he enquired sternly.

'Oh, jolly good fellows both,' said Marcus rapidly, knowing quite well that his uncle was bound to dislike them. 'Rhys Howell, lately a captain in the Lifeguards, and Fred Carnaby — you know Fred, he was in the Diplomatic himself until recently.'

'As well I know,' remarked Francis glacially, 'until

he was sent home for drunkenness and mislaying important dispatches. Hardly the sort of friend to bring here.'

'Well, too late now,' said Marcus cheerfully. 'Invitation already gone out.'

'And Howell, so-called captain,' pursued Francis determinedly, like a confounded dog with a juicy bone, thought his nephew irreverently. 'I have heard nothing good of him. A man is known by the company he keeps, Marcus, and your company is not nice.'

'You have forgotten what it is to be young, sir.'

'Oh, come, Mark,' interjected Almeria, trying to keep the peace. 'Thirty-four is hardly old, and you are already twenty-four yourself. Francis is right to wish you to settle down.'

'I'll make a promise,' said Marcus earnestly, who had made many promises before, and never kept one of them. 'If I find a splendid young woman here, I promise to pop the question and settle down myself— in Lulsgate Spa, perhaps! Will that do, sir?'

Francis regarded him with distaste. Perhaps he ought to throw him to Bel Merrick; it was all the young fool deserved. Question was, did she deserve him? And what an odd question that was to ask himself, he thought crossly.

'And I am to meet the pretty widow and some of the Lulsgate belles soon,' continued Mark, 'for Almeria has asked us all to accompany her on the trip to Beacon Hill tomorrow, and fortunate it is that I have brought my curricle with me. If I fall on my knees and say, Pretty please, Almeria, my angel, may I escort the charming young widow?'

'No,' said Francis coldly, before Almeria could answer Marcus, 'you may not, for I have already asked her to accompany me, and you are not a safe enough whip to escort any young woman. Confine yourself to conveying your disreputable friends about

Leicestershire. Their loss, should you overturn the
curricle and them, would not be felt by their relatives
or by society.' He turned to his half-sister. 'If you will
excuse me, I will leave you to change for dinner.'

'And what's the matter with him?' exclaimed Marcus
frankly, when his uncle had left them. 'What burr sits
under his saddle? Pretty widow not coming up to
scratch? More chance for me, then. Think I'll change
myself.' And he left whistling a cheerful tune, the
words of which were not known to Almeria, and just
as well, thought Philip, giving his wife an absent kiss as
she rolled her eyes at him, not knowing which gave her
the vapours most, silly young Marcus, or his unbending
uncle.

One reason for wanting Francis to marry Bel was
that she might take some of the starch out of him—but
it would not do to say so!

Bel, waiting for Francis to arrive the next morning, was
quite unaware that the plot was thickening as yet more
actors arrived on the scene. Mrs Broughton beside her
was all of a delighted flutter. Francis had said that he
would come for them in the Harleys' carriage, and Bel
would then be transferred to his curricle, the Harleys'
coachman taking over the responsibility of the carriage
in which Mrs Broughton would sit with the Harley
family. Henry Venn was driving his mother and Mrs
Robey in their carriage, and several other equipages of
varying age and fashionability would make up the
party.

Fortunately the day was fine, and even if Bel's spirits
were a little low at the prospect of being persecuted by
a haughty nobleman all day, the other prospect of a
picnic and a stroll in good countryside could still
attract. She would not allow him to destroy the
pleasure which she had come to feel in living at
Lulsgate Spa.

But he behaved himself perfectly when he arrived, handed Mrs Broughton in, and later out of, the carriage in fine style, and confided in them both that his and Almeria's nephew, Marcus Carey, Viscount Tawstock, had arrived with friends, and would be accompanying them on their jaunt.

Marcus Carey, the young fool who had proposed to Marianne and to whom she had been lending money! And what would *his* friends be like?

They were all assembled in Almeria's drawing-room, congratulating themselves on the fineness of the weather. Francis's hand was firmly on Bel's arm when he led her in, as though she might be about to desert him again at any moment, and she knew at once which of the three men whom she had never seen before was Marcus, the blurred likeness to Francis was so strong.

Marcus's candid appreciation of her when he was introduced did a little to mollify the spirits which Francis's treatment had wounded.

'Why, you dog, Uncle, is that what brought you to Lulsgate?' And he bent over Bel's hand with as much gallantry as he could muster, straightening up to stare at her in admiration, adding, 'We have not met before, I know, but I have the feeling, almost, that we have. You have a sister, perhaps? You certainly possess the look of someone I have known, but I should never have forgotten that divine shade of red-gold hair had I met it before!'

Bel could almost feel Francis's sardonic and mocking stare at Marcus's artless words. She was well aware that, although she had not greatly resembled Marianne in looks, there had been an indefinable resemblance between them—something in the expression, perhaps?—and that Marcus had seen it!

She judged it politic merely to smile; anything she said would be a lie, and, worse, might hang her later— and then she was being introduced to two men whom

she instinctively knew were Marcus's toad-eaters, mere
hangers-on whom only Marcus's presence there could
have brought into the vicarage.

Fred Carnaby was nothing, but, unworldly though
she was, she disliked Captain Rhys Howell on sight—
and did not know why. He was handsome in an easy,
obvious fashion, quite unlike Francis's severe and
harsh haughtiness, and his manner was as warm and
soothing as Francis's was abrasive. He held her hand a
trifle too long, smiled a little too easily, and she decided
that she disliked soft blue eyes and curly blond hair.
Besides, by his manner, she thought, Captain Howell
was a deal too fond of himself, and did not need
anyone else to be fond of him.

But she was all courtesy, and when Francis had
handed her into his curricle, a beautiful thing, picked
out in chocolate and cream, drawn by two matched
chestnuts, and they were starting off towards Beacon
Hill, Cassius up behind them, he said coolly to her as
he manoeuvred her through the light traffic of
Lulsgate's main street, 'A lady of great discretion, I
see. First to be such a diplomat when Marcus committed his unintended gaffe, and then your reception of
the dubious captain—I must congratulate you. Such
savoir-faire. A pity that you did not choose to settle in
London; you could have gone much further than your
sister, been a great man's public ladybird, the queen of
the *demi-monde*, no less.'

'Am I supposed to be flattered by that?' said Bel
curtly. 'Your compliment is as dubious as the
captain's.'

'Keep on remembering what you are is my advice,'
was his only reply, 'for, resourceful though you are, I
hardly think you carry enough armament to keep the
captain in order. And now shall we declare a truce? I
have a mind to enjoy my day in the sun,' and the look
he gave her as he said this was so warm and caressing

that it altered his whole face, transforming it so that
Bel had a powerful and sad wish that she could have
met him in different circumstances, and then their
whole intercourse could have been different, too.

She shook herself mentally, said coolly, 'If you wish.
I have no desire to distress Almeria, who is goodness
itself, and Philip also deserves consideration, to say
nothing of the children.'

This last sentence gave her a pang. She dearly loved
little Frank and Caroline, who in return loved Aunt
Bel, and the pang grew worse as she suddenly thought
that this renewed meeting with Lord Francis Carey
might yet mean that she would have to fly Lulsgate
and give up the happy life which she had created for
herself.

'Good,' said Francis, and then applied himself to
driving, for the roads around Lulsgate were not good,
and this part of Leicestershire, near Charnwood Forest,
was a little hilly—'For we are not so far from the
Pennines, after all,' he remarked, smartly negotiating a
difficult corner.

'I suppose you are what they call a whip,' offered
Bel, who had, much against her will, been admiring the
whole athletic picture which he presented.

'After a fashion,' he returned lazily. 'I have no
pretence to being a name in any way. My life has been
too busy for me to indulge myself in following fashion's
dictates—I have never wanted to rival a coachman on
the road or a pugilist in the ring. They are the pursuits
of men without occupation. Merely to do ordinary
things well is an aim worth following.'

Bel was suddenly determined to know more of him.
'And your occupation—what was, or is that?'

'At the moment,' he returned, 'I am a diplomat of
sorts. I was at the Paris Embassy, but I have been
recalled to act in an advisory capacity at the Foreign
Office, a duty which is neither here nor there, and if

that is what I am doomed to then I shall seek other duties. I suppose I ought to sit for Parliament at the next election and find my future there. The idea does not particularly attract.'

'And you have always been a diplomat?' Bel was curious. Something about his athleticism, the habit of command strong in his voice, had suggested quite otherwise.

'Oh, I see why you, and she, were so successful,' he remarked, breaching their truce a little. 'This gentle interest in a man's affairs, flattering as well as soothing. No,' he said hastily, seeing her expression grow stormy, 'I will answer you. I was in the navy, until there was no ship for me—was seconded to the admiralty, and from thence, by degrees, ended up in my present position.'

'The navy!' exclaimed Bel. It explained so much about him. His cold certainty—she could imagine him commanding a crew of recalcitrant sailors, quelling them with a look. 'Did you see action in any of the great battles in the recent wars?' and her voice was as eager as a boy's, not a girl's. 'Lord Nelson was quite my favourite hero. I used to dream of running away to sea and being a midshipman!'

'And a deuced hard life you would have found it,' was his answer to that, giving her a surprised glance on hearing this unlikely revelation. 'I was at Trafalgar, and allow me to tell you that sea battles are most unpleasant things, not romantic at all. You are better reading of them with Almeria, rather than taking part.'

'All the interesting doings in life are reserved for the male sex,' remarked Bel, a little aggrieved, 'such as being a sailor, driving a curricle, or a thousand other things. We are left with such milk-and-water occupations as sewing and tatting, no comparison at all!'

'But so much safer,' riposted Francis, using his whip to touch his horses lightly to make them turn more tightly than they wished. 'One rarely ends up with one's head removed by a cannon-ball while making baby-clothes.'

Bel could not help giving a fat chuckle at this. She had a vision of herself and Almeria sitting decorous in the vicarage drawing-room, dodging bullets, balls and grenades. Could one dodge them? She thought not. They 'arrived', one supposed, willy-nilly. She remarked so to Francis, who, rapidly looking sideways at her, registered a pang at the sight of her vivid face.

'Indeed, you are perceptive to understand that—there is no avoiding them—and I may add that driving a curricle is not the easiest thing in life. There are daring ladies who do, although most confine themselves to perch, or ladies' phaetons.'

Bel had a vision of herself, seated behind a pair of milk-white unicorns—for if one were using one's imagination one could surely imagine that—driving a curricle whose body was silver gilt, rubies set in the wheels, and the harness gold cord, and all the metal connected with it silver and gold, too.

Her face took on such an expression of pure happiness that Francis, despite himself, was touched. How did she do it? He had met many ladybirds, and not one of them could assume that look of enchanting innocence.

The day pleased Bel as well; the sun was at its kindest, golden and warm, with the faintest hint of mist in the distance taming the summer's heat. The greenery which surrounded them had achieved its final perfection before it began to fall into a golden or dull-ochre decay, the grasses becoming straw, losing their lushness.

Beacon Hill now rose before them. They were not to mount in their various carriages to the top, but to draw up on a flattish meadow at its base; last of all to be wheeled into position was the landau which contained the cold collation and the servants who would prepare and lay it out for them, once their masters had taken their pleasure, either by sitting in the shade or strolling up to the top to look out across the countryside towards Cold Ashby in Northamptonshire where the previous beacon to herald the Armada's coming had been lit, or northwards to the next.

'Stirring days, were they not?' remarked Bel to Francis, after his tiger had handed her down, and he had taken her arm, most proprietorially, she noticed. Anyone watching them would have assumed that Lord Francis Carey was indeed smitten by the widow's charms.

'And fortunate that the great Elizabeth and her sea captains won,' was Francis's answer, 'seeing that if they had not done so we should hardly be jaunting here — or might be speaking Spanish at the very least.'

'Only think,' said Bel, 'it would have been in the Channel that you won your spurs — if naval captains win spurs — and not Trafalgar, if you had lived then.'

'Spurs are for knights,' said Francis, 'of whom I am not one, not sailors.' And was that a reminder of their true situation? thought Bel, but she determinedly made nothing of it, particularly when little Frank, happy to be free again, came running to his uncle.

'You will give me a ride in your curricle one day, will you not, Uncle Frank?' he exclaimed. 'Perhaps you would let me sit on Aunt Bel's knee? She is quite my favourite aunt,' he went on, 'even if she is not a true one — a friend-aunt, Mama says. Perhaps — ' and he screwed his eyes up at his daring ' — you would make her a real aunt, and then I could have her all the time. Oh,' he said sadly, 'Mama told me not to say that to you, Uncle Francis, and now I have forgot — but,' brightening, 'I am sure you do not mind,' and he ran off again, his legs itching, his mama later said, after being confined in the carriage during their longish journey.

Bel, all blushes at the little boy's artless remarks, hardly dared to look at Francis, particularly when he remarked drily, 'You have won one male animal of the Carey family over, Mrs Bel Merrick, that is plain to see.'

Pricked, she could not help retorting, 'Oh, indeed? I thought, by your behaviour, that I had won two. One hardly pursues with such determination those to whom we are indifferent!'

Where all this was coming from Bel did not know. Ever since she had first met him, two years ago, she had begun to change from the milk-and-water creature who had gone to London and who had nearly been extinguished by the revelation of Marianne's career. The speed of change had slowed down during her time at Lulsgate, but since Francis had arrived so dramatically in her life again its pace had increased equally dramatically. There was something about him to which she responded, and whether that would have been so if she had met him as the respectable unknowing young lady she had once been she had no means of knowing. She only knew that in order to cope with him at all she needed all her wits about her, and those wits were sharpened every time she met him.

Marcus was approaching, Miss Robey on his arm, and Captain Howell with another pretty young thing on his—Kate Thomson, a manufacturer's daughter, visiting Lulsgate with her clergywoman aunt, and part of Almeria's circle in consequence, the clergywoman's late husband having been Philip's tutor at Oxford. And a less suitable partner than Captain Howell for a virtuous young woman Bel could not think of, but she assumed that Marcus had done the introductions and Almeria was helpless before them.

'Ah, Carey,' murmured Captain Howell, 'you had a good journey here, the roads not too tricky for a good whip?' And he waved a negligent hand at his own rather showy phaeton. 'And now for a walk to see the panorama—I am assured by the ladies that it is worth subjecting oneself to the sun and the insects to enjoy it. We shall shortly find out.'

Even his most innocuous remarks, thought Bel, appeared disagreeable when offered with such oily knowingness. She could almost feel Francis stiffen when addressed so familiarly by such a toad-eater, but there was nothing for it, and it was really, thought Bel unkindly, a little amusing to think that for once the great Francis Carey was being put down, even if she had to thank such a cad for doing so!

Almost as though he had divined her thoughts, Francis gave her arm a light pressure, similar, Bel thought, to that which he applied with his whip to his horses, saying, 'Shall we find our own way to the top, Mrs Merrick? Will Mrs Broughton allow you out of her sight? Surely in such a public view, with such a large party, I may be allowed to escort a young gentle-woman without adverse comment.'

Even as he spoke, Mrs Broughton walked towards them, fanning herself, her face already scarlet; being somewhat plump, she felt the heat of the day more than a little.

'You will forgive me if I do not accompany you both, but I wish to rest; the sun afflicts me, and I may help Lady Almeria with the collation. She needs to oversee it, she says, and I am to bid you to be back not later than two. The servants have placed the wine bottles in the stream, and the sandwiches will be greasy if you delay overlong. You may tell me of the view when you return, Bel. Philip, who has already set out, has promised to sketch it for me.'

Matchmaking, matchmaking, thought Bel of Mrs Broughton and dear Almeria both; if only you knew the truth! Almeria—Frank and Caroline running about her—waved her hand to them and made shooing

motions in the direction of the path up the hill. Henry
Venn, a disconsolate look on his face, his mother by
his side, proprietorial as usual, was apparently about to
escort the Harley children to the top, in default of
being allowed Bel.

'I like my niece and nephew,' remarked Francis, as
they set off, 'but feeling as I do they would be distinctly
de trop. I shall endeavour to make up for my defection
later. Almeria has packed a cricket bat and ball so that
we may have some lively entertainment when we have
recovered from luncheon, or nuncheon—I am not sure
what one calls what one consumes at two in the
afternoon, in the open.'

'A new word is needed, perhaps,' suggested Bel, as
they began their upward march after Marcus and his
companions, who could be heard laughing and talking
together, Kate and Miss Robey not finding Captain
Howell and his witticisms as unlikeable as Bel did. She
was aware that, since discovering what Marianne had
become, her knowledge of the world had increased so
greatly that she could never again be so young and
innocent as they were.

Curiously, the knowledge did not depress her. Young
women ought not to be kept in the same state as fools,
she decided, and this redoubled her intention not to be
cowed by Lord Francis Carey. Not that he was doing
much cowing of her at the moment, and when they
reached the top of the hill, where Captain Howell
was pretending to look for ash from the beacon—after
over two hundred years!—she noted that Francis was
careful to keep her away from Marcus and his friends—
whether this was for her protection, or theirs, she could
not decide.

In deference to the ladies, the whole party—a large
one, for others beside the Harleys' immediate friends
and relatives had come along—now sat for a moment.
Parasols were opened, and Bel's, a frivolous lemon-

coloured specimen, to match her loose gown, served to
protect Francis as well as herself. They sat at a little
distance from the others, and he pointed out to her the
various landmarks around them, and in the warmth of
post-noon Bel felt delightfully sleepy and relaxed, muttering um and ah at him, rather as he had done
yesterday when she had been telling him of the plants
and the fish.

'Why do I gain the impression that *you* are funning
me?' he said, the loose expression coming oddly from
him—his speech was usually precise, devoid of the
slang which Marcus and Captain Howell used so freely,
making the young women about them giggle and titter,
with cries of 'Never say so!', 'You are teasing me!', and
'Who would have thought it, sir?'

'Funning you? Never!' replied Bel calmly as though
she were discussing parliamentary matters with him.
'No such thing. I would not dare. Perfect respect is
what you always demand and are invariably given, I
am sure.'

'Said like that,' he returned lazily, 'it can only mean
that you are offering me perfect disrespect, secure in
the knowledge that, here, no condign punishment can
immediately follow. Take care. My memory is long and
payment will be required—later.'

The grey eyes mocking her were no longer cold, his
face, usually so set and stern, soft; whatever else, there
was no doubt that Francis Carey was enjoying himself,
and, had Bel but known, was doing so after a fashion
which he had not felt for years. The only flaw, he
considered, in the delightful sensation that being with
her was producing was the knowledge that consumma-
tion of it might take a little time.

Oh, the siren that she was! She need do nothing, but
nothing, to engage and trap him. She had captured him
from the moment he had walked into the study at
Stanhope Street, had merely needed to look at him

and he was lost. Oh, the pity of it that she was what she was. To have paid court to her properly, enjoyed her wit, beauty and fire in due form, *that* would have been something. And yet was not this sparring even more delightful with its undertones of the forbidden and the wicked carried on as it was in the presence of those who had no, or little, suspicion of what was going on in front of them?

If Bel were truthful, and had been informed of how Francis felt, she would have been compelled to admit that she shared much of his feelings. The spice which their unwilling conspiracy gave to all their encounters was having its effect on her—There must be more of Marianne in me than I thought, being her response as he helped her to her feet, and with one last look at the splendid view beneath them they set off for lunch, the last to leave.

'Come, we will follow a different path from the others. I don't want company,' commanded Francis, and, taking her hand, she following, he led her down a secluded track, shaded by some scrub, and, once well into it, out of view of the rest, he turned, took her parasol from her unresisting hand to place it on the ground, and before Bel could prevent him—did she want to prevent him?—took her in his arms, saying, 'First payment for me, Mrs Bel Merrick, a foretaste of what is to come,' and began to plunder her mouth.

Untried, unkissed, never before even touched by a man, Bel felt her senses reel. Beforehand she would have quailed at the thought of such an intimate caress as his mouth teased her own mouth open and his tongue met hers, causing such a roaring wave of sensation to pass over her that her knees sagged and she almost fell against him.

She should be shocked, revolted; she had not asked for this, did not want it, no, never—but yes, oh, yes, this was delightful, and when his palm cupped her right breast, stroking it through the light muslin, his thumb finding her nipple and doing dreadful things to it, so that this time the sensation produced had her gasping aloud, his mouth having progressed to the creamy skin below her slender neck, almost to the shadow of the cleft between her breasts, Bel said aloud before she could stop herself, 'Yes, oh, yes,' so that he withdrew, laughing, saying,

'The first plea of many from you, madam, I trust,' and the mockery in his voice rendered her wild—with rage now, not with passion.

'No,' she panted, 'no, not at all, you are quite mistook. Yes, you must stop, was what I meant.'

'Not, No, you must go on?' he riposted, eyebrows wickedly raised. 'I am sorry I may not pleasure you further now, but we risk comment. Later, perhaps, we may continue where we left off.'

'No, never!' raged Bel. 'I should not have come with you at all. I shall ask Almeria for protection. You are not to treat me so cavalierly. I do not deserve it.'

'But you wanted it as much as I did. Never say that you did not. A most willing encounter, by my faith. It augurs well for our future dalliance. Come.' And he picked up her parasol. 'Open it again, not to shield us from the sun, but the rest of the world from the spectacle of a well-roused woman. You look delectable, madam, but ripe for bedding at the moment.'

Oh, horrors! Bel knew the truth of what he was saying. Her whole body had become slack, relaxed, her mouth, even, had become almost slumbrous. She wanted more. Her body was on fire, not from the heat of the day, but from the heat of him.

This would never do. She opened the parasol and looked away, suddenly almost in tears at her body's betrayal of her. However much she thought that the cold mind ruled, once exposed to the fires of passion the body had taken its own wilful way. She could no longer deceive herself. She desired Lord Francis Carey most desperately, but if she could not have him in honour she was determined not to have him at all. He could not win his disgraceful campaign, however powerful the broadsides he fired at her.

This unintended nautical metaphor restored Bel's self-command and her ready humour. How apt it was to think so of a sailor. Did Lord Francis have a girl in every port? she wondered, and, thinking so, the face she showed him was one of Bel restored. Humour had replaced erotic passion, and he marvelled at her self-command. A mistress, a very mistress of the amorous arts, to recover so quickly. She was wasted living a pure life in Lulsgate; such art, such self-command would compel a fortune in London—and all to be enjoyed for nothing by Francis Carey. . .when he was ready.

Nonsense. He was ready now, but the open meadow was before them, cloths were spread on the grass, the food was waiting, the wine already being drunk, the ladies' lemonade being poured from glass pitchers, and he was handing Bel down, saying lazily in response to Almeria's slightly raised brows at their latecoming, 'I was enchanted by the view, persuaded Mrs Merrick to remain while I took my fill of it and beg pardon for dilatoriness.'

But the view which Francis Carey had been enjoying was that of Bel Merrick's enchanting profile, and for the life of him he could not have told his half-sister what he had seen from the top of Beacon Hill!

CHAPTER SEVEN

EATING in the open, delightful though it sounded in prospect, for she had never engaged in it before, was not so remarkably pleasant as Bel had thought it would be. True, the food tasted delicious in the open air; it was the other aspects of picnicking which were not so attractive.

First of all there were the wasps and flies, which were attracted by the food; secondly there was the difficulty of eating gracefully without making one's fingers unpleasantly sticky, or ruining one's gown; and finally the position was not so comfortable as one might have expected.

She said so to Francis, who was busy eating a chicken wing, and saving his glass of sparkling white wine from overturning on the ground.

'Alfresco meals sound delightful in novels,' she informed him, 'but are not so remarkably pleasant as I thought they would be.'

'Exactly so,' was his reply to that. 'Boring though it might sound, I always think food best eaten at a good table. One's cravat,' he said, rescuing a portion of chicken from his own perfectly tied butterfly fall, 'takes less wear and tear.'

Pleased to agree with him over something, Bel, who had recovered from her inward confusion after the encounter on the hill, began to listen to the conversation of the others. Inevitably, the news being what it was, the company had begun to discuss the delightfully scandalous business of the Bill of Pains and Penalties, instigated by her husband, King Geoge IV, against

Queen Caroline, the wife he loathed, accusing her of low behaviour culminating in repeated acts of adultery.

Discussion over this interesting event, sure to provide gossip for months, centred not on the question of the Queen's innocence, but on political grounds, those Tories favouring the King being adamant on the Bill's passing, and those Whigs who wished to see the King and the Government embarrassed wishing to see it fall.

The liveliness of the gossip was assisted by the fact that Marcus, Fred Carnaby and George Hargrove, another amiable but light-minded youth, had removed all the young unmarried girls, once lunch was over, to the other end of the green, and were playing childish games with them, leaving the seasoned men and women to gossip at will, Bel as a widow being included in the number.

Even Mrs Venn, that austere matron, was not averse to joining in, wagging her high-dressed head, her coiffeur a relic of her long-lost youth, deploring everybody, King, Queen and lords.

'And is the poor creature truly innocent, do you think?' asked Almeria of her brother. She could never bear to think ill of anyone.

'Hardly,' was Francis's dry response to that. He normally avoided joining in with such idle gossip, but the Queen's trial was more than that, it was politics, and who knew what might happen? Some doomsters had even suggested that the King's unpopularity might result in revolution, if the mob grew too restive. 'No one, not even those who support her, think that. I was at a dinner party, seated near Viscount Granville, George Canning's friend and adviser, and his comment was that the Bill indicting her would not pass the Lords, there not being sufficient evidence. Besides, he added, the majority would be for her, not on the grounds of her unpopularity, but of his. The answer to "Is she bad?" is "He is as bad". Guilt and innocence, he indicated, do not enter into it, and I fear that he is right. All the same, his friend George Canning fled to the Continent when the Bill was to reach the Lords, for fear that his relationship with the Queen might cause him damage, even though it was years ago.'

Captain Howell, not loath to show his own acquaintanceship with society gossip, commented, 'One wonders that Granville himself did not fly the country, since the Princess of Wales, as she was then, was one of his many conquests.'

'Ah, but Granville does not wish to be Prime Minister one day, and Canning does,' returned Francis unarguably, 'and he is now quite reformed—which Mr Canning is not.'

He did not add that it was reported that Lord Granville's clever wife had commented that if the qualification of the members of the House of Lords entitled to judge the Queen was that they had not had an affair with her then the House would be remarkably empty when the Bill designed to judge her was brought in!

Almeria said, 'One would like to believe her innocent. It is not right that vice should occupy the throne itself,' and then thought sadly that if that were so, then the Queen's husband, George IV, ought to consider abdicating.

'Yes,' said Francis, sanctimoniously for him, 'vice should never flourish; one wishes to see it gain the punishment it deserves. You agree with me, I am sure, Mrs Merrick?' he added, turning to Bel, who sat beside him, a little wary as this conversation had continued, waiting for some two-edged comment from him, and sure enough here it came.

She would not be daunted, not she. 'Oh, I do so agree with you,' she said. 'The wages of sin, as the Bible says, are cruel, and none of us, however high in rank, should be exempt from them. Although if there

is an element of revenge in the King's pursuit of his
poor Queen then I must add that I deplore that, too.
A most unworthy sentiment, revenge.' That should
hold you a little, she thought.

But no. 'Bravo,' said Francis, 'a most Christian sentiment and exactly what I would have expected from
you, Mrs Merrick, so absolutely does it sort with your
character as I have come to know it,' and this was said
with such apparent sincerity that not only Almeria but
others thought how partial Lord Francis was growing
towards the pretty widow.

Henry Venn, indeed, ground his teeth, seeing beauty
and a modest fortune slipping from him; Captain
Howell, still with the wine glass in his hand, sipped
from it thoughtfully and turned inscrutable eyes on the
subject of Lord Francis's apparent admiration.

The Reverend Mr Philip Harley, that saintly but
shrewd man, was the only person who did not quite
take Francis Carey's apparent compliment to Mrs
Merrick at its full face value. But he said nothing,
being wise as well as perceptive. Instead, tiring of this
lubricious gossip about a woman whom he considered
to be as unfortunate as she was ill-advised, he said
gently, 'You suggested a game of cricket, Francis, to
entertain Frank as well as the ladies. Enough time has
passed since lunch to enable us to perform without
difficulty.'

'Then we must round up Marcus and the rest,'
drawled Captain Howell, rising from his recumbent
position on the grass, to give him his due, thought Bel,
as ready to join in childish games as the less sophisti-
cated of the party. The servants were to be pressed in,
the coachman being a useful bowler for the Lulsgate
team, and the audience was to consist of the ladies,
and little Caroline, young Frank being allowed to field
under the eyes of his papa and uncle.

Somewhat to Bel's surprise, that haughty gentleman,

Francis Carey, joined in as enthusiastically as anyone else, taking off his beautiful cravat, his tight, fashionable coat, and rolling up his shirt-sleeves. She had not thought it of him, but Almeria, seeing her surprise, said, 'Oh, dear Francis excels at all sports and pastimes. He is a fine shot, and although he does not care for it Philip says he was a good pugilist—only practises it now to keep himself in trim.'

In trim he certainly was, was Bel's response. Losing a little of his outer clothing had served to reveal what a splendid body he possessed, emphasising its strength and its masculinity. Soft, self-indulgent Marcus looked almost effeminate beside his uncle. He, too, shed his coat and stock, and gave Bel his dazzling smile; she had to admit that he possessed his own charm, even if it were different from his uncle's, as he said, 'You will cheer for me, will you not? Francis must not be the only one of us here to gain your approval.'

'Bravely said,' remarked Rhys Howell, who had come up to them while Marcus was talking. 'Lord Francis must not be allowed to monopolise the only real charmer in Lulsgate Spa. You will allow me to call on you one afternoon, Mrs Merrick, will you not? I mean to further my acquaintance with you, to both our advantages, I hope.'

Was she mistaken—Bel hoped she was—but was there something a little two-edged in this remark of Captain Howell's; or was her doubtful association with Francis Carey beginning to colour every word said to her by anybody—however innocent they meant those words to be?

Bel shivered a little, bright though the sunshine was, but forgot her malaise in watching the men enjoy themselves. All boys again, was her reaction, as it was Almeria's.

'Difficult to think how serious Philip is and how

severe Francis is,' she said to Bel, 'when one sees them at play. I do believe all men remain boys at heart.'

Bel could not but agree with her. They were seated at some distance from the one stump at which the bowler was aiming, and she joined in the cheering when someone was out, or scored a good run by dashing towards Almeria's parasol, set upright in the ground instead of another wicket, there not being enough players to justify two batsmen at once, Philip said.

When Francis came to the wicket, the fun began. Almeria had been correct to describe him as adept at all sports, and despite herself Bel rose from her seat, the more easily to see him perform. Frank was jumping up and down, shouting 'Huzza!' every time his uncle lashed the ball into the distance.

'Bravo!' he shouted, after one splendid shot had sent the ball into the undergrowth and the fielders had spent some time looking for it, and the next ball Francis treated with even more disdain, striking it high into the air, towards the bevy of applauding women.

Bel never knew why she did it, but as the ball reached the top of its flight and began to arc towards her the memory of jolly days in Brangton with Garth were on her. She had purposely worn a dress whose skirts would not confine her, whose hem was unfashionably well clear of the ground, showing, as Francis had already noted, a pretty pair of ankles, and so she began to run towards the spot where the ball would land.

And then, as it was almost upon her, she saw that she would have to throw herself forward to catch it, and to catch Francis out was suddenly the most important thing in the world, so she launched herself forward, caught it, held it high, and then landed flat on her face, all the wind knocked out of her body, but the ball safely clear of the ground and Francis dismissed, stars in front of her eyes, and joy in her heart.

The only person not nonplussed by her extraordinary action was Francis himself. He flung down his bat and ran towards where she lay prone in the grass, unmoving, his face white. He threw himself down on his knees beside her, and why should it matter to him that Bel Merrick was not hurt? But all the same, before anyone else could arrive to help, he was assisting her, saying hoarsely, 'You have taken no harm?'

'No, none,' said Bel faintly, still holding tightly to the ball, 'and I have dismissed you, have I not?'

They were face to face, closer than they had ever been except for the brief embrace on the hill. So close that Bel could smell the warm masculine scent of him, the scent of a man engaged in powerful exertion, touched with a little fear for her safety, a smell uniquely that of Francis Carey; while he was equally aware of the unique flowery scent of Bel Merrick, and, all unknowing, his face was soft with love and concern for her.

Bel later thought that had they not been interrupted there might have been the beginning of healing between them. But then the world, in the shape of Captain Howell, was on them.

'Madam not damaged, eh, Carey?' he said, his face hard and knowing. 'A splendid catch, that, Mrs Merrick; should be a cricketer yourself. Bound and determined to get him out, were you?'

Their moment was over. Francis's face resumed its normal haughty aspect, and Bel's her look of slight withdrawal.

All in all Mrs Bel Merrick was quite the heroine of the afternoon, particularly so far as the gentlemen were concerned. The ladies, especially the younger ones, were not so sure. The pretty widow had stolen their thunder again.

'Oh, famous,' cried Frank, jumping up and down on the spot while Bel was tenderly carried by Francis to where Almeria gently straightened her dishevelled appearance, removed the dry grass from her hair, and generally restored her to her usual state of calm order. 'That's the very first time anyone has ever got Uncle Francis out when we've played cricket, and it was Aunt Bel who caught him! Would you like a go with the bat, Aunt Bel? Oh, do have a go with the bat—and then Uncle Francis can try to catch you!'

Everyone laughed at the little boy's enthusiasm, not least Uncle Francis and Aunt Bel, who laughingly declined, saying, 'I have had quite enough excitement for one afternoon, dear Frank, without putting myself in the way of allowing your uncle to gain his revenge. Another time, perhaps,' and she hardly dared to look at him while she spoke, helped a little by his nephew who flung his arms around her and tried to climb on her knee, disputing the favour with Caroline, who wished to offer Bel her new rag doll to play with.

'Pray, children, allow your aunt to rest,' instructed Almeria; 'she has had quite enough excitement for one afternoon,' amusing Bel a little, for she felt tremendously invigorated, if not to say uplifted, after giving haughty Francis his come-uppance—except that she could not forget the expression on his face when he had come to rescue her—so strange and gentle, almost loving.

Well, enough of that, she thought briskly, amused to note that Francis was so proprietorial with her, glaring at Rhys Howell when he tried to comfort her by saying, 'A fine opportunity for you to take Lulsgate waters tomorrow, to restore youself, Mrs Merrick. I understand that they are full of that rare stuff, sodium chloride.'

'Very rare,' snorted Francis, almost forgetting himself by being openly uncivil to a man he detested, 'seeing that sodium chloride is nothing but common salt, and would hardly restore Mrs Merrick to any-thing...other than giving her what I am sure she does not wish—a monstrous thirst!'

Captain Howell did not glare back, but said, rather wittily and pointedly, Bel thought—this was suddenly not Francis's day—'Well, Carey——' and she could almost feel Francis grind his teeth at this unwanted familiarity '—since the nobility and gentry see fit to rush to Brighton to bathe in and drink the salt sea-water there, it would not come amiss for Mrs Merrick to do the same, perhaps. Do I hope to see you there tomorrow, madam?' he queried. 'We could take the waters together; overfeeding in Town has rendered me a little bilious.'

Bel did not care for him at all—there was something false in his obsequiousness to her—but Francis Carey needed to be taught a lesson; that he could not dictate to Mrs Bel Merrick whom she should meet, and how she should conduct herself. So she smiled sweetly at Captain Howell, fluttering her eyelashes after a fashion she usually avoided, and said softly, 'Should I feel sufficiently up to an excursion to the Baths tomorrow, Captain Howell, you will be sure to see me in the Pump Room, and, if so, I shall be pleased to take the waters with you.'

She hoped that this would end the matter. The cricket match resumed again, for a short time only; the afternoon drawing on towards evening, and a late dinner beckoning, the party regretfully assembled for home, all the picnic stuff and cricketing paraphernalia having been packed. Francis, on his sister's instruc-tions, came forward to escort her home, Captain Howell being fobbed off with lesser attractions.

He said nothing until she was safely tucked in; for some reason both he and Almeria thinking that a young woman who had engaged in such minimal exertion as running to catch a ball and then falling over needed the utmost in tender, loving care—to the degree that they thought fit to muffle her in a blanket on such a warm day!

Bel was something in agreement with Cassius, whose sardonic expression before he hoisted himself on to his small seat behind them both told her what he thought of the coddling of such fine ladies as herself.

Coddling did not stop there. Having started off once more, Francis remarked in his most lordly voice, not so loud as the one he used on the quarter-deck to be sure, but full of the same command, 'You would be wise to have as little as possible to do with Captain Howell, Mrs Merrick. I tell you so for your own good. His reputation, particularly with women, is deplorable.'

'Oh!' Bel almost gasped; she was not to be lectured on proper behaviour by a man whose declared intent to her was so determinedly improper. 'For a man whose stated intentions towards myself are so dishonourable, I find such an...objurgation insufferable indeed. Am I to suppose that to be...deplorable to me is reserved strictly for you? Such hypocrisy! What would your poor sister say if she knew of the lengths to which you are going to reserve my ruin to yourself? Why should you care what Captain Howell does with and to me?'

She was well aware that Cassius was probably listening to every word she uttered, ears flapping, for she had not attempted to keep her voice down, but she did not care about that, not she! Nor apparently did Francis.

A look of fury crossed his haughty face; the hand holding his whip upright—they were driving along an easy stretch of road, his horses needing little direction— was shaking a little.

'Rant on, madam,' he said at last. 'I thought that perhaps you were a little nice in choosing those on whom you conferred your favours—or so you have suggested. I see that I was wrong—paddle in the mud with Captain Howell if you will; it is probably no more than I should have expected. I thought to help you.'

'Paddle in the mud! Thought to help me!' Bel was running out of exclamation marks. 'The public spaces of the Pump Room are not exactly muddy! And as to your notion of helping me—well, words fail me!'

'I cannot say that I have ever noticed any such phenomenon,' said Francis through his teeth. 'On the contrary, a longer-tongued shrew I have seldom encountered. You lack gratitude, madam. Stupid of me, I know, but I was only speaking for your own good.' He knew perfectly well that in the light of what he had promised to do to her he must sound ridiculous, but the mere idea of Rhys Howell, or any other man, laying a finger on Bel Merrick made him feel quite ill, and as for all the men she had. . .entertained before he had met her, well, he could have killed the lot of them . . .slowly.

The very last thing he had expected had happened to him. Standing there, his bat in his hand, watching her run to catch the cricket ball he had launched into the air, her beautiful face alight with joy, seeing her fall, had produced in him the most astonishing sensation. Inconveniently, against all reason, he knew that he had fallen hopelessly and desperately in love with a Cyprian of Cyprians, a woman whom, as he had seen this very day, men had only to look at to want. Henry Venn, young Marcus and his silly friends, Rhys Howell, and the rest of them, married and single, had all walked around her, their tongues hanging out, panting at the sight of her, and he was no better—no, much worse— than the rest.

How could such a thing have happened to him?

Oh, he must possess madam, and soon, to anaesthetise himself, to cool this terrible fever which he now knew had been burning him up since he had first seen her two years ago. *That* was the reason for his rage against her. But worse even than that was the dreadful thought that even to have her in his arms might not assuage his desire, but would merely serve to inflame him the more! For he hated every man who spoke to her, not simply the dubious semi-criminal he suspected Howell to be.

A mistress of the erotic arts, sitting beside him in his curricle, arguing with him wittily and unanswerably, refusing to be put down, robbing him of honour and common sense—how could he deal with her? He could go to his sister, tell her the truth about her friend, destroy her socially and for good—and make Almeria and all her family unhappy into the bargain. He told himself that he could not do it, because it would deprive him of the revenge which he had promised himself he would have if he ever encountered the sweet cheat again, but there was more to it than that.

He was drowning in love's cross-currents, for astonishingly he did not want to ruin her in *that* way, if he did in the other. Indeed, he hardly knew what he did want.

Why could she not have been chaste, so that he could have gone on his knees to her, instead of wanting her on her knees before him, to ask her to be—what? His wife? The second wife whom he had vowed he would never take, so determined was he to be faithful to the memory of his dear, lost Cassie.

His dear, lost Cassie! For the first time in years he had ceased to think of her; ever since he had first met Bel Merrick her poor shade had grown thinner and thinner; the years had done their work on him, and the boy who had loved and married and lost her was as dead as Cassie.

No! He would not be caught by madam; he had

made his intent known, and by God he would have her, and on his terms.

The silence between them stretched on and on. Francis's eyes were on the road, Bel's on her hands, now lax in her lap, now gripped together, for, like Francis, the terrible trammels of love were netting her about; she was a fish or a bird, caught in the meshes, unable to move in any direction. And, also like him, she hardly knew what to think, feel or do.

She told herself that she hated him, but knew that she lied, or rather knew that love and hate were now so inextricably blended that the power of decision had almost gone from her. As in the moment she had caught the cricket ball and had held it aloft she had felt regret for catching him, mixed with her triumph, so now she hardly knew where detestation ended and obsession began.

Oh, why could she not have met him in Lulsgate for the first time, been introduced to him as Miss Anne Isabella Passmore, the Reverend Mr Caius Passmore's virtuous daughter, on whom he could have smiled, with and to whom he would have spoken honourably, so that he would have been gentle with her, not reproached her in fierce despite?

They were entering Lulsgate again, passing the first new houses, and the even newer half-finished ones lining the road, tribute to the developing wealth of this part of Leicestershire. They were passing the Baths, reaching her home, he was setting her down, Mrs Broughton was being conducted home, too, and the day, so fraught with incident, was over. Lottie was coming out to greet her, exclaiming, 'Oh, Miss Bel, what have you done to your bonnet?' and Francis was bowing over her hand, saying in a low and stifled voice,

'I had forgot the truce I proclaimed; pray forgive me,' and she was replying, wearily, because although so little had happened on the way home she felt as though she had lived through years of emotion,

'And, I, too, forgot myself, Lord Francis. I thank you for the journey and,' she could not help herself, 'for the cricket. I had not played it for years, and found it strangely satisfying to catch a ball again.'

His strong face lightened at that, filled with somewhat unexpected humour as she lanced the tension which had lain between them. 'Oh, yes, you triumphed mightily, did you not? One act only, all afternoon, and you are immortalised in Lulsgate's annals. Allow me, if you would, to escort you to the Assembly Ball tomorrow evening,' and before she could reply he bowed over her offered hand as courteously as though they were what they appeared to be; a lady of spotless reputation and her loving cavalier—living for a moment, thought Bel, in the world of make-believe.

CHAPTER EIGHT

LULSGATE society called the next morning, either in their own person, or sending a footman, to ask whether Mrs Bel Merrick was fully recovered from her exertions of the previous afternoon.

Bel's amusement that such a mild event as her catching a cricket ball and falling over had caused such paroxysms of excitement was tempered by the thought that life in Lulsgate Spa was so tame that it needed only for a lady to be a little unladylike and take the consequences to send everyone into such regal fantods!

Only she knew what really lay behind her own respectable façade—that she was the sister of one of London's most notorious courtesans, and was being persecuted by a man whom everyone in Lulsgate Spa thought was her dearest admirer.

She had decided to take Captain Howell up on his suggestion that she join him during the morning in the Pump Room, and was debating whether to ask Mrs Broughton to go with her, that lady being truly overset after a day in the open and eating and drinking too much in the fresh air.

She lay wheezing on a sofa, and it was Bel who was tending her, rather than the other way round, when the knocker on the front door sounded, and the maid came in to tell her that Lady Almeria Harley was a-calling.

'Oh, I see you are in splendid fettle!' kind Almeria exclaimed when she entered, and then, remorsefully, to Mrs Broughton, 'I see that you, and not Bel, have been rendered *hors de combat* as the result of yesterday's adventures. You must not sit in the sun again, dear madam. Not wise, not wise at all. Have you taken

Epsom's Salts? I am persuaded that they are the very thing for the bilious.'

'Epsom's, and every other variety of salts, my dear,' replied Bel briskly; 'however, nothing but rest will answer, I fear.'

'I came to offer to escort you to the Pump Room, dear Bel,' offered Almeria, looking dubiously at Mrs Broughton. 'Shall you feel happy at leaving your companion?'

'Oh, pray, do not consider me,' said Mrs Broughton faintly. 'Dear Bel needs restoring, too. A cup or so of Lulsgate water will set her up for the day.'

Bel privately thought not. She thought Lulsgate water vastly overrated, but did not care to say so. Everyone in Lulsgate was convinced that drinking very salty liquid was a recipe for perfect health, long life, and a good complexion.

Mrs Broughton was, indeed, asking Bel to bring her a bottle back—'seeing that I have not the energy to go there to drink it in its proper surroundings. And you will change my book for me at the subscription library, will you not, dear Bel? Although I fear that you will not find anything to equal *Lady Caroline's Secret*; that was not only sweetly pretty, but exciting, too. So sad, poor Lady Caroline, but to marry dear Belfiori in the end, that was the best thing of all! I could not have endured it if he had continued to think the worst of her because she dared not tell him her secret.'

Bel wondered what unkind god in the Pantheon was arranging matters so that everything said and done these days seemed to cast its shadow on her own unfortunate condition. What Belfiori would spring from what trapdoor to rescue her from Francis's vengeance? And perhaps from Captain Howell—there was something in his manner to her which she did not like—and now she was being fanciful.

'Dear Mrs Broughton,' said Almeria affectionately,

as they left the house. 'I sometimes wonder whether you are her companion rather than the other way round. She is so easily overset and needs so much shepherding. It is you who wait on her, fetch and carry her library books, correct her tatting. You are a good soul, Mrs Bel Merrick, and Philip agrees with that verdict, I must tell you. He was praising you at dinner last night to Francis, almost as though he thought Francis needed to be told what a good creature you are, when he can see so for himself.

'Shall we go to the library first, and find something we can both enjoy, and which Mrs Broughton will cry over? Secrets, indeed! Real life contains very few, thank goodness, and Lulsgate Spa is not the place where people have them. Goodness and virtue may be dull, but think, my love, how appalling it would be to nurse a guilty secret. I am sure that I could not sleep if I did!'

This lengthy speech did not end until both women were safely inside the library and checking through the bookshelves, Bel reflecting sardonically that those like Lady Almeria who were born into wealth position and security could have little idea of how the rest of the world fared, so easily could she deny what lay all around her, for Bel was certain that others beside herself would not care for their entire life to be exposed to public view.

Filippo's Tower was finally decided on as a suitable book to comfort Mrs Broughton by making her flesh creep and her eyes drip salt tears, and which would serve to sustain her through her malaise; and then their destination was the Pump Room.

'I tried to persuade Francis to come with me,' remarked Almeria reflectively, 'but he says that an old sea-dog friend of his has settled near here, and that he proposed to visit him. He said that not even Lulsgate water could reconcile him to meeting Captain Howell for two days in succession!'

And I really do not want to meet him either, thought Bel. He makes me shiver, and I do not know why. He is not ill-looking after all, and although his manner is a little oily it is no more so than that of many other self-consequential men.

They finally entered the Rotunda, with its high glass dome, classical archways and statues of various gods and goddesses disposed in niches around the walls. The well was in the centre of the large room, and a series of spouts in the shape of shells were set in its high sides from which water flowed, to run into a low trough, be conducted away, or be caught in suitable receptacles to be drunk by those, like Bel, who might find it health-giving—not that Bel really thought any such thing.

Beyond them were the big double doors through which visitors who wished to bathe in the life-giving waters took their way. Bel had once surrendered to her doctor's wishes and gone there, but the springs which fed the baths contained a great deal of sulphur as well as salt, and she found them distasteful. She concluded that she was not at Lulsgate for its waters, whether sulphur-laden or not.

Fortunately for Bel, Captain Howell was not alone. He and Marcus and other young bloods were standing in one corner of the room, quizzing the passers-by, and laughing openly at some of the old men and women who chose to frequent the Pump Room, often daily. They were discussing the evening's dance at the Assembly Rooms—they were held twice weekly.

Entry to the Rooms was by a large subscription to keep out riff-raff, and, although Lulsgate had no powerful Master of Ceremonies to rule the spa as Beau Nash had once done at Bath, the MC who ran the Assembly Rooms, Mr Courtney, organised the events staged there very strictly, so that Lulsgate should not deteriorate socially, as some spas had done, losing their attraction for wealthy visitors and depriving the growing town of money.

Bel and Almeria both accepted glasses of Lulsgate water, Almeria being greeted by one of the church-warden's wives with demands to discuss the decoration of the church when Harvest Festival time arrived, and, offering Bel a smile of apology, Almeria was led away, leaving Bel to drink her water alone.

Rhys Howell must have had eyes in the back of his head, Bel thought crossly, for the moment Almeria was swept away he came over to greet Bel, and bowed extravagantly to her. 'Come, you must not be solitary, Mrs Merrick, when there are those who wish to entertain you.' And he escorted her towards some armchairs in the corner of the room, near to his cronies—he was one of those men who always attracted a small court around them—made up of victims as well as toadies of someone who they mistakenly thought was a man in the first stare of fashion.

'You are in looks today, madam,' he proclaimed. 'I am happy to inform you, Mrs Merrick, that you show no signs of yesterday's exertions. You hardly need the restorative properties of the water you are drinking.'

More compliments followed until Marcus, restless, said, rudely, Bel thought, 'You are as bad as Uncle Francis, Howell—and that is saying something—for monopolising Mrs Merrick. Allow me to entertain her for a little.' And he pushed Howell to one side, and sat in the next armchair to Bel.

'Have you lived here long, madam?' was his opening gambit. 'I would have thought Lulsgate a dull spot for such a charmer as yourself to grace for long. Were you ever in London?'

'A short visit, once only,' replied Bel, determined not to lie more than she need.

'Forgive me for quizzing you——' Captain Howell was taking the conversation over from Marcus Tawstock, whom he undoubtedly had in his toils, '—but you did not go into society, I collect.'

'No,' was Bel's short answer to that. She *did* object to his quizzing her, would much have preferred to speak with artless young Marcus, but could not say so.

'I thought not,' he said, offering her his wolfish smile. 'I should have been certain to have remembered you, so distinctive as you are, but I have been out of England these last few years—on business—and thought I might have missed you then.'

Bel gave him an ambiguous smile, which she also offered to his next remark. 'You intend to vegetate here, madam, not grace London with your. . .inimitable presence? One wonders why.' And again Bel did not like the expression he assumed when he had finished speaking.

'I enjoy country living,' was her short reply.

'Oh, indeed, so do I. For a short time, that is. And, of course, you gather useful admirers round you here, as you would in Town, do you not?'

Bel was suddenly certain that this conversation was, on his part, by no means innocent. She shivered a little, and was grateful when Mark intervened again.

'You are an inconsiderate devil, are you not, Howell? You knew that I wished to converse with Mrs Merrick, and here you are again, cutting me out. I particularly wished to ask her whether she would allow me to escort her to the Assembly Ball this evening, and since you will not leave us alone you compel me to ask her publicly, for if I leave you with her much longer, you are sure to be there before me.'

'Oh, indeed,' said Captain Howell and favoured Bel with his vulpine stare this time—she thought that perhaps with that tinge of red in his hair he was more fox than wolf, 'I shall ask her now, seeing that you were more concerned to reprimand me than to make your offer directly to her. Tell him, my dear Mrs Merrick, that you would much prefer me as a partner—seasoned men are always preferable to raw boys, as I am sure you are well aware.'

There was something so brutally suggestive in his manner of speech to her, so unpleasantly coarse, that Bel was sure he was offering her a double meaning— suggesting that she was a courtesan, or very knowing, at the least. She would much prefer Marcus, and began to falter, her usual calm on the verge of breaking down, as Captain Howell plainly saw, so that he said, quite softly, 'It would be wise, I think, Mrs Merrick, to accept my offer for tonight's Assembly, rather than Mark's here.' And this time his smile was almost a leer.

'Forgive me, Howell,' announced a new voice in the conversation glacially, 'but Mrs Merrick will be attending this evening's Assembly with me. I was beforehand, although you have not given her time to say so.'

It was Francis Carey, turned out completely *à point*, not for a cross-country journey as his half-sister had suggested, but wearing Town clothes of the most exquisite perfection.

'So you say, Carey,' said Rhys Howell smoothly. 'But Mrs Merrick has mentioned nothing of this. He seeks to pre-empt you unfairly, does he not, dear madam? Pray tell him either that you have changed your mind, or that he took your consent for granted!'

'Oh!' Bel was suddenly quite outraged by the behaviour of all three men, for Marcus, unseen by either Francis or Captain Howell, was mouthing something at her and pointing to himself, while Francis and the captain faced one another like a pair of mad dogs disputing a particularly juicy bone. And what was Francis doing here, anyway? Why was he not, as Almeria had said, jaunting about Leicestershire, rather than rushing here to tease her again?

She could think of nothing better to say than to ask him that!

'What are you doing here, Lord Francis? Almeria said that you were páying duty calls about Leicestershire.'

'I changed my mind,' he announced curtly. 'And, for your sake, a good thing too. I will not have you throw me over to go with another man.'

'Mrs Merrick does not confirm that she agreed to attend with you,' Rhys Howell began. 'I think you must be mistook——'

'No,' snorted Francis. 'It is you who are mistook, Howell. In decency you had better retire.'

'Oh,' cried Bel, suddenly beside herself at all this, and stamping her foot. 'I have not agreed to attend with anyone yet. You are both intolerable, Lord Francis for taking my agreement yesterday as read, without waiting for an answer, you to persist, Captain Howell, so mannerlessly, and as for Marcus, making faces at me behind you both, with such examples before him as the pair of you, I am not surprised at *his* conduct. No——' as both men opened their mouths again. '—I shall be going with...with... Mr Henry Venn,' for poor Henry had been besieging her for weeks to attend with him, and now she would inform him that she would be his partner this evening if he wished.

She had not the slightest wish to go anywhere with Henry, with or without his mother, for she was sure that Mrs Venn would attach herself to them this evening, but she was suddenly so enraged with both of them, and the attention which this altercation was causing, as their voices grew louder and louder, that she wanted nothing from either of them!

Both men suddenly realised that there was nothing left to fight for, and both said together, 'Then you will do me the honour of allowing me to wait on you this afternoon,' to which she replied shortly,

'Indeed no. I never receive on Wednesday afternoon. I have other duties to attend to, other matters to occupy me.'

Both men, unknown to each other and to Bel, were immediately struck with the same thought.

Other matters to which to attend! What could they be? Could it be that madam was still plying her trade in Lulsgate, discreetly, of course, but keeping in practice and earning a little money on the side? Both opened their mouths to try to make other arrangements. Francis's fury with both Bel and Captain Howell made him behave most uncharacteristically, as he later told himself dismally, Mrs Bel Merrick having such a devastating effect on his manners as well as his morals, but Bel was before them again.

'If you are trying to make an appointment with me,' she said crossly, 'you must both call at my door and take your chances, and that goes for you too, Lord Tawstock,' she added, seeing Marcus look hopeful at the prospect of cutting out his seniors. 'And now you will excuse me. I must return to Mrs Broughton with her latest novel, and you, Lord Francis, will proffer my excuses to your sister, for not returning with her, but I feel the need for something stronger than Lulsgate waters to restore me.'

She was completely unaware that, slightly flushed, her face animated, she had never looked so desirable, so that both men before her were in the grip of the strongest desire to enjoy the little widow whether she would or no.

Fortunately unknowing, Bel bowed and retired, anger lending grace to her carriage, elegance to her walk and fire to her eyes, so that every head in the room turned to see her go.

Well! she thought on emerging into the street again.

If I had thought to ensure for myself a quiet life by coming to Lulsgate, I certainly committed the biggest mistake of my life. What with Francis promising me ravishment and surrender in the distant future, and Captain Howell uttering veiled threats in the present, it seems that I must have all my wits about me, or I shall be sunk with all hands by Lord Francis, and be charged to destruction by Captain Howell. A plague on you both, gentlemen. But, oh, dear, she knew that that sentiment did not apply to Lord Francis Carey, however much it did to Captain Rhys Howell!

CHAPTER NINE

'So,' SAID Lady Almeria to her half-brother, 'you changed your mind about your day's activities.'

'Yes.' Francis was brief. He had no mind to explain to Almeria that he, who had dismissed women to the edge of his life, had been so haunted by Bel Merrick that he had been unable to leave Lulsgate Spa that morning knowing that she was likely to meet that ineffable swine Rhys Howell at the Pump Room.

Even Almeria, less so her husband, was surprised when, over luncheon, a cold collation as usual, Francis remarked, apparently idly, 'I understand from Mrs Merrick that she never receives on Wednesday afternoons, is otherwise engaged. With you on parish matters, I suppose.'

Almeria, as well as Philip, looked at him sharply. 'I really don't know, Francis. I only know that Bel is never available on Wednesday and Friday afternoon, and it has not occurred to me to question her on her activities. I know that everyone in Lulsgate likes to think that they know what everyone else is doing, but it is a cast of mind which I deplore.'

Nothing more to say on that, then! was Francis's glum internal comment. Nothing for it but to set Cassius to watching her, an ignoble act of which he was ashamed, but then his whole conduct lately had become shameful, and he shuddered a little at what Almeria might think if she knew, not only the truth about Bel, but how he was virtually trying to blackmail her into his bed—for he had to acknowledge that his actions justified no other description.

Luncheon passed without further discussion of Bel

Merrick, Philip contenting himself with discussing local matters, and commenting on the latest news in *The Times* about Queen Caroline and matters European, being determined to pick Francis's good brains while he was staying with them.

Only, when Francis had excused himself, ostensibly to change into riding clothes, but actually to brief Cassius—who had performed several such missions for him in Paris on behalf of some diplomatic subtleties, and was consequently able to disguise his tracking of others successfully—Philip looked up at his wife and said quietly, 'A private word with you, my dear.'

Almeria's expression showed her surprise when in response to her nod he said, 'Tell me, my dear, you know him well. Do not you think that there is something a little odd about Francis's interest in Mrs Merrick?'

'Odd?' repeated Almeria. 'Well, only in the sense that it is as long as I can remember since Francis showed an interest in any woman.'

'I think there is more to it than that,' observed Philip thoughtfully. 'I may be mistaken, but there is something in his speech and manner to her which is—to me, at least—a little strange, not at all like his usual conduct towards women.'

'I cannot say,' answered Almeria, 'that I have noticed anything untoward—and why should there be? Bel is a dear, sweet girl, and that should gain her nothing but approbation from Francis, surely.'

'Exactly so,' said Philip mysteriously, and decided to let the matter drop. He did wonder why his brother-in-law had bolted so rapidly from the room after asking pointed questions about Bel Merrick, and also wondered what he was doing now.

What Francis was doing was briefing Cassius, that close-mouthed Mercury, the messenger whom Francis could trust, who would never gossip, however bribed or tempted, because Francis had saved him from ruin and transportation some ten years ago, and he had served him devotedly ever since.

'Watch the house,' Francis concluded, 'and if Mrs Merrick leaves it follow her discreetly, find out where she goes, and then come and report to me immediately.'

Cassius nodded, saying aloud as he set off on his mission, 'And what's got in to you, cully? Never seen you so hot after a skirt afore. Not to say that this one ain't a prime piece of meat—and if you think she's a lightskirt, which I suspects as you do, then you're fit for Bedlam, sir, though I'll not tell you so!'

Francis, unaware of his judgemental servant's thoughts, decided to change, then rest a little in Philip's study until Cassius should return, hopefully with some useful information. Could Bel Merrick really be plying her trade in Lulsgate Spa? And if she were, why should it trouble him?

Bel set off on her usual Wednesday afternoon errand unaware that Cassius was on her tail—as he would have said. She had, he noted, no one with her, was plainly dressed in dove-grey and walked briskly along. She carried a covered basket, and took the road out of Lulsgate in the direction of that small and poverty-stricken village, Morewood, where the long depression after the late wars, coupled with the new machinery, had virtually destroyed the livelihood of the framework knitters there, so many fewer men being needed to operate the new machines, which were also capable of knitting much wider and longer pieces of cloth—a fact which still further depressed the wages of those fortunate enough to be employed to work them, whose old standard of living had been destroyed.

Occasionally some of those who had no work intruded into Lulsgate, their ragged children behind them, to try to beg from rich visitors to the spa, but the constables officiously ordered them back to their 'proper dwellings' and told them not to annoy their betters.

Well, thought Cassius sardonically, if m'lord thought madam was after trade, which Cassius suspected he did, then she was visiting an odd place to find it; and when Bel finally reached her destination he gave a long whistle before investigating further. The smile on his face as he hurried back to report was even more sardonic than it usually was, and the report he finally made to Francis more cryptic than it need have been — for Cassius was not averse to teasing the master who had saved him, but who he sometimes thought was too high-nosed for his own good!

Morewood! She was visiting Morewood! What the devil was she doing there? The sketchy report which Cassius had made had told Francis only that Bel had visited a small house on the further side of the little village, and that Cassius had no idea what she was doing there, or to whom the house belonged, he not liking to ask questions and draw attention to himself.

Francis had driven through Morewood once, and the place had depressed him. It contained only a few good homes, the whole village being given over to cottages with long windows in their upper rooms, the typical sign of framework knitters' homes, their machines always kept on the upper floors. The air of poverty saddened him, as it did Philip Harley, who tried, through Henry Venn who looked after the Chapel of Ease there, to alleviate the villagers' dreadful conditions. To small avail, for the villagers had turned away from the established church and favoured a Methodist ministry whose chapel was a tin tabernacle, very unlike the graceful Gothic building for which Henry Venn was responsible.

He decided to take his curricle to Morewood and

reconnoitre; the word sounded better than spying, somehow—which, after all, was what he was doing, but all in a good cause, he told himself sanctimoniously. But what good cause was that? The cause of Francis Carey's insatiable curiosity about everything which concerned Bel Merrick, of course.

The journey to Morewood, a silently gleeful Cassius up behind him, was soon accomplished, and just outside the village he left the curricle and the tiger concealed in a side-lane and began to walk briskly to where Cassius had told him Bel had made for.

The little house was modest enough—surely not a worthwhile customer there—and he stopped a sullen old man to ask him to whom it belonged, and his jaw dropped when the man said, 'Gideon Birch, the Methodee minister, o' course. Everyone knows that!'

The minister? What the devil was Bel Merrick doing with a Methodist minister? He stared at the little house, and then, on an impulse, hearing voices, he walked down the lane by the side of the house, to glare over a hedge at the garden from whence the voices—and now childish laughter—were coming.

There was nothing for it. That grandee, Lord Francis Carey, the pride of the Corps Diplomatique, was reduced to standing tiptoe in a lane and peering over a hedge. Worse was to come, for what he saw shamed him.

Sitting on the lawn, a group of small children facing her, was Bel Merrick. The children, of all ages from five to about twelve, so far as he could judge, were equipped with slates and pencils, and an impromptu spelling bee was in progress. The laughter was because as each child correctly spelt the name of an animal Bel was drawing it on the slate before her and showing it to them.

And while he stood there, fascinated, she drew an animal and then asked a small child in the front row to tell her its name, and spell it for her. Something strange seemed to happen, something passed from him to her, for as the child finished Bel turned her head slowly, to see him watching her.

A tide of colour washed over her face. She looked defiantly at him, said loudly, 'See, children, we have a visitor. Pray join us, Lord Francis, seeing that you have tracked me down. I could do with an assistant.'

Francis had never, in his whole life, felt so miserably helpless and ashamed. He shook his head, disembodied, he knew, the rest of him hidden by the hedge, only for her to cry, 'Never say you are shy, sir, nor that you have no feeling for these little ones. You have a duty to *me* now, having followed me here; pray fulfil it. There is a gate a little further on by which you may enter.' And now it was her look which challenged him, so that he shrugged; nothing for it. He could not retreat like a whipped cur—which was, astonishingly, how he felt, there was such a world of difference between what he had thought she was doing and what she was actually doing!

Bel felt indignation roaring through her, for how dared he spy on her, and follow her, especially after this morning? So that when she rose to meet him her face was brighter than ever, with a mixture of anger and scorn.

'Come, sir. You must meet my pupils. They are some of the poor children who have no work to go to. You do know that these little ones work long hours, and shame on us that we allow it. They need to learn to read and to write, and there is no school here, no dame to teach them, nor could their parents pay to keep one, so Mr Birch, the minister here, whom I met some few months ago, accepted my offer to teach these little ones, he having no aptitude for the task and having so many other duties.'

Francis tried to revive his scorn by assuming that Mr

Gideon Birch was some handsome young fellow of the artisan class turned preacher who might have some attraction for Mrs Bel Merrick, she presumably having come from that class of persons herself, but he despised himself for the thought, and sat on a white-painted wooden garden seat— 'where,' said Bel, scornfully, 'you may remain if you do not disturb us.'

The lesson continued, Bel, watching him, occasionally asking him a question, to include him in the lesson. One of the children read a small passage from the Bible, the story of Joseph, and then Bel asked them questions about it, as Francis remembered his governess similarly questioning him, long ago, in the schoolroom at the top of Tawstock House, something which he had long forgotten.

Outwardly calm, Bel was in turmoil. What business did he have to track her here? Could there be nothing left to herself, nothing private? For she had not even told Almeria of this. In her middle teens she had run, at her late papa's suggestion, such little classes for the poor children of Brangton, but Lulsgate, rich, important and comfortable, did not need such amenities; accidentally meeting Gideon Birch, she had discovered the need in Morewood for such help as she could give, and had offered to give it.

The little meeting ended, as Mr Birch always wished it, with all the class reciting the Lord's Prayer, heads bent, hands held together, and then the children filed out, the little boys bowing to Bel, and the little girls curtsying, and before they left through the gate they extended, at Bel's instructions, the same politeness to Francis.

'And now, sir,' she said, turning to him, 'why are you here?'

He had the grace to look awkward, she thought, and said, 'I was annoyed—I know that it was wrong of me—when you said that you were not at home this afternoon. I...was determined to find out what you were doing.'

'And now you have found out,' said Bel, almost contemptuously, thinking that for the first time the initiative in their meetings had passed from him to her, 'I think that you should leave, don't you? Unless you feel that there is some ukase, some edict you might like to pass to prevent me from lightening these children's lives a little.' Here, in this quiet garden, where she could see Gideon Birch through his kitchen window preparing to come outside, there was no place for his aristocratic scorn.

'Now you are being unfair,' he protested, watching an old man leave the house and come towards them, carrying a tray on which stood a pitcher of lemonade and three glasses. 'I can have no conceivable objection to the errand of mercy on which you are engaged.'

'No?' said Bel fiercely. 'I thought that you might protest that my presence might pollute them,' but, suddenly hearing Mr Birch approach them, she said more coolly, 'I think that I ought to introduce you to Mr Birch, even if I cannot explain your presence here to him, since I have no inkling of the reason for it myself.'

Mr Birch had placed his tray on a small wooden table, painted to match the bench. Francis rose as he did so, and bowed, saying—and it was all that he could think of in his very real distress and embarrassment, 'I have come to escort Mrs Merrick home,' after Bel had performed the necessary introductions.

No virile young suitor, Mr Gideon Birch, but an elderly man with a warm, concerned face, who said, 'You will do me the honour, Lord Francis, of taking a glass of my sister's good lemonade with us. She is unfortunately absent, so cannot welcome you. I am happy to learn that Mrs Merrick will have an escort today. I am never easy that she comes alone, although

I understand why she does. She does us a great kindness in offering her services to us, free of charge, especially as she is not a member of our church, although I am one of those Methodists who likes to think of himself as still part of the Church of England's fold, as John Wesley was.'

Bel noted that Francis was rapidly recovering his *savoir-faire* and spoke interestedly and informedly to Mr Birch, so that that gentleman thought what a gracious person he was, unlike many of the mighty whom Mr Birch had so far encountered.

'So,' said Francis, 'you were an Oxford man yourself before you heard George Whitfield preach and were converted.'

'Yes,' said Mr Birch mildly. 'I was offered a preferment in South Yorkshire, whence my family is sprung, but once I had been converted, had endured my private encounter on the road to Damascus, there was nothing for it, I had to follow my Master's call. Besides, there are many to succour the rich, few the poor. They need the Lord more in places like Morewood than in Lulsgate Spa.'

'Well spoken,' said Francis, now the grandee who could accommodate himself to any society, and plainly both interesting and pleasing the old man by displaying his knowledge without flaunting it, as Bel noticed.

She realised again, as she had often done before, that men were quite different when not with women, spoke differently, and had a range of interests rarely displayed in social intercourse. Whether she was glad or sorry at this she did not know, only that it was true, and wondered why so few women seemed to realise that it was so.

She was aware of Francis's eyes on her, answered a question of Mr Birch's, drank his excellent lemonade, and promised to be back on Friday to take the class again.

She made her adieus to the old man, picked up her plain bonnet, and put it on, and tied its ribbons, retrieved her parasol and the empty basket which Mr Birch had brought from the house.

'Mrs Merrick,' he informed Francis, 'always brings us some excellent cake. She says that it is surplus to her wants, would be thrown away if we did not accept it, but I suspect by its excellence that that is her way of bribing us not to refuse it, not letting us seem to sponge upon her kindness. She is a true friend—does good by stealth. I trust, sir, that you will not reveal to others what you have discovered.'

'Indeed not,' Francis replied, sincerity in his voice. 'if that is what you both wish.'

'I would not discommode her, sir,' said Mr Birch, 'for there are those who would not be pleased at what she does, and would gossip unpleasantly of it, and I am happy to learn that you are prepared to be discreet, will be careful to consider her interests,' and the old eyes on Francis were shrewd. 'We may meet again some time, sir, I hope. It is a long time since I was privileged to talk with a person as informed as yourself.'

They all bowed their farewells, Mr Birch retaining the formal manners of the eighteenth-century days when he had been a young scholar at Magdalen, Oxford.

'So,' said Francis, a little heavily, Bel thought, on their leaving the pleasant garden, 'I owe you an apology, Mrs Merrick.'

'For what you thought of me,' returned Bel shrewdly, 'or for following me?'

'Both,' said Francis, 'and I think you must agree that I could not possibly have guessed what you are doing. You will not hold it against me, and refuse a ride home?'

Bel looked about for his curricle, noting that when

he added, 'I have it down a side-street, Cassius attending,' he had the grace to blush.

'Diplomatic treachery at work, I see,' she commented sardonically. 'Was it Cassius who followed me? I am sure that it was not yourself!'

Francis chose to ignore this, saying instead as they rounded the corner to see Cassius staring at them, a knowing expression on his wrinkled face, 'I shall say nothing of this to Almeria and Philip, for had you wished them to know I am sure you would have told them. I do not think they would be displeased, you know.'

'Perhaps not,' said Bel a little curtly as Francis helped her up, Cassius attending to the horses, 'but I have no wish for gossip as Mr Birch says, and you must know as well as I do that the Methodist connection is not well seen, even if the Countess of Huntingdon has established a Connexion of her own. But I am not a countess, and my patronage would not be so honoured as hers, by no means.'

They were off, Bel's now empty basket on her knee, both of them unwontedly silent. Francis was wondering again about the strange nature of the courtesan he was driving home, and Bel was wondering about him. He had behaved so simply and properly to old Mr Birch; could it ever be that he might behave so to herself?

CHAPTER TEN

HENRY VENN, unable to believe his luck, did take Bel to the ball at the Assembly Rooms, and of course Bel was right: his mother did accompany them. Captain Howell and Marcus also claimed her for dances, but not Francis Carey.

Francis, in the oddest state of mind it had been his misfortune to suffer after the afternoon's contretemps—for that was the only way he could interpret it truthfully—could not bring himself to see Bel Merrick in public until he had recovered his usual haughty equanimity—if he could ever regain it, that was!

He hardly knew how he felt, and could not have believed the confusion of mind which he found himself in, and if anyone had told him a month ago that he would be in a mad frenzy of desire for a ladybird, was refusing to slake it by buying her, was not sure that he was other than in love with her, and was determined to have her in love with him, desperately and beyond reason, he would have called them a liar.

Seeing her in the garden with the children and later with Mr Birch had brought a new dimension to their relationship. What a paradox she was! He supposed that he should not be surprised to find that a loose woman was a practical and practising Christian, but he was.

Bel, for her part, was surprised to discover how sorry she was that Francis was absent. Whatever the reason, when he walked into a room she felt that he brought passion and vitality in with him, never mind that he despised her. All the other men she met seemed third-rate beside him.

'So, you have taken pity on poor Henry, then,' Almeria said to her in the interval between dances when Bel was alone. Henry had gone to fetch her a cooling drink, and his mama was busily engaged with three other mature matrons, destroying the reputations of any who incurred their displeasure, in the intervals of playing a game of whist in a small room opening into the ballroom itself.

'Francis refused to come,' she continued. 'He sent you his compliments, and hoped to attend, but said he was weary, needed an early night. Although what,' she added, 'he can have been doing in Lulsgate to weary him neither Philip nor I can think. London never seems to tire him so.'

'The country air this afternoon too strong for him?' said Bel, cryptically if a little naughtily.

'Perhaps,' said Almeria doubtfully. 'He did take a drive this afternoon—I believe he gave you a lift at the end of it; he seemed *distrait* when he returned.' She hesitated. 'He was a little as he was when his wife died. I feel that perhaps it would be right of me to inform you of his sad story. I know that he will never tell you, and Philip would say I was interfering, but I think that you ought to know; it explains him so much.'

She fell silent, and Bel said nothing. Francis was, or rather had been, married! She wondered what had happened, and her heart beat rapidly as she waited for Almeria to continue.

'He was only nineteen when he married his childhood sweetheart, Cassie—Cassandra Poyntz, Sir Charles Poyntz's daughter. They were so in love, and Francis was not a bit as he is now—a little forbidding, I must admit. He was so happy and jolly, rather like a more responsible Marcus. He was in the navy, as I suppose you know. They only had five happy months together, then Francis had to go to sea and left Cassie in Portsmouth; she was two months pregnant. He was on HMS Circe, which was sunk in action; he was transferred to another ship going to a West Indies station, and, what with one thing and another, instead of being back with her in a few months to be there when the baby was born it was a year before he saw Portsmouth again.

'And when he reached home she was five months dead, and the baby too. She was a little thing, very sweet and gentle, and the birth was something like poor Princess Charlotte's and the outcome was the same. Mother and child both dead. Poor Francis. You can imagine what it did to him. He quite changed. Jack, our brother, said he grew up in an hour, and that it was a pity it was so quick, for he refused all consolation, would never speak of her, and took occupation and duty for his wife, would hardly look at a woman—indeed, he has spoken to and shown more interest in you than in all the other women in his life since Cassie died put together.'

Almeria fell silent; she had promised Philip that she would not interfere, but she had felt that Bel should know the truth about her half-brother.

Oh, poor Francis, what a terrible story! was Bel's immediate and pitying reaction. It gave him no right to treat her as he did, but she could understand why he would never give his heart away again, seeing what had happened to him when he had done so before—everything gone in an instant when he had been looking forward to wife and child both.

She guessed, too, and guessed correctly, that duty and shunning the fair sex had brought Francis to the point where he had come to see women as enemies, waiting to hurt him again.

She grew quiet, thoughtful, and when Henry returned the bright sparkle of her early evening manner had gone, so much so that on Henry's showing his displeasure at Captain Howell for coming to claim her

for their dance she dismissed it as absently as she did
his further criticism of the raffish captain, as he termed
him, after he had returned her. In the same *distraite*
fashion she had agreed to Rhys Howell's insistence
that he visit her the following day.

That night, lying in bed, she thought over her
relationship with Francis, and bitterly regretted the
anger which had seized her when he had burst in that
first day, and the reckless deceit with which she had
cheated him. She was compelled to admit that her own
conduct had helped to provoke him into believing that
she shared her sister's profession, and that at no time
had she given him any reason to think otherwise than
that she was a courtesan, too.

Well, in the words of her old governess, she thought
ruefully, You have made your bed, Bel, and must lie
on it, and then her usual bright wit conquered her
ridiculous self-pity, as she added the gloss, and you
must try to prevent Francis Carey from lying on it, too.
Unless he offers you a wedding-ring, that is. And,
thinking of him, she let sleep take her into a land
where regrets and hopes were transformed into other
symbols and she was running through a wood, tears
streaming down her face, looking for something—
what?—and, panting, woke to the realisation that, treat
her as he might, it was Francis Carey, so sadly
bereaved, for whom she was weeping. Or was it
herself?

Bel had no desire whatsoever to entertain Rhys
Howell. She felt an instinctive distrust of him and all
his works, and was sorry to see what a firm friend he
was of silly young Marcus's; for all her youth, she had
discovered that she possessed the power to read people
aright. She wondered again if Marianne had shared it,
and wondered further if it had helped to make her so
successful.

She waited for the sound of the knocker all morning, quite distracted, causing Mrs Broughton to say mildly, 'You are hardly yourself today, my dear. I do hope that you are not sickening for something.'

'No,' said Bel rapidly, and to stop further comment picked up *Filippo's Tower* and said, 'Pray allow me to read to you, madam,' only for Mrs Broughton to look at her, scandalised, and remark, 'In the morning, my dear?' for she had been brought up in a household where novels were allowed to be read provided only that they were indulged in in the afternoon, when all one's duties were done.

'Oh, yes,' sighed Bel, and picked up the little night-dress she was working, and began to hem industriously, an occupation which had one drawback: she had the time to think both of Captain Howell's unwanted visit, and of Francis Carey's being either cold and haughty, or unwontedly amorous—both expressions seemingly reserved for Mrs Bel Merrick!

The doorknocker duly reverberated through the house. Mrs Broughton looked up from her plain sewing—canvas work, like novels, being reserved for the afternoon, and said hopefully, 'I do hope that that is dear Lord Francis come a-calling. I do declare I am quite in love with the man. Oh, to be twenty-five again!'

But it was, as Bel expected, Captain Howell whom the maid announced, and Captain Howell who came in, his black cane with its ivory top in his hand, his clothes just that little bit too fashionable in a flash way. Indeed, in another world, of which Bel knew nothing, he was known as 'Flash Howell' and valued accordingly.

'Ladies.' He was all good manners this morning: he put down his hat and his cane beside the chair which he was offered, made small talk for a moment, and then said, almost carelessly, leaning forward to give

Bel the full benefit of his smile, 'My dear Mrs Merrick, I wonder if you would allow me to have a few words alone with you? I have some private messages for you, from your sister, which she has asked me to deliver, concerning your family. You will forgive us, madam, will you not?' he said, turning his doubtful charm on Mrs Broughton.

'My sister?' queried Bel, trying to keep her voice steady. She had had but the one, Marianne, also known as Marina St George, and to hear Captain Howell speak of sister and messages filled her with nameless dread.

'Your dear sister Marianne,' said Rhys Howell sweetly. 'You have but the one, I believe.'

Had was the proper tense, thought Bel distractedly, but looked at Mrs Broughton; if Rhys Howell proposed to speak to her of Marianne—and how had he tracked her here, and how did he know that she was Marianne's sister?—she had no wish for Mrs Broughton to be present.

'No matter,' smiled Mrs Broughton, determined to love every gentleman who seemed to possess a *tendre* for dear Bel. 'I will take a turn in the garden. I see our neighbour is there; we may discuss the prospect of a good plum crop together. Plum tart is a favourite delicacy of mine,' and she drifted through the glass doors to the garden.

'What an obliging soul,' remarked Rhys Howell, looking after her, an unpleasant leer on his face.

'My sister, you said,' offered Bel, desperate to get this over with, an indelicate expression used by her maid Lottie for anything from taking physic to listening to a tedious sermon in church.

'Ah, yes, your sister,' drawled the captain. 'Dear Mrs Marina St George, such a high flyer; you may imagine how I felt when I came back from urgent business on the Continent to discover her unexpectedly dead. her sister inherited, the house sold. I was desolate. We were partners, she and I. I cannot for the world understand how she came to forget me in her will. Why, she owed her start in her. . .way of life to me, and an apt pupil she certainly was.'

He paused. 'You were about to say something, *Mrs* Merrick?' and he trod hard on the word Mrs, his expression sardonic.

Bel would not be put off by his odious mixture of innuendo and familiarity.

'Mrs Marina St George?' she began. 'I know of no such person.'

'Oh, come, my love,' said Captain Howell, closing one eye in a wink so lubricious that Bel shuddered before it. 'No need to try to flim-flam me, my dear Miss Passmore. A useful invention, Mr Merrick, I am sure. You share your dead sister's wit and inventiveness; we should be splendid partners, you and I. Clergymen's daughters make the best whores, should they decide to go to the bad, and your sister went to the bad most spectacularly. Now you, you could rival her—you have managed to preserve a delicacy and innocence which are quite remarkable.'

'You have lost me,' said Bel, rising. 'I ask you to leave. I have no idea of what you speak.'

'Won't do, you know,' leered Captain Howell confidentially, putting a hand familiarly on Bel's knee. 'Father the Reverend Mr Caius Passmore, sister the late and talented Marina, servant named Lottie, who was close-mouthed, for a woman, but felt compelled to write to her great-nephew, upon whom she dotes, where you are and what you were doing. . . You see I speak no lie; your sister and I were so close she told me everything of you. Now what, I wonder, would that upright gentleman Lord Francis Carey think, if informed that the virtuous little widow was the sister of the fair Marina, and probably a dab hand at the

game herself? Wouldn't like him to know, would you—
eh, would you?' And his voice rose menacingly.

Bel had a desperate desire to laugh, seeing that Lord
Francis also shared the delusion of her lack of virtue
with Captain Howell, and would not be in the least
surprised at whatever Captain Howell chose to tell
him.

'And the aristocratic sister, and the parson husband—what would they think of their pious home's
being a haven for such as yourself, my dear? Worth
something to keep me quiet, do you think? That is if
you don't want to resume Marina's partnership with
me, eh?' His wink grew more grotesque by the minute.

Had Marianne really been this low rogue's partner,
thought Bel, and did it matter if she had? In the here
and now he was perfectly able to ruin her socially and
financially, and would have no scruple about doing
either.

She rose, deciding to put on a brass face and deny
everything. 'I am still at a loss,' she replied, her voice
freezing, 'and I ask you to leave immediately. I am not
accustomed to being insulted in my own home.'

Captain Howell put his finger by his nose. 'Oh, I'm
patient, sweet, patient. I mean to stay in this dull
backwater a while longer, and you, you'll go nowhere,
for you've nowhere to go. I shall remind you of my
wishes, madam, until reckoning day, when you'll either
give me what your sister morally owed me, or I shall
tell Lulsgate Spa of the serpent in their bed of flowers.
Until then, madam, adieu.'

He picked up his hat and cane, walked to the door,
bowed mockingly and added, 'Allow me to congratulate you, madam. I do believe that you are as cool a
piece as the great Marina herself, and you deserve his
haughty lordship as a prize, yes, you do. But beware,
madam, beware. I know these high-nosed gentlemen.
Should he discover who and what you are...' and he

wagged his head commiseratingly at her '. . .*that* would be an interesting day, a most interesting day. Till we meet again, madam, for meet we most assuredly shall— to do good business together, I hope—you must not keep all the rewards to yourself!'

CHAPTER ELEVEN

Bel hardly knew whether to laugh or to cry: to laugh at Captain Howell's notion of the shock which Lord Francis Carey would receive over the knowledge that Bel's sister was Marina St George, something which he already knew, or to cry over the fact that two men now knew her secret—and the second a malignant creature who would not hesitate to harm her in any way he could in order to get some, or all, of Marina's fortune for himself.

And there was no one whom she could tell or to whom she could turn for advice or help. She was quite alone, and the strange thought struck her that the vile way in which Captain Howell had spoken to her, not only the manner of his speech, but the way in which he had looked at her, held his body, revealed how different a man Francis Carey was from the unpleasant captain, even though he despised her for being, as he thought, a courtesan.

Bel even realised that in other circumstances she might have gone to Francis for help and protection, something which was now impossible.

Pondering this, she heard the knocker go again, and voices in the hall. The door opened and the little maid stood there, only to be swept aside by Francis, his face ablaze, saying, 'I must see Mrs Merrick, and at once.'

Bel wanted no more scandal, and said coolly, feeling that she had exchanged one tormentor, Captain Howell, only to gain another, Francis Carey, 'Yes, you may see me, Lord Francis,' so that the little maid bobbed at her and departed. She turned to him, lifted her brows and, still cool, said, 'Well, sir, what brings you here in such a pelter that you have forgotten your breeding?'

Francis made no response to this last. Lip curling, he said, 'So, you have been entertaining the captain alone? Remarkable, seeing what a pother you made over walking with me in the garden with Mrs Broughton playing nearby dragon!'

'It is no business of yours. . .' began Bel, only to have him fling at her,

'It is not only your reputation for which you should have a care, madam, but your safety which you should also consider. The man is, I am certain—nay, I have reason to know—little more than a common criminal. He left the Life Guards under the most dubious circumstances, was forced to flee England because he cheated his criminal associates, performed the same unwise act in France, and was compelled to return—which is why he is here, rather than London, to escape vengeance, one presumes—and you, madam, see fit to entertain him alone!'

He ran out of breath, and about time too, thought Bel, the courage with which she always faced life strong in her as he moved towards her. She had been standing by the glass doors when he entered, about to rejoin Mrs Broughton, whom she could see, head bobbing, talking with their neighbour—about plum tart probably! This prosaic thought, against all the suppressed violence which had been going on in her quiet drawing-room, made her want to giggle.

Francis saw the smile blossom on her face, misinterpreted it, and said furiously, 'A joke, madam? You think Rhys Howell's unsavoury reputation a joke!'

'I am wondering,' said Bel, her heart hammering, 'why, knowing this of him, you do nothing about it. The man should be before the Justices, surely, if half of what you say of him is true.'

'Oh, indeed,' he almost snarled, 'I should have

known that your light-footed wit would have you firing broadsides at me. Well, let me tell you, my legal-minded lady, that I have no evidence of this to satisfy a court, but, being in France when he was, and at the Embassy, I knew a deal more than I should about such. . .persons, even if little enough to do anything about it, except to be wary, and warn my friends.'

'Your friends!' Bel's contemptuous snort of laughter would have graced a Drury Lane melodrama, so fine was it. 'Am I, then, to count myself one of their number? You surprise me, sir. I thought that I was only fit to be thrown on a bed and ravished, or tied to the cart's tail as a common whore to be whipped!'

'Oh.' Poor Francis was breathless. Armoured with rage at both men who were in their different fashions blackmailing her, Bel had never looked so lovely. Her luminous green eyes flashed fire; even her red curls seemed springier; the tender mouth quivered voluptuously; her whole beautiful body, although she did not know this, seemed to be straining against the light muslin dress she wore. It was enough to drive any red-blooded male mad with desire. Francis Carey felt a very red-blooded male indeed. 'I come to warn you, help you, madam, since you seem to need it, and what reward do I receive? A lawyer in skirts, instructing me of my duty.'

He was almost upon her, and a dreadful mirth, akin to hysteria, Bel knew, began to inform her. She dodged away from him, into the room—she dared not let him pursue her outside, for fear that the anger which consumed him might cause him to be unwise before Mrs Broughton and reveal all, which would never do.

In her haste to remove him from the revealing window she caught against the little occasional table on which her workbox stood and knocked it over, the child's nightdress and the contents of the box cascading across the floor, pins, reels of cotton, her thimble, crochet hooks and all the paraphernalia which accompanied a lady's sewing spread out between them.

To Bel's surprise this minor disaster seemed infinitely more important than all the dreadful threats which the two men in her life had thrown at her.

'Oh, no,' she wailed, 'now look what you have made me do!' and she fell plump on her knees on the carpet, grieving over each pin and hook as though she were recovering the treasures of Midas, at least.

Francis was nearly as fevered as she was. Jealousy, desire and frustration held him in thrall, and the sight of her on her knees on the carpet, lovely face distressed, overset him further.

To his own subsequent astonishment—what could have got into him to behave so uncharacteristically?—he found himself on his knees before her, to the ruin of his breeches, his boots and his common sense, none of them assisted by the violence which he was doing to them. 'Oh, no,' he crooned, clumsily trying to pick up pins, 'do not grieve,' and then, as she stared at him astonished, the little nightgown in her hands, a crystal teardrop running down one damask cheek, he was going mad, wanting to write poetry—to a whore, yes, a whore, but what did that matter? He put up his hands to clasp her face in them, saying tenderly, 'Oh, do not cry, I beg of you, do not cry, pray let me kiss that tear away,' and before she could stop him he licked up the salty pearl and began to suit his actions to his words.

He had forgotten that he had promised himself that she would be on her knees begging him, not the other way round, but no matter. While Bel. . .

While Bel what? She should be thrusting him away, telling him to take his mouth where it was wanted, but each delicate moth-like kiss made it harder and harder for her to do any such thing. She was so near to him that she could see that his eyes were not a pure grey but had little black flecks in them, like granite. Could granite melt? It seemed to be doing so.

She gave a little moan, dropped the nightgown among the scattered pins and needles, and gently, very gently, as he lifted his mouth from her eyes to transfer it to her mouth, she kissed him back—and then sanity prevailed.

Mrs Broughton might come in, and she hated him, did she not? He thought her a whore and would shortly, if she were not careful, be treating her as one, here on the carpet, among the pins and needles; and what would Mrs Broughton think? For his hands had left her face and were beginning to pull her dress down. So she pushed him away before her body could betray her, and sprang to her feet, to leave him among the needles and pins; it was all that he deserved.

'Oh, you are all the same,' she raged at him. 'Show a little weakness, and you are all over us. And how can you, with all that you have said to me, be in the least surprised that I should wish to favour Captain Howell? If all diplomats are such muddled thinkers as you are— and naval captains, too,' she flung in for good measure, 'no wonder it took us so long to win the war, and to win allies, such mad heedlessness as you show, with Mrs Broughton in the garden and likely to interrupt you at your work any minute. Shame on you!'

Francis, still on his knees, stared up at her. Paradise so near, and now so far away. He wanted to pull her to the carpet, but Mrs Broughton's name was like cold water to him, whereas the sight of the angry Bel served only to rouse him further. He ached, yes, he did, and damn his treacherous body which had now overtaken the cold mind which had ruled it for so long, and mastered it quite, so that Bel Merrick walked through his days as well as his dreams.

And that came, he tried to tell himself sternly, from over-continence; Marcus was right, he should have indulged himself more, pleasured a few bits of muslin, and then this one bit of muslin would not inflame him so.

Useless talk—it was Bel Merrick he wanted and none else, and now she must know it, the witch, and would tantalise him the more, if he knew women.

He rose, conscious that for once all his haughty pride had fled from him—and she had done that, with one tear; one damned tear, and he was undone.

'You wrong me,' he began, and what a stupid thing to say—could he think of nothing better? 'I had meant to console you merely, but you do not seem to need consolation.'

'Oh!' exclaimed Bel. 'Consolation! I am not so green as to think that *that* was what you were about. Unless you were consoling yourself, that is!' She was rather proud of that last statement; it was quite fit to be one of La Rochefoucauld's witty *Maxims*, she thought.

Francis said, through his teeth, 'You are pleased to reproach me, madam. Believe me, you cannot reproach me more than I reproach myself.'

'For failing in your fell design to ravish me, presumably,' flashed Bel, on whom adversity seemed to be bestowing the gift of tongues. 'I cannot believe that you are feeling ashamed of so accosting me—*again*!' And her eyes flashed fire and ice.

That usually resourceful nobleman Francis Carey had no answer to this. He had never found himself in such a position before, and had certainly no experience to call on to advise him. God help me, he thought, if I were the womaniser she must think me, I should know what to do—unknowingly in the same case as Bel, who was as innocent as he was!

They stared at one another, each crediting the other with a past as lurid as it was imaginary, and each so strongly attracted to the other that they were compelled to call the emotion they were mutually experiencing hate, for they dared not admit that it was love.

'I think that you had better leave, at once, sir,' declaimed Bel, all dignity, rivalling Mrs Siddons in her best dramatic fit, to have him reply humbly, for him, ·

'You will remember a little what I said of Captain——' to have Bel retort,

'Oh, this is brave, sir, brave,' more in the line of Dorothy Jordan expressing grief at a wanton social misunderstanding than Siddons as Herodias about to demand John the Baptist's head on a platter.

Francis walked to the door, head high, past Bel, also head high, both principals congratulating themselves firmly on their recovered self-command, both painfully aware that in their recent passage they had given themselves away completely.

To think that I could find myself in love with such a haughty peacock who thinks all women are fair game, raged Bel inwardly, as Francis reproached himself for falling for a lightskirt, and then behaving towards her like a bullyboy whom Captain Howell might despise.

'Oh!' Bel let out a long breath, sank into a chair, as Mrs Broughton finally arrived, to prattle vaguely of plum tart, Lord Francis missed, *Filippo's Tower*, the changing weather, and how delightfully well Bel looked.

'All this social junketing must agree with you, my dear. You never looked so when we led a quiet life. You bloom, you positively bloom, I do declare!'

Lord Francis Carey was not blooming. Furious with himself for his loss of self-control—or was it that his loss of self-control had not gone far enough?—he strode down the main street of Lulsgate Spa, cutting everyone right, left and centre in his determination to reach his nephew and warn him of the captain. A letter which he had sent to London had brought him a reply,

giving him further, worse information about the man—
hence his visit to Bel, and his anger at seeing Howell
visit her, apparently in her confidence.

He strode into the taproom at the White Peacock
unaware that his expression was thunderous, and
whether his rage was directed at himself, Marcus,
Captain Howell or Bel Merrick he did not know.

Marcus was seated at one of the tables, a tankard in
front of him, smoking a clay pipe, an experiment he
was beginning to regret. There was no sign of his usual
court of hangers-on. He looked up in mild surprise as
his uncle entered.

'Didn't know you favoured this sort of entertainment, sir,' he offered almost reproachfully.

'I don't.' And Marcus could not help noticing that,
saying this, his uncle was even more glacial than usual.
Oh, Hades, another sermon, he thought glumly, and
prepared to be lectured again. What was it this time?
He did not have long to wait to find out.

'I am glad to find you alone,' began Francis, refusing
the chair which Marcus pointed out to him. 'Thank you,
no, I have no intention of staying. I have come to warn
you that Captain Howell is not a fit person for someone of your station and expectations to make a friend
of, never mind a boon companion,' he continued, his
temper not helped by Marcus's eyes beginning to roll
heavenwards.

'I know that I am no longer your guardian——'

He got no further, for Marcus said petulantly,
'Amen, to that, sir, and, that being so, I am in no mind
to be lectured by you. Rhys Howell is no better and no
worse than a hundred others in society, and I find him
amusing.'

'Then your taste is deplorable.' Francis was not
prepared to give way on this. 'I must warn you not to
play cards with him. I know that you frequent the
tables at Gaunt's Club on Bridge Street, and it has

come to my attention that you have already lost large sums to him; you must be aware that you cannot afford to do so.'

'Win some, lose some,' yawned Marcus aggravatingly. 'I won last week, he wins this week, next week the luck will turn again. All square at the end, Uncle, the odds see to that.'

'They do if all the players are honest——' began Francis, only to be interrupted again.

'Oh, damn that for a tale, sir, begging your pardon,' said Marcus. 'No reason to think Rhys other than straight. Sing another tune, sir, this one's flat.'

Francis could think of no tune which he could sing that would please anyone he knew. Even Almeria and Philip were looking at him a little sideways these days, especially Philip, and as for Bel Merrick...so it was not surprising that Marcus was recalcitrant—he should have expected nothing else.

'Very well,' he said, preparing to leave. 'I have done my best to warn you, but if you refuse to listen...' And he shrugged his shoulders. 'I would have thought that the man's character shone on his face—that, and the fact that he has come to Lulsgate at all.'

'He came because I did,' returned Marcus impudently. 'Is it so very strange, Uncle, that someone likes me, does not spend his time dooming at me like some messenger fellow in that damned dull Greek stuff they forced down my throat at Oxford?'

Francis turned and stared at his nephew, wondering how his clever brother Jack could have spawned such an ass. 'If you had listened to that damned dull stuff more carefully,' was his cold reply, 'you would have discovered that fools in them got short shrift for their folly. I leave you to Captain Howell. You deserve one another.'

And I was no more successful with Marcus than I was with Bel Merrick, he thought, but at least she was intelligent in her waywardness, whereas Marcus... All that he possesses to recommend him is a pretty face and a willingness to be cozened.

Listening to Mrs Broughton read *Filippo's Tower* to her did absolutely nóthing to restore Bel to her normal tranquil state of mind. The determined silliness of Bianca dei Franceschini's every response to the predicament in which she found herself roused her, for once, to tears rather than laughter.

How could she be so stupid as to take refuge with vile Federigo Orsini and fly the noble and improbably virtuous Rafaello degli Uberti? Real people did not behave like that, not at all. Why, even she, inexperienced as she was, could recognise Captain Howell for the villain which Lord Francis had confirmed him to be.

Her anger with Francis Carey was not for pointing out to her what she already knew, but because he seemed to think that he was the only one allowed to prey on Bel Merrick! Not that she saw Francis Carey as wicked; no Federigo Orsini he—that role was reserved for Rhys Howell. It was merely that he was morally blind when it came to reading Bel Merrick. And that was partly her fault, was it not? That blind moment of temper in Stanhope Street had unleashed all this on her.

Not that she could blame Rhys Howell's villainy on Francis Carey, since the captain would presumably have tracked her down even if Francis Carey had never existed, and she was now caught in two nets, not one, with no idea of how to extricate herself from either.

But one way or another, she promised herself, I will. And how inconvenient life was, that real people were not hopelessly virtuous like Rafaello, but more of a mixture, like Francis; and presumably, then, even Rhys Howell was not as completely villainous as Federigo

Orsini was, even though he might be so towards herself and Marcus. . .

Bel gave up, allowed Mrs Broughton's soothing tones to pour over her, like treacle from a jar, and when that lady put the book down, sighing, 'Oh, how delightful, even better than *Lady Caroline's Secret*,' Bel did not scream at her, Oh, what bosh you talk, madam. You know as well as I do how ridiculously improbable all that we read to each other is. For it passed over her in a wave, or even as a revelation, like one being smitten by God, as Mr Birch would have said, that Mrs Broughton and all those who read the Minerva Press's productions were seeking refuge in them from the intolerable demands of a world in which Mrs Broughton, if not employed by Bel, would have slowly starved to death in genteel poverty.

To live in a world where right always triumphed and virtue was its own reward—but also gained a fair share of the world's goods as well—must always be not only soothing to the nerves but an aid to sleep; and happiness achieved that way felt no different from happiness achieved in any other.

Bel could not help smiling to herself as she thought this. I am truly a parson's daughter, she decided, to moralise and think such things, and I don't believe, although pray God I shall never be put to it to find out, that I could ever have followed Marianne's way of life.

And then, again, revelation struck. But suppose I had been tempted by Francis, without the cushion of Marianne's ill-gotten wealth behind me; how would I have behaved then? For face it, Bel, if he desires you, as he plainly does, then you desire him, and if that were a way out of poverty and misery, what then, Bel Merrick, what then?

CHAPTER TWELVE

OF COURSE, life had to slow down a little, Bel thought; it could not go in the same hectic fashion that it had done since first Francis Carey and then Rhys Howell had arrived in Lulsgate Spa.

Neither of them made a move in the strange three-cornered game she was playing with them—or they were playing with her. The somnolent peace which had prevailed in Lulsgate during the two years in which she had lived there resumed; it was as though nothing had happened, or would ever happen.

Bel attended the St Helen's sewing circle, arranged the flowers in the church, took her daily walk, visited Lady Almeria and Philip, spoke coolly to Lord Francis when she met him, bowed distantly to Captain Howell—she could not afford to cut him—joked a little with Marcus, finished *Filippo's Tower*, took out *The Hermit of San Severino*—the Hermit being someone who vaguely resembled Francis Carey, all haughty pride, straight mouth and hard grey eyes, as well as his overbearing rectitude towards everyone except the heroine.

The heroine was not a bit like Bel; true, she was virtuous, but she had no spirit at all, allowed the Hermit to walk all over her, scorning her, although she was so determinedly proper that she was only fit for a saint. Bel was quite out of patience with her. She really ought to give the Hermit what for, as Garth used to say.

Coming out of her little class at Morewood one day, the late August rain pelting down, she found Francis Carey waiting for her at Mr Birch's gate, a large green umbrella in his hand. This unromantic sight amused her—was this part of his strategy to bring her to her knees before him? If so it seemed a strange one.

'You will allow me to drive you home, I trust? It is really not at all wise for you to walk through this downpour. You will catch a cold.'

What could Bel say? She could not bring herself to send him away when he had been standing in the rain waiting for her. She could see Mr Birch hovering in his little bow window; he had expressed his distress that she should be going home without proper protection. 'You will be soaked before you get very far.'

Bel could not make out the expression on Mr Birch's face as Francis held the umbrella over her head and walked her to the curricle, Cassius, his withered face impassive, water dripping off his little top hat, standing behind.

'Poor Cassius,' she said. 'He will be soaked through by the time we reach Lulsgate.'

'His fault,' said Francis curtly. 'He insisted on coming. I told him that he was not needed. He said that he was always needed.' His expression lightened a little. 'I could not make out who Cassius thought needed the chaperon, you or me.'

'Oh, you!' exclaimed Bel, relieved that matters were light between them. 'He does not heed me, I am sure. He is protecting you from me.'

Francis knew this not to be true. He had been aware ever since they had reached Lulsgate that both Cassius and his man, Walters, disapproved of him and his dealings with Bel. Cassius had said to him, indeed— and how he knew of Francis's belief as to Bel's lack of reputation Francis could not imagine, 'You're wrong, you know, *sir*——' and the 'sir' was insulting. 'She's a good woman, Mrs Bel Merrick, none better,' and then had turned his back on his master.

'I,' Francis had said frostily to the turned back, 'am

not interested in your opinions about any woman, good or bad.'

Cassius had muttered something rude under his breath, and when ordered to fetch the cattle, and see them properly harnessed, had announced that he would be up, 'whatever.'

Francis rarely pulled rank with his servants. They and he usually knew exactly how they stood with one another. 'A hard man, but fair', was Cassius's usual description of him to the staff in the houses which they visited. Faced with this act of mutiny, he said coldly, 'You will do as I order you, man. For God's sake, who is the master here?'

Cassius, already donning his hat and its red and white cockade, Francis's colours, said, 'You'll do without me, then, for good, sir,' and turned steady eyes on his master.

Francis drew in his breath and readied himself to use his best quarterdeck voice, designed to make Satan on his throne quail, but something in the steady eye Cassius turned on him stopped him.

'I do believe,' he said, face and voice incredulous, 'that you are constituting yourself her protector when I drive her in the curricle.'

'She needs one, then?' returned Cassius, giving no ground at all. 'You wish me to leave your service, *sir*?'

Francis cursed beneath his breath. He had no mind to lose Cassius, and why that should be was another mystery. The little man always went his own way, and this was not the first time such an act of insubordination had occurred.

'Get up, then, damn you,' he finished. 'You may have the privilege of being soaked to the skin, and if you take a rheum do not expect me to nurse you, or give you sympathy!'

Cassius rolled his eyes heavenwards, did as he was bid, and all the way to Mr Birch's home and back again Francis could feel his beady eyes boring into his back.

'You have thought of what I told you of Captain Howell?' And then, seeing Bel's face flush with anger, he added hastily, 'I have reason to believe that Marcus has begun to lose large sums of money at Gaunt's gaming house to the captain and his dubious friends. Howell allowed him to win when he first came here — a common trick to catch pigeons and pluck them, and now Marcus sits about waiting for his luck to turn, which it never will.'

He did not know why he was telling Bel this — except to reinforce his warnings about Howell, and when she said, 'Have you spoken to your sister of this?' he replied wearily.

'Yes, and he will take no note of *her* warnings, either. The trouble is, the man comes from a reasonably good family, and Marcus is innocent enough to think that that alone is a guarantee of his good behaviour. But Howell tarnished his good name and reputation long ago, although that has never prevented him from ending up with some young fool in tow.'

Bel thought for a moment. She was genuinely sorry for Almeria's sake that Marcus was being so stupid, but could not help saying, 'When we first met, you were of the opinion that I was about to pluck the pigeon myself. Does this confidence mean that you have changed your mind?'

'Only to the extent,' he said kindly, but with his usual air of effortless superiority, 'that I do not think that Marcus is now your target — not rich enough, I think.'

'Oh', said Bel, exasperated, 'then who, pray, is my target? I should like to be enlightened. I hate to think that I am working in the dark.'

Overhearing this, Cassius gave a series of strangled coughs, like a small horse neighing.

'Myself, of course,' said Francis, pulling back on the

reins to indicate that they were to stop, Bel's front
door being reached. 'Richer, more of a prize; not such
a good title perhaps, but better than you might have
hoped to achieve. Not that marriage is necessarily
your——'

At this point what he was about to say was drowned
by a coughing fit from the dripping Cassius, so noisy
that Bel turned, said sympathetically, 'Oh, poor
Cassius. How heartless of you, Lord Francis, to drag
him out in such weather, without any means of protection. You must see that he has a hot lemon drink with
rum in it when he goes in.'

Francis turned to stare at Cassius, and said grimly,
'His fault entirely if he dies of a rain-induced fever. He
insisted on riding behind, in defiance of my orders. I
have to say that it is bad enough to be bullied by my
tiger, without my would-be doxy putting her oar in,
and requiring me to nurse my servant, instead of the
other way about.'

'You have not been sitting in the rain, inadequately
clothed,' replied Bel incontrovertibly, 'so the question
of his nursing you does not arise.'

'No more,' said Francis wrathfully. 'I insist, Cassius,
that you hand Mrs Merrick down before she orders me
to carry you to bed. I do believe the pair of you are
hatching some damned conspiracy against me.' And
then, seeing Bel's laughing naughty face at having provoked him to lose his temper, 'Why, madam, do I
understand that you are roasting me? Has your impudence no limits? I should marry you off to my tiger here
as a suitable punishment for the pair of you.' Then, on
hearing the tiger's coughing laughter as he prepared
to hand Bel down, he was seized—again—with the
most dreadful desire to do her a mischief—the sort of
mischief which involved removing her clothes and...
and...

Francis thought that he was going mad. He pushed

Cassius to one side, took Bel by the arm, and half ran down her little front garden to her own door, and, regardless of watchers, said goodbye, or rather kissed her goodbye, tipping her face up to do so.

The kiss, contrary to usage, began fiercely and ended gently, and when Bel said, eyes wicked as he straightened up, 'You had best hurry, Francis, or Cassius will drown,' he replied with a half-sob,

'Oh, you witch, Bel, you witch. What is it that you do to a man? When I am with you, all sense, all honour flies away from me.'

'I?' said Bel innocently. 'I do nothing, Francis. And while you are about it you have provided Mrs Venn with enough ammunition to aim at us for the rest of the season. If you have no care for your reputation, Francis, you might consider mine. I know that you think I do not possess one—but Lulsgate is my home, and so far I have led a spotless life. Should she say anything, I will inform her that she was mistook—you were removing a smut from my eye. Her sight is notoriously bad.'

'And you, my dear doxy,' said Francis, delighted at her quick wit, 'are as devious as you are desirable. You are right to remind me not to be over-fierce with you publicly. I have no mind to ruin you—yet; but if you smile at me like that I shall not answer for the consequences,' and he bent towards her again.

'Cassius,' said Bel firmly, and pushed him towards the gate, where Cassius stood patiently, holding the horses, his eye on his master. 'He thinks that you need protecting from me, in which of course he is quite wrong, the reverse being true.'

But you, my dear Mrs Bel Merrick, thought Francis, striding back to his curricle, do not have the right of that, for, improbably, Cassius had constituted himself your protector!

*   *   *

'Bel,' said Lady Almeria carefully as they sat side by side in the Harleys' drawing-room, working busily away, waiting for the rest of Lulsgate Spa's sewing circle to arrive, 'a word to the wise. Mrs Venn is a little of a viper for gossip, as I'm sure that you are aware, so it would be better not to give her occasion to circulate any.' She fell silent again, staring at her hem stitching.

Bel knew at once that Mrs Venn had been busily spreading the news of Francis Carey's public and stolen kiss around Lulsgate, that some kind person had gleefully retailed the gossip to the vicar's wife after such a fashion that Almeria felt that she had to counsel a young friend.

The sturdy independence which lay behind her decorative appearance reared its head; she bit her thread in two and said quietly, 'Perhaps such advice ought to be offered to your brother rather than myself, the man usually taking the lead in such matters. I think I know to what Mrs Venn referred, and she was quite mistook.' She was astonished at how easily the lie flowed from her lips, but she was not about to be destroyed by a combination of Francis's folly and Mrs Venn's jealousy of herself as a possible wife for her son—self-preservation was the order of the day. 'Francis gave me a lift home the other afternoon. He saw me to the door where he removed a smut from my eye for me. Doubtless Mrs Venn, in her enthusiasm to spread gossip around Lulsgate, misinterpreted what she saw.'

'Oh, dear.' Almeria coloured to her hairline, looked distressed, and put down her sewing. 'I should have thought before I... I should have known you both better, but I only wished to help you; you are after all so young, and Mrs Broughton...' She almost began to stammer, and Bel felt remorse that her lie should overset poor Almeria, but she had not asked for the kiss, or, rather, she *might* have done so, but never in such a public place. She knew that Francis had lost control for a moment, but could hardly tell his sister so.

She put out a hand to Almeria, the younger woman comforting the older one—there were times recently when Bel felt that she was ninety—and murmured gently, 'Do not distress yourself; you were right to counsel me if you thought that I was being indiscreet. I promise you, my dear friend, that I know how to treat your brother—or any other man, for that matter. Trust me.'

Almeria's face changed again. 'Oh, dear Bel,' she said, 'you are so alone, with no relatives to whom you may turn for advice, and, although you have always behaved with the most perfect discretion, as a woman you are vulnerable, and as your friend I would always wish to help you. Forgive me if I have hurt you by believing a falsehood.'

Bel, from being cool, a little distant, was herself again, charmingly impulsive, even if her impulses were controlled. She rose, kissed Almeria on the cheek and went to stand before the window, looking out across the garden, which backed on to Bel's own, tears filling her eyes, hating herself for the lie and at having caused Almeria distress by telling it.

Oh, Francis, she thought, if only we could have met after a proper fashion, introduced at a ball or in a drawing-room where the strong attraction we feel for one another could have taken its due course. Or if only I *had* been a lightskirt, so that we could have taken our pleasure together, heedless of consequences. As it is, we are trapped in a situation nearly as fraught as those of the novels I take home for Mrs Broughton, and with no easy way out, no author to wave a magic wand and bring all to a happy conclusion.

She resumed her seat, for she could hear the others arriving, and when they came in, Mrs Venn among them, she was her normal self again. Bel was not to know that when Francis entered the vicarage drawing-room later that day, telling Almeria that he would not be in for dinner, he intended to spend the evening at Gaunt's gaming club, she said quietly to him, something which Bel had said having struck home, 'Francis, a word with you.' She was a little fearful at his reaction to what she was about to say, for he was a formidable man, and no mistake. 'Lulsgate Spa is a small place, and gossip abounds, some of it not nice. I know that you seem attracted to my good friend, Mrs Bel Merrick, and I trust you to do nothing which would hurt her, or destroy her standing here.'

Francis stood stock-still, rigid. What could he say? Like Bel, he was reduced to a lie. He could not reply, *The woman is not what you think*, and, *being what she is, has no reputation to destroy, and sooner or later I intend to take my long-deferred pleasure with her, and damn the consequences!*

To his horror, shame ran through him. He tossed the gloves he was holding on to an occasional table, and, like Bel, walked to the window, but saw nothing. Through numb lips he said, 'I will never do anything to hurt a lady, Almy, dear, you may be sure of that.'

He hated himself for the equivocation. What a weaselling declaration! Bel Merrick being far from a lady, he might treat her as he pleased, but his half-sister would take his statement at its face value.

Like Bel, he wished that things had been different. He could, he knew, solve his problems by leaving Lulsgate Spa, forgetting her, but he could not. He was in her toils; what had begun as simple revenge had become something much more complex—he wanted Bel Merrick, most desperately, all of her, and he wanted her to come to him; he would not go to her, he would not, never.

Thinking so, he turned. 'Any more good advice, my dear?' And, although he did not know it, the face he

showed her was hard, inimical, the face of a man
staring down an enemy.

Almeria was horrified. Philip had warned her against
meddling. She had meddled, and—what had she done?

'Oh, do forgive me,' she stammered, 'I had not
meant. . .'

Like Bel, he leaned forward, face softening a little,
to kiss her on the cheek. 'I know,' he said. 'But the
road to hell is paved with good intentions—and there
is a limit to what vicar's wives may or can do.'

It was a rebuke, Almeria knew, and one more proof
of Philip's wisdom. She would not meddle with Bel and
Francis again, and she would listen to her husband's
quiet advice in future—in the present she must learn
to live with the knowledge that something more than
simple mutual attraction lay between her friend and
her brother.

Gaunt's gaming club was, as usual, well patronised:
husbands, fathers, brothers and lovers were busy enjoying themselves. Francis looked around for Marcus and
his low friends when he entered, but there was no sign
of them. There were a few persons present whose
acquaintance he had made in Lulsgate, including an
old friend from his boyhood days, George Stamper,
now a fat squire with a fat wife whom he had deserted
for the night, having met Francis earlier in the day and
offered to introduce him to Gaunt's.

'Good to get away from the women,' he sighed. 'See
you had the common sense not to marry, Frank.' He
had no knowledge of Francis's short marriage to
Cassie, and Francis did not choose to enlighten him.
He agreed to make up a four for whist with two cronies
of George's, and looked around Gaunt's while introductions were being made.

It was quite a reasonable gaming hell, as hells went,
and if one had to gamble outside one's home, seeing

that it could only be done in clubs in private these days, Francis supposed that Gaunt's was as good a place as any.

The room he was in was respectable enough, although there was another down a short corridor, George told him, where there were girls and 'other possibilities'—to do with the girls, presumably. Francis wondered, briefly, if Marcus was already there, but the 'other place' did not open until nine of the clock, and it was now only seven.

Along one wall a huge sideboard ran, on which were set out plates of excellent food, which came free, once the heavy entrance fee had been paid. On a small table stood a large silver wine cooler, full of bottles of good white wine; red wine stood on a shelf beneath the table, and rows of glasses were stored in a cupboard whose doors were perpetually open.

The four men about to play whist ate and drank first. Francis attracted a good deal of attention. A member of a distinguished noble family, he was something of a pasha in this company, and his very air of cool indifference to others added to the impression of effortless superiority which he always gave off.

Even George Stamper was affected by it, and sought to dispel the unease it created in him by clapping Francis on the back and behaving as though they had been uninterrupted boon companions in the sixteen years since they had last seen one another.

Eating over, they carried their wine glasses and a plate of ratafia biscuits to their table and began to play. Francis's luck was as good as his skill; his attention was not on the game, however, but on the door, and it was almost with a sense of relief that he saw Rhys Howell enter.

Marcus did not, at first, appear to be with him. But, suddenly, in the small group which comprised Howell's raffish court, and which followed him in, Francis sud-

denly saw his nephew being held erect by two knowing
rogues. Marcus was half-cut already, his face flushed,
and as he walked, or rather staggered, to the table
where hazard was being played it was evident that he
was a pigeon ripe for the plucking.

Rage with Howell, coupled with annoyance at
Marcus for being such a weak young fool, consumed
Francis, but little of it showed. He kept an unobtrusive
eye on the goings-on at the hazard table, and became
convinced that Howell and the man who ran the table
were in collusion, and that Marcus was their joint
victim. Marcus was playing against Howell, and Francis
could hear the rattle of the dice box behind him, and
Marcus's blurred voice cursing as luck constantly
favoured Howell.

'Dammit, Howell, the devil's in the dice that I do so
badly,' floated across the room towards Francis as the
round of whist ended.

'Excuse me, gentlemen,' said Francis, rising, his face
hard and angry. He pushed the money he had won into
the centre of the table. 'I fear that I must leave you,
and you may share what I have won between you as a
recompense for spoiling your game, but I have a duty
to perform.'

He turned towards the hazard table, where Marcus,
face purple, was sprawled in his chair, peering angrily
at a smiling Rhys Howell, who was plainly sober. The
whole scene was reminiscent of a print from a sequence
rightly called *The Rake's Progress*, showing the young
fool of an heir being despoiled by his hangers-on.

On impulse Francis picked up a bottle of wine and a
glass as he passed the wine table on his way towards
Marcus. He ignored Rhys Howell, who stared at him
insolently, saying, 'Want to throw a main, Carey?
Thought you was only interested in old lady's games
like whist, haw, haw!'

'Marcus,' said Francis, not quite in his quarterdeck

voice, but near it. 'Time to go home, I think. You're hardly up to hazard or any other game in that state.'

Marcus peered at him owlishly and muttered, 'Death's head at the feast again, Uncle, are you? Want to stay until the luck changes. You go home to bed if you want. . .'

One more drink, thought Francis dispassionately, might have him unconscious, judging by his appearance. He disliked Howell intensely, but did not want an open fight with him; however, behind Francis's back, Howell was saying in a jeering voice, 'Man's of age, Carey. Can do as he pleases. Not yours to run any more.'

Francis decided on another ploy. He poured a bumper of what he suddenly saw was port, not a light red wine, from the bottle he was holding, and held it out invitingly to his nephew.

'Come on, old fellow,' he almost crooned. 'I'm not such a bad chap after all. Drink a toast with me. No heeltaps, and God bless Queen Caroline, and all who sail in her.'

This was so uncharacteristic that Marcus took the proffered glass with a crack of laughter, and, throwing his head back, drank the lot down, watching his uncle swallow his share from the bottle.

Francis's own draught was smaller than any of the spectators realised, and as Marcus, the drink safely down him, shuddered and fell forward, his eyes rolling, and purple face turning ashen, Francis, praying that he had not overdone things, caught him, and swung his nephew over his shoulder, head on one side, legs on the other.

Even Rhys Howell, he thought, could hardly complain at his removing a victim who was now dead drunk; but he underestimated the captain.

One hand plucking at Francis's sleeve as he manoeuvred his way to the door, he hissed for the room to hear, 'Damn you, Carey. You did that deliberately. He owes me this game.'

Francis, enraged at the hand on his arm, and Howell's unwanted familiarity, swung round to face the man who was robbing and exploiting his nephew.

'Oh,' he said, his face ferocious, the face of the man who had boarded French war ships, pistol in one hand, cutlass in the other, 'you mean that you wanted him drunk enough to fleece, but not so drunk that he was unconscious and you couldn't ruin him?'

Everyone in the room heard the insult. A deathly quiet fell. Howell's face turned black with fury, and Francis, who had broken his own rule of not provoking trouble, was so buoyed up by anger that he hardly cared what he said or did.

'Satisfaction!' cried Howell. 'I'll have satisfaction from you for that, damn you, Carey. No fine gentleman insults me with impunity.'

'No?' said Francis through his teeth. 'Well, let me inform you that I have no need to prove my courage, and I have no intention of fighting such as yourself. Rummage through the gutter if you want a fight, but don't come near me.'

'You'll pay for this. I swear you'll pay for this, Carey.'

'By God,' said Francis, swinging around again, treating Marcus's dead weight as though it did not exist. 'Call me Carey in that familiar way once more, and I *will* kill you. Now be quiet, and let me get this young fool home to his aunt's. Tell the White Peacock he'll not be returning there. My man will call for his traps tomorrow.'

He was out of the door and in the street, his companions holding back the raving Howell, Francis's late whist partners staring after him.

'Well,' said George Stamper, happy at this interesting diversion which had lightened the drab domesticity of Lulsgate Spa, 'I heard that Frank Carey had turned into a tiger when he went into the navy, but this beats all. That feller,' he said, pointing at Howell, 'ought to be glad Frank won't fight him. A devil with pistol or swords, they say. A man would be a fool to provoke him.'

Which was the general epitaph agreed to by those present as the evening now settled back into its usual calm, and George Stamper treated himself to one of the girls in 'the other place' as a reward for having introduced Frank Carey to Gaunt's gaming club, and given the company there a rare treat.

'Oh, Bel,' wailed Almeria to her friend, 'we have never had such goings-on in Lulsgate in all the years we have lived here. So quiet and, yes, dull. And it is all Francis's fault—and he is usually so proper. First of all he excites everyone just by being here—Lulsgate is not used to such fine gentlemen—and then Mrs Venn accused you and him of kissing in public, and now this to-do over Francis, Marcus and Captain Howell at Gaunt's! You have heard about it?'

Yes, Bel had heard about it, as who had not?

'I suppose it has all been exaggerated—like the kiss,' Bel offered, and she was devious enough to laugh at her own duplicity—for the kiss had been true, and doubtless Francis had done all that gossip said he had in Gaunt's—not less.

'I cannot think what has got into Francis. There is a look about him which I have never seen before. It is as though——' and Almeria hesitated, but she had to speak to *someone* '—as though he is sowing all the wild oats he never sowed in youth. Not that he is chasing women, not at all, he seems interested only in yourself, but otherwise, I mean. Do I know what I mean?' Almeria finished distractedly.

Bel knew only too well what had got into Francis

Carey. It was Bel Merrick, and the fact that she was refusing him herself. It had got into her, too, and was affecting everything she said and did, especially since, being virtuous, although Francis thought that she was not, she could not offer him herself. Of course, being a woman, she had learned self-control in a hard school; but Francis, she suspected, was a passionate man who had held his emotions on a tight rein for so long that now that he was sorely tempted and unable to do anything to satisfy himself his passion was taking its revenge by provoking him into unwise action elsewhere.

But she could hardly tell Almeria that, simply said gently, 'I suppose that Francis thought it was the only way to protect Marcus—who really does seem to need protecting.'

'Hush,' said Almeria feverishly, not wanting to be thought to be interfering again, but if she did not talk to Bel about all this she would burst. 'Here they come, quarrelling as usual.'

They were sitting in a little open-fronted summer-house, set at an angle to the path, so that they could hear the men's approach, but not see them, as Francis and Marcus were equally unaware of their presence. It was plain that they were, as Almeria had said, quarrelling.

'I tell you, I won't be kept in leading strings, Uncle.' Marcus's voice was petulant. 'You had no right to do what you did. Rhys told me that you deliberately gave me that drink to push me over the edge. A fine way to go on.'

'It was necessary,' Francis said coldly, one difficulty in arguing with him, Marcus found, being that Francis rarely lost his temper, which made his recent conduct the more baffling, 'quite necessary, if you were not to be fleeced by the cheating toad-eater you call friend. I would prefer that you stay here, at the vicarage, and not return to the Peacock.'

'You cannot stop me. . .' began Marcus, and then hesitated, on Bel's giving a giant cough to warn them they were overheard. 'Oh. Excuse me, Aunt Almeria, Mrs Merrick, I did not see that you were there.' And he gave them both an embarrassed bow.

Francis also bowed, the marks of anger plain on his face. Anger conferred even more power on him, thought Bel, fascinated. She had a sudden dreadful wish that she had seen Francis in Gaunt's, Marcus, dead drunk and incapable over his shoulder, insulting Captain Howell, his face on fire, power radiating from him, she was sure. It certainly made a change for him to be insulting someone other than Bel Merrick!

But how strong he was, how impressive! She had another vision of him, jumping on to the deck of a ship in battle, waving a pistol—or would it be a sword?— magnificent in anger against the French.

Almeria, desperate to mend matters, said nervously, avoiding looking at Francis, 'I could not help overhearing what you were saying, Marcus. I do beg of you to stay here. Philip and I would like it of all things—so much better for you than an inn.'

This emollient request had a stronger effect on Marcus than Francis's stern orders. It was hard for him to be rude to kind Almeria.

'I am imposing on you, I know,' he began, only for Almeria to respond rapidly,

'Not at all. Philip was saying that you really ought to be with us, one of the family as you are. You could put your groom up at the Peacock, for we haven't really room for him here.'

She thought ruefully that since her passage with Francis she had rarely quoted her husband so often, and even he had noticed that her usual cheerful and managing habits had changed lately.

Marcus looked at the two women, said doubtfully, 'Well, if you really say so, then I will, but you are to turn me out if I become a burden, mind.'

'Good,' said Almeria, regaining a little of her normal cheerfulness. 'Now you may take me for a walk into Lulsgate to visit the mercer and then the apothecary, and Bel, my dear, perhaps Francis might like to visit your shrubbery for a turn there; there is an entrance at the back through our dividing fence, Francis.' And this, she thought, would give Francis a chance to recover a little of his normal self in Bel's company—and did not know how much she was deluding herself.

She and Marcus set off down the path away from them, leaving Bel and Francis face to face.

'You heard my sister,' he said. 'The least that you can do is entertain me as she wishes. Now how I might wish you to entertain me is, of course, a little different. But lead on, my dear Mrs Merrick, pray do. Of all things I wish you to provide me with enjoyment in your shrubbery.'

'Oh!' gasped Bel, thinking how right Almeria was. The devil was in Francis these days. One eyebrow cocked at her, his head bent in mock-humility, his arm held towards her with exaggerated and mocking courtesy, safe in the knowledge that none could overhear them, he felt free to indulge in his passion for her.

Last night he had woken up in a fever of desire, his whole body roused, her image in his mind; and now, seeing her, only the strongest exercise of self-control was preventing him from falling on her at once. He wondered how private the shrubbery really was, and how long it would take Almeria and Marcus to do Almeria's few errands.

There was nothing for it, thought Bel exasperatedly. Almeria was sure to ask him of the shrubbery and would think it odd to learn that Bel had refused him his treat. His treat? Inspecting the shrubbery, a treat?

Bel suspected that Francis's notions of what a treat in
the shrubbery was did not encompass a mere oohing
and aahing and recital of Latin names, and admiring
the gloss on the leaves and the state of the few
blossoms.

Oh, no, it would be the gloss on Bel Merrick and *her*
state which would engage him, she was sure, and as
she led the way she prattled as lightly as she could of
the difficulties of the true gardener she was in restoring
a garden which the previous owner had neglected.

Talking so, she felt Francis bend down and deposit a
kiss on her sun-warmed neck, and she said crossly,
'Now you are to stop that at once, sir. I cannot properly
explain the garden if you carry on so.'

They were by now through the opening in the fence,
always left there so that Bel and Almeria could visit
one another freely, and were standing on a secluded
path, surrounded by plants of all sizes and shapes,
overlooked by nothing, as secret a place as even
Francis Carey might wish to find himself in with his
prey.

'I have not,' murmured Francis, 'the slightest wish to
have the garden explained to me. Gardens are made
for other purposes than botanising, and it is those
purposes which I wish to explore.'

'Almeria,' said Bel severely, 'told me to show you
the shrubbery, and that is what I am about to do.' They
had reached a cross path where an old wooden bench,
painted green, stood, where they would, Bel knew
despairingly, be even more secluded.

Even the shade was green, and here everything was
quiet, the scents of late August were all about them,
the summer visibly beginning to die. Francis said, still
gentle, although at what cost to himself only he knew,
'Pray, let us sit, my dear Mrs Merrick. I wish to be at
one with nature—in every way known to man.'

And that is what I am afraid of, thought Bel, but

allowed him to seat her gently, hoping perhaps that
what he was saying might be more aggressive than
what he might be about to do, and so it proved—at
first, that was.

'Now I wonder why you are in such a pother, my
dear doxy?' he said, leaning back and surveying her
enchanting face and form lazily. 'Can it be that you are
a trifle hopeful that dallying in gardens might be pro-
ductive in other ways than gathering flowers fruit and
vegetables?' And he picked up her hand and kissed it.

Bel pulled it away furiously. 'You are not to call me
that, sir.'

'No? But that is what you are, is it not? A doxy, and
dear to me, for the moment at any rate,' and as she
rose to leave him, crying,

'I have shown you the shrubbery, and so you may
tell Almeria,' he caught at her to detain her, saying,

'But I wish to see so much more than the garden,'
and, using his strength, pulled her on to the bench
again, took her in his arms and began to kiss her,
gently at first, and then more and more passionately.

Bel began by fighting him off—or trying to, but as
his kisses began to stir her, so that his arousal fuelled
hers, she found herself drowning in the strangest sensations, quite unlike any she had experienced before.

They involved her whole body, not just her mouth,
and then, when his kisses travelled down her neck,
found the cleft between her breasts, and he began to
caress her there, she threw her head back so that
without her meaning to not only did she give him a
better access to her body, but she was able to gasp her
pleasure the more easily.

Reason had fled, and she felt that she could deny
him nothing. Worse, her hands were beginning to
caress him, and when he lifted his head for a moment
she began to kiss him in the most wanton manner.

He had stopped kissing her only to give himself

easier means to pull her dress down, as he had done
on Beacon Hill, and this time she did not stop him,
and he did not stop either, so that he was now stroking
and kissing her breasts, taking them into his mouth, so
that the sensations which he produced in her were so
violent that Bel thought she was about to dissolve.

She writhed beneath him, so that he gave a soft
laugh, and now, lifting her slightly, he began to pull
her skirts up, his right hand travelling up her leg,
beyond the garter on her stocking, to stroke the soft
inside of her thigh—and she was not stopping him, no,
not at all; she wanted him there, wanted the hand to
travel further still, so strongly did she ache for him;
shamefully she wanted all of him there—not just his
hand—there, where no man had ever been.

Oh, madam is ready for me, thought Francis exultantly; she is as on fire for me as I am for her, and she
is as sweet as I had thought her—sweeter—and it is
she, Bel, I desire and none other, no one else will do—
and then he remembered his vow that she should plead
for him, and not he for her, and now, so wet and
wanton was she, so far gone, that surely this, too, he
would have.

'Feel me, Bel, feel me,' he said hoarsely. 'Feel how I
need you,' and he took her hand and pressed it against
his naked chest where she had unbuttoned his shirt, so
that she could feel the fever which gripped him. 'And
you, I can tell how much you need me. Say it, Bel, say
it; say, Francis, pleasure me, please, beg me to do so,
and then we may be in heaven together.'

As before, his voice broke the spell. In agony as she
was, body trembling, on the very edge of a spasm of
pleasure so strong that it would consume her quite,
wanting most desperately the man in whose arms she
lay, some strong core of integrity, so powerful that it
willed her to refuse to be used by him as an instrument

of revenge when she wanted to be an instrument of love, asserted itself.

'No, Francis! No! Never! I will not be used in despite, to prove what you think of me is true. I will not plead. You must plead for me, and in honour, not take me here as you might the doxy you call me, to boast later of how you had me—without payment.'

And the last phrase was the cruellest thing that she could think of to say to him, and as he pulled away, face blind and soft with desire, she added, 'Such a man of honour as you are, to save your nephew one day, and then despoil me another.'

The pride which ruled him, even at the last fence of all, was strong in him. Believing her to be otherwise then she was, he had told himself that he could not love a whore, but every fibre in his body told him that he did. That it was not, as he wished, mere lust which moved him, but that, against all reason, he loved Bel Merrick—and did not wish to hurt her.

And, that being so, he could not do what many another in his case might have done, and that was to take her as she lay before him, whether she consented or no, since, she having consented so far, a man might do as he pleased with the whore with whom he lay.

He could not resist saying as he sat up, and allowed her to free herself from his grasp, 'Not honest of you, madam, to progress so far, so willingly, and then refuse me at the last gasp of all.'

How to say, I am not experienced, did not know how quickly we should arrive at such a pass that my very virginity was on the point of being willingly lost? Had you not spoken, reminded me of how matters really stand between us, that I love, and that you only desire—for Bel had no knowledge of what time and propinquity had done to Francis—then I would have been lost in an instant, no better than poor Marianne—indeed worse, for she was betrayed by a man who she thought loved her, whereas I. . .I know perfectly well that that is not so.

Instead Bel lowered her head, said numbly, 'I am sorry. I was carried away.'

Francis stared at her. 'Carried away! You cannot expect me to believe *that*?'

'Believe what you please,' she returned. 'And now you have had what you came for, or most of it, and you may safely tell Almeria that you have seen the shrubbery, without the necessity of lying.'

Bel was straightening herself, repairing the ravages of passion as she spoke, and Francis was feeling the worst pangs of passion die within him, the physical pain which refusal had produced abating a little.

'You will excuse me,' she said, on the verge of tears, not wishing to shed them before him. 'I must go. You know the way back, I believe.'

Francis had one final parting shot for her like a crippled ship able to fire one last ball at the enemy. 'Oh, yes, my dear doxy, I know the way back; you have made me take it so often now.' And the smile he gave her as he left was rueful, not reproachful, no enmity in it.

And Bel? She knew now beyond a doubt that blindly, inconveniently, what she felt for Francis was love, and that what had begun in light-hearted mockery of him at Stanhope Street was ending on quite a different note in Lulsgate Spa.

CHAPTER THIRTEEN

LULSGATE SPA had not known such a season for years. Bumbling along in its quiet middle class way, few great ones visiting it, it was a haven for minor gentry and tradesmen; the aristocracy, the upper gentry, the flash coves and Cyprians of the *demi-monde* usually passed it by. But in 1820 all were present and sensation followed sensation.

Marcus provided the next delightful bit of gossip. Living at the vicarage, he could not drink and ruffle as he had done, and, being sober most of the time, he suddenly, as Francis had hoped he might do, saw through Rhys Howell and his cheating ways.

Smoking was not allowed by Almeria, and his boon companions stank of smoke as well as drink, which he came to find distasteful. Clear-eyed physically, Marcus became so mentally, and one evening at Gaunt's it was Marcus who challenged the captain over his honesty at dice and cards, and not his uncle.

According to rumour, high words followed, and Marcus, imitating Francis, declined to give the captain satisfaction. 'You have had enough of my tin,' he had declared, 'and in future I shall play cards at the Assembly Rooms.'

'Go there, then,' roared Rhys, and swore at him, seeing his pigeon fly away, and funds running low. 'Shuffle the pasteboards with the tabby-cats and dowagers. Bound and determined to turn parson yourself, are you? Having a genuine one for an uncle and a defrocked monk for another not enough for you?'

Marcus ignored the insults, said sturdily, 'No need to

shout at me, Rhys. I shan't change my mind. Uncle
Francis was right about you, dammit.'

There was nothing Rhys Howell could do. The damage was already partly done. To be proven a cheat at
cards or dice would brand him pariah for life, and he
had no mind for that. Best to let it go, accuse the
young fool of being light in the attic, trying to excuse
his own bad luck and less skill by attacking another's
honesty and reputation.

Of course, there was always Mrs Bel Merrick to fall
back on, for others were declining to play in any game
in which he was taking part. Lulsgate was slowly growing too hot to hold him, but he did not wish to leave
yet. He felt safe in such a backwater, thought that his
enemies from London and Paris might find it hard to
track him down and harm him there.

Bel was sitting in her drawing-room when the doorknocker rattled and a man's voice was heard. Mrs
Broughton, reading yet another romance, *The Curse of
the Comparini* this time, looked up hopefully, and said,
'Lord Francis?'

Bel shook her head; it was a week since Francis had
nearly had his way with her in the shrubbery, and they
had met only in public, and both of them had been
glacially proper, so much so that Almeria had sighed
at the sight. Oh, dear, yet another chance for Francis
to make a happy marriage seemed to be disappearing.
What could have happened? Ever since she had asked
Bel to show him around her shrubbery an arctic frost
seemed to have descended on both of them.

She had always thought shrubberies were places
where romantic interludes took place. Obviously Bel's
had had no such effect on her and Francis. It was not
that they were not speaking at all, but they were going
on as though they were both ninety.

To Mrs Broughton's dismay, Bel was right, it was
Captain Howell who was announced, and she did not

like him—not the person to pursue dear Bel at all. She
had seen the captain's eye on her mistress, and had
interpreted his interest wrongly.

Not completely so, for, having an eye for a pretty
woman, Rhys Howell not only wanted a good share of
Bel Merrick's fortune, he also had an eye to her body.
Now, if she possessed half Marina's possibilities. . .why,
they would both be in clover.

'Your servant, ladies.' And he gave them his best
bow, which did not mollify Mrs Broughton. She would
rather have read *The Curse of the Comparini* than
entertain the captain.

Bel rang for the tea-board; it was not long since they
had dined, and she assumed that the captain had dined,
too. They made unexceptional small talk, and Mrs
Broughton looked longingly at the clock.

Her salvation came early, and Howell's intention to
rid them of her presence was so boredly naked that
Bel feared that even Mrs Broughton might notice how
thin his excuse was. 'I have further private news for
you,' he said bluntly, raising his eyebrows at the
unwanted companion, so that Bel was compelled, flush-
ing slightly, to indicate that she should leave.

Fortunately, for all her vague ways Mrs Broughton
was discretion itself, never gossiped, but she must be
beginning to ask herself what unlikely bond existed
between Bel Merrick and Rhys Howell, that he should
be bringing Bel private messages!

'You grow bold,' said Bel severely. 'Even Mrs
Broughton will notice your cavalier manner to me and
wonder at it.'

'Oh, as to that,' said the captain carelessly and
beginning to roam round the room, picking up orna-
ments and staring at them, inspecting the bookshelves
as though he were a bailiff pricing goods for distraint,
'you have the remedy in your own hands, my dear.
Either hand over the dibs in large quantities, or join

forces with me to our mutual advantage. I am surprised that you should wish to remain in this dull hole.'

Bel went on to the attack, that being the best form of defence.

'And I am surprised, sir, that you should wish to stay here, or should come here at all. The pickings must be small, compared to what you might hope to gain in London.'

'As clever as you are beautiful,' he remarked with a derisive bow. 'But you are a little off the mark. You are providing me with one reason—or rather, Marina's small fortune which you inherited, and your own person, more remarkable than I had dared to hope. I could make you Marina's best, you know. And also it suits me to be here at the moment.'

Bel knew nothing of the criminal underworld, but prolonged reading of the novels which Mrs Broughton loved had given her some insight into the nether side of life. 'London too hot for you?' she enquired politely.

He was across the room in one fell stride and had gathered her into his arms.

'Come, you bitch, are you lying to me as well as to the rest of the world? Are you still in touch with your London cullies, that you know such a thing?' And, pressing his lips roughly to hers, he forced a brutal kiss on her, so that Bel's senses reeled, not with the erotic passion which Francis's touch produced, but with the utmost revulsion.

If she had ever feared that any man's touch might stir her sexually, Rhys Howell had shown her in a moment that that fear had no basis.

As he forced her mouth open, she allowed him to do so, in order that she might bite hard on his invading tongue.

He reeled back with a curse, clapping his hand to his bleeding mouth.

'Damn you for the hellcat you are! I was right about

you, I see. All that parade of virtue a mockery. I've a mind to proclaim what you are to the world from the steps of the Butter Cross.'

'And what a mistake that would be,' said Bel, heady with a feeling of sweet victory, even if it were to be temporary and unwise. 'For you would undoubtedly ruin me—at the expense of the possibility of gaining anything for yourself.'

The hard eyes which surveyed her were full of an unwilling admiration.

'By God, you're the shrewdest piece it's been my good fortune to meet. You remind me not to let passion rule reason. Now, madam, let us come to terms. If you wish to leave here with reputation intact, you must be seen to go with me willingly, for I have a mind to take you and your fortune both. My bed and my future assured at one go. With me to run you, there is no telling where we might end. No, do not turn away.' For Bel, sickened, had thrown out a hand, and walked to the fireplace, where, hands on the mantel-piece, she bent her head, staring at a hearth filled with flowers. 'No, I would not ruin you. Better, I would marry you. Thus I would gain everything—and you lose nothing. Refuse me, and you lose everything.'

What to do? Frantic, Bel stared blindly at the flow-ers. There must be something. She would not agree to this, she would not. If all else failed she would let him destroy her reputation rather than agree to such a bargain. But could she not, somehow, cheat him of both alternatives which he presented to her? The spirit, the courage with which she had so far triumphed over everything in her short life was strong in her still.

She would appear to agree with him. By what he said he did not intend to leave Lulsgate Spa yet, and it was to his long-term advantage to have her retain her reputation, if only that he might sell her more profit-ably in the end—for Bel had no doubt of his intentions.

.

Ever since she had learned what Marianne had done, had read her letters, the letters of her lovers, examined her books, she had known of the harsher side of life usually concealed from young gentlewomen like herself. She had no illusions at all, none.

Yes, she would appear to give way—and then would scheme an escape—even if giving way meant that she would have to endure Rhys Howell's hateful company.

She swung around to face him. His handkerchief was at his mouth, the eyes on her were inimical, baleful. She drew a deep breath, summoned up all her arts. He had said that she was Marina's best. She would be Marina's best.

'Yes,' she said. 'Yes, I will do what you want; I have no alternative, it appears.'

His whole face changed, became darkly triumphant. He strode towards her, to assault her again, no doubt. Bel put her hands on his chest to push him away as he reached her.

'No,' she said. 'No. Most unwise. If you wish to take me away, my reputation intact, to be your wife, then you must court me in proper form, so that all will be deceived. No liberties, no hints or innuendoes. You are struck dumb by my virtue, sir. My apparent innocence is what you are after, is it not? Preserve that by your manner to me. Go slowly at first, and even after; a modest admiration will deceive all.'

He stepped back, and his face was full of an unwanted admiration for her. 'I was right,' he breathed. 'By God, we shall rule the world together, you and I. Between us there is nothing that we might not do. It was an unholy parsonage which spawned you and Marina, to be sure.' He made her a grinning, derisive bow. 'It shall be as you so wisely advise. I don't want that damned canting swine of an aristocrat after me over you, as he charged at me to deprive me of his thick-headed nephew.'

He took her hand and kissed it with the greatest solemnity, though winking as he straightened up. 'You will do me the honour, my dear Mrs Merrick, of taking the air in my phaeton this late afternoon, will you not? I have a mind to drive a little beyond Morewood. One of the grooms from the inn will be my tiger, to retain propriety's demands. You see how well I know the manners of the world which I intend we shall despoil.'

He released her hand, strolled to the door. 'Until five of the clock, madam. Oh, I know that we shall enjoy working together.'

He was gone. Bel sank into an armchair, her head in her hands. She had gained herself a reprieve—but for how long? And at what a cost. What would Francis Carey think, when he saw her at such ins with Captain Howell, but that she was exactly what he thought her to be?

The faint hope that somehow she could convince him of her purity and that they could begin their relationship all over again on a better footing had been destroyed forever this afternoon. And Lady Almeria and Philip—what would they think of her, to consort with such a creature as the captain was? Would it not be better to have done, let him destroy her, rather than have them all despise her——?

She jumped to her feet. No! This way, she might yet escape him. The other way, she was doomed forever. Any hope that she might yet have Francis in honour would be gone forever—and she knew one thing, and one thing only. What she felt for Francis Carey was so strong, so powerful, that she would do anything to have him hers, to try to ensure that what she felt for him he would feel for her.

Meantime she must appear in public with Howell, and then this evening she was to sup at the Harleys'— and she could only imagine what would happen then. Best not to; best to take each moment as it came, and trust that the God who presided over all might yet spare Bel Merrick.

So, another splendid piece of gossip for everyone to chew over. Mrs Bel Merrick, that virtuous widow, pillar of the church, best friend of Lady Almeria Harley, a lady to her fingertips, was seen riding down Lulsgate Spa's main street in Captain Rhys Howell's flashy phaeton, with only a groom from the Peacock to act as chaperon!

And naturally, thought Bel despairingly, the first person whom they passed was Lord Francis, driving his curricle, who gave them both the coldest stare a man could, before cutting them stone-dead in full view of half of what Lulsgate Spa called society. By six that evening Mrs Venn had been told the delightful news and trumpeted at poor Henry how lucky he had been to escape the widow's toils, a view which Henry did not exactly share.

Bel walked into Almeria's drawing-room that evening, Mrs Broughton by her side, well aware of the furore she had caused, and defying Almeria to say anything.

She was dressed to perfection and beyond in lemon silk, the waist a little lower than had been fashionable at any time in the past fifteen years, seed-pearls sewn into the boat-shaped neck of her dress, Marianne's half-moon jewel in her hair, her fan a dream of a thing, lemon in colour with painted porcelain panels showing birds of paradise—it had been Marianne's, and in her state of anger and defiance of all the world Bel had deliberately carried it in as a kind of trophy.

Her red hair she had brushed into defiant curls; her usually ivory pallor was charmingly enhanced by a wild rose blush, for she would not be set down, she would not, and, ruined or not ruined, she would be Bel Merrick still.

Francis's eyes ran insultingly over her, his glance mocking, as much as to say, We have shown the world our true colours, have we not? But he said nothing; indeed, *everyone* determinedly said nothing, although Bel could feel that everyone was thinking everything.

What a strange world it was, that one indiscreet act could ruin one for life, she thought, but was as pleasant as ever, speaking to Marcus, whom Almeria had placed by her, and to Phillip, who was on her left at the head of the table, and with all the cool command of which she felt herself capable.

Marcus, indeed, conscious of having saved himself—he gave no credit to Francis—from Rhys Howell's clutches, said to her in a low voice, 'My dear Bel—you will allow me to call you Bel, Mrs Merrick; Almeria does, and it does so suit you—I would wish to have a private word with you before you leave us this evening—after supper, perhaps, when the tea-board comes round?'

Francis, who sat opposite, bodkin between Mrs Robey and her daughter, frowned his disapproval at what he saw as a tête-à-tête between Marcus and Bel, which had the effect of making her begin to flirt desperately with his nephew, just to show how little she cared for all the lowering glares he was throwing in her direction.

'Did you ever visit Astley's when you were in London, Lord Tawstock?' she enquired sweetly, fluttering her eyelashes at Marcus, who began to think that, widow or not, travelling in Howell's phaeton or not, the little widow might be worth pursuing.

'Marcus,' he replied gallantly, 'do call me Marcus, I beg of you,' and he said this loudly enough for Francis to hear him and to grind his teeth as madam brought her trollop's ways to the sanctity of the vicarage supper table. Was she thinking of Marcus as a possible protector? Were Howell and himself not enough for her to try her claws on, without attracting his ass of a nephew?

Marcus went on to recite the delights of Astley's at some length to an apparently entranced Bel, who could not resist laying a pretty hand on his arm, and fluting at him with much eye-rolling and grimacing, 'Oh, never say so, Lord Tawstock—I mean Marcus,' when he told her of the pretty female equestriennes who ended their act by standing on one leg on the back of their prancing steeds. 'I should feel quite faint at the sight. But you, I suppose, would enjoy it. Female and hippic beauty in one joyful caracole must always be a delight.'

Bel knew that she was behaving badly, and that she was leading Marcus on in the most dreadful fashion, but the sight of that damned canting aristocrat, the unfrocked monk, as Howell had dubbed Francis, was responsible for her wickedness; it was not her fault at all, it was he who was provoking her, and he who, once the meal was over, would, she was sure, be pouring recriminations, and unwanted advice over her, while being himself ready to fall on her in the most disgraceful manner, ready to relieve her of her virtue in quick-march time.

Philip spoke to her too, quietly and kindly, which made her feel a little ashamed, and she tailored her response to him, being the sedate Bel Merrick she had always been until first Francis and then Captain Howell had arrived to deprive her of sense by pursuing her, each in his own inimitable way.

Not that her measured replies, and discussion of her helping to decorate the church for the following Sunday, brought her any credit with Francis; rather, indeed, his expression as he surveyed her grew more and more sardonic, so that when she turned to speak to Marcus again she was wilder than ever.

Fortunately for Bel, when the meal ended it was Marcus who escorted her out, almost pushing Francis

over when his uncle made a dead set at Bel, taking Bel
into a corner of the room, to say confidentially, 'I know
you will not take this amiss, Bel, I only speak for your
own good, but I understand that you went driving with
Captain Howell this afternoon. Ladies are not aware
of such things, I know,' he added sagely, as though he
had suddenly acquired the wisdom of Solomon, 'but
the man has a wicked reputation and you should avoid
him by all means in your power, not encourage him.
You do not mind my saying this,' he went on anxiously,
'but a lady alone. . .'

'No, not at all,' said Bel, amused that Marcus, in
Rhys Howell's toils until a few days ago, should now
constitute himself a protector of the innocent. It was,
she thought, almost flattering that Marcus should see
her as such an innocent.

'I am always——' she began rapidly, laying her hand
on Marcus's arm again, for she saw that Francis had
stopped hovering and was advancing on them, a determined expression on his face, ready, she assumed, to
hand her yet another sermon to digest, and she thought
that she and Marcus might hold him off.

No such thing, for, interrupting her, he said through
his teeth, in his most high-handed way, 'My dear
nephew, you have monopolised Mrs Merrick all
through dinner; now you must let someone else have a
turn with her. Good manners require no less.'

'Suppose, Lord Francis,' retorted Bel sweetly, 'I told
you that I preferred to continue my discourse with
Marcus, rather than move on to another?'

'Then,' said Francis glacially, 'I should be compelled
to conclude that the lack of wisdom which impelled
you to share a carriage with such a blackguard as
Captain Howell was still working in you this evening,
madam.'

'Steady on, Uncle,' protested Marcus. 'No way to

treat a lady, and Bel has a right to stay talking to me, if she wishes to do so.'

'Do you wish me to read you a lesson on good manners, too?' asked Francis, aware that he was behaving as badly as Marcus and Bel, but unable to prevent himself. 'Go and help Almeria hand out the teacups— that should cool you off, and provide you with an occupation which, if not as exciting as whispering nothings to Mrs Merrick, is at least useful.'

This pedantic speech, delivered in Francis's best manner of captain reproving a misbehaving midshipman, had Marcus retreating and muttering, and Bel wanting to giggle, the manner and the matter being so at odds with one another.

Francis, seeing her mouth twitch, said dangerously, 'And what is amusing you, madam? The spectacle of yet one more of your victims caught in your toils? What a mermaid you are, to be sure. Have you tired of respectability, that you should allow Rhys Howell to ferry you about? Where was all that noble virtue you used with me the other afternoon? Left behind on the couch where you entertained him, I suppose.'

This was delivered in low tones and through his teeth, after such a fashion that, no one being near to them, no one could have any idea what he was saying to her.

The most appalling and delightful rage ran through Bel. How dared he, how dared he say such things to her? And then he said, again through his teeth, 'I warned you about Howell, madam, I told you that I knew him to be a villain of the first water, but what notice did you take of me? Recklessly, wantonly, you put yourself in the way of danger. . .'

'Pray stop,' said Bel, also in low tones, reduced to whispering for fear that if she raised her voice it would be to tell him, and the room, exactly what she thought of Lord Francis Carey, unaware that love, desire, a care for her safety and plain green-eyed jealousy were all at work in her tormentor.

Francis opened his mouth again, and what would come out this time? thought Bel despairingly. She must stop this, she must, for her sake, and Almeria's and kind Philip's—she could see his thoughtful eye on them and was suddenly persuaded that he was understanding more than he ought.

Invention struck. She dropped her fan, gave a loud wail, clutched at her bosom—was that the right place to clutch? she wondered—said faintly, 'Oh, dear heavens, what is coming over me? Oh, I feel so faint; the heat——' and, speaking thus, her voice dying away, she allowed her knees to sag, and began to fall forward, head hanging, into Francis's arms. He, face disbelieving, caught her as, eyes rolling into her head, she willed herself to turn pale, by holding her breath, which had the effect of her turning purple, an even more awful sight, while Francis, enraged, certain that madam was at her tricks and doing this to confound him, was perforce compelled to carry her to a sofa and deposit her reverently on it, with Almeria fetching smelling salts, which did cause Bel to turn pale, and various gentlemen, Marcus the loudest, then to offer contradictory forms of assistance.

Marcus caught his uncle by the arm and hissed at him, 'And what were you saying to poor Bel, to overset her so?' for he had been watching them like a hawk, and was sure that Francis had been bullying her; he knew that look of his uncle's very well, having had to endure it so many times himself.

'I, you damned young pup?' returned Francis. 'I have said nothing to cause this. I'd take a bet there's nothing wrong with her but a desire to attract attention.'

For one moment Francis thought that his tongue had run away with him to the degree that Marcus was about to strike him, but Marcus restrained himself with difficulty, contenting himself with saying, 'What the devil do you mean by that?'

To which Francis replied wearily, 'Oh, never mind,' turning to look at Bel, who was now propped up against some cushions, offering the company a weak and watery smile before closing her eyes and moaning gently.

He had to hand it to her. What a devious bitch she was, to be sure. She had stopped him in his tracks—or anyone else who might try to reproach her—and had thoroughly disarmed everyone. He was not deceived by all this, and tomorrow he would let her know, and no mistake.

Bel opened one eye. She closed it again hastily when she saw Francis's disbelieving stare trained on her. 'I really do feel,' she announced bravely, 'a little better. I cannot think what came over me. It was all so sudden. One moment——' and she sighed as though words were too much for her '—I felt quite well, and then the next moment. . .' And she gave a delicate shudder as she spoke.

Privately she was again appalled at her own deviousness—and wondered, as before, where all this was coming from. It was Francis Carey's fault, she was sure. If only he would let her alone—or rather would *not* let her alone, but would treat her as he should, respectfully and lovingly—then she could go back to being well-behaved, innocent Bel Merrick again. As it was, she had to protect herself, and if throwing a fainting fit in Almeria's drawing-room was the only way to do it, then so be it.

'Let me assist you upstairs to my room,' said Almeria, who had no reason to doubt the truth of Bel's behaviour. 'And then Francis can take you home when you are feeling a little better. I shall send Mrs Broughton on to prepare a warm bed for you, and a restorative cordial. I have a splendid bottle of my own brewing which I shall give her—excellent with a little brandy before retiring—it always ensures a good night's sleep.'

Privately, and irreverently, Bel thought that a good draught of brandy might accomplish that for her without the cordial, but said nothing, only sighed gently, and when Almeria called on Francis to carry her upstairs she smiled up at him so limpidly that he almost began to laugh himself. Just let him get madam alone, and she would find out his opinion of mermaids who behaved as she did, he thought, as he laid her lovingly on the bed—he could not help but be loving, only wished that he could stay to...to...and he hurriedly left her to Almeria's ministrations before he forgot himself completely.

CHAPTER FOURTEEN

'You are better today, then?' Almeria asked Bel anxiously the next morning. Bel was lying on the sofa looking prettily *distraite*—she thought that she had better keep up the farce of being a little unwell. Not only Francis, but Captain Howell, could be kept at bay by it.

Mrs Broughton had been reading *The Curse of the Comparini* to her when Lady Almeria had arrived, and Bel replied to her question by saying in a low voice, 'Oh, I am a little recovered. Rest will assist me...I think,' and she lowered her long dark lashes over her eyes in what she hoped was an interesting fashion.

'I bring messages from us all,' went on Almeria, a concerned expression on her face. 'Marcus was particularly disturbed by your malaise—and Philip and Francis, too, it goes without saying. I am sure you are in good hands,' she ended, looking at Mrs Broughton.

'Oh, yes,' said that lady vaguely. 'I am breaking the habit of a lifetime by reading dear Bel a novel in the morning to comfort her.' And she waved a hand at *The Curse*, which was lying open on her knee.

This distracted Almeria, who picked it up, said eagerly, 'Oh, the Comparini—too exciting, dear Bel, for an invalid, I would have thought. That scene where the cowardly and dastardly Paolo Neroni blackmails poor Sophia Ermani...words fail me—such a brute. I thank God we live in dear quiet Lulsgate Spa where such dreadful events do not occur.'

Bel thought that, though she and Almeria might laugh together at the goings-on in Gothic novels, Almeria also enjoyed them on a different level...and

189

what would she think if she knew of the pother Bel was in? It was not so different from Sophia's. Oh, if only there was someone in whom she could confide!

She thought that if Philip Harley had not been her friend's wife and Francis's brother-in-law she might have gone to him for advice, but, as it was. . .no such thing.

Later that afternoon, putting on a big bonnet, and venturing out when no one was about, she went to her little class, not so much to teach, but to ask the advice of Mr Birch.

Unworldly he might seem, but Bel thought there was an iron core to him, seldom shown, revealed a little when he had recently queried Francis's intentions towards her, in the most discreet fashion, of course.

After she had dismissed her class, taken indoors, for the weather was growing chilly, Mr Birch brought her a cup of tea and a slice of the cake which she had brought with her.

'What is it, my dear?' he asked her mildly. 'I cannot help but see that you are troubled in spirit. May I assist you in any way?'

Well, that showed percipience, Bel thought wryly, since no one else about her seemed to have noticed *that*.

'I have a problem,' she said simply. 'But it is not one which I can properly confide to anyone.' She paused, and said, 'Is it ever proper, or truly Christian, to deceive people, even for the best of motives?' For this was one of the questions which occupied her thoughts more and more; it was a series of deceits, undertaken mostly with the best of motives, which had landed her in her current predicament.

Worse, she was beginning to feel more and more uncomfortable about the false face she presented to Almeria and her Lulsgate friends, the face of a widow, not the young untried girl she really was.

'As a Christian and a minister,' said Mr Birch gently, 'my answer must be, of course, no, as you are well aware. But, as a man of the world, living in the real world, the answer cannot be so clear-cut. Suffering human beings may feel it necessary to engage in them. I have to say that if they do so they must be prepared to take the consequences which must inevitably follow.'

'Yes,' said Bel, in a hollow tone, heart sinking. 'And suppose, only suppose, that one's heart is fixed on someone who may have the wrong view of one——' for this was, she felt, as far as she could go '—what then, Mr Birch, what then? Should one abandon one's feelings, or try to overcome the error?'

Mr Birch, as Bel suspected, was no fool. 'If,' he said, 'your object of affection were someone like the gentleman who has called for you lately, I would think it unwise to try to trick him. Perfect candour would answer better. From his looks and conversation he is upright to a fault, if a minister may properly say such a thing.'

Bel's answering, 'Yes, I suppose so,' was hollow again. 'Then one should never do a wrong, however slight, hoping that good might come from it?' she asked feverishly, feeling that her conversation was becoming more and more obscure, but, paradoxically, feeling also that Mr Birch somehow knew exactly of what she was speaking.

'Truth is always the best,' he answered, 'although sometimes it may be inconvenient to tell it. Only you, my dear, and no one else, save only God, can help yourself. I may advise you to be perfectly candid, but if, in your opinion, being so would be destructive to yourself, then in the real world one might have to think again. On the other hand, you may find that truth and only truth can save you. Put your trust in God, and he will tell you what to do.'

Bel took his old hand and pressed it. 'Oh, you are

kind,' she said fervently, 'and wise. For many in your condition would simply have given me a stern answer without understanding how difficult my situation might be. You will forgive me if I do not tell you exactly what it is, but. . .' She hesitated.

Mr Birch looked at her agonised face. 'My dear,' he said, 'we have been friends for nearly two years, you and I, and I know you to be that rare thing, a good woman. But you are a woman on your own. I understand that you have no near relations, no family on whom to fall back, who might advise you, and, that being so, your conduct has been admirable. But you are very young, and the young may be foolish, impulsive. It is for you to try to remedy that by letting your head as well as your heart advise you, and God is there for you to ask for succour.'

Bel withdrew her hand and drank her tea. Having spoken to him, her heart felt lighter, even if he had only told her what she already knew.

'Thank you,' she said, voice low, for him to answer,

'My dear Mrs Merrick, you know that here you may always find refuge, should you need it. The children and I owe you at least that. You bring sunshine into our lives every week of the year.'

Well, that was that, she thought, walking home, and even as she breathed relief she heard carriage wheels and knew that Francis had been waiting for her to leave Mr Birch's cottage, and that the hour of reckoning for last night's naughtiness was on her.

Francis stopped the curricle, leaned down and said roughly, 'Come, you cannot refuse my offer of a lift. Almeria said that you were too overset to do anything today, but I was sure that you would not neglect your children. What a strange mixture you are, to be sure.' His face was rueful, and she knew that he was as tormented as herself, but for quite different reasons.

'No more so than another,' she said quietly, only to be met by his disbelieving face.

'And what does the old man make of you, madam? I should dearly love to know. And the trick you played on me and the company last night—what would he have made of that?'

Bel thought of the conversation which she had had with Mr Birch, decided to tell Francis the truth—or at least a little of it. 'I could think of no other way of quietening you,' she said. 'Another moment and you would have ruined the pair of us.'

His eyebrows rose haughtily. 'Ruined me, madam? I can see how I could have ruined you, but how should I have ruined myself?'

'To let the company know of what you think is the truth of me would be also to admit that you had known of that truth for some time, and had said nothing, had allowed the woman you think of as a Cyprian not only to continue as Almeria's friend, but as the friend of her little children, polluting a pure home,' Bel said, wondering why this had not occurred to her before. 'What would Almeria think of your conduct then?'

Francis, mouth tightening, stared at the passing scenery, then, 'Not only a witch, madam, but were females allowed to be diplomats you would make a masterly one. Your mind is as sharp as it is devious. You admit, then, that you were shamming last night?'

'For a good reason,' said Bel wearily, 'although I do not think that Mr Birch would agree with what I did, were I to tell him of it.'

Francis was silent again, then finally he said in a stifled voice, 'Since I met you again in Lulsgate I think that I have run mad. I think only of you, want to talk only with you, be with you, want only you in my bed, wish that you were. . .honest, that we could have met in some other way. *That* is my ruin, madam, and you have worked it.'

How strange, thought Bel; last night I blamed Francis for destroying my usual good conduct, and today he is blaming me for doing the same thing to him, and his thoughts are my thoughts: he wishes, as I do, that we had met under a different star.

'And now I must say again what I have said before,' he went on. 'That you should have nothing to do with Captain Howell. Most unwisely you choose to receive him, drive out with him, and I suppose that I shall be hearing next that he is taking you to the grandest Assembly of the year—the September Ball.'

Bel was silent, for that lunchtime a note had been delivered to her from Rhys Howell, stating that he expected her to attend the September Ball with him as a proof of her good faith.

Francis read her silence aright. 'No!' he exclaimed violently. 'Do not say that I have hit the nail on the head! You *are* going with him. Why, Bel, why? You, with your excellent judgement, must know that the man is a blackguard—will ruin you...' He fell silent, suddenly conscious of the absurdity of what he was saying.

'Now, how can that be,' wondered Bel, 'when according to you I am ruined already? What a mass of contradictions you are, Francis.'

'No contradictions at all,' he almost groaned. 'I cannot bear to think of you in his arms, or, indeed, in any man's. There. I have said it. You have wrung it from me. I shall not be answerable for the consequences if you go with him. I know what he is, I see the way in which he looks at you. He wishes to run you, to be your pander, to sell you to the highest bidder, that is plain to me, as plain as day, and do not ask me how I know, for I cannot tell you. Do you wish to be run by him, Bel? Do you wish to out-Marina Marina? Are you not content to stay virtuous in

Lulsgate Spa? Does that…life…still attract you, call you back?'

She could not tell him that his intuitive guess about Rhys Howell's intentions towards her was correct. It trembled on her lips; she almost told him of Captain Howell's blackmailing of her—but could she trust Francis, either?

Had their relationship been different, been what she knew it ought to have been, then and only then could she have asked him for help. As it was… She hesitated and was lost; the moment passed. She saw his grim face. No, she must solve this problem herself. She could not beg for help from a man who thought her a trollop; pride alone prevented that.

They had reached her home. He helped her down, said, hoarsely, 'Remember, Bel, if you go to the ball with Howell I shall act. What I shall do, God help me, I don't know. But I saved Marcus from him, and I do not intend to do otherwise with you.' He saluted her with his whip, and was gone, Cassius at the back clinging on for dear life, favouring her with a wink as he flew by, which had her laughing despite her very real misery.

Oh, damn all men, good and bad, thought Bel as she entered her home. How much better if this world were peopled only by women, and the odd notions of men did not obtain, and babies did appear under the gooseberry bush—and all of them female!

Just to make life more exasperating than ever, Mrs Broughton met her with a long face. The postman had been and brought her a letter from her sister. She was ill, and Mrs Broughton was needed to help her, for her sister's husband was an invalid, the housekeeper had deserted them, all was at sixes and sevens, and only Mrs Broughton's presence would help.

'Dear Bel, you will allow me leave to go, I trust. I

would not ask if the case were not dire. I shall return as quickly as may be. And you do have dear Lottie.'

Bel refrained from pointing out that dear Lottie was growing old, was nearly at pensionable age, if not beyond it, but she had no mind to do other than accede to Mrs Broughton's wishes, even though she used that lady as a bulwark against the man she loved and the man she hated.

'Of course you must go,' she said, 'and of course I shall manage. Stay as long as is necessary, my dear. Lottie will help you to pack. You wish to go on tomorrow's stage?'

'Indeed, as soon as I may. You will be careful when I am gone, dear Bel. You are usually the soul of discretion, though I cannot say that I fully approve of this new friendship of yours with Captain Howell. I do not feel that he is quite the thing. Lord Francis, however. . .' And she trailed up the stairs, murmuring benedictions on Bel, Lord Francis and Lady Almeria — already seeing me as Lady Francis, I suppose, thought Bel ruefully. Oh, dear, what a tangled web we weave, when first we practise to deceive. I never thought much of that verse in the past. . .but now. . .

Bel was thinking of this again while waiting for Captain Howell to call for her to take her to the Grand Assembly. She had not seen Francis in private again; she did not know that he was almost afraid to be alone with her, and when they met in public they were icy cold to one another — anything less and there was the danger that they might be in each other's arms, and for their own reasons neither wanted that until the difference between them was resolved.

'Oh, dear,' mourned Almeria to her, 'I am so disappointed that you and Francis have not taken to one another; at first I thought. . .' And then, mindful of Philip's strictures, she said apologetically, 'I do not mean to meddle, but you seemed so suited to one another.'

She wished that she could ask what had gone wrong, but sitting with Francis at breakfast that morning she had thought that one of the things which he and Bel had in common was an indomitable will, allied to a pride which was so strong that it could almost be felt.

Perhaps *that* was what was wrong, thought Almeria; they are too much alike, so strong, so independent. For she had begun to see beneath the surface gloss of Bel's gentleness to the steel core it covered.

The doorknocker went in the middle of Bel's musings over this conversation and Lottie came in.

'That nasty piece is here to take you to the dance,' she said bluntly. 'I cannot imagine why you encourage such a low creature.'

And what to say to that? I have no alternative but to do as he wishes, so do not pester me with reproaches? Instead Bel said gently, 'He asked me before anyone else did, and it was difficult for me to refuse him without offence.'

'You have never found much difficulty in holding off those you do not care for before,' returned Lottie with incontrovertible and inconvenient truth.

'No matter,' said Bel, drawing on her long lace gloves, and seeing that the small circlet of silk flowers in her hair was in place—she was as fresh and lovely as she ever was, even though all this was put on for her to be escorted by a man she despised. For Francis was there, and she wished to be absolutely *à point*, even though he was not to know that she had dressed for him, and thought it was all for Rhys Howell.

Bel had long since lost the wish to provoke Francis Carey—except, of course, when he deliberately set out to provoke her.

'Oh, you are magnificent tonight, my dear,' sighed the captain gallantly over her hand, admiring the delicate blue silk of her dress, the creamy gauze which covered it, the new way in which she had made Lottie dress her hair—that unhappy servant trailing along behind them on the short walk to the Assembly Rooms, to sit with the other servants in an ante-room until the dance was over, seeing that there was no Mrs Broughton to protect her mistress.

They were early. The party from the vicarage had not yet arrived. Some of Rhys Howell's disreputable court were leaning against the wall, yawning, such small beer of excitement as Lulsgate could provide already boring them. Several more hangers-on had arrived during the week, although one hard-faced gentleman whom Bel had seen disputing with the captain in Lulsgate's main street was not there; nor, she discovered, did he later favour the dance with his presence.

Slowly, the room filled up. The Venns arrived, and Henry, on seeing Rhys Howell leave Bel to join one of his boon companions for a moment, and then go to the supper-table for a cool drink for them both, took the opportunity to come over to her to say, 'Is this wise, my dear? Your escort, I mean. My mother. . .'

Bel was tired of being hectored by everybody from Francis Carey downwards, all of whom seemed to know her own business better than she did herself.

'Your mother never approves of anything I do, as you well know, my dear Mr Venn. Now if she were to approve, you might trouble me about the matter. Otherwise, I will take her censure as read.'

Henry turned a dull red. 'She and I only mean you well,' he said stiffly, 'whereas I doubt whether the same can be said for Captain Howell. You choose your companions badly.'

The worst of it was, thought Bel, that so far as Rhys Howell went he was in the right. But all this was handed down from on high, and she also knew quite well that if

Henry knew the truth about her—and Marianne—he would throw her over without a thought.

'I will take note of what you say,' she replied, attempting to be a little conciliatory, 'but it is for me to make my own decisions, as you, Mr Venn, make yours. I do not choose to lecture you on what you are to do.'

'But then I am not a young woman who needs advice lest she be led astray, women being so prone to that if not guarded with loving care,' was his swift response.

Fortunately, before Bel could say something unforgivable, Rhys Howell returned, a glass of lemonade for her, and a cold stare for Henry.

'Happy to see you are guarding Mrs Merrick for me,' he said. 'Now that I am back I thank you, and you may return to your mama.'

Henry turned red again, bowed stiffly and walked away to speak to the said mama, who turned her baleful and disapproving gaze on Bel.

I shall be ruined before Captain Howell gains his ends, she thought, and then had not time to think more, for the vicarage party arrived, Almeria and Philip leading, Francis and Marcus behind, Francis throwing every other man in the hall into the shade, and consequently had every female eye, married and unmarried, young and old, on him.

He was quite unmoved. Took it as his due, doubtless, thought Bel exasperatedly, and was far more exasperated when Captain Howell, who, seeing Francis's eye, even more baleful than Mrs Venn's, upon them, said loudly, 'Come, my dear Bel. Stand up with me, I beg. It is the waltz next, and none but your humble servant shall dance it with you.'

Bel tried to hang back, began to mutter some feeble negative, only he turned *his* baleful stare on her, saying, 'Remember what I have promised you, my dear, if you fail to co-operate with me.'

There was nothing she could do. Resigned, if inwardly mutinous, Bel stood up with him, and as the small group of musicians began to play she and the captain were the first on the floor, every eye upon them, as he had intended.

Bel was quite aware that if she allowed the captain to monopolise her it was as good as announcing that she and he were an engaged pair—or that she, Bel, was on the loose side of good behaviour. Lulsgate Spa was as narrow-minded as most small provincial towns, and breaches of etiquette were severely frowned upon.

She could almost feel Francis's eyes boring into her back, and was relieved when Mr Courtney, the Master of Ceremonies, waved his hand and the music stopped. Fortunately, she and the captain were not near the small group from the vicarage, and she was walked back to her seat by him, feeling that she was treading on eggshells or grenades, at the very least.

The captain began small talk, in the middle of which she saw Marcus Carey crossing the floor towards her, a purposeful look on his face.

He reached her, bowed, and said, 'You will allow me to reserve a dance with you, my dear Bel. I am sure that your card is not yet full.'

Bel's card, given to her as she entered the hall, was hanging from her wrist; she detached it and began to examine it, only for the captain to take it, saying, 'Mrs Merrick's card is reserved for me tonight, Tawstock.'

'No,' Bel protested without thinking, 'not so. I shall be happy to stand up with you in the quadrille, Marcus.'

'Marcus, is it?' said the captain nastily, snatching the card from Bel's hand and beginning to write his name beside every space. 'Well, you may stand up with this popinjay for the next dance, but the rest will be mine.'

'You are a very oaf, Howell, and how I endured you

for so long I shall never know,' said Marcus indignantly. 'I shall speak to the MC. I understand that such
monopolies are not allowed at Lulsgate Spa's
Assembly Rooms. Things are done in proper form
here. You have no right to take Bel's card from her.'

Bel, who was by now on her feet herself, furious
with the captain, who she suddenly realised intended
to compromise her hopelessly, so that she would be
compelled to receive his protection, decent society
being sure to cast her out once it saw her apparent
relationship with him, said, 'Dear Marcus, I will stand
up with you, and as for the card, rest assured that I
shall dance with whom I please.'

'Not so,' said the captain again with a grin, 'and
dancing with raw boys without manners or money is
not what I intend for you at all.'

To Bel's horror, she saw Marcus begin to square up
to the captain in protest at the manner which he was
using to her, but before he could do anything a new
actor arrived on the scene.

It was Francis Carey. His baleful stare took in the
three of them.

'You are in danger of becoming the talk of the
ballroom,' he said coldly. 'Are you at your tricks again,
Howell? I understand that Lord Tawstock came over
to ask Mrs Merrick to dance with him. The rules of the
Assembly say that it is her choice with whom she
dances. What is your wish, Mrs Merrick?' And his hard
eyes were on her, pitiless, challenging her, she was
sure, to state her position.

'I have already said that I will dance with Lord
Tawstock,' Bel replied, as cold as he. 'You will hand
me back my programme, Captain Howell. No one but
myself shall fill it in.'

It was a declaration of war, and Bel knew it. She
also knew that, faced with Francis Carey, Rhys Howell

might not go so far as he had done with Marcus, and she read him aright.

For all his bravado the captain had no wish to fight with a man who reputation was as great as Francis's. Francis had, he knew, killed the man who had wantonly shot down one of his young officers in a duel not of the young man's making, and his bravery as a naval officer had been recognised on more than one occasion.

The captain had come to the Assembly Rooms with the half-formed idea of ruining Bel Merrick on the spot by his behaviour to and with her—but not at the risk of being killed himself. He would wait to finish her off when the mealy-mouthed aristocrat seeking to protect her was not about.

But Francis's expression was so grim that Bel feared for a moment that worse might befall, except that the MC, Mr Courtney, whose duty it was to see that such scenes did not occur, now joined them.

'Gentlemen,' he said, severely, 'may I remind you that before you were allowed to share in the pleasures organised here you signed a set of rules which demanded certain standards of behaviour and agreed to adhere to them? It is my duty to see that you do so. You will observe them, will you not?'

Mr Courtney was, in many ways, a silly, pompous man; nevertheless in a town like Lulsgate Spa the wishes of the MC were law. Those not agreeing to be bound by them were banned from the official festivities of the place, were banished from the very society which they had come to enjoy.

All the gentlemen, including Rhys Howell, bowed together to signify their submission to the MC's wishes. Marcus took Bel's hand to lead her on to the floor as the music began.

Like all reformed rakes and gamesters, Marcus wished to reform others. 'Dear Bel,' he said, 'you must know what a blackguard Rhys Howell is, as I now do, and I cannot understand why you should give him such encouragement.'

His voice was so sorrowful that Bel did not know how to answer him, and was reduced to saying, rather cryptically, 'I fear that he asks me for more than I wish to give, and it is hard to refuse him.'

Marcus mistook her meaning a little. 'Oh, you have no man to protect you,' he said. 'Why do you not ask my Uncle Frank to look out for you? I am sure that he would be only too pleased to do so,' and when Bel shook her head he said ingenuously, 'Oh, he is such a good fellow, I am sure that he would not mind. Look how he cared for me, and I am sure that I did not deserve it, whereas you. . .' And he paused, his artless face aglow with new-found goodwill.

Bel could see Francis watching her as she danced. He was almost the only man in the room not on the floor, and she could almost feel what he was thinking of her, and she was sure that it was not favourable. But at least he and Marcus, by their intervention, had saved her, for she was certain that the captain was frightened of Francis, and Marcus had given Francis the opportunity to intervene without it appearing that he was doing it for himself.

Marcus said nothing more after that, concentrating on the dance, until, the dance over, he said to her, 'Join us, Bel, dear; you surely do not wish to remain with a man who treats you in such a fashion.'

Bel hesitated; then, looking across at the captain, who was now talking angrily to one of his cronies, she knew that, whatever else, he would not ruin her tonight. He was too frightened of Francis and what he might do to him. He had backed down over Marcus the night that Francis had taken him away, and tonight he had let her go without making any real threats.

If she joined the Harleys' party she was sure that he

would make no attempt to haul her back this evening, but would do so on another day.

Well, that other day was not with her yet, and—who knew?—by then she might have thought of something to thwart him in his designs on her. What that might be she could not foresee, but meantime Marcus was offering her salvation.

'Thank you,' she said. 'You know, I really do not care for him at all, Marcus, but he asked me to come here tonight before anyone else did, and in politeness it was difficult to refuse.' Which was, she thought, as good an excuse as any, and was the one which she had offered to Lottie.

Marcus nodded, satisfied. He knew how strict were the rules of etiquette which governed women's conduct, and that lone women like Bel were at particular risk. They were, by now, with Philip and Almeria, who both rose, Almeria saying, 'Oh, I am so happy to see that you no longer wish to remain with that man. Come and tell me what you think of *The Curse of the Comparini*. Did Mrs Broughton find time to finish it before she left? It is a pity she had to go. Captain Howell could not have been so particular with you had she been present.'

Bel nodded agreement to all this, before Almeria carefully seated her beside Francis, who was as glacial as ever. When Philip and Almeria had taken the floor, and Marcus had engaged Miss Robey, he said to her coldly, 'You put yourself in a false position, Mrs Merrick, accompanying such a creature as Howell is. Young Marcus did well to lead the column of relief for you.'

'Oh,' said Bel. 'The pair of you manoeuvred that, then?'

Francis nodded. 'I admit I was the instigator, once I saw that you had come with him as you had said that you would. But Marcus needed little prodding. He is thoroughly converted to good behaviour at the moment, is disillusioned with all such as Howell—and how long that will last is another matter. But you— what has got into you, unless it is a hankering for your old ways?'

'My old ways!' said Bel vigorously. 'I have no old ways—as one day you will realise.'

'And you will promise to avoid Howell from now on and save...Almeria...and myself from worry in the future.'

Bel went white. 'I cannot promise you that,' she said faintly, knowing that the captain would begin his campaign to persuade her to throw in her lot with him, once Francis was not about.

'I cannot understand you,' he said passionately. 'Until he arrived you were discretion itself, in your public life at least. Now you worry all those who care for you by your odd conduct.'

'And do you care for me?' queried Bel, eyes agleam, for oh, how wonderful it would be if he did, if he could abandon the false belief he had of her—which to be fair to him was one which she, and none other, had created. Oh, how she regretted the hasty words at Stanhope Street with which she had deceived him— and the trick which she had played upon him.

Francis wanted to cry, I more than 'care for you', I adore you, but I cannot tell you so. I want to protect you, as well as love you, and now I know that my love for you is more than lust I am beside myself.

Controlling himself almost visibly, he said instead, 'I do not care to see anyone exploited by such a cur as Howell,' and she had to be content with that, and with his invitation to her to dance the next waltz with him, to which she agreed with alacrity.

Oh, bliss for Bel to be in his arms, to be so near to him, and yet purgatory that she could be no nearer— and Francis? He, too, felt as Bel did. The intoxication of the music, the passionate feelings both were experiencing were, unknown to them, written on their faces; all the signs of their profound and mutual love gave them away to the watchers.

By God, the monk's in love with her—and she with him, thought Rhys Howell savagely, having taken a little more port than he ought in an effort to forget that he had once again given way to Francis Carey, while Philip and Almeria—and a hundred others—came to the same conclusion.

How lovely she is, thought Francis distractedly, and how brave, even in her wilfulness. The red hair, the green eyes, the damask cheek, the. . . I grow maudlin. While for Bel the athletic body, the strong face, straight mouth and hard grey eyes of the man whom she had come to love were more pleasing to her than the softer features of the other men who surrounded her. And each thought with longing of the other: male and female both *beaux-idéals* of beauty and strength.

The dance over, Francis led her back, thinking hard, at the last, of anything but the woman he so inconveniently loved, lest his arousal betray him to all the world. A period away from her and a cold drink might restore him, he thought wildly, and so he said to Almeria, who had been watching them, 'A drink, perhaps, Almy, and you, too, Bel?' and, the two women assenting, he and Philip strolled off to the supper-room together.

Neither Bel, Almeria nor Marcus, who stayed behind with them, to talk lightly of Queen Caroline, the weather, and various inconsiderable topics, ever knew exactly what passed in the supper-room, which stood at some distance from the ballroom itself.

The supper-room was laid out with tables containing food more substantial than, if not so fashionable as, the light fare found at similar places in London. As in London, long sideboards containing drink stood at the

side of the room, and Francis and Philip made for
these.

Rhys Howell, his pack of toadies about him, had
abandoned the dance-floor and was drinking fairly
steadily, even though he was, as yet, still relatively
sober. His eyes were ugly as he surveyed the brothers-
in-law choosing their partners' drinks after drinking
themselves—Philip sticking to lemonade, Francis taking a glass of port.

'Enjoying the pretty widow, are you, Carey?' he said
jeeringly; he could not restrain himself at the sight of
the man he disliked, but was content to address
Francis's back—though not for long.

Francis swung round. 'I told you before not to call
me Carey, Howell,' he said coldly, 'and I will also
thank you not to speak of any lady before the scum
whom you call friends.' He felt Philip's hand on his
arm and threw it off. The anger mixed with jealousy
which he always experienced when he thought of Bel
having anything to do with this piece of filth was strong
in him. He was sure that Howell wished to be Bel's
pimp, and the desire to kill him with his bare hands
was almost overwhelming.

Howell went purple. Even he could hardly swallow
such an insult.

'Damn you. . .Carey. I'll call you out for that.'

'As I told you before,' returned Francis, 'I'll not fight
you, ever. A horsewhip, now that would be a different
matter. Shall I send for one?' If this was Drury Lane
heroics, he thought savagely, then he was enjoying
them. He felt Philip's restraining hand on his arm
again, and threw it off again.

'By God,' swore Howell, 'if you think to continue
insulting me with impunity, you are vastly mistaken,'
and, made bold by the drink he had taken, he threw
himself on his tormentor, to be met with Francis's iron
fingers on his throat.

'Francis, think what you are doing!' Philip was trying to pull his brother-in-law off his victim, who was slowly turning purple; men were shouting, and, fortunately for Howell, the MC himself came bustling in, mewing fearfully,

'Gentlemen, gentlemen, remember where you are. There are ladies near by. Shame on you, sir,' he addressed Francis, and, strangely, the MC's fluttering tones restored him to sanity.

Francis let go of Howell, who fell to his knees, clutching his throat and croaking, 'By heaven, Carey, another minute and you'd have killed me.'

'Pity I didn't, for the sake of all the men you've cheated and the women you've seduced,' retorted Francis, cold again, and when Mr Courtney said, tremulously, looking at the pair of them,

'I shall have to ask you to leave, both of you, and you must seek my permission before you are admitted again,' Francis replied in a more normal voice,

'I regret, sir, that what I did was done here. I cannot regret the doing. All the same, I beg your pardon, and I shall leave at once.'

He swung towards his brother-in-law. 'You were right to try to stop me, Philip, and you will give my apologies to Almy and Bel, but whenever I see that man——' and he indicated Howell, who was being led away by his cohorts '—reason seems to leave me.'

Philip nodded. In all the years he had known Francis, he had found him stern but always perfectly in control of himself, and the savage who had nearly strangled Howell was unknown to him. His belief that there was more than met the eye between Francis, Bel Merrick and Rhys Howell was further strengthened.

As if he knew what Philip was thinking, Francis said ruefully as Philip walked him to the back door, 'Pray forgive me but it is most unlike me to behave as I did. The devil seems to be in me these days.'

Philip thought, but did not say, that since Bel Merrick had come into Francis's life his whole world seemed to have turned upside-down, but it was Francis's problem, not his, and Francis would have to solve it.

Meantime he must return to Almeria, Marcus and Bel, and try to gloss over what had happened in the supper-room, and over the fact that Bel Merrick was the main cause of it—for of that one thing Philip was quite sure.

CHAPTER FIFTEEN

BEL, however, was soon made aware that whatever had happened in the supper-room between Francis and Rhys Howell must in some way have concerned herself.

She had suspected it ever since Philip Harley, in his quiet fashion, had told them that the MC had asked Francis and Captain Howell to leave. She remembered what Francis had said—that if she persisted in attending the September Ball with Rhys Howell he would take action. The stares and curious glances which she received all evening, the triumphant expression on Mrs Venn's face, and Henry's mild, forbearing one, almost as though he were saying, I told you so, at a distance, carried their own message.

She was determinedly gay, but the gaiety had something febrile in it. She was almost sure, now, that Philip Harley, alone of all the people she knew in Lulsgate, thought that there was something a little strange, subtly out of place, in her relationship with Francis, and it was that which troubled him, as much as her apparent friendship with Rhys Howell.

Suppertime arrived, but she could not eat or drink, and suddenly everything seemed intolerable, even Almeria's kindness and protection, for, while the Harleys approved of her, Lulsgate would always accept her.

She rose, saying to Almeria, 'You will forgive me if I leave you early. I have a headache coming on, and an early night will suit me.' She had stayed long enough, she knew, to remove suspicion that the fracas in the supper-room had driven her away early, and

Almeria, looking at Bel's suddenly white face, had not the heart to persuade her to stay longer.

'Of course,' she said, then, 'Bel, dear, do not worry over what passed tonight. Francis has been...impulsive, I know, but I am sure that whatever he did was done to protect you. Most unlike him to act as he did, but I believe that that, and only that, lay behind his conduct.'

Bel saw Philip Harley, almost unconsciously, nod agreement. She fought an impulse to cry, knowing that what Almeria said was true—despite his suspicions of her, the mixture of desire and hostility which were the staple of Francis's dealings with her, he genuinely wanted to save her from Rhys Howell. She almost wished that she had confided in him.

'Thank you, Almeria,' she said through stiff lips. 'Now you will excuse me, I trust. I will go and fetch Lottie. It is time that she went home; she is growing too old for late-night sessions such as these.'

'And that is what I like about Bel Merrick,' remarked Philip as they watched her go, bowing to those who bade her goodnight, 'she has a true consideration for all those about her. I suppose,' he added slowly, 'that that might account for her taking up with such an unlikely person as Rhys Howell. . .' But he did not believe what he said.

Bel found Lottie, looking weary as she had expected, but also surprised at Bel's relatively early departure from an event which was the height of Lulsgate's small season.

'I thought that you were going home with him, or with the Harleys, Miss Bel,' was all she said when it became apparent that she was Bel's sole escort.

'No.' Bel was brief. 'I am tired, and do not wish to stay longer. You may accompany me home. After all,

the journey is not far, and Lulsgate streets are safe at
night.'

Once home, bone-weariness took over. She felt as
though she had run the sort of race she had done as a
youthful hoyden before ladylike considerations took
over to make her the model of a parson's good and
proper daughter.

When Lottie would have followed her into her bedroom to ready her for the night, she shook her head.
'No, we are both tired, you more than myself. You
may go to bed at once. I will look after myself.'

She thought that Lottie was growing old, and would
have to be pensioned off, found a little home, but she
was the last link with her old life and she did not wish
to lose her. She watched the old woman struggle
upstairs to her bedroom on the second floor. The
temporary loss of Mrs Broughton had never seemed
more annoying, for it had thrown more responsibilities
on to her old servant.

Sighing, she pushed open her bedroom door, the
candle she held throwing strange shadows about the
room, her own, monstrously distorted, moving with
her. She placed the candle on the dressing-table, undid
her pearl necklace—only to see a movement in the
shadows reflected in her mirror.

Startled, Bel swung around, a scream on her lips as
she saw that a male figure was seated in the armchair
by her bed, a scream she stifled when she saw that it
was Francis, his face white and drawn, his whole mien
one of barely suppressed pain.

'You!' she exclaimed. 'How came you here? And,
more to the point, what are you doing here?'

He answered her second question, not her first,
standing up as he did so, all his usual formality of
manner quite gone.

'I came through the connection between your garden
and Almy's. I noticed the other day that one of the

glass doors in your drawing-room had a faulty lock. It was the work of a moment to force it and to enter. I have done no permanent damage. In any case, for your own safety the lock needed replacing.'

There was nothing apologetic about him. Nothing to suggest that the last thing he ought to have done was to break and enter a house, force his way into a lady's bedroom.

Shocked though she was, Bel could not help saying sharply, before she asked him to leave at once, before she called for the constable to remove him, 'You took a great risk. Suppose Lottie had come in with me—she usually does? What would you have done then?'

'Then I should have hidden in the curtains, or in the closet yonder, until she left.' He gave a humourless smile. 'You see, where you are concerned, Mrs Bel Merrick, I am full of wicked invention, and I have no conscience or honour left at all. You have deprived me of it.'

'Oh, I see,' said Bel, fascination replacing fear. 'It is all my fault. I might have expected that. I have provoked you to this dishonourable conduct, unworthy of a man of your reputation, character and station in life.'

Why was she bandying words with him? she wondered. She must order him to leave, although how she could compel him to go if he chose not to she could not think. To scream, to call for Lottie, or Ben, the boy who did the odd-jobs for her—a handyman rather than a footman—would destroy the last shreds of her reputation in Lulsgate Spa, to say nothing of the humiliations which such an act would heap on Francis himself. A supposedly honourable man who had arrived, uninvited, in a lady's bedroom, presumably to force her...or so the world would think. She did not really believe that that was why he had come.

'Yes, you have provoked me,' was his reply to that, 'by encouraging that damned swine Howell. God forgive me, I nearly killed him tonight, after seeing you with him. You must know only too well what a black-guard he is, that he can only mean you harm——'

'And what harm do *you* mean me?' flashed Bel. 'It is you who are in my bedroom, uninvited, at nigh on midnight, not Rhys Howell—who, of course, I know to be a villain, and one who means me harm. And now I ask again that you leave me, at once.'

'Not before you have heard me out,' he replied hoarsely, his face full of an almost physical pain. 'It has been murder, pure murder, for me to watch you tonight—aye, and all the recent days when I have seen you with *him*. Do you not know how you affect me, madam? Oh, Bel, I burn for you, feel how I burn,' and he grasped her hand, held it against his forehead for a moment, and it was true, he was on fire.

Bel wrenched her own hand back, for through it the fire had passed from him to her, and she was suddenly shaking, consumed by the same flames. Her breath had shortened at his touch, and the sight of him, here in her most secret place, the room where she had dreamed of him so often, was rousing her to the same pitch of excitement which Francis was suffering—or enjoying. . .perhaps the two sensations were the same, pleasure so exquisite that it was almost pain.

Francis saw her state, saw everything about her as though she had become transparent, open to him, felt her desire for him in the same measure that he felt his for her.

'Oh, you feel as I do!' he cried exultantly. 'Oh, Bel, you must not torment me longer. The more you hold me off, the more you inflame me, particularly when I know that you are deceiving me when you deny me. I vowed two years ago that I would enjoy you without paying you anything, that as a punishment for cheating me you would lie with me willingly, would beg me to do so, as I am now begging you. I told myself that I hated you for being a cheating whore, but I was wrong. I cannot pretend any more. I wish to be in your arms so strongly that I will gladly pay any price you name to be there.'

He loved her with all the passion of a passionate nature long denied, but he could not say so. He could not confess that he loved a Cyprian, and the sister of a Cyprian so notorious that two years after her death her name was still remembered—that was beyond him. Besides, he feared that she might laugh at him if he made any such confession; she had mocked him so often for much less than that.

Bel swallowed at his words, especially at the one word 'price'. He *still* thought her a whore after all these weeks together. How could he, oh, how could he? Her unconsidered acts of two years ago had ruined the future for both of them. Suppose she had said then, I am Marina St George's innocent sister, and can prove it—then they would not be standing here, dying of love for one another, and unable to do anything about it without each violating his or her most inward self.

For if Francis felt that he was betraying himself by loving a whore—for Bel now had no doubts that he loved her—she too would betray herself, destroy her own virtue, by consenting to lie with him in other than honourable marriage, because now she knew that she loved him beyond life, beyond reputation.

Love's cross-currents flung them now together, now apart—except that tonight, alone at last, hidden from the prying world, Bel knew that nothing could prevent her from giving him what he wanted so desperately to take—and she as desperately to offer.

He would not, she knew, keep her, take her as his mistress. She knew that his dead wife stood between him and a lesser permanent union. He would have her for one night, she thought—to assuage what? Was he strong enough to love her and leave her—was she strong enough to accept him as a lover, without marriage, risking social disgrace, and perhaps pregnancy—which was possible from even one night's loving?

And if she gave way to herself, as well as to him, what price would she demand of him—and of herself?

Francis had grasped her hand again, and again she pulled it away. She said coldly, denying the passion within her, 'Why do you ask me, Francis?' and her voice was almost cruel. 'We are here alone. You may take what you wish, with or without my consent. Many would not hesitate to take a whore without her consent. Why do *you* hesitate, Francis, thinking so little of me as you do?'

'Oh, God, not that, no, never that,' he said violently, putting his hands over his eyes. 'Not rape, Bel, never rape. Only with your consent, ever. You must accept me willingly, or not at all. If not for love, then for money, and you may name your price.'

She could not take him in the name of love—for she thought that he might not believe her if she told him that she loved him, and that would be to dishonour love. Knowing that, she also knew that in the end she would take him for the lesser reason. For, against all logic, all common sense, she was as determined to have him as he her, and if that meant the surrender of her chastity, then so be it—but he must pay in another coin first.

'Then beg me, Francis,' she said fiercely. 'Would you care for me to give you brandy, as you gave it to me at Almeria's table, that first night? Beg me, Francis, beg me on your knees for me to take you to my bed, if you wish to lie with me, for whore though I *might* be,' and she stressed the might, 'though any may offer me payment, I and only I choose who may visit my bed— and I am not yet sure that I wish to choose you.'

Francis fell on his knees before her, put his head in her lap, before looking up at her to see her face almost saintly in the halo created by the candlelight behind her.

'Oh, Bel, be merciful. Would you have me walk through the fire as well as burn?'

As I would walk through fire for you, and as I burn for you, was her unspoken reply. Yes, I would have you do that, so that we might be equal.

Instead, she answered him gently, 'No, not for mercy, Francis, but for payment. Whores have no pity, look only for payment. Your payment is—that you should beg again.'

Bel thought for a moment that she had gone too far. He lifted his head, stared at her, rose; pride had returned. He saw her white face, disembodied in the mirror, saw with astonishment that she was suffering as he did, for she was beside herself, lost in her own torment—and feeling his.

He was not to know, even though some strong message, unspoken, passed between them, informing him of the depths of her feelings, that, untried, chaste though she was, she would have taken him in love and was now, as she thought, prepared to take him in despite, seeing that there was no other way in which she could accept him.

Francis had no means of knowing this. Love's cross-currents were now so strong that both were drowning in them.

'I ask you, Mrs Bel Merrick, for I have no other name for you, to take me, Francis Carey, as I am, as your lover, for whatever reason, for love, for pity or for money, so long as we may enjoy together what I now see that we both so palpably want. Beyond reason, beyond honour, what I feel for you—and I have no name to give it—is so strong that you alone can give me something which I never thought to feel again.'

He fell silent, and Bel knew that, mistaking what she was, it was as near to a declaration of undying love as he could make to her. She thought of his dead wife and child, of her dead sister, and all doubts, all hesitations and resentments, were burned away.

'Yes,' she said simply. 'Yes, Francis, you need say no more. No payment of any kind is needed. Now it is my turn to beg you to come to me, to assuage *my* longing, *my* desire, for I, too, am beyond reason and honour and need no payment for what I so dearly wish.'

Francis's eyes, wide already from his body's arousal, widened still further, for he had thought that she was about to inflict the final humiliation on him—either refusal, or an acceptance so insulting that their loving would be bitter.

'*You* beg *me*?'

'Yes, Francis,' she said quietly, her voice so full of love for him that he ached at the sound, her face as soft as an angel's in a painting. 'That was what you wanted, was it not? For me to beg you? Shall I beg you again? Love for love, Francis, not hate for hate. No payment needed on either side. We are to meet as willing equals.'

Bel saw that she had cut the Gordian knot, broken down all the barriers which had arisen between them. She had, at one stroke, freed them from the hateful past, for now his eyes were glowing, triumphant, but loving, too.

'Equals, Bel? You mean that?'

'Equals, Francis. As though we meet for the first time, no taint of our mutual past upon us, free to enjoy one another without bitterness, revenge or the desire to hurt.'

'Then I kneel to you willingly,' he said, and proud Francis Carey went down before her, and this time when he took her hand she let him keep it. He kissed it, and said, looking up at her, 'Oh, you are generous, my heart, and now let me see all of you; not only that which you show the world, but the treasures which you normally hide—except from your lovers, of whom I am humbly one.'

Bel shivered under his ardent gaze, internally quaked at the thought of stripping herself before him. But, after all that she had said she could not refuse him, even though her modesty shrank before the act.

She stood up, he still kneeling, pulling her dress over her head, removed her underclothing, her stockings, until she stood naked before him. His gaze on her had never wavered. His eyes were wider than ever, and as her last garment fell away, and she instinctively dropped her hands to cover herself—there—he was there before her, had clasped her round the knees and was kissing her where the red-gold fleece hid her most secret parts.

'Oh,' he said fervently, looking up at her perfect, unspoiled body, a very chaste Diana as she was, although he was not yet to know that, 'you are even more lovely than I had dared to hope. Bel, you are *belle* indeed,' and he rose, saying, 'And now you may prepare me for the sacred rite we are about to undertake, for there shall be nothing between us, nothing, all subterfuge stripped away.'

Again Bel could not deny him, and it was she who undid his cravat, peeled off his coat, undid the buttons of his shirt, and then, when he bore her to the bed, between them they reduced him to the same state as herself, so that now she saw all of him, and as they came together nothing, no, nothing lay between them, symbolic of the fashion in which they had mentally stripped themselves before beginning the physical act of loving and finally offering to one another two perfect bodies.

The fierceness of her passion surprised Bel, who had thought herself a calm and reasoned soul. But she could not have enough of him, as he wished to have all of her; mouth, hands, legs, eyes and voice, all played their part, and as he loved and caressed her breasts and her mouth, so she too rejoiced to stroke his hard body, kissing and caressing his torso, the muscles which stood on his arms and shoulders, ran her hands up his inward thighs—as he had done to her—so that as she cried out for surcease, so did he, and finally his passion, so long restrained, could be held in check no more and he entered her.

To find, too late, that she was the virgin she had always said she was. But there was nothing he could do; the very shock of the forced entry brought Francis relief, a relief so strong and fierce that Bel, too, shared in it, immediate though it was, for the strength of their passion and their preliminary loving, and the frustrations of the previous weeks, would brook no delay for either of them.

Time and space disappeared. The sense of separateness disappeared, too, as they achieved the truest union of all, not given to many to experience. Francis was too far gone in sensation to register his shock at finding his lightskirt, his ladybird, his bit of muslin, his courtesan a virgin, although when, shuddering and gasping, the first transports were over, Bel, who regretted nothing, found him still shaking, but this time in grief, not in love.

'Oh, God forgive me, Bel, for you never can, for what I thought, said and did to you. I have wronged you for months in thought, and now in deed. I have seduced an innocent girl. I am Rhys Howell's worst.'

Bel clasped him to her. 'Oh, Frank,' she said, the pet name coming naturally to her lips, 'my darling Frank, there is nothing to forgive. I misled you first, and tonight I freely invited you to love me, as we both wished, and there is nothing you say which can change that.'

He lifted his ravaged face from the pillow in which he had buried it. 'Oh, you are an angel, my darling, to speak so, but for weeks I have miscalled you, taunted you, and now...I have ruined you. Now you must marry me.'

'Marry you!' Bel sat up. 'Oh, I cannot do that. You cannot marry me. It would not be fitting. I bring you a dishonoured name. I have told so many lies, not only to you, but to all the world. You must marry someone truly innocent. Captain Howell...' she began, then hesitated, finally said resolutely, 'Captain Howell has been trying to blackmail me, about Marianne and my supposed past; that is why I was compelled to endure his advances. You cannot wish to marry someone who may have other such creatures arrive in the future to soil your good name.'

'My good name?' said Francis bitterly. 'And what is that, pray? I have, in effect, seduced you, bullied you until you gave way to me. If you marry me, then I will protect you from any who might try to harm you—or me. Oh, my love, you should have come to me for protection from him—but how could you, speaking to you and treating you as I did?'

He does not say that he loves me, thought Bel—but then he turned towards her, kissed her, and said hoarsely, 'Oh, I worship you, Bel, worship you, so gallant as you are. Why did you pretend to be the same as your sister, *why*?'

'Because,' said Bel, inwardly joyful at the declaration which he had just made, 'I was so angry when you treated me as a courtesan that I pretended to be one—and then cheated you, something which I have regretted ever since, for after that you could never believe me innocent. But I had no idea that I should ever meet you again, or that you had affected me so strongly, so quickly—as you did. You see, I am shameless where you are concerned.'

'Then,' said Francis, kissing her on the cheek, 'with

you feeling as you do, I fail to see why you refuse to marry me.'

'You could. . .keep me,' said Bel gently, to have him say, violently,

'No, indeed. It is bad enough that I have ruined you, without proclaiming it to all the world; besides, it is not a thing I am prepared to do. I despise the immorality I see all around me, and now you may laugh at me for saying that, in view of my behaviour to you. I fail to see why you cannot accept my honourable proposal when you have accepted my dishonourable one— against all your beliefs, I am sure.'

'Because I love you,' Bel said, 'and because I accepted your dishonourable one, then the other is forbidden to me, and besides, although I come from a good family and my father was a parson, think of what my sister was, and what you are. You cannot marry such as myself.' And she leaned forward and kissed him on the cheek.

They were both now sitting up, and he took her face in his hands and said, 'It is not your sister whom I hope to marry, but you. Let me try to persuade you other-wise,' and he kissed her on the lips, gently at first, and then with renewed and rising passion, so that, all his good intentions forgotten, he turned her beneath him again, and they resumed where they had so recently left off. Only this time he treated her with such loving and patient care that in her transports she almost wept beneath him.

And when, sated, they lay in one another's arms, and he would again have asked her to marry him, Bel put her fingers on his mouth and said, 'Go to sleep, Francis, let us have tonight.'

He nodded his head, but replied, 'But I must leave soon, I must not ruin you completely,' and they fell asleep, sitting up, propped against the pillows, arms

round one another, as though to be parted physically
was death itself.

Bel slept as she had not done for weeks, and Francis
too, so deeply that dawn came and went, and the door
opened, for Lottie had knocked, and Bel had not
answered, nor did she wake until her old servant,
worried, entered the room——

To see Francis still there, sleeping, his head now on
Bel's breast, and Bel's gaze, steady, unashamed, meeting hers, left hand to her lips commanding silence, for
she knew, instinctively, that Francis was at peace as he,
too, had not been for years.

The old woman, who had seen even more of the
world than Bel suspected, nodded her head and left,
but the closing door broke Francis's slumbers. He sat
up, looked at Bel, saw the daylight through the curtains, and said, 'My God, Bel, whatever is the time? I
said that I would not ruin you, but I am like to do so,'
and he sprang out of the bed, alternately pulling on his
clothing and demanding that she marry him.

Bel rose from the bed, pulled on her dressing-gown
and began to help him, buttoning his shirt, tying his
cravat, assisting him into his tight, fashionable coat,
shaking her head, finally saying, 'Then give me leave
to think on the matter, Francis,' for him to begin to
kiss her passionately.

'Yes, my darling, for that answer is better than last
night's refusal, but not enough!' And then, 'But I must
be away, before I am seen.'

Together they stole downstairs—it was now eight-
thirty on a fine morning—and Bel let him out through
the glass doors in the drawing-room, for him to escape,
not by the way to Almeria's garden, but through a
small gate to a side-alley, so that he might steal back
unseen—after claiming yet another kiss.

Then Bel went back indoors, to meet Lottie's

reproving stare. 'I might have known,' said the old woman resignedly. 'You are not your sister, but you are loving enough. Could he not wait for you, then, or were you only too ready to make him your lover without so much as a wedding-ring, or a betrothal?'

'He has asked me to marry him,' began Bel, 'but——'

'But?' said Lottie. 'What but is there? The man is besotted. Has been since he met you as was plain for all to see—who had eyes, that is, and were not full of their own consequence. To be Lady Francis—what "but" can there be? Your wits are addled, Bel Passmore, for I will not call you by a name that is not yours. Does he know that yet?'

'No,' said Bel, 'and I do not think that he cares. I have promised to think on the matter.'

'Think for one minute and then say yes before he changes his mind,' said her servant acidly, for Bel to walk by her, clutching to her the memory of the night, and with the intention of considering carefully what she ought to do. Impulsiveness had brought her to this day; would careful thought do better for her?

Francis made his way to the vicarage as warily as he could. No one was about, and he knew that neither Almeria nor Philip would rise early after last night's junketing. With luck he could slip in—he possessed a door-key—and be up the stairs before anyone stirred.

Good fortune was not with him. Little Frank had been ill in the night, and though he took all the care in the world Francis had no more luck than to start up the stairs just as Philip and Almeria arrived on the landing, early risers after being awake most of the night caring for the little boy.

They both stared at the sight of him, still in last night's clothes for the ball, dishevelled, not at all his usual orderly self, walking in after a night spent— where? To try to explain would make matters worse.

Neither his half-sister nor his brother-in-law said anything. Francis smiled ruefully, and continued on his way. It was only too patent that he had spent the night away from the vicarage. He shrugged his shoulders. Well, that could not be helped; after all, he was more than of age.

Only to meet Marcus's accusing stare as he, too, arrived to see his uncle coming in after a night's debauch. Marcus's smile was knowing, almost derisory, and the only consolation was that not one of the three of them could have any idea in whose bed he had actually spent the night.

'Celebrating?' said Marcus, thinking he had caught his high-minded uncle on his way home after a bout with one of Lulsgate Spa's rather seedy Cyprians. Never say the old fellow has turned human at last! was his inward thought.

Francis cursed his ill luck, said, 'Good morning,' as cheerfully as though he were not rumpled, unshaven, and full of a goodwill brought on by a thoroughly satisfactory night's loving—of which he could say nothing to anyone. Neither Marcus's broad grin, nor Almeria and Philip's faint expression of shock, had the power to move him. He was suddenly sure that his heart's desire would be granted, that Bel would agree to marry him, and his lonely years would be over.

Bel did not have long to debate over Francis's proposal, or over her own surrender of her virginity. She had expected to feel some faint regret, but could only feel pleasure. Francis's loving had been so kind and careful, as well as passionate—exactly what she might have expected it to be.

But could she really accept him? Eating breakfast, dressing for the day, a sense of well-being lapping round her, she was coming to feel that perhaps she could—but that she must not hurry her decision.

Just before luncheon, however, Lottie came in, her face one big O, bursting with news. 'Oh, Miss Bel, you would never guess what has happened!'

'No,' said Bel, smiling, 'I refuse to guess, for I am sure that you are determined to tell me.'

'It's that Captain Howell. He was found shot dead in his room at the White Peacock not an hour ago. They had to break his door down when he failed to rise this morning, and his man could not make him hear. Such a thing to happen! And him taking you to the ball, last night! I can't say that I'm sorry to hear the news, I disliked the man greatly, but I hope no one thinks Lord Francis had anything to do with it, after his quarrel with Captain Howell last night.'

'Goodness!' said Bel. 'That's the most unlikely thing I ever heard,' only for Lottie to look at her, and say,

'Well, at least, Miss Bel, *we* know that Lord Francis couldn't have murdered Captain Howell. . .' And she almost winked at her mistress.

Bel was not surprised that Captain Howell had been murdered. Given the way in which he had behaved towards her, and what Francis had hinted about his career in London and Paris, it was perhaps to be expected that someone should see fit to dispose of him.

One more thing which I do not need to worry about, thought Bel. I don't like to be relieved that a man, even a man like Rhys Howell, was murdered, but his death has saved me from further difficulties—and perhaps may change my intentions about marrying Francis.

She suddenly had a desperate, aching desire to see him, to be with him, and her resolve not to marry him was shaken. Oh, to love someone was so all-consuming, how could she bear to wait to see him again? Thank God, she thought, that I am to dine at the vicarage tonight, when we may meet at last in friendship, even if we are not able to acknowledge our love openly.

Her smile was so purely happy that Lottie, looking at her, thought wisely, No need to worry about Miss Bel. He's an honourable man, for all that he got her into bed before he asked her to marry him, but he'll do the right thing by her, I'm sure, and whatever she says I'm sure that she'll accept him.

She sighed sentimentally. She knew that she should have been shocked, but the sight of Bel with Francis in her arms had warmed her, not shocked her, for Lottie's view of life, like that of many servants, was earthier than that of the gentry whom they served. I know Miss Bel, she thought; she'll make a good wife, and a good mother, not like Miss Marianne—she always wanted things easy...not surprising that she went wrong in London.

Which was Marianne's epitaph and Bel's eulogy.

CHAPTER SIXTEEN

CAPTAIN HOWELL provided Lulsgate Spa with as much scandalised and excited gossip in death as in life. From the moment he was discovered on the floor, a pistol thrown down by him, which had been held close to his body when it fired, presumably to muffle its noise of the shot, speculation roared about who had done the deed. Opinion was divided between whether the murderer ought to be hanged—or rewarded, the innkeeper's belief inclining to the latter since it turned out that Captain Howell had left nothing behind him with which to pay his huge bill.

Inevitably the discord between Lord Francis Carey and the dead man, ending in the fracas the night before the murder, was also discussed in gleeful tones. Among those worried by the news was Almeria, remembering that Francis had spent the night away from the vicarage—of course he could not have murdered Captain Howell, could he? But where had he been, what had he been doing?

Speculation even invaded the vicarage itself at the dinner which Bel attended. There had been talk of sending for the Bow Street Runners, but Mr Thomas Fancourt, a local landlord, who was one of Lulsgate Spa's magistrates, said that he had been informed by Sir Charles Walton, the chief of them, that that would probably not be necessary—he knew no details, but Sir Charles had been on his high ropes, had said that the identity of the murderer would cause great excitement, and he would not move against him until he was sure of his case.

Mrs Venn informed the table, 'The sooner that such

a creature is apprehended the better; we are none of us safe in our beds.'

Ever inwardly inflamed by Mrs Venn, Bel wanted to retort, On the contrary, we are all safer now that he is dead, and he has probably been killed by someone whom he has bammed, this last delightful piece of slang having come from her latest novel from the subscription library, partly set in London's underworld, *The Bells of St Giles.*

Almeria had sat her by Francis, and his speech and manner to her at dinner were so loving that Bel almost feared that they would cause comment; but no such thing—everyone was too busy dissecting the dead captain. For once she saw little of Francis after the dinner, the men congregating together to discuss the day's news; and the women, too, in their own excited huddle, wondered at it, and said how little surprised they were, the dead man having become universally disliked, although a few had favoured him at first.

Over the tea-board, Francis took the opportunity to pass her cup to her and sit beside her, saying in a low voice, 'You have thought of what I said? You have reached a decision?' and the hard grey eyes were suddenly so soft and full of hope that Bel hardly knew him. She could see Philip and Almeria watching them, presumably also hopeful, and she felt compelled to say,

'Not yet, Francis, not yet. I have had no time to think.'

'No time?' he said tenderly. 'You have had since morning. An eternity. If all time passes as slowly as this while I wait for you to make up your mind, I shall have a white beard down to my knees by the week's end.'

Bel choked back a laugh, said, severely, 'You are as naughty in your admiration as you were when you despised me.'

'No,' he said, suddenly deadly sincere in his manner.

'I never despised you, however hard I tried—that was the trouble. Oh, I cannot see why you hesitate; we are two halves come together, and my life will be incomplete without you. Ever since my dear Cassie died I have lived without love—and now I see what a half-life it was, and how hard it has made me. Marry me, Bel, and save me.'

Almost she said yes on the spot, but Mrs Venn came up, spiteful eyes on them. She did not want Henry to have Bel, nor did she want Francis Carey to succeed with her either.

'So,' she said to Bel, 'you have lost your admirer, Mrs Merrick. Not that I can say I cared for your taste, but then Lulsgate Spa probably contains few who can please you, you being so discriminating in all things.' The last was said in such a manner that it indicated Mrs Venn believed that Bel was nothing of the kind.

Bel was fearful of what Francis's reactions might be, but he merely bowed—he had risen on Mrs Venn's approach—and said lightly, 'I believe that Mrs Merrick has always a good reason for even her lightest decisions, and one must remember that, whatever else, Captain Rhys Howell once held the King's Commission.'

That Mrs Venn was annoyed at Francis's refusal to be ruffled went without saying; she tossed her head and moved on, Francis remarking mildly when she was out of earshot, 'I am so near to happiness today that even such arrows as Mrs Venn cares to loose at us cannot touch me. Have we reached harbour, Bel? Say that we have, I beg of you,' and even though she shook her head at him her eyes were giving him another message—and it was the one he wanted. Paradise seemed near.

Those around them thought so, too. Almeria kissed Philip when Francis had retired for the night, said joyfully, 'I do believe, my dear, that my good little Bel is going to make Francis a happy man. You could not but notice his manner to her, and hers to him. And you must not say that I interfered to arrange it, for I followed your instructions, and left them to solve their problems together.'

'Better so,' said Philip gently, 'and I agree that Bel will do Francis the world of good. He was in danger of becoming a lost soul, and I feared for him a little.'

'So, we go to bed happy,' said Almeria gaily, kissing him again, 'and the thought that Francis will have someone, as I have you, and will no longer be lonely, is a comforting one.'

Bel thought of Francis's proposal the next day when she sat reading a letter from Mrs Broughton, who said that although her return was delayed it would not be many days before she was with dear Bel again. Bel put the letter down, and thought that if she accepted Francis he would almost certainly help her to find a place for Mrs Broughton somewhere in his vast establishment. Almeria had told her of his wealth, and the great house in the north which his mother had left him.

Which means, she told herself joyfully, that I have made up my mind to accept him, for he is right, we are two halves, and must come together. I am foolish to let what Marina was come between us. After all, we came from a good family, and in normal circumstances there would be no bar to our marriage. We love each other, our minds meet as well, and that is all that matters in the end. Oh, I can hardly wait to tell him.

A comic thought struck her: and Cassius will be so pleased that we have stopped wrangling, so there is a good thing! She must remember to share that joke with Francis. She knew that he would appreciate it, and now they would share their jokes, not hurl them at one another—as she hoped they would share everything else.

While she had been reading there had been noise in the street, and now she heard the sound of running footsteps, and the door flew open.

It was Lottie, her face white. 'Oh, Miss Bel. Such terrible news. Sir Charles is at the vicarage, with the constables. Betty from the kitchens has told me that the pistol found by Captain Howell's body was Lord Francis's. He says it was stolen from him in Paris, but they knew that he was out all night, will not say where he was, and they are threatening to arrest him for murder, for all the world knows how much at outs he was with the captain, and that he had attacked and threatened him only the evening before. Betty says that were he not who he is they would have had him in the lock-up by now!'

Bel rose to her feet, mouth trembling. 'Francis, murder Captain Howell! Are they all run mad? Besides, he can have done no such thing. He was with me all night, as you know. Oh. . .!' And the implications of *that* struck her immediately, and she knew, though no one else did, why Francis would offer no explanation of where he had spent the night.

It was her honour, her reputation which he was protecting, at the expense of his freedom—possibly of his life.

White to the lips, her whole body shaking, she said hoarsely, 'You must be mistaken, Lottie. Sir Charles cannot believe that Lord Francis would do such a thing.'

'And so he apparently said, Miss Bel, but the evidence is so strong. . . Why? What are you about to do?' For Bel had picked up her shawl, thrown it around her shoulders and was making for the glass doors and the back path to the vicarage.

'Do?' said Bel energetically. 'Why, go there at once, and tell them the truth—that he was with me.'

'No,' said Lottie, barring her way. 'Oh, no, Miss Bel.

Think; your reputation will be gone in an instant. You will be no better than poor Miss Marianne. You will have to leave Lulsgate.'

'I cannot allow them to try Francis, possibly hang him, for something which I can prove he did not do,' said Bel, her heart sinking into her pretty little kid slippers at the thought of what telling the truth might do to her.

But Mr Birch had told her that there might come a time when she ought to tell the truth, and now she had no choice—that time had come.

Ironically, what Francis had thought of her would shortly come true. She would be a pariah, a light woman, not fit for society. She would almost certainly have to leave Lulsgate, forfeit her friendships here, and her good name...but what was that against what might be done to Francis if she kept silent?

She could not allow him to do this, she could not, and, pushing by Lottie, she ran towards the vicarage, praying that she was not too late.

Francis, at bay in the vicarage drawing-room, Philip and Almeria with him, was at his haughtiest.

He had laughed contemptuously at what he called the so-called evidence, said that the pistol with his arms and initials on it was one of a pair stolen from him in Paris, and he could prove it, that he was certain that Howell had been killed by someone he had cheated, almost certainly from outside Lulsgate. And no, he could not deny that he had not been in his bed at the vicarage the night that the captain was murdered, but would not, on any account, say where he *had* been.

'You leave me no alternative but to arrest you, Lord Francis,' said the harassed Sir Charles. 'You threatened him more than once, before many witnesses, the last time on the night before the murder when you had to be pulled off him before you killed him. Your pistol is found by his body, and you refuse to say where you were—hardly the action of an innocent man.' He refrained from adding that were he anyone but *Lord* Francis he would not be debating the matter at such length before taking a man with such a wealth of evidence against him to the lock-up.

'Francis,' said Philip gently, 'is there nothing you can tell Sir Charles of your whereabouts on the fatal night? Nothing at all?' He was suddenly sure where Francis had been that night, but, in the face of Francis's own silence, he too could say nothing, could offer no hint.

'Only,' said Francis, and his voice was stone, 'that I was troubled in my mind, and spent the night walking and thinking.'

'All night?' said Sir Charles, with Philip's expression echoing his words. 'You must see that that beggars belief.'

They had reached this impasse when there was the sound of an altercation outside, the door was unceremoniously thrown open, and Bel almost threw herself into the room.

Francis took one agonised look at her and knew why she had arrived, what she was about to do. The haughtily indifferent languor which had infuriated Sir Charles and his brother-in-law flew away in an instant.

'No, Bel,' he said, walking towards her and seizing her hands. 'No, you have no business here. You know nothing of the matter,' and then he saw her implacable face, felt her trembling at what she was about to say, and said loudly, 'No, I forbid it, you understand? I positively forbid it. You are not to speak.'

He swung on the startled spectators, his face anguished. 'Tell her to leave. She has no place here,' and he tried to push her to the door. Neither Philip nor Almeria had ever seen him so moved before. Stern, implacable Francis Carey had disappeared.

Bel freed herself from his clutching hands. 'No,

Francis, I cannot allow this. You must not lie yourself to the gallows by refusing to speak.'

She turned to Sir Charles, who knew her a little and was staring at her wild manner and informal dress with astonishment. Not in such a fashion was Mrs Bel Merrick wont to be seen abroad in Lulsgate Spa.

'Do I collect, sir, that the gravamen of the case against Lord Francis is that he cannot prove, or will not say, where he was on Thursday night when Captain Howell was murdered?'

Sir Charles nodded. 'Yes, madam, but I fail to see——'

'You will see this, sir,' said Bel steadily. She was aware, for all the world suddenly seemed hard and clear, that Francis had sunk into a chair, his head in his hands, compelled to realise that nothing he could say or do would stop his gallant love from ruining herself for him. 'Lord Francis could not possibly have killed Captain Howell, for he spent the entire night with me. I arrived home with him a little time after eleven of the clock, and we were together until gone eight the next morning. He is refusing to speak in order to save me, but I cannot allow him to do so at the expense of his freedom and his life. I must tell the truth.'

The world, from being so sharp, became dull and blurred. She heard Almeria's indrawn breath, saw Philip's kind and understanding face, and Sir Charles's almost disdainful one as she finished speaking.

Francis lifted his head, said hoarsely, 'Not so, I say. It is good of her to do this, but she is lying to save me,' and Sir Charles, seeing how matters must stand between them, began to say,

'Just so——' only for Bel to interrupt him, shaking her head and looking steadily at Francis.

'It is useless, Francis,' she said gently, 'for you must know that my maid Lottie came to my...room while you were still sleeping in the early morning, and I was awake and she. . .saw you there. And so she will testify. I appreciate the sacrifice you have been making in order to save my reputation, but it is your life which might be at stake, and I cannot allow you to save me at such an expense.'

She saw Philip's approving nod, heard Almeria give a half-sob, but nothing mattered to Bel except that Francis must be saved. The passion which had ruled since Lottie had told her of Sir Charles arriving to arrest Francis, and his refusal to say where he had been, was beginning to fade. There was a ringing in her ears, and she was fearful that she would disgrace herself by fainting. And this time the faint would be a true one. . .

Philip, indeed, looking at Sir Charles, moved forward and took her hand; he could see that she was *in extremis.*

'Look at me, my dear Bel,' he said gently, an expression of infinite pity on his face which had her fighting against tears. 'You are telling the truth, are you not? You are not simply trying to save Francis by sacrificing yourself?'

Bel looked at him, beyond him to where Francis had turned his back to them all, and was, she knew by his whole stance, fighting for his composure.

'Yes,' she said, and her voice was suddenly strong. 'I have told you so many lies, dear Philip, as you will shortly discover, but I am not lying to you over this, I swear it.'

Philip looked over the top of her head at Sir Charles, said, 'I am sure that Mrs Merrick is speaking the truth. Everything which she has said bears the stamp of veracity, and, that being so, it would be most unwise to arrest my brother-in-law before her servant has been questioned. Best to make enquiries about the theft of the pistol as well. You really have no case against him now.'

He released Bel's hand, but not before, with a look of infinite compassion on his face, he had kissed it. Almeria was looking from Bel to Francis, and the glance which she gave her half-brother was a fierce one, all the usual affection which she felt for him quite banished.

Sir Charles bowed to them all, gestured to the two constables to leave with him, not before saying stiffly to Francis, 'You will forgive me the accusation I made, but your refusal to answer me, or to divulge your whereabouts, made it inevitable that I did so. Mrs Merrick's evidence, given that her servant supports it, leaves you innocent of all accusations relating to Captain Howell's death. I shall make enquiries about the theft of your pistols. I am inclined to the belief that if they were, as you say, stolen in Paris, then someone from that city may have come here to murder him. I understand, and not only from yourself, that his reputation was a bad one.'

And so it later proved. Captain Howell's death was a nine-day wonder, ended only when it appeared that he had been engaged in criminal activities in both Paris and London, and his associates, whom he had cheated, had found means to dispose of him—Francis's pistol, bearing his initials and arms, being a useful red herring.

The door closed behind them. Bel, around whom Almeria had placed a protective arm, had begun to shiver. Francis swung towards her, his face ravaged.

'Oh, my darling Bel!' he exclaimed. 'You should not have done what you did—the accusation against me could never have stood, I am sure—but oh, how I honour you for it.' And he fell on to his knees before her, clutching her hand as he did so, ignoring Philip and Almeria who stared at him in wonder.

Proud and stern Francis Carey, almost fighting tears, was saying to the woman he loved and who had destroyed herself for him, 'You cannot refuse to marry me now, Bel; it is the least that I can offer you. . .if I thought that I loved you before, think what I feel for you now.'

Bel snatched her hand away, and turned impetuously from him to face Philip and Almeria. 'No! You cannot marry a ruined woman, and one of such a bad reputation. I must tell you all the truth, I must.'

She was thinking of what Mr Birch had said as she poured this out. 'I have told you so many lies. I am not even Mrs Merrick—there is no Mr Merrick. I am Bel Passmore, a respectable clergyman's daughter, but I am also the younger sister of Marina St George, the noted courtesan, as Francis knows, and until two days ago I was virtuous, but am no longer. Francis cannot marry such a woman, a woman whom Rhys Howell felt free to blackmail. No, do not argue with me, Francis; you know that what I say is true, and that is why I refused to marry you two days ago, and do so now.' And before any of them could stop her she ran from the room.

Francis rose, started to follow her, but was stopped by Philip, his face stern. 'No,' he said. 'leave her alone, Francis. You seduced her, did you not? And that you wished to marry her afterwards does not mitigate what you did.' And Almeria's eyes were as accusing as her husband's.

Francis turned towards them again, his face a mask of torment, tears in his eyes, quite changed from what he had been.

'I love her to distraction,' he said hoarsely. 'I first met her two years ago, shortly after her sister died. I never thought to meet her again, and then here she was in Lulsgate. I thought at first that she was unworthy, but it is I who am that, not my dear Bel. You are both right to despise me. And now you must let me go to her, for I shall not rest until she consents to become my wife. I have mourned my dear Cassie too long; it is

time to let her go—in any case she would hate what I
have done to Bel as much as you do. I cannot spare
her scandal, but with my name she may face the world
down.'

'Oh, you do love her, Francis,' said Almeria wonder-
ingly. 'Why did you seduce her, then? All you needed
to do was offer her honourable marriage.'

Francis could make no reply to that without giving
away the tangle of his relationship with Bel. He saw
Philip raise warning brows at his wife, and then, like
Bel, he ran through the door, out into the garden to
take the path to Bel's glass doors. To find her, to ask
her to forgive him—and become his wife.

Almeria turned to Philip, bewildered. 'I do not
understand him at all,' she complained. 'If he loved
her, and wished to marry her, why did he do what he
did? He had no need——' And then, as Philip looked
at her steadily, she said, 'Oh, you always thought that
there was something odd about them, did you not?
And you would not wish me to pry, I understand...or
rather I don't.'

'There are some things about others,' Philip said,
'which it is best for us not to ask about, or even to
know. I said once before that Francis and Bel must
solve their own problems, and despite all that has
passed this morning I think that they are about to do
so. And now we must think of other things—and try to
stop Lulsgate from tearing them both to pieces, for this
morning's doings will be all about Lulsgate in the
hour.'

But Francis discovered that Bel was not at home, only
found Lottie there, who had just confirmed Bel's story
to Sir Charles, for if Miss Bel had sacrificed her good
name to save Francis then she could do no less than
tell the truth.

'Where is she?' they both said together, Francis recovering himself first. 'She has not come here?'

'No,' said Lottie, staring, 'I thought that she was still with you.'

'Oh, God,' said Francis frantically, 'where has she gone, if she has not come back here?'

'And why should I tell you anything,' said the old woman fiercely, 'seeing that you have ruined her with your wickedness? Such a good girl, my dear Miss Bel, not at all like that silly Miss Marianne. Shame on you if you thought Miss Bel was no better.'

'You cannot despise me more than I despise myself,' said Francis humbly. 'Have you no idea where she may have gone?'

Lottie shook her head, and Francis ran back to the vicarage, his head on fire, to enquire frantically, 'Oh, Almy, my dear, do not look at me like that. I have no idea where she has gone, and I must find her, I must.'

'Before every tabby-cat in Lulsgate rips her to bits when today's news leaks out, as it will,' said Almeria. 'I hardly know you, Francis. Such a good girl as my dear Bel was. How could you treat her so?' And then was silent, remembering what Philip had counselled.

'But none of this helps me to find her,' said Francis grimly, and he looked so distressed that Philip, who had come in while they were talking, pushed him gently into a chair, pouring him a glass of wine from the bottle which he had brought in with him, then handing the glass to his brother-in-law who pushed it away.

'No,' said Philip gently, 'drink it. You look as though you are about to drop dead any minute. Think, Francis, think. You know her as well as anyone. Where in Lulsgate Spa could she have found refuge?'

Francis drank the wine, shuddering. Something in Philip's words struck him, and he stared at him. Even Almeria was beginning to show a little pity for him in his distracted state.

'Not in Lulsgate Spa,' he said slowly, 'but in Morewood.'

'Morewood!' they both said together, then Almeria, 'Why Morewood?'

'Because,' said Francis, 'and I see that you do not know this, she helped the Methodist minister, Mr Birch, to run a small dame school for poor children at Morewood twice a week. She extended her love and compassion to them—as she did to me.'

'On Wednesdays and Fridays!' said Almeria. 'Which explains why she was always unavailable on those days.'

'Exactly,' said Francis, colour returning to his cheeks. 'Morewood, I am sure of it. To the old man there. I know that he thinks a great deal of her, and she respects him. I will go there at once. Not in the curricle. To take that would be to emphasise the difference which once existed between us.' And before Philip and Almeria could stop him he ran out of the room again.

Almeria turned to Philip, shocked. 'I would never have believed it,' she said slowly. 'He adores her, that is plain. And if so, why did he ruin her? For that is what he did. I shall never understand him, ever. So upright he was, and now this.'

'He is human,' replied her husband, 'and he has been so severe with himself for so long—and now he must try to find his salvation—for that is what Bel is, I suspect. And, as I said before, he must do it himself.'

Francis followed Bel, who, as he suspected, had gone to Mr Birch at Morewood for succour. Like her, he ran through the streets unheeding, surprised spectators turning to follow his progress, as they had followed Bel's.

Bel, indeed, had had only one idea in her head, and that was to get away from everyone, and find absolution with Mr Birch. Why this was so she did not know. Only, at the moment when she had told the truth about the night which Francis had spent with her, she had had a kind of revelation—that it was important to tell the truth about everything; there must be no more lies, however good the reasons she might once have had for telling them.

She must go to see Mr Birch, to tell him what she had done, and only then could she allow herself to think about Francis and his needs—for she knew that she could not abandon him, only that before she could speak to him again she must clear her conscience, and she could only do that when she had spoken to the old man. Philip Harley would not have done at all, for it was not Philip to whom she had earlier hinted of her dilemma, but Mr Birch.

Mr Birch was in his garden when Bel arrived, panting, her eyes wild, nothing of the refined young lady left. She threw open the garden gate and ran to him, half sobbing, 'Oh, Mr Birch, dear Mr Birch, pray let me speak to you.'

He put an arm around her, led her gently into the house, sat her down in his big Windsor chair, and brought her a glass of water to still her shaking and sobbing.

'Now what is it, my dear? How can I help you?'

'I have told the truth,' she wailed, 'and I feel worse than ever. Not only am I ruined, but I have told the whole world of it, and more beside.' And she broke into the sobs which she had held back for so long. 'And it is all my fault. Oh, dear Mr Birch, I did a wrong thing two years ago; I told a great lie—or rather implied it—to the gentleman who has come here for me several times, and though I love him dearly I cannot marry him.'

'He rejects you, then,' said Mr Birch gently. 'I told you I thought that he was not a man to play with.'

'Oh, no,' said Bel, showing him a tear-stained face. 'He wishes to marry me, but I feel so unworthy.'

Mr Birch looked puzzled. 'But you said that you were ruined. You mean that there is another suitor, of whom you have not told me?'

'Oh, it is all so difficult,' wailed Bel again. 'I allowed him to ruin me because I loved him so, and he thought that I was not virtuous, but then he found out that I *was* virtuous after all, and now he wishes to marry me. But it would not be fair to him. Oh, I have done my duty, and even that does not answer.'

This muddled explanation served to enlighten Mr Birch a little. He handed poor Bel a man's large handkerchief and said, 'And if you truly care for him, my dear, and he wishes to marry you, and you are—or were—virtuous then I do not see your problem. But always remember that virtue and telling the truth are their own rewards—although sometimes God sees fit to give us more.'

He had hardly finished speaking when there was a hammering on his front door. Bel heard the house-keeper answer it, and then Francis's agitated voice echoed through the house.

Bel rose to her feet, turned towards the door, and said to Mr Birch, 'It's Francis.' Her lip trembled. 'Should I see him?'

'It is your life and your decision, under God, of course,' said the old man gently.

'Yes,' said Bel, and as Francis came through the door he saw them together, Bel's hand in Mr Birch's, a look of peace on her face such as he had never seen before.

And what did Bel see? She saw that Francis had in some strange way found his peace, too. The mixture of desire and pain which had driven him ever since he had first met her had disappeared.

He bowed to Mr Birch, and said, 'You will allow me to speak to Mrs Merrick, I trust.'

'Miss Anne Isabella Passmore,' said Bel. 'I must not deceive either of you, or the world, any more. I am the daughter of the Reverend Mr Caius Passmore, sometime rector of Brangton in Lincolnshire, who was cousin to Sir Titus Passmore of Dallow in Cheshire. It is little enough to claim, but I must tell you at last who I really am.'

'Miss Passmore, then,' said Francis gravely. 'I have something which I wish to say to her privately, sir. We have had too much discussion in public today.'

'If Miss Passmore wishes it,' said Mr Birch, 'then it shall be so. It is your wish, Miss Passmore?'

'Yes,' said Bel, suddenly and unwontedly shy. 'If Lord Francis wishes it.'

'Then I will leave you,' said the old man, and, as he reached the door, 'May the Lord be with you both.'

Francis bowed again. His punctiliousness and care for the old man pleased Bel more than she could say. All his pride and hauteur seemed to have leaked out of him. She thought that they might return, but that he would never again be entirely as he was.

And now he bowed to Bel. 'I am pleased to make your acquaintance, Miss Passmore,' he said, as though they had never met before. 'I have something to say to you, to which I hope you will give your most earnest consideration. You will allow?'

Bel bowed her head, signed for him to continue. She felt barely able to speak.

'Yes,' she achieved, 'pray do,' as though, she thought, they had not so recently been together, as close as a man and woman might be.

'Miss Passmore, I have known you long enough now to be aware that above all things I would wish you to be my wife. You are the woman I have always wanted to meet: kind, brave and generous. You have borne my recent intolerable behaviour after a fashion so admirable that it gains my utmost respect. More, I know that I love you as I have never loved any other woman.

'What I felt for my dear Cassie was quite different, if no less true. Today you honoured me by offering up your reputation in order to save me obloquy, pain and possible death. If you can bring yourself to accept my suit you will make me the happiest man in Britain, as I hope to make you the happiest woman. I cannot say fairer than that.' And he took her hand and kissed it, bowing his head, then lifting it to show her his eyes, brimming with love. 'Please, my dear Miss Passmore, marry me, as soon as possible.'

Bel could not speak. Her throat had filled. What he had said to her was said so humbly, so differently from all his previous offers to her, either honourable or dishonourable.

She lifted his hand to her lips, kissed it, and said, 'If you can bring yourself to offer for me, Francis, knowing my true circumstances, then, loving you as I do, I cannot refuse such a noble offer. Yes, I will accept you.'

Francis broke on that. The perfect courteous calm which he had shown to her ever since he had entered the room was suddenly gone; he took her in his arms and began to kiss her, kiss away the tears which ran down her face—tears of joy, not of sorrow.

'And you will not regret this,' said Bel, pulling back a little, 'knowing of me, and mine, what you do?'

'I would regret not asking you,' he said. 'And if you can bring yourself to forgive me, then some time, perhaps, I can forgive myself.'

Bel put her hand on his lips. 'The fault lay in both of us,' she said, 'and we have a lifetime to repair it. And now, sir, we must be decorous. It is Mr Birch's home we grace, and it is time that we informed him that we intend to behave honourably in future.'

'Indeed,' he said, putting an arm around her, and kissing the top of her head. 'We must behave ourselves now, until we marry. I shall go to London for a special licence, and Philip shall marry us if you think you can face the world here. If not, we can be married at my home in the north.'

'I think,' said Bel steadily, 'that it would be only fair to Philip and Almeria, whom we have both deceived, to be married here as quietly as possible.'

As she spoke, there was a knock at the door and then Mr Birch came in, carrying tea-things for three on a small tray.

He looked at them shrewdly, and said, 'I thought that you might like to celebrate with me. You *are* about to celebrate, are you not?'

Francis and Bel stared at him, astonished. He gave a dry chuckle. 'Come,' he said, 'I have lived in the world these many years, and I know the faces which men and women assume. You are a man and a woman of sense; I could not but think that you would behave sensibly in the end, and so it proves.'

He handed the cups around, and said, 'I toast the pair of you, and I firmly believe that you will soon be Lord and Lady Francis, and happy together.'

Francis Carey had never expected to become betrothed to the woman whom he so passionately loved in a Methodist minister's shabby parlour, nor that the minister's prophecy would come as true as it did when he forecast a happy life for him with the Cyprian's sister.

NOTES FOR THE READER

MARIANNE PASSMORE's death from a 'fulminating stomach' was, in modern terms, from a burst appendix. Appendicitis in the early nineteenth century usually resulted in death.

In the early nineteenth century, the notorious courtesan Harriette Wilson blackmailed her famous lovers just as Marianne did in the novel. She was also in league with dubious adventurers of good family, come down in the world, very similar to Rhys Howell.

Lulsgate Spa is an imaginary town: it does not exist in Leicestershire or any other country. Its environment, social life and characteristics are based on many of the spas which were popular in the eighteenth and nineteenth centuries. The MCs in such towns were very powerful people who controlled social life in them, keeping it respectable.

Morewood also is imaginary, although again there were many small and depressed villages like it in the Midland counties, both during and after the Napoleonic wars. Beacon Hill, however, does exist, and may still be visited.

A COMPROMISED LADY

by

Francesca Shaw

Dear Reader

We were thrilled to hear that *A Compromised Lady* had been selected for the Regency Collection, celebrating the enduring popularity of the Regency novel. Just as readers—and TV viewers—adore the elegance, style and vitality of this era, so we find it a continuing source of inspiration—and a pleasure to write about. It has all the romance of the past yet the sense of being almost close enough to our own time to feel we could reach out and touch the characters.

This novel is a particular favourite of ours, and not only because we fell instantly in love with the hero, Jervais Barnard. It was intriguing to explore how two people, deeply attracted to one another and thrown together in extreme circumstances on the battlefield of Waterloo, could be kept apart by a misplaced sense of duty and honour.

In working out the love story of Jervais and Caroline we discovered that they both shared a sense of humour which rescued them when events, and other people, conspired to keep them apart. In the end, love conquers all, and we had the fun of reconciling two passionate and independent spirits.

We hope you enjoy reading the story of Caroline and Jervais as much as we enjoyed discovering it for ourselves.

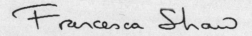

Francesca Shaw is not one, but two authors, working together under the same name. Both are librarians by profession, working in Hertfordshire, but living within distance of each other in Bedfordshire. They first began writing ten years ago under a tree in a Burgundian vineyard, but although they have published other romances, they have only recently come to historical novels. Their shared interests include travel, good food, reading and, of course, writing.

Other titles by the same author:

Master of Winterbourne
Miss Weston's Masquerade
The Unconventional Miss Dane
The Admiral's Daughter

CHAPTER ONE

THE guns had ceased their incessant booming, but the sound was still echoing in her head with the clamour of battle and the screams of men and horses.

The girl shifted restlessly and pain shot down the column of her neck, bringing her awake with a jolt. As she opened her eyes, the sensation of noise faded away leaving a silence almost as deafening. A sparrow flew across the dusty space above her, flitting in and out of the shafts of sunlight which streamed through the rickety timbers of what she could now descry to be a barn.

She stared up at the cobwebbed beams. A barn? She had no recollection of coming here. Nor was she alone: as she blinked in bewilderment her eyes met the baleful brown stare of quite the ugliest horse she had ever seen. Its iron grey flanks were streaked with mud and it stood awkwardly, favouring its left hind leg which was scabbed with blood. It soon lost interest in her, dropping its head and blowing heavily at the pile of hay at its feet. The sound was loud in the dusty space as it pulled disconsolately at a mouthful.

Disconcerted, she put up her fingers and pushed the tangled black curls off her forehead. She winced, then her fingers moved more cautiously, exploring the egg-shaped bump on the back of her head. That explained the headache which made it so hard to think...but where was she, and where had that horse come from?

Now that she was fully awake the barn no longer seemed silent: the corners were full of scufflings and more sparrows chattered overhead. The hay on which she was lying scratched and tickled her shoulders and a spider scuttled across her bare ankle. Bare? Where were

253

her clothes? She straightened up on the makeshift bed, realising she was dressed in only her shift and covered by a thick black cloak.

Something large moved the straw beside her. All pain forgotten, she twisted round and stared, open-mouthed, at a man—unconscious, totally unknown. Her horrified gaze took in the tousled chestnut hair, the lean tanned face smudged with dirt and sweat, the mouth and chin masked with reddish stubble.

He was deeply asleep, yet there was nothing vulnerable or unguarded in that face. His restless movements had dragged the cloak from his shoulders revealing muscular shoulders and chest, paler than his face, one upper arm wrapped in a stained, clumsy bandage.

With a gasp of horror, the girl sat up, drawing back against the rough boards of the manger behind them. The movement was enough to rouse the fourth occupant of the barn, a large shaggy hound which, she could now see, lay guarding its master's flank.

The young woman began to edge cautiously away from the man, then froze as the action was met by a low, blood-curdling snarl from the dog, its lip curling over threatening canines.

'Good. . .dog,' she whispered, but the result was not encouraging. The hound's head came up and its ears pricked.

'Quiet, Percy.' The man spoke without opening his eyes as if he were used to such behaviour. In response, the hound put two enormous forepaws on his chest and licked his master's face with gusto. 'Down, sir! Detestable animal!' He pushed at the big hairy body with both hands, then swore viciously at the effect on his wounded arm.

The girl gasped at the oath and both dog and master turned as one to stare at her. 'Hell and damnation, I'd forgotten you were here,' the man remarked amiably, his eyes openly admiring the soft swell of breast above her scanty chemise.

'Sir!' she protested, scandalised at the frankness of his admiration. Her hands shot up to pull the cloak up to her bare throat, but the heavy garment was wrapped around the man's legs and came up no higher than her waist.

Her hands tried in vain to cover herself and she felt beneath her fingers the hot blush spreading up to the tips of her ears.

The man's smile widened, revealing even, white teeth. The grin did not reassure; nor did the unashamed gleam in his dark eyes. 'Why so coy, sweetheart? There's no need for play-acting with me; your charms are well worth displaying, as you are very well aware.'

Before she could respond, his left arm gathered her efficiently against his bare chest and he kissed her. Hard lips explored hers, stubble rasped her cheek and, where her bare skin met his, she was shockingly aware of the warmth of him and his strength.

As unceremoniously as he had taken her, he released her. Outraged blue eyes blazed into his, her slight frame aquiver with fury. His obvious amusement only inflamed her more.

'Sir! How dare you! I. . . I. . .' She fought to express her shock and said the first thing that came into her head. 'We have not been introduced. I do not even know your name!'

The man threw back his head and laughed, startling the horse. It was some moments before he composed himself, scrubbing a dirty, bruised hand across his face as if to straighten it. He made her a mocking half-bow from his reclined position. 'Ma'am, I do beg your pardon. I have obviously misjudged your. . .status. Permit me to introduce myself: Captain Jervais Barnard, Eleventh Light Dragoons, your humble servant.' He picked up one of her hands in his and raised it to his lips. 'And whom do I have the honour of addressing?'

She flushed angrily at the heavy irony in his tone. 'I am. . .' She shut her mouth as words failed her, then tried again as thoughts ran incoherently through her brain, a jumble of names, one of which must be hers, none of which sounded familiar.

He saw the panic in her eyes and was serious at once. 'Can't you remember?' he prompted gently, all the mockery gone.

'No,' she whispered in horror. 'I cannot remember who I am, how I came here. . . Please, help me!'

As she started to shiver in reaction, he sat up and pulled the cloak round her shoulders, gathering her against him. She stiffened, then relaxed: in a frightening, unfamiliar world this big man was the only rock to cling to.

She held him, feeling his unkempt hair tickling her brow, his breathing steady and reassuring under her cheek. It felt right, familiar, to be held against a man like this. But the strong young man in her memory had no face, no name.

When the officer spoke the words echoed under her ear, although they were soft and thoughtful. 'I have seen this happen before after a blow to the head or the shock of battle. Your memory will come back in time, you must not strain for recollection. But we can deduce something.' He gently sat her back against the manger and picked up her right hand. 'Your name, for example.' There was a ring of coloured stones on her middle finger and he pointed to each gem in turn. 'Coral, amber, ruby and opal spells CARO. Does that seem familiar to you? Could you perhaps be called Caroline?'

Could she? The name was not unfamiliar, yet. . .the mists swirled in her brain again. . . No, the name meant no more than any other. She shook her head, then winced. 'I cannot say, I have no remembrance.'

'No? No matter, it will do for now and I must call you something.'

'Very well. It is strangely comforting to have a name, even if it may not be my own.'

He looked into her face consideringly. 'It suits you. What else can we surmise? No wedding ring, nor trace of any mark on your finger.'

He turned her hand over so it lay in his big brown one. 'Your hands are white and soft, and your face under the paint. . .' Jervais smiled and ran one finger down the smooth, unlined skin of her cheek. 'Your face is that of a beautiful woman, no more than perhaps eighteen.'

Caro raised her eyes to his and felt her heart contract with a sensation she knew instinctively was new to her. She didn't understand it, had no name for it, but the warmth of it filled her and for the first time since she'd woken, she felt a stirring of happiness and trust.

'As for how you came to be here,' Jervais continued, 'that is simple to recount. I found you near midnight on a track off the Brussels road lying senseless in a rut full of water. I surmise you had fallen from a cart, although what one was doing off the main highway I do not know. And at the time I did not greatly care—it was dark, Caesar was almost on his knees and I was still losing blood.' He tossed aside the blanket and she saw his overall trousers were torn and soaked with blood.

Caro rubbed her forehead as if the action would call back her memory. 'Then there was a battle? I remember the guns and the ground shaking and I was searching . . .searching.'

'Yes, there was a battle.' Jervais laughed, but without humour.

'Who won?'

'We did, the Allies—if you can call such a slaughter victory.'

'Wellington. . .' Caro said hesitantly '. . .the Duke and

Napoleon. . .and there was fighting at Quatre Bras. Why do I remember that?' she demanded angrily, 'when I cannot remember who I am, or why I came to be close to a battle?'

'Quatre Bras, that was Thursday the fifteenth. Of June, 1815,' he added, glancing at her to see how much was familiar. When she shook her head he shrugged and went on, 'This is Monday the nineteenth and we routed the French at Mont St Jean last night. Wellington and the Staff are probably at their HQ at Waterloo. Which is where,' he added ruefully, 'I should be.'

His obvious concern for his own duty was lost on Caro, deep in her own preoccupation. 'But how came I to be so near a battle? And why are we here?'

'It was the nearest shelter I could find. It's a farm of sorts, although the house must have taken a direct hit. The inhabitants—if they are alive—will be out there cutting the throats of any Frenchmen they come across.'

She shuddered and pulled the cloak more closely round her shoulders. 'Why so delicate?' Jervais was suddenly hard. 'As a soldier's woman you must have seen a battlefield before. You know what follows after.'

'As a soldier's woman?' Caro echoed incredulously. 'Sir, you are offensive!'

'My apologies.' The mocking tone was back. 'An officer's woman I should have said, from your obvious quality. But what other explanation can you offer? The only Englishwomen on that road were campfollowers or members of the muslin company sent back to Brussels for their safety and to clear the lines. You have paint on your face, no wedding band on your finger, and as for your clothes. . .'

He gave the hound an unceremonious shove and pulled a crumpled garment from the floor where the dog had made a bed of it.

Caro spread out the carmine silk gauze of the dress upon the hay. The bodice was the merest wisp of fabric, expressly designed to display not conceal. The skirts were cut to cling to the wearer's limbs and would scarcely need damping to become totally transparent. 'Where are the petticoats?'

'You were wearing none,' he said drily. 'I have to say I have the greatest admiration for the taste of your. . . protector.'

Could it be true? Caro sat and thought over what he had said. She could not recognise herself in his description, yet she knew that campfollowers existed, that officers would offer protection to young women—the muslin company—some of them of good birth, as she felt herself to be. Captain Barnard must be correct, for some instinct told her that sheltered young ladies would know nothing of such things as she was discovering she did.

There was a very long silence, both Caro and Jervais deep in their own thoughts, then they both spoke at once.

'I must get back to my regiment. . .'

'I cannot stay here. . .'

The Captain looked at her consideringly, then said, 'I can take you to the Brussels road, put you on the first wagon we come across. Once you are back in Brussels someone will recognise you.'

'Will you not come with me?' Caro felt a sudden panic at the thought of losing him, which was not entirely fear for her own safety.

'I must find my men, there will have been orders to rally. I should go to HQ and find out what is happening.'

Jervais was getting to his feet as he spoke, but as he put his weight on his left leg, it gave way and he fell back to his knees in the hay. 'Hell and damnation!' Sweat stood out on his brow and he grimaced in pain. The big hound pushed him with his muzzle, whimpering softly. 'Get off, Percy! Damn this leg, it must have been a deeper thrust than I thought.'

'Let me see.' Caro kneeled beside him, pulling aside the torn fabric of his grey overalls to expose a raw, jagged cut. She winced, but managed to say with composure, 'It needs cleaning and binding. Lie still,' she added sharply as he tried to sit up. 'You will set it bleeding again.' Suddenly there was a familiarity in this role of ministering to a man. . .

Caro scrambled to her feet, heedless of displaying her bare limbs in the scanty shift, and pulled on the red dress without a second thought. A pair of insubstantial satin slippers were under it and she thrust her feet into them. 'There must be a well outside. We need water—I will look for a bucket.'

'Take care!' Jervais tried to get up, then fell back with a gasp. 'Percy: Guard!' The dog trotted obediently after Caro, his great head pressed against her thigh.

With caution she pulled open the door a crack and peered out. The farmyard was deserted, the house indeed a smouldering ruin. The smell of burning was rank in the warm sunshine, yet incongruously the skylarks were filling the sky with song. She jumped at the sharp crack of a rifle, but it was some distance away.

In the centre of the yard was a well, mercifully with bucket and rope still intact. With an effort Caro winched up a half-full bucket, sniffing suspiciously at the water before realising that the unpleasant smell in her nostrils was being blown from the body of a horse lying dead across the gate.

Back in the barn she set the bucket down by Jervais. 'Here, you must drink or you will take a fever. I think the water is clean. Do you have a saddle bag?'

He nodded towards the great horse, still standing patiently in the shadows. 'Over there, by the saddle. Is there still water for Caesar in the trough?'

The charger moved over obediently as she slapped his shoulder and Caro realised she was used to horses and not afraid of them. It was a small thing but she was coming to treasure every scrap of self-knowledge.

The saddle-bags yielded a pair of clean shirts and a neckcloth, a hunk of dry bread, a greasy bundle which proved to contain a piece of bacon and, right at the bottom, a silver flask.

After a brief struggle she managed to tear one of the shirts into strips. 'I had better look to your arm as well,' she said firmly, steeling herself to remove the grimy bandage. At the sight of the torn flesh she quailed momentarily, feeling slightly sick, then forced herself to continue. This was no occasion for a fit of the vapours.

'Here.' Captain Barnard pulled a knife from the top of his boot. 'Cut the cloth with this.'

She worked quickly and with grim determination, cleaning the wounds and bandaging them tightly. As her hands moved deftly over his body, she acknowledged that this close familiarity with the male form must confirm what Jervais had told her about herself.

That she had touched a man's skin, was familiar with the feel of leg muscles, of the weight of a man supported against her shoulder. . .all proved that indeed she was some man's mistress.

She looked up from tying the bandage tight around his thigh, her blue eyes puzzled. 'I think my. . .protector must be an older man than you. His skin is not so. . .' She broke off, finding to her confusion her fingers were skimming his bare chest, sensing the hard muscles beneath the supple surface.

Captain Barnard smiled laconically. 'Hell's teeth, don't tell me I've spent the night with a general's mistress. Not the way for an ambitious officer to gain promotion.'

He narrowed his eyes and scrutinised her more closely as she bent to her task again. She was an enigma to him. . . No unmarried lady of breeding would handle a semi-naked stranger with such calm efficiency, yet her voice, her bearing, her obvious education shrieked 'Quality'.

The orphaned daughter of an officer, perhaps, he mused. Fallen on hard times and choosing to put herself under the protection of a man rather than starve. A sad, but not uncommon state of affairs after years of war.

She was a piquant little thing, too: that slender, almost virginal figure in that outrageous dress, her blushes and indignation when he'd kissed her had seemed real enough but must be artifice. Perhaps her protector liked that appearance of girlish innocence.

'Here, put this on.' She had finished bandaging his leg and was holding out the second clean shirt. 'You need a good wash and a shave, but this will have to suffice.' Her hands were gentle as she eased his bad arm into the sleeve and buttoned up the garment.

Captain Barnard looked down at the tousled dark head, dismissed all prudent thoughts of irritable senior officers and tipped up her chin. 'Thank you, sweetheart.' This time his kiss was welcomed and answered with soft lips that parted under his and arms that snaked round to encircle his neck.

The feel of his mouth on hers felt strange, frightening, yet Caro had no urge to pull away from the warmth and pleasure of the embrace. She had no recollection of kisses in the past, yet she knew she had never been kissed like this before. Jervais was responding to her willingness, bending her back over his good arm so that she arched against his chest, their hearts beating together.

He moaned huskily, his mouth trailing hot kisses down her temple, teasing her ear-lobe with his teeth, then nuzzling through the soft cloud of her hair to her bare shoulders.

Caro closed her eyes and felt reality begin to float away on a tide of sensation; her entire body was suffused with warmth, where his lips touched her skin burned and her fingers tightened involuntarily in the clean linen of his shirt.

She was laying back on the hay now, breathless as his weight shifted above her. Part of her knew this should not be happening, although she could not remember why that should be so. But she trusted, desired, this man she did not know. . .

Jervais gasped in pain and fell back against the hay. 'I'm sorry, sweetheart, but I do not think I can acquit myself with any distinction with these damned wounds! I must have lost more blood than I knew.'

Indeed, he did look dreadful. Pinched and white around the mouth, the lines tight around his eyes as he struggled with the pain.

'I should never have behaved so. . .' she stammered, suddenly overcome with guilt and shame, mixed with fear for Jervais.

He opened one eye and managed a slight grin. 'Indeed we should not have, it might upset the general.'

'Oh, never mind the general!' Caro would have stamped her foot had she been standing. Why she was suddenly angry with him she did not know, but the irritation was helpful.

They could not stay in this barn much longer. As if to underline the thought, the sharp crack of a rifle sounded, much closer than before.

Jervais pulled himself painfully to his feet. 'They are probably just shooting looters and wounded horses, but we cannot be sure. I've no intention of surviving the battle only to be shot by a French sniper. Come on, my lovely, we must be on our way.'

Between them they got Caesar saddled. Jervais led him round in circles, scrutinising the wounded leg, but after a few stiff steps the big horse loosened up and pricked its ears eagerly. Jervais slapped its dusty flank with affection. 'Come on, old lad. One last pull and it's a stable and oats for you.'

He limped back to the makeshift bed and found his uniform jacket, shrugging it on with a grimace. The dark blue cloth was stained and dirty, the silver lace tattered. Jervais smoothed down the buff facings and fastened the buttons, then began to buckle on his sword belt, tugging the sabretache to hang beside the curving scabbard of his sabre.

Caro was watching him when he looked up, her blue eyes fierce with the effort of memory as she stared.

'Is this uniform familiar?' he asked.

'No. . .' She shook her head doubtfully. 'No, his is a red jacket, gold lace.' There was no face to the figure she was remembering so hazily. Jervais stooped and picked up his shako. The plume was missing from the black, peaked hat and the silver cords were tangled. 'And the shako is wrong, it should be more like a helmet.'

'First Dragoon Guards, I think.' He was tying his scarlet and gold sash around his waist, his face unguarded as he thought back to the battle. 'They were in the centre, to our right.' He didn't add that they had taken heavy losses; this girl watching him with troubled eyes might be more alone now than she knew.

'Come, take the cloak. That dress is not fit for riding in.'

Caro could only agree with him as they emerged cautiously into the farmyard and the strong sunlight rendered the flimsy silk almost transparent. She was suddenly self-conscious, although if what Captain Barnard had suggested of her calling were true, why she should be so shy was a mystery.

Captain Barnard hoisted himself painfully into the saddle and surveyed the chaotic yard until he saw the mounting block. Caro found herself sitting behind him on Caesar's broad back with little trouble and her body responded easily to the steady walk.

'I have ridden before,' she remarked, tightening her fingers in Jervais's sash.

They rode on in silence down the rutted cart track, away from the farm and through scrubby woodland. Caro was aware of her companion's vigilance as his head turned to scan the trees, wary of every sound. It was a relief to emerge into the open and they stopped for a moment, looking north towards Brussels.

What had been standing fields of rye and wheat only days before were now muddy trampled wastes, across which limping figures made their way to the road. The highway was congested with a stream of wagons bearing the wounded back to the city, and mounted officers rode up and down shouting orders to try and speed the flow.

Jervais kept Caesar to the fields to make better progress, but he was watching the officers as they went and Caro guessed he was looking for someone of his own regiment to ask for news.

They were almost within sight of the city when he reined in and shouted 'Harding!' A captain in the same buff and blue wheeled his horse away from a mired wagon and cantered over, his face breaking into a broad grin as soon as he saw who had hailed him.

'Barnard, my dear fellow! I thought you were dead!' Peeping round Jervais's back, Caro saw a stocky figure with a cheerful, plain face.

'What news of the brigade?' Jervais demanded urgently. 'What losses did we suffer?'

'Less than you might think. Perhaps a half-dozen officers gone, including poor Stewart, and under a hundred men. When I think of that charge up to the French guns: we must have been insane!'

'Couldn't stop more like,' Jervais remarked grimly.

'Anyway, I've been detailed to try and order this shambles, the rest are mustering at Nivelles, in case Bony tries a counter-move. Unlikely in my opinion: the

French were done for the moment the Old Guard turned and ran.'

'Captain Harding, get back to your duty, sir, and stop gossiping like a schoolroom miss!'

A bellow from an approaching rider caused the captain to wheel his horse, getting a sight of Caro as he did so. 'By God, Barnard, you lucky dog! What a little sweetheart!'

'Damn you, watch your mouth,' Jervais snarled with a sudden ferocity which alarmed Caro and obviously surprised Harding.

'No offence, old chap! Take care...' Harding cantered off, giving a wide berth to the approaching officer, who nodded curtly in acknowledgement of Jervais's salute.

'Good to see you, Barnard. Wounded, I see.'

'Yes, Major. I'll get it dressed and return to the regiment. We are mustering at Nivelles, Harding said...'

'You will do no such thing. That leg's bleeding badly and you have hurt your arm by the look of it. Your brigade's in good enough shape: they don't need you slowing 'em down. Get into the city and find a surgeon, then you might be of some use later.'

The Major nodded curtly and tightened his reins. 'At least you still seem to have your wits about you. The quality of your battlefield souvenirs appears to be improving.'

Before Jervais could respond, he had ridden off back to the road. 'What did he mean?' Caro demanded.

'You. I have the reputation of collecting odd things from battlefields. Caesar from Salamanca, Percy from a nameless skirmish outside Lisbon. Neither of them, you must agree, a very beautiful sight.'

For a moment Caro felt a little flicker of pleasure at the somewhat backhanded compliment. Then she felt anger. So she was just some battlefield memento, was she? To be compared with an old war horse and a scruffy mongrel? Whatever else she might be, she was no man's just to take, she knew that! Irritably, she poked him in the ribs. 'Well, don't just sit there! Your leg has begun to bleed again and I cannot pick you up if you fall off...'

He nudged his heels into Caesar's side and the horse walked on. 'I have every intention of getting us both safe back to Brussels and into bed.'

Caro flushed at the mocking warmth in his words. 'You are most certainly going back to bed, Captain Barnard! You have no strength to do anything else, as I recall.'

'*Touché*,' he murmured and fell silent as they entered the city gates.

The streets were chaotic, a mass of overturned carts and tumbled furniture, abandoned as panic-stricken residents had tried to flee in the face of the French onslaught they believed was coming. The relief was plain on every face they passed and many people waved and called out to the Allied troops straggling in.

Caro twisted and turned to try and see a familiar landmark, but nothing struck a chord. Surely she would remember something: a street, a shop, a church? After all, the army had been billeted in Brussels since Wellington had arrived in April in response to Napoleon's escape from Elba. There was another piece of intelligence she knew, another confirmation that her protector had been a military man.

Sighing, she sat patiently as Caesar made his way through back streets and across a small square, its market stalls deserted, through an arch and into a respectable street of modest houses.

They halted before a door and almost as they did so, a skinny youth ran out calling, 'Tante Elise, Tante Elise! Le Capitaine Barnard!'

Jervais dismounted stiffly and helped Caro slide down

to the cobbles. 'Here.' He tossed the reins to the lad. 'Take Caesar and Percy, make sure they are both fed and comfortable and put a poultice on that hind leg.' The youth nodded eagerly and led the horse away, Percy trotting behind.

'Monsieur, you are hurt!' A plump, respectable-looking woman was hurrying down the steps towards them, wiping her hands on her apron. Her expression of concern froze as she took in Caro who hastily wrapped the cloak around her all-too-revealing dress.

'This is Mademoiselle Caroline who has suffered a severe blow to the head and has lost her memory. I am relying on you, Madame, to help her.' Jervais smiled warmly at the bristling Belgian landlady. 'I told her that we could depend upon your kindness.'

He turned to Caro, adding, 'Madame Briquet has made a home from home for several lonely British officers and we all look upon her as a favourite aunt.'

The look Madame returned was hardly that of a favourite aunt and Caro registered how very effective Jervais's charm could be. At the same time, she was very conscious of the reason for Madame's coolness. Young women such as she herself appeared to be were not welcome in respectable homes. Why she was not hardened to such a response she did not understand; perhaps her military protector had sheltered her from the censorious world.

Humiliated, Caro followed Madame Briquet into the house and waited while a manservant helped Jervais up the stairs. Now that he had got them safely back, the sheer strength of will that had sustained him deserted him, and Caro realised with a sudden pang of fear how seriously he was hurt.

'I will call my own physician,' Madame announced, firmly shutting the bedroom door on the two men. 'You may have this room, Mademoiselle. I will send my maid up with hot water and some more. . .suitable clothes.'

Left alone, Caro sat on the bed, hands clenched in her lap, fighting down the tears that threatened to overcome her. In a barn on a battlefield, anyone might be excused for feeling confused and uncertain. Now that she was sitting in a placid, bourgeois home surrounded by all the trappings of everyday life, her lack of memory became even more frightening.

What would be the fate of a young woman in a foreign country with no money, no past, no connexions? Her only friend was Jervais and he was seriously ill. Men died from wounds such as that, she knew. Loss of blood, infection, shock—all could be fatal.

But her fear for him was not purely selfish. True, he believed her to be a woman who sold her favours in return for a man's protection—it seemed it must be so, for there was no other explanation—but if she were to lose Jervais, she would have lost far more than a protector.

Caro shivered and realised she was touching her lips lightly with her fingertips: whatever else she had forgotten, or would forget, the memory of Jervais's mouth hard and sure on hers would never leave her.

There was a tap on the door and a maidservant slipped in, a bowl and ewer in her hands, a plain dark gown over her arm. The look she gave Caro was not unfriendly, but held a wealth of curiosity that made her flush.

Caro spent the rest of the day closeted in her room. The bustle of the doctor's arrival brought her to the door, urgent questions on her lips, only to be shooed back inside by Madame.

In the late afternoon the widow came in briefly. 'He is sleeping now,' she said, not unkindly. 'The wounds are bad, but Doctor Degrelle is hopeful that with rest and good nursing, he will make a full recovery. And he is strong,' she added with a sly glance that brought a flush to Caro's cheeks.

'I must help nurse him. . .' she began, getting to her feet.

'I do not think that is wise.' Madame was firm. 'You must be discreet and remain in your room: there are several other officers billeted in this house. The maid will bring you your supper within the hour. I bid you good evening, mademoiselle.'

Rebuffed, Caro moved restlessly to the window and pushed at the shutters. The room looked out over the courtyard at the rear of the house where long shadows cast by the late evening sunshine patterned the cobbles. Percy was lying in a last pool of warmth, his great shaggy head on his paws, one eye cocked at the yard cat who slunk insolently around just out of reach.

The whole house was quiet and still. At long last the echo of the guns had gone from her brain, but no helpful thoughts came to fill the space left by the sounds of the battlefield. She was tired it was true, she tried to console herself, and worried about the man who had snatched her from danger. . .

It was quiet now; perhaps she could slip across the landing and just look at him. He was bound to be asleep, the doctor would have given him a sleeping draught, so she must take care not to disturb him.

Gathering up the skirts of the drab gown Madame had given her, Caro eased open the door and peeped out. Up above her a door banged. As she glanced up, startled, she caught a glimpse of scarlet uniform and the jingle of spurs as someone ran down the stairs. Caro drew back and the man was past without noticing the door standing ajar. One of the other officers billeted here, no doubt.

Once more the house was silent. Caro counted sixty under her breath then crept across the corridor, slipping into Jervais's chamber, holding her breath for fear of discovery.

She need not have worried: he was alone and asleep.

The room was shuttered and dark, save for a shaft of light from the gap between the wooden slats which slanted across his face. Caro moved softly to the bedside and stood looking down.

Under the tan his skin was pale from loss of blood, the bone structure of his face honed by pain, dark shadows under his closed eyes. They had made no attempt to shave him and the light caught red glints from the stubble that was now almost a beard.

Caroline put out tentative fingers and gently pushed back a wayward strand of hair that had fallen onto his forehead. His skin was hot and dry to her touch and her heart quickened with anxiety. He was running a fever — perhaps one of his wounds was infected. . .

She was looking round for a water jug to bathe his face when Madame's voice floated up the stairs, sending her hurrying back to her room. 'Sit with Monsieur Barnard tonight, Henri. You know what to do, and call me immediately if there is any change.'

Reassured that Jervais would not be alone, Caro undressed and climbed wearily into the narrow bed. The bolster was firm, and as her head touched it a sharp pain lanced through her neck. Cautiously she massaged the large lump on the back of her head: no wonder she had no memory, it was a wonder she had any wits left after that blow! If it felt no better tomorrow, she would ask Madame if she might consult her doctor.

She had expected to lie awake worrying half the night, but as soon as she settled herself sleep swept her into deep oblivion.

CHAPTER TWO

HE WAS drunk again, Caroline realised with disgust, as she stood regarding him from the top of the sweeping staircase. His scarlet face, lined and jowly, stared up at her, the weak blue eyes struggling to focus.

Moved by exasperated pity, she ran down to assist the valet who was supporting his master and urging him to mount the stairs. Caroline put his arm around her shoulder, slipping her own across his back. Mercifully he was not a corpulent man, but the drink had made him clumsy and the two of them could hardly manage him between them.

The scene blurred and shifted in her sleeping mind and Caro tossed restlessly. Now he was sprawled on the big half-tester bed and she was tugging the nightshirt over his head while the valet pulled off his master's boots.

'Darling Caro. . .my dear girl,' he was muttering drunkenly. 'What would I do without you? You're a good girl to put up with an old man like me. . .had a drop too much. . .make it up to you. . .pretty necklace, eh?'

The incoherent ramblings faded away as Caro's head moved restlessly from side to side on the unyielding bolster. But as she slipped back into deep, dreaming sleep again, the face that came to her was no longer old.

The soldier standing framed in the doorway was young, handsome, glowing with pride in his new uniform. She ran to him, running her fingers over the gold lace, the gold and crimson braid, proudly adjusting the sash round his slim waist.

He put his arms round her and held her close as she kissed him, trying not to show her fear for him and spoil his moment of pride in his commission.

'Do not be fearful, darling,' he murmured into her hair. 'I will be back soon, safe and sound. And if something should happen, well, you'll be taken care of. . .'

'No, no. . . I do not care about that. . .' Caro said out loud in her sleep, but the young man had gone leaving only a name on her lips. 'Vivian? Vivian?'

He came back into her dream as though called. This time they were both happy, drinking champagne, the bubbles fizzing up her nose, the taste sharp on her tongue. He held up his glass. 'To us, Caro!' and she knew she was happy.

She fought to see the details of the room, but it was a blur of candlelight on fine crystal, of panelling hung with paintings and long windows swagged with damasks.

'Vivian?' she murmured again, but he had gone and in his place was a lovely woman, her face painted artfully, her hair teased into locks which tumbled enticingly over her voluptuous shoulders and daringly exposed bosom.

Her own voice echoed through the dream, confused, questioning. 'But what of love?'

'Love?' The other woman laughed shortly. 'Oh no, my dear, we may not love. That is not part of the bargain. We sell ourselves for protection and security for as long as it lasts. Women in our trade guard only two things: the money we gain and our innermost feelings.' The carmine lips twisted slightly. 'Fall in love and you regret it forever, for they never truly love you in return.'

Caro woke with a start to find her cheeks wet. She rubbed the back of her hand over her eyes as she fought to keep hold of the dream, but it had faded leaving only the name 'Vivian' and the sickening certainty that Jervais had been right about her profession.

At the window she breathed deeply, struggling with the feelings her dream had evoked. It seemed she had been the mistress of at least two men, two very different men. Why then was she so shamed by the knowledge?

Servants were moving about the yard. As she watched Percy walked out of the shed, stretching each leg out with a great effort then trotting purposefully off to the kitchen door. Conscious of her nightgown, Caro pulled the shutters closed and washed rapidly in cold water from the ewer before scrambling into her borrowed dress.

Her hair was knotted and tangled from her restless night and it took several painful minutes before the glass to tame it into some semblance of order.

For the first time since she had regained consciousness she was able to regard herself in a mirror. Caro's first thought was how dreadful she looked in bottle green, how the shade did nothing for her pale complexion and black hair. It even succeeded in drowning the blue intensity of her eyes.

Her glance strayed to the crimson gown tossed on the end of the bed. No, she thought regretfully, she would never be allowed to visit Jervais wearing that!

Twisting her hair back into a severe knot that made her look positively dowdy, Caro ventured out in search of Madame. If she looked demure enough, perhaps the widow would relent and let her move about the house.

Downstairs, all was activity. A hubbub arose from the dining salon where Caro could see officers crowded around the table, talking non-stop while they demolished the first good meal most of them had seen in days.

She slipped past into the kitchen and almost collided with a maid carrying a jug of porter in one hand and a platter of ham in the other. Madame was in the centre of the kitchen, sleeves rolled up, apron swathing her gown, giving orders.

'Ah, mademoiselle—take care! That hot water upstairs for Lieutenant Hargraves, Henri, then back here for the Colonel's shirts, he rejoins Lord Wellington's staff this morning.'

Taking refuge behind a chair as the servants scurried around her, Caro asked tentatively, 'May I help, Madame?'

The widow seemed about to refuse when a maid enquired, 'Am I to take up Monsieur Barnard's breakfast, Madame?'

'I will take it,' Caro said eagerly, reaching for the tray.

Madame sighed, then nodded her assent. 'Better that than you remaining down here with so many officers in the house.'

Caroline was stung by the implication that she could not be trusted, but was mollified when the widow added, 'Perhaps I was mistaken in my opinion last night. I would not wish you to receive any unwanted attentions from these gentlemen.'

The other manservant put his head round the door and reported, 'The army surgeon has been and dressed Monsieur's wounds, Madame. He seems quite satisfied that the crisis is over, but he wishes a word with you in the parlour.'

Caroline seized the opportunity—and the tray—and hurried upstairs. Jervais was propped up in bed looking, if anything paler than he had the night before. When he recognised her, his face broke into a smile that lightened her heart like magic until he spoke.

'Caro! Where did you get that dress?'

'Madame felt it to be suitable,' she said stiffly, placing the tray beside the bed and shaking out the napkin.

She was suddenly shy with him, and tried to cover it with light conversation. 'Do you not care for it?'

'If I were looking for a governess, no doubt I would. No, give me the bowl,' he ordered as she lifted a spoon. 'I am quite capable of feeding myself. What is this?'

'Gruel, I think. And bread and warm milk.'

Jervais gazed into the bowls with horror. 'And there was I thinking that the morning held no worse terrors than the gentle ministrations of Surgeon-Major Fortescue.'

'Was it very bad?' Caro busied herself at the shutters, not meeting his eyes. What had seemed natural yesterday in the enforced intimacy of the barn was discommoding now. To be alone in a man's chamber, to be alone with a man who was to all intents and purposes a stranger, was embarrassing. She did not want to look at him, to remember as she saw the clean white bandages against his bare skin the feel of that body against hers.

'Well. . .' Jervais was laconic '. . .after he decided he was not going to cut my leg off, things improved, but on balance I think I would rather fight the battle again.'

'Eat your breakfast,' Caro urged, steeling herself to turn from the window and not think about what he had had to endure. 'You need to eat to restore your health.'

'This will do nothing to help,' he grimaced, spooning the pap up distastefully. 'I need good red meat and a bottle of claret.'

'Eat it,' Caro wheedled, forgetting her self-consciousness in her concern for him, 'and I will see what can be done for luncheon, but red wine and red meat will only inflame the wounds.'

'Quite the little nurse,' he mocked her. 'You speak as if you have a knowledge of sick-rooms.'

'I believe I have,' she said slowly, stung by his harshness, but the memory of the older man from the dream refused to clarify into anything more substantial.

'Do not you remember anything more? I should have asked, how are you this morning?'

'My head is sore if I touch it, but it no longer aches. I had a dream last night. . .' her voice trailed off.

'A dream? That is promising.' She had caught his interest. 'Here, take this thing—' he pushed the tray aside '—and come sit by me.'

Caro hesitated for a moment, then sat right on the edge of the bed, as far as possible from him.

'What do you recall?' he urged.

'An elderly man, I believe. . .he was drunk or ill. . . drunk, I think. I helped him to bed. No, it is gone again.' She shook her head helplessly.

'Your general, no doubt.' Jervais was tart. 'Come on, what else?'

Caro rubbed her forehead. 'A young man, in uniform. Younger than me, I think. He was so proud, and alive—vital. So handsome.'

Jervais pulled himself more upright on the pillows. 'When you have quite finished eulogising this paragon, try and remember something more to the point. After all, the army is full of young cubs you would no doubt regard as well-favoured. I can hardly be expected to identify him from that!'

She looked at him with hurt in her eyes and he felt a momentary irritation at her, sitting there so nun-like in that dreadful gown, confidently expecting him to deliver her back to some young puppy. Damn and blast the pain that was making him so short.

'Look, Caro,' he said more gently. 'I'm trying to help, but let us be frank with each other. Which of these two was your most recent. . .protector? Returning you to the wrong one would hardly be tactful.'

Caro sat pleating the coverlet between her fingers. She didn't want to be returned to anyone. All she wanted was to remember who she was.

She lifted her eyes to the lean, laconic face. She did

not know him well enough to interpret his expression or the wry twist to his lips as she said, 'Vivian. That's all I recollect.'

'Vivian?' His eyes were narrowed in thought. 'Surely you cannot mean Major-General Sir George Vivian? I would not have thought you were in his style.'

'No, the younger man is called Vivian, of that I am sure.'

'That is a source of some relief,' Jervais said drily. 'The thought of enquiring tactfully of Sir George whether he has mislaid his mistress makes my blood run cold.'

'I do not feel like anyone's mistress.' The beautiful, unsettling blue eyes were raised to his again.

'Well, at the moment you are not, are you?' He saw her flush and wondered at himself for his restraint. She really was a piquant little thing. Even dressed in that frightful gown her slender figure was alluring. . . Why he was so reluctant to offer her his protection he was uncertain. Despite what he had said to her, the thought of dealing with an enraged senior officer gave him no qualms, and he had recently parted company with a charming Portuguese mistress with no hard feelings on either side.

As he thought, Jervais rubbed his hand across his jaw, grimacing at the scrape of stubble. 'Damn it, I feel like a hedgehog. I cannot recall when I was last shaved.'

'I can do it for you.' The words were out before she could stop them.

'Can you indeed?' His eyebrows rose. 'I am very attached to my ears and I have a fancy to keep them.'

'I have done it before, quite often, I believe. . .' That wretched, elusive, memory! Caro shook herself and stood up briskly. 'I will go and get some hot water.' She was already regretting her unthinking offer which would necessitate such enforced intimacy, but to change her mind now would seem missish.

When she returned with hot water and a towel, Jervais gestured at his saddle-bags, still propped against the wall. 'My kit is in there.' He watched as she opened the canvas roll and pulled out one of the pair of ivory-handled razors. 'Take care for the edge. . .'

Even as he cautioned her, she was testing the edge of the blade competently with her thumb. 'Good, it is very sharp, I never could strop them properly, it is quite an art.' Caro was aware of Jervais watching as she moved purposefully about to hide her apprehension, setting the basin by the bed, whisking up a lather and draping the towel around his shoulders.

She had to perch on the edge of the bed, close against him, forcing herself to concentrate on her task, a trace of delicate colour mantling her cheeks.

With resolution Caro dipped the badger-hair brush in the soap and began to lather his face. Jervais sat very still, and she strove to seem quite unconscious of his eyes watching her.

Her fingers were firm and cool as she pulled the skin tight over his cheekbone and began to run the razor with apparent confidence down through the stubble. Jervais saw the concentration in her eyes, the way her teeth caught the fullness of her underlip as she wiped the blade on the towel and began on his chin.

Caro twisted round as she tried to reach his right cheek. The height of the bed and the size of the man in it made getting the correct angle difficult. She hesitated. She could hardly leave him half-shaved. . . Without giving herself time to think what she was doing, she kneeled up on the bed and leaned over him. She worked steadily and silently, the only sounds in the room the scrape of the blade, his breathing and the occasional creak as Caro shifted her balance on the mattress.

'There!' She sat back on her heels, rather breathless, and wiped the razor for the last time. 'Just a last bit of soap here. . .' She reached across him and dabbed with the edge of the towel at the point of his jaw.

Their eyes met and the towel fell unheeded from her fingers. They were as close as they had been when she had woken in the barn, but now he was no longer a stranger. This was Jervais. . .

Caro's breath caught in her throat and her heart drummed in her ears until she felt dizzy. She was caught by the intensity of his gaze, trying to fathom the question his eyes were asking her.

Jervais reached up and cupped the softness of her cheek with one hand, his fingers moving round to pull her gently down into his embrace. She went with no resistance, almost fatalistically. Caught against his chest, held in the circle of his unwounded arm, Caro raised her face trustingly to his.

The kiss was gentle, slow, almost leisurely, yet the warmth and tenderness was insidious. Caro's very bones felt formless, her body was weightless, floating as Jervais deepened the kiss. She responded without artifice, knowing she had never been kissed like this before.

The very artlessness of her response was a provocation. Jervais groaned, deep in his throat, his mouth moving on hers, the pain in his wounded arm as if nothing as he tightened his hold on the slim body. Caro's trust, her air of innocence, was intensely erotic: he was damned if he was giving her up to any other man.

He freed her mouth, murmuring into the softness of her throat, 'Take off your gown for me, damn this arm—I cannot do it for you.'

'Your wounds!' His voice recalled her part way to reality. 'We should not. . .'

'I doubt I can,' he said ruefully, 'but come back to bed, my darling Caro, and let me give you pleasure.'

Her hands moved obediently to the fastenings of her gown, yet even as they did so, she was conscious through the turmoil he had aroused in her body that in one corner of her mind a small voice said coldly, clearly, 'No'.

Caro stared at Jervais as he smiled back at her, his mouth warm, promising tenderness and delight. 'Jervais. . . I. . .' She sprang from the bed and ran.

In her own room she slammed the door and turned the key in the lock, resting her flushed cheeks against the wood. Fighting down the clamouring of her body, she forced herself to think. Ever since she had woken in the barn she had been doing things she could not remember having knowledge of. She could ride a horse, dress her own hair, shave a man. Yet when Jervais invited her to his bed, there was no knowledge there—and never had been. She had never known a man: and if that were so, then everything else she had come to believe about herself in the last two days was untrue.

Caro sat down on the bed, her legs suddenly weak. She gazed round the small room seeking something, some clue as to who—or what—she was. She was frightened: it had been bad enough before, having no memory, but at least Jervais had offered her some explanation that she could hold on to. Now she knew nothing.

The room yielded no inspiration. A gloomy print of Daniel conversing with a number of cross-looking lions did nothing to raise her spirits. Voices floated up from the courtyard and suddenly Caro needed sunshine, warmth, people.

Snatching up a pelisse, she hurried downstairs. There was no one about in the hall. Should she leave Madame a note? No, she had to get outside and the widow might try and stop her. Caro slipped through the front door and looked up and down the street. Nothing seemed familiar, she could recognise no landmarks. After a moment's hesitation she turned left and followed where most of the passers-by seemed to be heading.

Ten minutes of brisk walking brought her to a wide market square, hedged with tall gabled buildings, its centre a bustling mass of servants with baskets amid the stalls.

'The Grand Place!' she exclaimed out loud, causing several people to turn and stare at her. Excited, Caro looked round, realising she could name the King's House, the Town Hall, that the masses of statues decorating the house fronts were familiar. She hurried across the square looking for more landmarks, hoping against hope she might see a face in the crowd she knew.

At the edge of the pavement she paused. If she could remember this place, perhaps she could remember her name. But it would not come. Tears of frustration welled in her eyes, she clenched her fists in a physical effort... As she turned from the road a voice rang out, shrill with excitement across the hubbub.

'Caroline!'

Caro spun on her heel, searching for the source of the voice. Her shoe slipped off the kerbstone, vainly she flailed her arms for balance, then fell. A sharp, familiar pain lanced through her head, then darkness enveloped her.

She came to, lying across the seats of a barouche, her head pillowed in the lap of a slender woman in her late twenties.

'Flora!' Caroline gasped.

Her aunt smiled with relief, stroking Caroline's cheek with a hand that shook slightly. 'Darling girl, we have been frantic with worry for you! Where have you been? What has become of you?'

Caroline struggled to sit up, wincing at the pain in her head. 'What has happened? Where am I?'

Her aunt took in the gathering crowd of gawping bystanders. 'Drive home, Jacques!' She delved into her reticule and produced a bottle. 'Here, sniff this, the fall has shaken you out of your senses.'

Caroline waved away the sal volatile, wrinkling her nose. 'Flora, please, it makes me feel dizzy.' She closed her eyes, seeing lights dance against the lids as she fought against nausea. After a moment she blinked and sat up slowly against her aunt's supporting arm. 'This is the Grand Place, isn't it? But I don't remember coming out today. And why,' she demanded, catching sight of her skirts, 'am I wearing this dowdy gown? It is not mine.'

Lady Grey glanced at the back of the driver and gestured to Caroline for discretion. 'You have had a dreadful bump on the head, dear, just lie back and close your eyes until we get home.'

The elegant town house in the quiet square was familiar and welcoming as Jacques helped Caroline down from the carriage. Her aunt wanted her to lie down, but she was too confused and full of questions to rest.

Flora insisted on bathing the lump on the back of Caroline's head. 'It looks as though you struck your head twice when you fell,' she commented, gently parting the black curls. 'There are two nasty bumps here.'

'Ouch!' Caroline protested. 'Oh, please let it alone, Flora, and tell me what is happening! I cannot even recall going out this morning.'

'This morning!' Her father's only sister sat down abruptly on the end of the bed and stared at her aghast.

'My dear girl, you have been gone since Saturday noon and it is now Tuesday morning!'

'I have been missing for three days?' Caroline was equally aghast. 'But where have I been?'

'But I do not know! You took your horse and went to ask Colonel Jones, the Military Commandant, if we should leave, do not you recall? I became concerned because of the rumours that our army was retreating and you said we should stay because of Vivian. . .'

'Vivian! How could I have forgotten him!' Caroline was half off the bed in her agitation. 'Is the battle over? Is he safe?'

'Your brother is quite unscathed,' her aunt assured her, her calm tone belying the tired, drawn cast of her face. 'Tired, filthy and very hungry, but without a scratch, thank God. He called by for an hour this morning. He was half-mad with worry about you, but he had to go back to his regiment.'

'At Nivelles?'

'Yes, but how could you know that?'

Caroline looked at her bleakly. 'I do not know, I just do not know. I cannot recall leaving the house or where I have been these past three nights. . .' She could feel the colour ebbing from her cheeks. Nivelles. . . there was something about Nivelles. Then it came back with a clarity that shocked her: her arms around Jervais's waist, the movement of Caesar beneath her, the voice of the other officer giving Jervais the news of victory and of the troops reassembling at Nivelles.

'Oh, my dear, you have gone such a strange colour!' Flora cried in distress. 'I must send for the physician— I fear you are succumbing to a brain fever.'

'No. . .no, please do not. It is simply that it is so distressing being unable to recollect what has occurred.' It was the exact opposite of the truth: at that moment Caroline felt she would give almost anything to be in ignorance once again, to consign to oblivion the remembrance of waking in the barn, in the straw with a man beside her!

And how had she come to be there? There was still Saturday noon to Monday morning to be accounted for; that part of her memory was still hidden behind a closed door in her mind and, struggle as she may, she could not open it.

Her aunt came and sat beside her on the bed, a slight flush staining her cheeks. 'Caroline, my dear.' She took her niece's hand and sat smoothing the skin over her knuckles. 'I hardly know how to put this into words for fear of offending you...but you are not even wearing the clothes you left in. Did anything occur... are you... I mean to say...' She looked away, her flush deepening. 'Are you unhurt?'

'My head aches.' Then Caroline caught her aunt's meaning and blushed scarlet, the question striking home to the most mortifying memories of her experience. 'I am quite unharmed! Nothing is amiss. I am certain I would know...if...' She, too, could not continue: the thought of her forward behaviour, of her willing surrender to Jervais's kisses in the barn and later, of that moment in his bedroom when she so nearly capitulated to his passion, was too searing to face. How could she begin to explain to Flora how she had abandoned every tenet of modest behaviour? How could she begin to explain to herself?

'Of course...forgive me, you understand why I had to ask.' Her aunt smoothed her gown in her agitation. 'Now, we will not refer to it again. I am sure the solution to this conundrum is quite simple: you must have had an accident and been cared for by a respectable Belgian family. That would explain the modesty of your gown and how you came to be in the city.'

Flora seemed quite satisfied at her explanation and Caroline grasped at such an innocent theorem. She hated the thought of lying to her aunt but the outcome of revealing the truth was beyond contemplation.

There was a tap at the door and a maidservant came in with hot water. 'I will leave you to rest, dear, and go to write some notes. I must let Vivian know you are safe, and Colonel Jones, also. Since I reported you missing he has set people to look for you.' She paused, her brow furrowed. 'Perhaps it were best we say you were stunned as a result of a fall, and unable to give the family who found you your name and direction.' She closed the door behind her with a worried backward glance at her niece.

Caroline fidgeted about the bedroom as the maid tidied up after her bath. She had replied very confidently to her aunt's delicate probing, but how could she ever rest easy in her own mind until she discovered how she had spent those missing two nights and a day before Jervais had found her, and why she was clothed in that indecorous gown?

She smoothed the peignoir at her throat, and with the touch of her fingers on the bare skin a sudden flash of memory transfixed her again. His lips on her throat, grazing, caressing the softness. . .

Jervais! Jervais kissing her so intimately. No, she must not think about him! If only she could believe that the blow on the head was causing her to hallucinate. . . No man other than her brother or father had ever done more than kiss her hand in a respectful salute until Jervais.

She stared into the mirror, expecting to find she had changed, but the face that looked back at her was indubitably that of Miss Caroline Franklin: twenty years old, single and likely to stay so. The example of her parents' mismatched union and her own notorious discrimination—which some had chosen to characterise as over-particularity—had kept her from accepting the many flattering proposals which had come her way in three Seasons.

Miss Franklin might be warm, vivacious and friendly, but none of her suitors, however ardent, had made the mistake of presuming that she was fast. If the slightest whisper reached the ears of Society that she had spent the night unchaperoned with Captain Barnard, she was ruined beyond redemption. Her fingers strayed over her throat again as though seeking to recapture his touch. The only comfort was that this would remain forever her secret, for he did not know who she was and never would.

All this time the maid Evangeline had been patiently waiting, a simple lawn day-dress over her arm. Its fresh sprig pattern was in sharp contrast to the dull stuff of the gown she had just discarded. Flora had at least been correct in her assumption that some respectable Belgian had come to her aid: she regretted her inability to send word to the widow that she was safe. Despite Madame's censorious demeanour, she had been kinder than Caroline could have expected.

At dinner that evening Caroline forgot her own intimate worries in hearing news of what had occurred in the city whilst the battle had been raging.

'It was chaos, Caroline, and so frightening.' Her young aunt shivered at the memory. 'We knew not what to do for the best. Rumour was rife...we had won...we had lost...the Corsican Monster was at the gate...the Guard was defeated... I could not leave because I expected your return at every moment. I kept telling myself the crush was so great in the streets you could not get through, but all the time I was reproaching myself for ever having let you go.'

Her aunt's distress was so apparent that Caroline pushed back her chair and came to comfort her. More like an elder sister than an aunt, her father's widowed sister was a scant eight years older than herself.

When her elderly husband Lord Grey had died, two years after the wedding, Flora had pressed her niece hard to come and live with her. But Caroline could not bring herself to leave her father. His behaviour, always rakish, had been increasingly dissolute since the death of his wife, the only restraining force upon him.

'It must have been intolerable for you, Flora.' She bent to kiss her cheek. 'My disappearance on top of all our worries for Vivian! Oh—I had quite forgot to ask after Major Gresham! Is he safe?'

Flora coloured, the smile in her eyes making her seem eighteen again at the mention of her suitor's name. 'Quite safe, just a scratch on the cheek. And so tired and worried for his men as all the officers are.' She was suddenly serious. 'He says there was no glory in the victory, the carnage was terrible on both sides: I fear we have lost many friends and acquaintances.'

Flora returned her embrace and Caroline returned silently to her place. There was no need for words, they knew each other too well. It seemed selfish to be happy, but at least her brother and Flora's suitor were not counted among the dead or the wounded.

They had made many acquaintances in the three months they had been in Belgium, lured—as so many of the *ton* were—by the prospect of safe travel on the Continent again after so many turbulent years of conflict.

It was half past nine and the butler had just brought in the tea tray when the two women heard the knocker bang on the front door. Booted feet clattered on the tiled floor of the entrance hall and spurs jangled as the wearer ran upstairs.

Caroline sprang to her feet as the double doors flew open and her brother strode across the room to gather her into his arms.

'Vivian. . . Vivian. . .' was all she could say, so overcome was she to see him. They clung together and she could sense he was as affected as she at the reunion.

At last he broke the embrace and held her at arm's length. 'Let me look at you. Caro, wherever have you been? I could make no sense at all of Flora's note, although never have I been so thankful to receive a billet!'

Caroline made much of settling her brother in a chair and pouring him a cup of tea while she collected her thoughts and schooled her face. Vivian would never believe she could lie to him; if only she could reassure him, all would be well. If he discovered the smallest part of the truth he would call Captain Barnard out, of that she was certain.

'I must have been thrown from my horse,' she confessed, after explaining how she came to leave the house. 'And after that I know nothing.' She saw the consternation on his face and hurried to reassure him. 'Flora and I have settled between us that I was rescued by a respectable Belgian family. Except for the blow to my head I am quite unharmed and I was wearing the most dowdily respectable gown you have ever beheld!'

'Quite frightful,' Flora interjected, laughing for the first time that day. 'We can rest assured that whoever was looking after your sister had the most decorous taste!'

'You make it sound like an insult,' Caroline teased, forcing herself to keep the conversation light.

'I would not dream of putting even a governess into that gown,' her aunt countered.

'Flora, that is the second time you have said I looked like a governess in that gown: there is no need to remind me what a dowd I looked!'

'No, it is not,' her aunt insisted.

Caroline rubbed her forehead. 'I was certain. . .' No, the voice that echoed in her brain was not her aunt's light tone, it was Jervais's: masculine, deep and sardonic.

'Caroline?' She realised her brother had been speaking to her. She must guard her tongue, her thoughts, every moment or she would betray herself. It was hard to be dishonest with the two people she cared most for in the world.

'I am sorry, Vivian,' she apologised. 'I keep having these unsettling moments of abstraction.'

They talked long into the evening, hardly noticing as the servants came in to light the candles and set a taper to the fire.

Tired as she was, Caroline was reluctant to go to bed. She was happy and secure, home at last, Vivian was safe... She smiled hazily at him as the firelight flickered on the gold lace of his uniform.

The room tilted around her and she clutched the arm of the sofa to steady herself. The figure of her brother in scarlet and gold was overlain by another in blue and silver. The images shifted and merged and she threw up her hands to cover her eyes.

'Caroline!' Her aunt was by her side and Vivian was bending over her. 'I thought you were about to faint. It was foolish of me to let you stay up so late. You should feel the bump on her head, Vivian!'

Caroline fell asleep as soon as Flora blew out the candles and left her room. And with the sleep came the memories and the dreams of Jervais. His arms were tangible as he held her to him, his mouth hard and demanding on her yielding lips, and she was drowning, drowning in sensation.

In the velvety darkness her lips parted and she murmured, 'Jervais, Jervais.' But there was no one there to hear her.

CHAPTER THREE

IT HAD been one of those unexpectedly warm days England often experienced in early October, but now the sun was sinking and a vicious breeze was getting up.

Looking down from the drawing-room window on the first floor of the house in Brook Street, Caroline watched as the under-footman struggled to gather up the fallen leaves he was attempting to clear from the front steps.

'Is there any sign of him?' Flora was sitting beside the fire, a tambour frame in her hands. 'We cannot wait tea much longer.'

'You mean, is there any sign of them?' Caroline teased, turning away to smile at the blush mounting to her aunt's cheeks. Ever since Vivian and Major Gresham had arrived back in England for a month's furlough, the senior officer had been a frequent visitor to the widow's London residence.

Anthony Gresham had been very good to Lieutenant Sir Vivian Franklin, introducing him to his club and taking him about Town. Flora maintained stoutly that this was merely the kindness of an older man for a promising young officer in his regiment. 'He has simply taken him under his wing,' she would protest to Caroline's teasing.

'I think it has more to do with the fact that Vivian is under your roof,' Caroline had replied. Although Vivian and she frequently twitted Flora about her suitor, they were both very glad that, after over five years of widowhood, she was finding happiness at last. She had dutifully married her elderly husband at twenty: although no words of complaint had ever escaped her lips, Caroline guessed it had not been an entirely happy marriage.

'It seems an age since we were in Belgium,' Flora mused as she held up a tangle of green silks to the light. 'Despite all the horrors of the battle and the worry of your accident, I am glad we decided to yield to Lady Blatchett's persuasion and take a house in Brussels as she did.'

'Indeed,' Caroline replied warmly. 'It was such a refreshing change to travel out of the country. And we had all the benefits of a change of scene, but with the company of so many of our old friends.'

'Oh, yes!' Flora agreed. 'The picnics, the expeditions, the balls—why, even the Duchess of Richmond's ball, agitating though it was with all the officers leaving for the battlefield. . .' She sighed and returned to her needlework. 'We seem to live very quietly now.'

'I assure you, Flora, that the tranquility of this household is still most welcome to me,' Caroline assured her.

Brother and sister had moved in with their youthful aunt two years ago after the death of Sir Thomas Franklin, their father. The calm and order of Flora's home was still a source of wonder and comfort to Caroline after the turbulance and alarums of life with the baronet.

'We may not burn the candle at both ends, but we contrive to entertain ourselves most satisfactorily, do we not?'

'Unfortunately, my dear, your experience of one who did burn the candle at both ends was not a happy one.' They both knew to what Flora alluded. 'To have had the burden since the age of fifteen of your unfor-tunate father's habits—of having to assist him to his chamber bed night after night when he was in his cups and to lie awake listening to noisy card parties in the salon below was quite insupportable.'

Caroline's lips twisted with wry recollection. 'Frankly, aunt, that was the least of it. The mortification of having tradesmen dun one on one's own doorstep was a far greater burden.'

And even, on one occasion, a discarded and disgruntled mistress had forced her way in, although she had no intention of telling her aunt of that, even several years after the event.

Caroline had been more intrigued than shocked by her scandalous visitor, and had offered the woman tea after explaining that her father had gone to Newmarket for the races.

The woman's painted face and brassy manner belied her age and Caroline had felt a strange liking for her. They had talked long into the evening and she could remember asking about her protectors. 'Do you not love them?' The girl had laughed shortly and explained her very practical philosophy of life. When she had finally departed with some of Caroline's guineas in her reticule, she had left a thoughtful young woman behind her.

No wonder she had understood so many of the allusions Jervais had made to the 'muslin company'! Life with Sir Thomas and the revelations of one of that sisterhood had only served to confirm Caroline in her observation that marriage was a state to be entered into with extreme caution. This reserve had led her to refuse an earl's son for his propensity to gamble, a baronet for his short temper towards servants and one wealthy young man for his lack of intelligence.

As though reading her thoughts, Flora remarked, 'I cannot help but feel I have failed in my duty since you have been in my care. If only I could see you suitably bestowed. . .'

'Why, Flora, if I cannot catch myself a husband in

three Seasons, I am at my last prayers and destined to be an old maid!'

'It is not a subject for levity,' Flora scolded. She was despairing of seeing Caroline married, especially after her rejection of the future earl. But she recognised the impossibility of persuading her niece against her will: Caroline could be very obdurate.

'Why not ring?' Caroline suggested, turning back to her idle scrutiny of the street. 'They will not be much longer on such a cold day.'

She sat on the window-seat and continued to watch the street below. Although four months had passed since Waterloo and her mysterious disappearance, Caroline still felt very strange. Occasionally she felt dizzy. Her head had long since stopped aching, although the loss of the time after she had left the Brussels house persisted, as did the dreams which came every night.

Emotionally, she felt drained and deeply unsettled. The dreams were always of Jervais, although the scene changed: sometimes they were on his horse together, sometimes they were in his chamber. One feature was constant: when she woke she could still feel the touch of his lips on hers and an aching sense of loss that he was gone.

'Here they come!' The two uniformed figures were strolling from the direction of Grosvenor Square, cloaks swirling in the rising wind, collars turned up against the cold. Flora tugged the bell pull, then hurried to the glass to tease out her curls more becomingly. Caroline was just turning from the window when she saw the pair stop and hail someone.

Curious, she turned and looked. A big, raw-boned grey horse was pacing up Brook Street from the direction of New Bond Street, a scruffy hound trotting at its heels. From above the rider was unrecognisable.

But the animals were instantly familiar. The world

tilted and swayed and Caroline clutched the muslin drapes for support, straining to see. Astride Caesar was a man in riding clothes, his hand raised in greeting as the horse and men converged to meet under the window. The rider reined in the grey, holding it with a strong hand as it fidgeted in the wind.

Looking down, Caro saw the chestnut brown hair, ruffled as he raised his hat; the long, capable hands on the reins; the broad shoulders under the dark cloth.

'Jervais.' The name was almost soundless as the man from her dreams dismounted and shook the hand of Major Gresham.

'What is keeping them?' Flora enquired, still primping.

'They have... I think they have met someone they know.' Caroline hardly knew how she got the words out, or how her aunt had failed to notice her extreme agitation. Her heard was thudding so hard she felt sick and the curtain was knotted hard in her fist.

'Another military man?' Flora walked over to join her.

'Yes.'

'But, my dear, how can you tell? He is not in uniform. What a hideous horse!'

'Oh, I just assumed...by his bearing, I mean.' Fortunately her aunt had eyes only for Major Gresham and still did not notice her strained demeanour.

The two young women watched the tableau below in silence, Flora smiling happily at the handsome picture her tall Major made, Caroline with her heart in her mouth. Vivian was obviously urging Jervais to enter the house, and Major Gresham was adding his entreaties. Jervais, after a moment's polite hesitation, allowed himself to be persuaded and handed the reins to the waiting footman.

'Oh, my heavens!' Caro whispered under her breath, turning in agitation from the window. Her first reaction

had been of incredulous pleasure and recognition, soon
engulfed in apprehension as the reality of the situation
came over her. How could she possibly receive this
man? Her last encounter with him had been in his
bedroom—virtually in his bed, certainly in his arms!
She had to escape before he came in: surely, even if he
were enough of a gentleman to say nothing, nothing
could disguise his amazement at finding one he
believed to be of the 'muslin company' in a fashionable
house in Mayfair!

'Flora. . .one of my dizzy spells. . . I must have got
up too suddenly. Please make my excuses to Major
Gresham. . .' She was already halfway to the door,
panic lending her speed.

Flora asked anxiously, 'Should I ask Peters to send
for Dr Shepherd?'

'No, please. . . I will lie down for a while, it will pass
. . .but I am not fit for company.' Caro was out of the
door and fleeing up the stairs even as booted feet
sounded in the hall below.

Safe on the landing she peeped down through the
curling acanthus leaves of the banisters as the three
men came upstairs. She wanted to see Jervais so much,
discover if he was well again: she pressed her face up
against the metalwork the better to observe him.

The men paused outside the salon door and Jervais
suddenly glanced up, as though he could feel her eyes
upon him. Caro recoiled into the shadows of the unlit
landing, but even so his gaze seemed to follow her.
Then Vivian opened the door and the three disappeared from view.

In the safety of her own room Caroline paced up
and down, wringing her hands in perturbation. Her
mind was so full of remembered images she could
scarcely order them, never mind comprehend the enor-
mity of Jervais's presence.

'I cannot think!' she said out loud, sitting down, then

springing to her feet again. The memories were filling her brain, clamouring. With Jervais downstairs, rational thought was impossible. The sensible thing would be to stay where she was until he had gone: that was what a prudent, well-brought-up young woman would do. There was no reason why she should ever see him again after all. The meeting had been a chance one; he was not one of Vivian's friends.

Calmer, she went and sat at the dressing-table, smoothing her hair and dabbing a little lavender water on her temples. Yet, perhaps she was not as safe as she thought. He was obviously a friend, or at least an acquaintance, of Major Gresham, and the Major was surely on the point of making Flora a declaration. Captain Barnard could well become a regular visitor to the house and she could not plead a dizzy spell every time he called.

She should go to Longford: that would be sensible. Vivian rarely used the country seat he had inherited, preferring London life to the rambling manor in Hertfordshire with its unhappy memories of their father. She could use that as an excuse to leave London, say she felt the house might be neglected and the servants needing supervision.

Then the flaws in the plan struck her. She could hardly stay at Longford for ever, and besides, Flora would soon become suspicious and would descend to find out what was amiss.

No, she must beard this lion now, while she was prepared. At least she had the advantage of being forewarned and the shock of seeing him had spent its force. Caroline looked steadily at her reflection in the mirror: perhaps he would not recognise her. She certainly looked different from either the painted, bedraggled demirep of the barn or the drably dressed young woman of the Brussels house.

Her afternoon frock was a simple affair of figured

muslin, but the elegant lines imparted by a fashionable modiste were quite unmistakable in the tiny pleats at the waist and the pretty puffed sleeves. Her hair was glossy and freshly cut in the latest mode, with demure curls escaping provocatively from a gauze ribbon to frame a complexion owing everything to nature and nothing to art.

No, there was every chance he would not recognise her. He would never expect to see her in the setting of a tonnish town house, furnished with every appurtenance of elegance. And besides, although their encounter was memorable for her because it had been so shocking and intimate, for him she was probably just another young woman amongst a host.

No—it was worth hazarding: before she could lose her nerve Caro ran downstairs and opened the salon door. Flora was bent over the tea-tray, the Major attentively at her side. Vivian had his back half-turned to the door as he made conversation with the Captain. Jervais Barnard occupied the sofa, nodding in agreement with something his host had just said.

They all turned at the sound of her entrance so that only Caroline saw the look of stunned recognition on Jervais's face. Vivian jumped to his feet and came to take her hand, saying in low tones, 'Are you feeling quite yourself again?'

Caroline nodded, not trusting herself to speak, maintaining a polite social smile learned during the course of several Seasons. There could be no doubt that Captain Barnard had recognised her, but by the time she brought herself to look at him he had his face well schooled.

'Caroline, this is Lord Barnard who has lately returned from Belgium. Lord Barnard, my sister Miss Franklin.'

Jervais was on his feet, bowing over her proffered hand. Caroline forced herself to look at him. His face was politely composed as it should be, meeting a young lady for the first time. But his eyes reflected his thoughts and she read there a message of reassurance that she met with a look of blank incomprehension.

As she met his gaze without a sign of recognition, his brows drew together, then his expression cleared and became politely bland. Yet aware of him as she was, Caroline recognised a flash of something else in those brown eyes. Puzzlement perhaps, which she could understand, but also a hint of anger which confused her.

Caroline was determined to press her advantage while she was so composed. If she could only establish beyond a doubt that she remembered nothing of their previous encounter, then as a gentleman he would have to accept that. To say anything of their Belgian adventure would be to humiliate and embarrass her in front of her friends and he would have to assume she would deny everything angrily if her loss of memory was genuine.

I do so hope he will keep silent, she prayed inwardly, and that he is sufficient of an actor not to betray that he knows me. If Flora or Vivian were to discover what had really happened during those missing days in Belgium, she and Jervais would find themselves married out of hand. She might try and refuse, but no honourable gentleman would hesitate to do the decent thing, having compromised her so thoroughly. It was a bitter twist of fate to find a man to whom she was attracted and found so intriguing, only for him to prove to be the last one she could honourably consider marrying.

She sat down beside him on the sofa, accepting a cup of tea from Major Gresham with a word of thanks. If she could only maintain the pretence, Jervais would find it impossible to broach the subject of their adventure and they would both be safe.

'Were you in the army in Belgium, sir?'

'Yes, Miss Franklin, but I sold out last month. I am now a man of leisure.' He was speaking lightly, but Caroline could almost hear his mind working on the problem she was presenting him.

'Take no notice, Miss Franklin,' the Major said jokingly. 'One would scarcely call the management of an estate the size of Dunharrow a sinecure, Barnard. It's no secret that your late cousin let the place fall into wrack and ruin.'

Caroline pulled herself together. She had been in such a state of turmoil she had missed the significance of Jervais being introduced as Lord Barnard. 'You have recently come into the title, then? I do not believe I knew your late cousin: were you close?'

'He died two months ago, and no, we were not close. In fact, Cousin Humphrey was best described as a curmudgeonly old recluse.' His mouth twitched at a sudden memory. 'I used to pay him duty visits; I was the heir, after all, but he did not welcome my opinions on the state of the land. Last time he threatened to set the dogs on me.'

'How sad that you were estranged,' Caro commented coolly. She was rather taken aback that he should seem so unmoved by his near relative's lack of affection. 'So, inheriting the title caused you to sell out?'

Jervais regarded the polished toe-cap of his riding boot. 'I had been in the army for many years, it was time to settle down. And with Napoleon defeated, the army will be a very different place now.'

'Did you fight at Waterloo, my lord?' Caroline was astounded at her own coolness, yet it would seem unnatural to avoid the subject.

'Yes,' he replied shortly.

'And was honourably wounded,' the Major supplied.

'Oh, not badly, I hope?' Caroline said without thinking, then bit her lip. This was too near the knuckle for comfort, she could feel the blush staining her cheeks.

'It was not pleasant at the time,' Jervais said evenly, his eyes on her face. 'In fact, the entire aftermath of the battle was a strangely confusing experience.'

Caroline put her cup down with a rattle. What devil had prompted her to turn the conversation in this dangerous direction? And how was she to get out of it? 'Another cup of tea, Captain Barnard?' She picked up his cup and her own and took refuge beside Flora.

Waiting while the tea was poured, she watched him from under her lashes as he talked easily with her brother. This was the man she had dreamed of so feverishly night after night. She could feel his skin under her fingers as she lay in his arms, the touch of his lips on hers. . .

He was watching her like a hawk across the room, his face inscrutable. Caroline writhed inwardly with embarrassment. He must never, ever, know she remembered what had been between them. She must guard her tongue and hope this was the last she ever saw of Lord Barnard.

He got to his feet as she returned with the cups and she noticed with a pang of relief that there was no sign of any stiffness in his leg.

'And where is your estate?' she enquired politely.

'Hampshire. . .' he was beginning when they were interrupted by a commotion outside the door. After a moment it opened and the flushed face of the under-footman appeared.

'I'm sorry, I'm sure, Ma'am, but I can't do a thing with this dog. . .'

As if to prove the point, he was almost sent flying by the hound in its eagerness to find its master. It bounded over, tail thrashing perilously near a pie-crust table covered in enamelled boxes, and prostrated itself at Jervais's feet.

'Sit!' Jervais glowered at the beast which immediately

obeyed. 'I do apologise, Lady Grey, I left him tied up in the hall.'

The big hairy head turned to look reproachfully at his master and then saw Caroline. With a soft 'wuff' of recognition the dog flattened his ears and sank his muzzle on her knee.

'Hello, Per. . .boy,' she caught herself just in time, but no one seemed to have noticed the near slip.

'Anyone would think he knew you,' commented Jervais in a low tone to Caroline, dragging the big dog off by its collar. 'He is usually very wary of strangers.'

'I like dogs. I think they can tell, do you not agree?' She was determined not to show him how flustered she was feeling. Percy's greeting had told him nothing he did not already know: she must not allow herself to be panicked into betraying herself.

The party broke up shortly afterwards, Major Gresham announcing he was almost late for a meeting at the House Guards and Jervais rising to accompany him.

'I hope you will call again, Lord Barnard,' Flora invited warmly. 'Any friend of Major Gresham's is welcome in this house. We are usually At Home on Wednesday and Friday afternoons.'

'I would be honoured,' Jervais bowed over her hand. 'Perhaps I can persuade you and Miss Franklin to drive with me in the Park one day?'

'But surely you will be returning to Dunharrow?' Caroline asked, too abruptly for politeness. 'You must have so much to overlook if the estate has been so neglected.'

Flora shot her a quelling old-fashioned look, then turned, beaming, to the Captain. 'We would enjoy it immensely, would we not, my dear?'

'Yes, of course.' Caroline tried to sound enthusiastic. 'How kind.'

As soon as the door had closed on the gentlemen,

Flora turned on her niece in a swirl of skirts. 'Really, Caroline, that was almost rude! I could despair of you sometimes! Here is the most eligible man to enter our acquaintance for months—so good-looking, too—and you treat him as though he were a boring young subaltern.'

Caroline recognised one of the rare occasions when her aunt was annoyed with her. 'He might not be eligible,' she protested. 'He could have a wife and ten children for all we know.'

In reply her aunt pulled a thick, red bound book off the shelf and ran her finger swiftly down a page. 'Baldock, no, Ballard. . .here we are. Barnard. Well, he was not married last year, and as he has been in the army he will have had scant chance!'

Caroline recognised when she was beaten. 'I am not seeking for a husband,' she insisted stubbornly.

Flora sprang to her feet and began to pace upon the hearth-rug. 'Really, Caroline, I do not know what to do for the best!' She took a deep breath the better to remonstrate with her niece about her obdurate behaviour but was arrested by the sudden change of expression on Caroline's face. 'What is it?' she asked, alarmed.

'Those words. . .you used the self-same words in Brussels, that day I left the house. Why, I remember now what happened!'

'But we had already settled upon what must have happened, my love—' Flora began.

'Yes, I know. . .but now I remember.' It was true. Whether it was the shock of seeing Jervais or whether the echo of Flora's despairing words as panic had seized the city, she knew not, but it had been enough to recall that frightening morning when neither of them knew what to do for the best.

'Caroline!' Flora pressed her down onto the sofa. 'Sit down and tell me all about it.'

Caroline took a deep breath and tried to organise her thoughts. She could have kept her counsel, she supposed, but she did not like to deceive Flora and watching her tongue endlessly would be very wearing. Yet she could not tell her aunt everything—no mention of Jervais must cross her lips.

'You know I went to enquire about the wisdom of our leaving Brussels?' she began.

'Yes, of course, and you took Gypsy from the stables because you said it would be quicker to ride rather than to walk with such crowds on the streets.'

'It was a foolish decision. I should have remembered he had not been out of his stable all week, and he has always been nervous of loud noises.

'I got lost.' She frowned at the remembered frustration. 'So many streets were blocked with carts and refugees and I tried to avoid the main roads because of the troop columns. I must have taken a wrong turn, for I found myself near the outskirts of the city in an area I did not recognise. And by then it was already mid-afternoon and I was so tired and frightened.'

'But why did you not turn back?'

'I was going to. I realised I must be heading towards the battlefield because no one was going in that direction, but then a horse came bolting down the road and panicked Gypsy. I managed to hold on, but it was all I could do to stay in the saddle.'

'I knew that gelding was too much for you,' observed Vivian who, unheard, had re-entered the room.

'He was not!' Caro protested indignantly. 'I would have liked to see you fare any better.'

Her brother grinned wickedly, but stopped teasing. 'Go on, Caro, what happened then?'

'We went for miles, I thought he would never stop. At last he began to tire: I was so relieved for I thought we were going to find ourselves in the middle of the battle!'

Flora exclaimed in horror. 'Thank heaven you managed to control him at last!'

'It was due to no skill of mine,' Caroline admitted ruefully. 'He stumbled in a pot-hole and threw me right over his shoulder into a deep muddy puddle.'

'And you let go of the reins?' Viaian demanded from where he stood at the fireside.

'I must have done.' She shook her head. 'Poor beast, I wonder what became of him.'

'If he was not killed, he was no doubt appropriated by a grateful soldier. The carnage among the horses was appalling, several people had more than one horse shot away from under them.' Vivian's face darkened as it always did when he spoke of the battle.

Flora took her niece's hand. 'My dear, it must have been a nightmare! What did you do next?'

'I. . .' Caroline's voice died away. The door into her memory had swung to once again. 'I suppose I picked myself up and started to walk back the way we had come.

'You can recall no more?' demanded Flora, shocked.

'No, there is still a void. I think I can remember it getting dark and being very tired, but being afraid to stop. It must have been as we supposed and some kind and respectable people found me and helped me back to Brussels.'

'But what I do not understand is why you did not come straight back to the house when you reached Brussels,' Flora said.

'Why, because Caro had lost her memory of who she was,' Vivian interjected. 'It is no wonder she cannot remember,' he added. 'A fall like that is enough to rob a strong man of his senses, let alone a young woman.'

'Of course, I am becoming so muddled trying to piece it all together.' Caroline could only be grateful for her aunt's vagueness, it prevented her from asking more awkward questions.

'I do wish we knew who had helped you,' Flora continued anxiously. 'I would like to write and thank them. Still, we must be thankful that the conundrum is gradually resolving itself. No doubt it will all come back to you in due course.'

Indeed, Caroline hoped most fervently that it would be so. Comforting though it might be to have more of her memory restored, these recollections did nothing to explain how she had come to be found by Jervais wearing a most immodest gown and with paint on her face, nor where she had been for two nights.

There was a silence while they sat and mused, each lost in their own thoughts, then Vivian asked, 'But how did you come to be in the Grand Place?'

'I must have left my rescuers' house thinking a walk might prompt some recollection, or that someone I knew might see me.'

'Thank heavens it was I,' exclaimed Flora. 'Can you imagine the scandal if anyone else had found you! As we said before, you must be careful, dear, to speak of this to no one. What would people think if they knew you had spent all that time in circumstances we cannot account for? How tongues would wag!'

Caroline nodded meekly and sat back against the cushions, relieved that some, if not all, of the truth was out and that her family accepted her explanation of what had happened. But her precarious peace of mind was short lived.

'Caroline, we must go out tomorrow morning and buy that handsome bonnet we saw in Miss Millington's shop yesterday,' Flora announced: her train of thought appeared to have moved on from Caroline's adventure.

'But we agreed it was far too dear!'

'Nonsense, it would be just the thing to set off your new walking outfit. You want to look your best, after all.'

'Why?' Caroline enquired mutinously, knowing only too well.

'For your drive with Lord Barnard, of course,' Flora said unanswerably.

CHAPTER FOUR

'THEY are all most handsome: do you have a preference, Caroline? For myself, I cannot choose between them.' Flora turned from the shop window to smile at her niece.

'I care for none of them,' Caroline declared flatly.

'But you admired that one in green so much the other day,' protested Flora with a sinking heart. Persuading Caroline to visit Miss Millington's exclusive establishment in Conduit Street had proved suprisingly easy: she should have known better, with Caroline's strange new mood, than to believe the rest of the expedition would go as well.

'I cannot imagine what I was thinking of, it is positively dowdy.'

'Dowdy? Surely not? Well...perhaps we could ask Miss Millington to exchange the grosgrain ribbon for some curled plumes in a darker green. That would give it a touch quite out of the ordinary and it would look very becoming with your new walking dress and pelisse.'

'Very well,' conceded Caroline, nodding to the young woman who opened the door for them. If the truth be told, she was not averse to buying a stylish new hat, but being dressed up to be paraded in front of the one man in London she wanted to avoid was galling. Although not as galling as the knowledge that in other circumstances she would have needed no persuasion at all!

Miss Millington darted out from behind the tasselled velvet curtains which concealed her inner sanctum and a workroom full of apprentices. 'Lady Grey, Miss Franklin. . .what an honour. Drusilla!'

Miss Millington fluttered like the small bird she resembled while her assistant, a willowly young woman, arrayed gilt chairs and a small table for the comfort of the two ladies. 'A glass of ratafia, Lady Grey?'

'Are you seeking a hat for a particular occasion or would you care to see our latest creations?' the milliner enquired once the ladies were settled.

'Oh, all the latest ones, please,' Caroline asked firmly.

'But, Caro dear,' Flora hissed out of the corner of her mouth, 'you know why we are here! A hat for your drive in the park!'

'But we may as well see the new ones,' Caro wheedled. 'Oh, now do look at this one—it will suit you admirably.' And indeed the rose pink villager-style bonnet with its deeper pink ribbons would set off Flora's brunette prettiness to perfection.

'I am not in need of any new bonnets,' Flora said, with a hint of wistfulness.

'Major Gresham would admire it so much. . .' Predictably, Flora blushed and dropped her long lashes over her dark eyes in confusion. People often thought that aunt and niece were sisters, although those who knew them well could see Flora's resemblance to her brother, Caro's father, in his younger days, while Caro had inherited her mother's dark blue eyes and much of her slender grace.

'We will see,' was all Flora would say as Drusilla brought in more stands displaying the dashing new modes.

At the end of an hour's agonising debate, the ladies had settled on two bonnets apiece—including the pink villager for Flora. Miss Millington bowed them out with promises of speedy delivery of three of the hats, whilst a page boy carried the green bonnet safe in its ribboned box out to the waiting barouche.

Flora and Caro settled back under the snug carriage rug, warmed by the glow of a successful shopping expedition. 'Shall we call at Hatchard's?' Caro suggested, as they turned into Regent Street.

'More books, dearest? You will be thought bookish if you do not take care!' And will never catch a husband, was Flora's unspoken warning.

'Why, I found you sighing over the most frivolous novel only the other day!' Caroline riposted. 'And I want to see if Miss Austen's lastest book is available yet.'

Flora raised no more protests and climbed down with willingness when their coachman drew up outside the busy bookshop. Despite the relatively early hour of their visit, the bench outside the bow-fronted shop was already occupied by a number of liveried footmen awaiting their employers who browsed and gossiped within.

Flora and Caroline arrived back at Brook Street eventually with not only a book apiece and the hat box, but a myriad of parcels containing silk stockings, ribbon, some embroidery floss for Flora's latest project and two pairs of kid gloves found at a bargain price.

'Take those directly to my chamber, William,' Flora was directing when her eye fell upon a number of calling cards on the salver on the hall table. 'We have had several visitors whilst we were out, Caro,' she commented, flicking over the rectangles with a gloved finger. 'Mrs Rivington and that sulky son of hers. . . Aunt Lloyd—oh dear, we will have to pay a duty visit, there is no avoiding it now she is back in Town. It is most reprehensible of me to say so, but I had so hoped she would find herself suited in Bath with Mrs Chatto as companion. Who else. . . Caro! Look, Lord Barnard has left his card with a note. He begs the honour of taking us for a drive in the park this afternoon.'

She turned to Caroline, her eyes shining. 'I knew I was correct in my view of him! And so considerate to ask me, too—so many young men would fix upon the object of their interest and quite ignore any other ladies. Not that I shall go, of course.' She was already hurrying upstairs, stripping off her gloves as she went. 'How providential that we brought the green bonnet back with us. I shall get Jackson to press your new walking dress and pelisse at once.'

'But I have not yet decided to go,' Caro protested. 'I am certain it is going to rain and I want to read this new book. . .'

'Caroline, will you please join me in the small sitting-room?' Flora said, directing a quelling look at her niece and closing the door firmly behind them. 'Now what reason can you have for acting in this contrary manner? There is not a cloud in the sky, no sign of rain and you can read your book at any time.'

Caroline was fidgeting with some small boxes on a side table, not meeting her aunt's eyes. Flora took her by the hand and forced her to look into her face. 'I can understand you wishing to be careful in your choice of husband. After all, we both know that your poor mother had much to bear. . .'

'And you yourself,' Caroline said gently.

'Lord Grey may have been a little older than I. . .' Flora began hesitantly.

'Nearly thirty years older,' Caroline said indignantly. 'And I know he was very indulgent, but you cannot deny he was a difficult man when he had the gout.'

'We are not speaking of Lord Grey,' Flora replied with some dignity. 'And you cannot compare a man in his fifties to Lord Barnard. Why, he is handsome, intelligent, well-bred and obviously much taken with you. What more can you ask for? I warn you, Caroline, if you persist in this attitude to your suitors you will get a name for yourself and no one will want you. No man enjoys being humiliated.'

'And I find the whole Marriage Mart humiliating!' Caroline countered with spirit. 'It is all anyone talks of—who is engaged to whom and how much the settlements are. Who has refused whose proposal, which men have not come up to scratch. I tell you, aunt, I am heartily sick of it!'

Flora was taken aback by Caroline's vehemence, then rallied. 'Well, the sensible thing is to find a man you can respect and admire and accept his proposal—and I fail to see what there is not to respect and admire in Lord Barnard.' She subsided into an armchair, flushed and ruffled.

'Oh, I am sorry, Flora.' Caroline came and sat at her feet, resting her head on her aunt's knee. 'I do not wish to provoke you or seem to be ungrateful for your concern. But I know him not at all; we have scarcely exchanged half a dozen words and you have us married off already.' It was not the truth, of course; she knew far more than was either wise or comfortable about Jervais Barnard!

There was a long pause then Flora patted Caro's head absently. 'It is most curious. It had not come to me before, but the reason I think you would be so well suited is the feeling I had that the two of you knew each other already. A rapport like that must surely mean something.'

Caroline caught her breath. It was serious if Flora, not given to introspection, had sensed a familiarity between herself and Jervais. She forced herself to sit still and conceal her agitation. Of all the ill fortune to be rescued by this man when it seemed, because of his friendship with Major Gresham, she was fated anyway to meet him in London. Thousands of men could have found her on the battlefield and would have treated her as well—if not better—than Jervais Barnard.

If she had met him for the first time yesterday there was every chance something might have come of it. Now she was totally confused: was he asking to see her because of what had occurred in Belgium or because he was genuinely a suitor? But whatever his motives, as a gentlewoman it was her duty to see matters went no further. He was her rescuer and it was her duty not to compromise him by revealing what had passed between them.

Duty had never seemed quite so bleak, but without a display of quite shocking bad manners she could not refuse his invitation. With a resolution she was far from feeling, she scrambled to her feet and smoothed down her dress.

'Very well, I will go. You are right. It would be ill-mannered to refuse. Now, we are both in need of a little luncheon and then you shall help me change and ensure my new hat looks its best.' The two linked arms and went through to the dining-room in perfect amity.

Caroline was sitting, pretending to read a volume of poetry, one of her new purchases, when the knocker sounded at half past two. Her heart leapt with an unpleasant lurch, but she forced herself to carry on scanning the lines until the footman announced, 'Lord Barnard, my lady.'

She put the book down with studied calm and waited while Flora greeted Jervais.

'Lord Barnard, what a pleasure to see you. Will you take a glass of sherry?'

'Thank you, no.' Without appearing to stare, Jervais noted with interest Flora's attire: she did not appear to be dressed to leave the house in Brook Street that afternoon. Caroline, on the other hand, was becomingly attired in a dark green walking dress and a neat pair of buttoned kid walking shoes peeped from under the hem.

He walked over to shake her hand, noting how the richness of the gown brought out lustrous tints in her dark hair. The demure elegance could hardly be a greater contrast to how he had first seen her. Her eyes dropped before the frank admiration in his.

Caroline could feel Flora willing her to make polite conversation and break the silence that had fallen. 'Will you not sit down, Lord Barnard?'

He sat, picking up the discarded volume of poetry as he did so. 'Do you admire Byron?' He flicked the uncut pages with his thumb. 'Perhaps not, as you do not seem to feel it worthwhile to go past the first page!'

'I bought it only this morning,' Caroline said, angry to find herself sounding so defensive. 'And perhaps it was a foolish choice: on the whole I find his work overrated. Quite impossibly Romantic.'

'And you do not believe in Romantic adventures?' he asked with a dangerous twinkle that caused the corners of his eyes to crease.

'Certainly not.' Caroline was brisk. 'The sort of adventures heroines in novels have always sound dirty, dangerous and thoroughly disagreeable, and I cannot conceive how they ever get themselves into such a plight in the first place!' She caught Flora's eye and subsided. Her aunt's expression said clearly that if anyone had had an adventure recently, it was Caroline and the less said on the subject the better.

'Well, if I cannot interest you ladies in adventuring, perhaps I can offer a gentle drive in the park in my phaeton.' He turned politely to Flora. 'Lady Grey?'

'I am afraid not: I must visit my aunt who is unexpectedly come up to Town from Bath. Please forgive me, Lord Barnard.'

'May I drive you both to your relative's house?' Caroline liked the way he accepted the refusal so graciously and was about to agree with relief when Flora intervened.

'I would not dream of spoiling your afternoon by taking you so far out of your way as Cavendish Square. No, do not alter your plans—I have already ordered the carriage to be sent round for me later. Caroline, dear, go and get your pelisse and bonnet.'

That was neatly done, Caroline mused, as she went to her room: she had not realised Flora possessed such tactical skill!

When she joined him in the hall Jervais congratulated her on her promptitude.

'It is chilly,' Caroline replied calmly. 'I would not wish you to keep your horses standing.'

The phaeton was waiting, the groom at the head of a neat pair of match bays.

'You do not drive a high-perch carriage?' Caroline enquired as he handed her up and adjusted the rug over her knees.

'I did not think it suitable for two ladies, but I will bring it next time if you wish.'

So there was going to be a next time, was there? Caroline thought grimly. Part of her thrilled to be sitting there beside him, so close their elbows almost brushed, but every time she saw him the pain of knowing she must rebuff him grew stronger.

She realised he was talking to her. 'I do beg your pardon, my lord, I quite missed what you just said.' Her attention was wandering into the most dangerous paths; it was time to direct it firmly back or she would be in danger of betraying herself.

'I was asking if you drove yourself—you seemed knowledgeable about carriages. And I wish you would call me Jervais.'

'But, my lord, that would be most improper on such short acquaintance!' Caro knew she was blushing hotly: she only hoped he would interpret it as maidenly modesty and not a recollection of what had occurred in the short time they had spent together. Hastily she tried to turn the subject. 'I have driven a small carriage down at Longford, but only with my old pony between the shafts and he is so slow that "slug" is too active a description for him! I should like to learn,' she added wistfully.

'Then I will teach you with pleasure, if Lady Grey permits it.'

The traffic was heavy and Caroline did not answer at once, sitting silently watching his handling of the team as he threaded expertly through the crowded streets between Brook Street and Tyburn Lane while she tried to think what to say. The bright, cool afternoon had brought out many driving parties to take advantage of the parks before the true onset of autumn and she could have had no better demonstration of Jervais's skill in driving.

'Green Park or Hyde Park, Miss Franklin?' he enquired as they reached Hyde Park Corner.

'I have no particular preference,' Caroline replied, then realised she had still not responded to his offer. Much as she yearned to accept, it was too dangerous. 'And thank you, I would very much like to learn to drive, but I do not think my aunt will permit it. She is very nervous of open carriages.'

Jervais negotiated the turn into Hyde Park without replying. Caroline hoped she had struck the right note: she would hate to be thought ungracious in refusing— and indeed she earnestly desired to learn—but the thought of the intimacy it would thrust upon them made her shiver.

Stealing a sideways glance at his gloved hands as he steadied the team she could almost feel them closing over hers, the strong fingers guiding and tutoring. That thought was too disturbing to be pursued. . .

'Indeed, Lord Barnard,' she stated firmly before she

could weaken, 'I would be reluctant even to raise the subject with my aunt, she is so nervous about it.'

'She must have had a most alarming experience in the past,' he said sympathetically.

Well, that was one danger avoided, Caro thought, stifling her regret at the missed lessons. 'How quickly the leaves are turning now,' she observed brightly. 'And how beautiful they look with the sunlight upon them.'

'Yes, it is a pleasure to see an English autumn again. I have spent so much time abroad these past six years, it almost feels like a foreign country to me.'

'Surely autumn on the Continent is not so very different to our own? The countryside of Belgium struck me as very similar whilst I was there.' As soon as the words were out she was regretting them. She had given Jervais a perfect conversational entrée, yet how could she ignore the dramatic events of the past year? To studiously avoid all mention of Belgium and the battle would be highly suspicious and it would seem rude to ignore what must have been a momentous time for her companion.

'You were in Belgium long?' he enquired casually, raising his whip to acknowledge a passing rider.

'We went out in April. Vivian, my brother, had just been posted there and Lady Grey thought it would be an ideal opportunity to travel on the Continent. So many of her friends were planning to go: after all, who could have foreseen Napoleon's escape?'

'Indeed! None of the Allied governments, that seems certain!'

'We found Society in Brussels very pleasant, and we made several delightful short outings.' Caro found herself babbling like one of the featherheaded debutantes she despised, yet she could not stop herself. 'Bruges is so picturesque and quaint have you been there?'

'I did not have much time for pleasure trips once the regiment reached Belgium,' Jervais remarked drily.

Caroline racked her brains for a safer conversational topic than the Belgian countryside. 'I had heard that the British officers contrived many impromptu parties despite the rigours of camp life.'

'I would not have expected a young lady to know anything of the rigours of camp life.' Jervais flashed her a quizzical glance which, with her secret knowledge, filled her with consternation.

'Why, only what Vivian has told me, of course,' she returned lightly. 'Oh, look over there—is that someone waving at us?'

'At you, I believe,' he observed, reining in the horses, allowing the other phaeton to approach. 'I am not acquainted with any matrons of quite such a formidable aspect, I am happy to say.'

'Caroline!'

'Oh, no! It's Aunt Lloyd—and Cousin Frederick driving.'

'And Lady Grey, overcoming her terror of open carriages in the most courageous manner, I observe. Although I must say,' he added *sotto voce*, as the two carriages drew up alongside each other, 'she would have felt safer with us than with that cow-handed youth.'

'Caroline, my dear! What an unsuitable bonnet! And who is this, pray? Introduce us, girl!' Caroline's great-aunt had never felt under any obligation to say anything other than precisely what she thought on any subject and swept on, ignoring Caroline's obvious embarrassment. 'Well, young man? Cat got your tongue?'

'Jervais Barnard, ma'am.' Knowing him as she did, Caroline realised he was amused—and not in the least discomforted by the rude old lady.

Flora hastened to intervene. 'Aunt, let me introduce

Lord Barnard. My lord, Lady Lloyd, my aunt. And may I make her grandson, Mr Frederick Lloyd, known to you?'

The Honourable Frederick bowed stiffly in acknowledgement. His grandmother had made her intention that he marry his cousin Caroline very clear and he had no desire to lose the old lady's good graces—and handsome allowance—by being cut out by a rival.

The fact that Caroline had never given him the slightest encouragement had not deterred him: he was too thick-skinned to fear that any lady might rebuff him. But equally he was not stupid enough to fail to recognise at a glance the threat that Jervais Barnard posed.

Somehow Caroline got through the next five minutes before her great-aunt announced it was far too cold to sit around gossiping—and she was much too busy to do so.

'I do apologise,' Caroline said, red-cheeked, as soon as they were out of earshot. 'But I assure you she made no exception in your case—she is always that rude, even to her closest friends.'

'Think nothing of it, we all have relatives we blush for—only consider my late, unlamented, cousin. He wore a ginger wig and was a virtual stranger to soap and water.' Caroline giggled at the picture he painted.

'Is that the cousin from whom you inherited your estate?'

'The very same. Fortunately, he was buried in the wig and I was not compelled by the terms of the will to wear it myself.'

Caroline was so preoccupied with stifling her laughter that she was caught completely off-guard when he said, 'I'm filled with admiration for your Aunt Flora. Such poise in concealing her fear of open carriages in order to do her duty. . .'

There was a long silence, punctuated by the hoof

beats on the tan surface. Caroline swallowed hard, reviewed several implausible excuses and decided frankness was the only answer.

'Lord Barnard, I have dissembled. . .been less than honest with you. . .'

'Well, I did suspect as much.' He was smiling down at her in a most disconcerting manner.

'Oh dear, how can I put this. . .you must believe I am not normally given to falsehoods. . .'

Jervais pulled up the team and sat watching her as she pleated the skirt of her gown with nervous fingers.

'I wondered when you were going to tell me,' he said gently putting one hand over hers to still the fidgeting.

'Oh dear, was I so obvious?' Caroline made herself meet his eyes, but let her hand remain under his. His expression was curiously tender, certainly his demeanour was more intimate than seemed warranted by the occasion of the confession of her small fault.

'Not at all. In fact, I was wondering whether I was imagining things,' he said quietly.

'What I said about Flora being too nervous to allow me to learn to drive. . . I am afraid that is not the truth. She does not enjoy driving, but she does not mind me doing so, and she would never prevent me learning if she believed me in safe hands. . .'

'Ah.' Jervais's expression was now unreadable, but she had the strangest feeling she had disappointed him. He released her hand. 'So why do you not want me to teach you to drive?'

'Well, I was afraid I had sounded as though I were angling for you to offer to teach me,' Caroline improvised feebly.

'Not at all,' he assured her firmly, moving the team into a walk again. 'You gave me no such impression and I am delighted to have found something I can do that would give you pleasure.'

There was no response to that other than to accept gracefully, but the seemingly innocuous words evoked that heady moment in his arms in his room in Brussels. Her cheeks were flaming and Caroline turned her betraying face away from him as she fought to regain her composure, a task made more difficult by the knowledge that she was blushing, not out of maidenly shame, but because she wanted to relive that moment when he had invited her to his bed.

'Is your new home in good hunting country?' she finally managed to ask before the silence became oppressive.

'Moderately good, although the coverts have been neglected—my cousin was not remotely interested in the chase. If I hunt this autumn, I intend to join some friends in a rented hunting box in Leicestershire.'

If! Why could he not be more definite about his plans? Then at least she would have the comfort of knowing he would soon be safely away. Her memories of Belgium seemed dreamlike and unreal, despite having the flesh and blood man sitting beside her: knowing what was the right thing to do, the safe way to behave, was far more difficult than she had imagined.

'No doubt you are like my brother and not over-fond of balls and parties,' she said lightly, trying to keep the conversation going along a safe path yet test how likely he was to stay in London. 'Will we be seeing you at Almack's, perhaps?' The thought of Jervais in satin knee breaches, submitting meekly to the scrutiny of the starchy patronesses, was an unlikely one. Nor could she imagine him performing a quadrille or country dance!

'It is a distinct possibility. I enjoy dancing and have had little opportunity of recent months.' The amusement was back in his eyes as he sensed her surprise. 'The Duchess of Richmond's ball was the last occasion.'

'You were there, too?' Caroline asked in amazement. There was no good reason for her surprise: every officer in the vicinity who could be spared had been at that glittering dance on the eve of Waterloo.

'Indeed, I was.' He looked at her, speculation in his eyes. 'How strange that we should not have met then and been introduced.'

'Surely not, it was such a crush! And no doubt, like the other officers, you had to leave early.' Was it coincidence or was he leading the conversation at every turn back to Belgium, back to their first encounter? 'But it is a coincidence that you should know Major Gresham and we should meet in London.'

'And it is always so important to be properly introduced,' he added smoothly. 'Are you cold? You are shivering?'

He was too acute, too aware of her for comfort. 'The air is a little chilly, perhaps we should return.'

Jervais turned the team out of the park and into the busy traffic of Oxford Street. Caroline felt an enormous relief now his attention was off her and concentrated upon negotiating the throng of carriages and pedestrians making their way home as the day drew in.

'I have kept you out too long, Miss Franklin,' he remarked, his eyes still on the road.

So, he was as aware of her as she was of him. 'Not at all,' she protested. 'Why should you think that?'

'You sighed just then. If you are not tired, is anything wrong? Perhaps I can help.' Jervais sounded warm and concerned and the temptation to admit that she remembered everything that had passed between them in June and end this tense charade was almost overwhelming. She wanted to be friends with him, perhaps when they knew each other better, more than that...

No, she pulled herself together sharply, he was a gentleman. If he knew she remembered, then he would have no choice but to marry her and she would never know whether it was his free choice or not.

'No, nothing is wrong,' Caroline replied stiffly. 'And I hope I would never presume to trouble a mere acquaintance with my concerns.'

They had reached the house in Brook Street as she spoke. Jervais reined in the bays and sat looking down at her. 'But I hope I may become more than a mere acquaintance before much longer.'

He was not to be rebuffed. Caroline was used to suppressing pretension with a few cool words, but Lord Barnard was too self-assured to be fobbed off like a callow youth.

The footman was running down the steps to help her down, but neither Jervais nor Caroline noticed him. Jervais picked up her gloved hand and held it for such a long moment that she raised her eyes to his in confusion. As she did so he lifted her fingers to his lips and brushed them lightly.

Caroline felt her own fingers tighten in his and recalled herself hastily. Compared with what had passed between them in Belgium this was insignificant, yet her heart was beating and she could hardly formulate a few polite words of thanks for the drive.

'When may I call again?' he enquired as she reached the flagstones safely and glanced up at him.

'I. . . I do not know. I cannot say what our plans are now my great-aunt is in Town. But if we are not at home when you call, we may, after all, meet at Almack's.'

'Miss Franklin? It's a cold wind, Miss. . .' The footman was patiently waiting with the front door open. Caroline realised she was standing gazing down the street after Jervais as he skilfully took the corner into David Street.

Really! She must be losing her senses! Caroline gave herself a brisk mental shake and passed through the front door with a word of thanks to the footman. What if someone were to see her standing like a moonstruck girl in a public street?

'Is Lady Grey at home, William?' she enquired, handing him her hat and gloves and drifting towards the sitting room.

'Not yet, Miss Franklin. She sent to say she would probably be late at Lady Lloyd's and not to wait dinner for her.'

That was a relief. She would not have to face Flora's enquiries until she had reduced the drive to a commonplace incident she could speak of comfortably. None the less she felt a pang of guilt at the thought of her young aunt having to endure single-handed the interrogations of Aunt Lloyd.

Caroline sat down on the sofa with the book of poems and a paperknife to cut the pages. Half an hour later, when the tea tray was brought up, she realised with a start that they still remained uncut and her thoughts were quite elsewhere.

CHAPTER FIVE

Lord Barnard called at Brook Street on three occasions over the next fortnight, finding the ladies not at home on two and engaged with an animated tea-party on the third.

Caroline, who had looked for him in vain on the several occasions she had danced at Almack's, could not help but feel piqued that he had not called more frequently, although for a recent acquaintance his behaviour was most correct.

She no longer suffered from the fevered dreams which had come every night in the months following her return from Brussels. Now the real man was close he was filling her waking thoughts and disturbing her equilibrium in a way she found difficult to counter. The nagging mystery of how she had come to wake up beside him in that barn remained but Caroline was learning, for her own peace of mind, not to dwell on it.

When Jervais finally found them at home, ten days after the drive in the park, she was in the act of passing a cup of tea to Miss Babbage, a serious-minded debutante with somewhat of a reputation as a bluestocking.

'Lord Barnard, my lady,' Dorking the butler announced, causing Caroline to spill tea into the saucer as Flora shot her a meaningful look.

'Lord Barnard, what a pleasure,' Flora beamed, rising to shake hands. 'May I hope you will join us for tea? Whom may I make known to you?'

As her aunt performed the introductions, Caroline noticed that beside her Miss Babbage, bluestocking or no, was not immune to the arrival of a good-looking man. There was a slight pink tinge to her complexion as she patted her curls and her face fell a little as, the introductions complete, Lord Barnard took himself and his tea-cup to join Major Gresham at the window.

Caroline watched Jervais discreetly under cover of handing round a dish of almond macaroons. She rather regretted that as he was no longer a serving officer he could not wear the uniform of the Eleventh Light Dragoons that suited him so well. But there was no doubting that the coat of dark blue superfine cloth showed off his broad shoulders to admiration and his long, well-muscled legs could stand the fashion for tight trousers better than many gentlemen.

Caroline turned in her chair to place the empty plate on a side table and was startled to find Jervais at her side. 'You have given them all away,' he said, low-voiced. 'And almond macaroons are quite my favourite.'

'How did you know,' she said without thinking, her eyes flying to his face, 'when you were not even looking?'

He seemed not to notice the implication that she had been covertly watching him. 'But how could I be unaware of the presence in the room of my favourite . . .delicacy?' he asked gravely.

'You are teasing me, Lord Barnard,' Caroline riposted. 'I do not believe you gentlemen really care for such sweetmeats, but to test you I shall ring for more—and I shall expect you to eat several!'

The chair beside Caroline was free, Miss Babbage having joined Flora to admire some new prints. 'May I?' He scarcely waited for her murmur of agreement before dropping into it. A long silence ensued, long enough to goad Caroline into speech.

'You are very silent, my lord!'

'I do beg your pardon, Miss Franklin, I was not aware you were desirous of conversation and I was preoccupied in anticipation of the macaroons. You notice I dare give you a hint that you have not called for more as you promised.'

'Why come and sit by me if you do not wish to converse?' she demanded, tugging the bellpull, too rattled to be polite. 'And do not say it is because of biscuits!'

'For the pleasure of your company, Miss Franklin, why else?' He smiled, white teeth mocking her.

'Yet you do not wish to talk to me?'

'Being near you is enough,' Jervais replied blandly.

What game was he playing with her? Perhaps he was just determined to tease her. Taking a firm hold on her temper which was rising dangerously, Caroline managed a sweet smile and enquired, 'Are you by any chance flirting with me, my lord?'

'I never flirt, Miss Franklin. I would scarce know how. You behold in me just a bluff soldier, unused to feminine company.' He managed such a look of pained innocence that Caroline nearly choked on her tea. Unused to feminine company, indeed! She had never come across anyone who seemed more familiar with it! She suppressed a snort of indignation.

'Miss Franklin, I fear you are laughing at me,' Jervais reproached her.

'Indeed I am,' she responded, smiling despite herself. 'I have never heard such a tarradiddle: I am certain you have laid siege to the hearts of young ladies across the length and breadth of Europe.'

'But never one like you...Caroline.' He had dropped his voice so that they could not be heard and the ring of sincerity sent a shiver down her spine. She could not even reproach him for using her Christian name.

'Lord Barnard...'

'Jervais, please.'

'Really, my lord, I could never address you so...'

'Never? Very well, as you wish, but I shall call you

Caroline when we are driving. I cannot shout at you if I have to address you as Miss Franklin in every sentence.'

'Shout at me!' Caroline was indignant. 'And why, pray, should you shout at me?'

'I shall have no compunction if you jab my horses' mouths or take my hat off with the whip!'

'Then I shall not come out with you! I shall ask Cousin Frederick to be my tutor.'

'Without wishing in any way to be disrespectful of a relative of yours, I have to tell you that he is cow-handed to a degree.' Try as she could, Caroline could not school her mouth to the expression of severity his levity deserved. 'And there is also the consideration that I do not believe you would willingly be alone with your cousin.'

'And I would have no such compunction with you, sir?' Caroline's chin came up challengingly.

'You have shown none in our acquaintanceship thus far.' He reached for a macaroon whilst keeping his eyes on her face.

The colour flooding her cheeks, she said, 'How could. . .?' before she checked herself, realising she had nearly betrayed herself fatally. He could not, surely, have intended such a blatant reference to what had passed between them in Belgium? 'I cannot feel that one drive alone in the park can be taken as an indication of my willingness to be alone with you, Lord Barnard.'

'As you would have it. These macaroons really are excellent. Would you consider me totally without self-control if I asked for another?'

He was laughing at her, she was sure, although his face betrayed nothing beyond polite enquiry.

'I am certain your self-control is beyond reproach, my lord.' Caro said waspishly. 'Now, if you will forgive me, I must see to my other guests.'

The party began to disperse soon afterwards, the young ladies casting demure glances at Lord Barnard as they went. Caroline, watching them with well-concealed irritation, remarked quietly to Flora, 'All off to tell their mamas to add a new name to their invitation lists, no doubt!'

Flora arched her brows. 'My dear Caroline, I do declare you are jealous.'

Before Caroline could riposte, Major Gresham and Lord Barnard came to take their leave.

'I have a favour to ask you, Lady Grey,' Jervais said, bowing over her hand.

'Indeed, sir?' Flora, warmed and flattered by the affectionate attentiveness of her beau at her side, was inclined to be gracious.

'I was hoping for your permission to teach Miss Franklin to drive. I believe she is desirous of learning and I imagine her brother has little leisure at present.'

'What an excellent scheme! If you are certain it would not be an imposition. . .?'

Jervais bowed slightly. 'It would be a pleasure, ma'am.'

'I see no objection. What is your opinion, Major?'

'I am entirely of your view. There is no man in London at present with a better pair of hands.'

'You flatter me, sir.'

The Major noticed with amusement Miss Franklin's delicate blush and downcast eyes. So, his beloved Flora was quite correct in her belief these two would make a match of it. So much the better! He was having the devil's own job to persuade Flora to agree to marry him while her niece was unattached.

'You will use only a quiet horse—and not a high-perch phaeton?' Flora asked anxiously.

'You may rest assured. Miss Franklin has told me how nervous you are of open carriages. I would do nothing to alarm you, or to put Miss Franklin in danger.'

Caroline shot him a darkling glance which he blandly ignored. Flora, unaware she was supposed to be nervous in carriages, merely looked somewhat puzzled at this solicitude for her nerves.

'Shall we say tomorrow at ten, Miss Franklin? If the weather is fine we can go to Richmond Park where it will be quieter for you.'

'That will be delightful, my lord.' Caroline recognised when she was beaten.

The next morning dawned bright and sunny, dashing Caroline's craven hope that poor weather would postpone her first lesson. Yet despite her qualms at being once more alone with Jervais, she could not suppress a frisson of excitement at the memory of his hands on hers last time they drove together.

She again wore the dark green costume, this time with a pert curl-brimmed hat newly delivered from Miss Millington's emporium. It was a fetching deep gold in colour with no feather to tangle in her whip and a coarse veil to shield her complexion from the wind.

Flora, pausing on the landing on her way to inspect the linen cupboard, walked round her niece tweaking invisible creases from the soft fabric. 'There!' she announced, just as Caroline was reaching the limits of her patience. 'You look charming. Now, do you have those new tan gloves? Will you be warm enough? It would be a shame to spoil this outfit by having to wear a mantle.'

'Flora, please! I am simply going for a drive, not being presented at Court!' Caroline reined in her fraying temper and managed a conciliatory smile, recognising it was not her aunt who was responsible for this irritation of her nerves. 'I shall be quite warm enough: the wind has dropped since yesterday.'

Any further conversation was curtailed by the sound of the knocker. Caroline, anxious that Lord Barnard should not come in and be engaged by Flora in a conversation which might prove embarrassing, caught up her skirt and was almost out of the door before she called back, 'Goodbye, Flora!'

She paused on the step to catch her breath and saw Jervais half rising from his seat. 'Please do not get down, my lord,' she said, nodding her thanks to the groom who was now handing her into the carriage.

'Thank you, Cooper, there are no errands this morning,' Jervais said, dismissing the groom who touched his hat with one finger before walking off down Brook Street. 'Once more you are most prompt, Miss Franklin, and, if I may say so, in great beauty.'

Behind the veil, which did nothing to conceal the slight flush which mounted to her cheeks, he saw her flash him a quick glance, half-flattered, half-suspicious.

'If I am prompt, sir, it is because I am looking forward to my lesson and do not wish to keep your horses standing.' She could think of no suitable rejoinder to his blatant flattery, so ignored it. 'That is a very fine pair of bays: have you had them long?'

'They were one of the few possessions of my late cousin which showed any sign of taste or discrimination!' Jervais's eyes narrowed as he concentrated on a corner partly obstructed by an approaching coal wagon. 'They are rather more docile than I would have chosen for myself, but that makes them ideal for our purpose today.'

As if to belie his words the nearside horse shied violently as the coal heaver tipped his sack down a coalhole in the pavement with a rush and a cloud of dust.

'Steady!' Jervais skilfully reined in the nervous animal.

'Perhaps they are fresher than I realised. But the drive down to Richmond will shake the fidgets out of them, there is no need to be nervous.'

Caroline, who had neither shifted in her seat, nor grasped the side of the carriage, replied composedly, 'I am not at all nervous, my lord.'

She was conscious of his narrowed, sideways glance which seemed to convey more than mere approval. 'I think it would take a good deal to rattle you, Caro.'

He had used the one word above all he could have chosen to rattle her. 'No one but my family ever calls me Caro, sir,' she said coldly. Her heart was beating uncomfortably hard at the memory of the hay bed in the barn and Jervais spelling out her name from the jewels in her ring.

Involuntarily she glanced down at her had, but she had left the ring off that morning before pulling on her tight-fitting gloves so as not to stretch the leather.

'And was it your brother who gave you your ring?' he asked casually, his eyes fixed on the road ahead as they neared the river crossing.

'My ring?' Caroline said feebly.

'The one you usually wear on your middle finger with the stones which spell CARO,' he said patiently.

'How observant you are, sir.' Caroline swallowed hard, half fearing the moment had come when he would drop the pretence that they had never met in Belgium.

'I notice everything about you, Caroline.' That statement was unanswerable. There was a long silence while she contemplated telling him once again to stop addressing her by her first name, then she gave up: he would take no notice. And besides, she liked the sound of it on his lips: it was a dangerous, indulgent pleasure.

By the time they reached the entrance to the park and Jervais reined in to show his ticket of admission to the keeper at the gate the bays were trotting calmly without a sign of skittishness.

Caroline looked round admiringly at the rolling grass, still verdant under the autumnal trees. 'Richmond Park always puts me in mind of the countryside around our home at Longford; I never tire of coming here.'

A group of strollers admiring a small herd of fallow deer was visible under the nearest stand of trees. Further off another phaeton bowled along one of the numerous carriageways which crisscrossed the parkland, but otherwise they seemed to be alone.

When they were well into the park and away from the entrance, Jervais reined in the horses.

'Now, have you ever driven a pair before?' He shifted on the seat to look at her, his manner serious now he had begun to teach.

'No, only a pony in a dog cart about the estate—I told you about that.'

'It will take a little time to become accustomed to the feel of two sets of reins. Here, hold them thus.' He handed her the reins, adjusting them until she could feel the gentle tension from the horses' mouths to her hands.

Caroline had expected to be very conscious of the touch of his fingers on her own, but in the event was concentrating so hard on his instructions and the horses, it was no more disturbing than if her brother were her tutor.

Following his directions, she allowed the pair to move forward in a gentle walk whilst she concentrated on the signals she was receiving from the animals: it felt very strange to be controlling two animals after dear old Rollo who plodded obediently along the lanes of Longford which he knew better than she did.

For half an hour Caroline walked the team around the park, totally absorbed in what she was doing, scarcely aware of the man by her side except as a reassuring presence. She was quite oblivious that he watched her face as much as her hands, smiling as she caught her lower lip between white teeth in concentration or muttered instructions to herself under her breath.

So intent was she that when he spoke she jumped slightly and the nearside horse jibbed.

'You look quite fierce, Caroline,' Jervais said, sounding amused.

'I know,' she admitted ruefully. 'It is a very bad habit. Vivian tells me I scowl horribly when I am concentrating and Flora warns me I shall have dreadful lines by the time I am five and twenty.'

'An unlikely prospect,' Jervais murmured, looking unashamedly at the smooth skin of her brow. 'Here, give me the reins for a while. You will find you are more tired than you imagine.'

'Indeed, I am quite stiff,' Caroline exclaimed, easing her shoulders with relief and flexing her fingers as he took back control of the horses. 'I had no notion it would prove so taxing.'

'You must learn to relax both your hands—indeed, your whole body—or you will become very tired.'

This reference to her form was quite unseemly and Caroline reacted sharply. 'That is a most improper remark to address to me, my lord!'

'Either I will teach you to drive as I would teach a man, Caroline, or I will not teach you at all!' His voice was curt. 'I had believed you an intelligent woman. . .'

'I am!' she said indignantly.

'Then you must understand that it would be unsafe to modify my tuition to compensate for your sex. Unless, of course, you were not serious in wishing to drive a pair.'

Caroline flushed at the open rebuke. His good opinion was important to her. 'My lord. . .'

'Can I not persuade you to call me Jervais, at least whilst we are alone?' He still sounded irritated with her, which perversely made his request seem innocuous: he certainly was not flirting now!

'Very well, Jervais,' she capitulated, 'but only whilst I am having my lessons.'

'But of course,' he said smoothly, bowing slightly. 'Now, are you fatigued, or would you like to try trotting?'

The increased pace was invigorating and seemed quite safe on the smooth, straight track with Jervais at her side, only occasionally now intervening to correct her handling of the reins.

Looking back on it afterwards, Caroline realised she had become over-confident, that her concentration had become blunted by the novelty of the experience.

'There is a bend approaching,' Jervais cautioned, 'steady them now as I showed you.'

But Caroline hardly heard him. The team seemed steady under her hands and the bend looked innocuous enough to take with scarcely a check. Perhaps it would have been if it were not for the sudden eruption of a stag from a thicket of thorn on the apex of the curve just as Jervais said sharply, 'I said steady!'

The horses shied violently, breaking into a canter, sending the phaeton swaying dangerously around the bend. Jervais grabbed for the reins, but in trying to release them, Caroline let them go and they fell to the floor of the carriage in a tangled heap.

Without any control the pair bolted in earnest, throwing both Caroline and Jervais violently to the left. Caroline seized hold of the side with both hands as Jervais flung one arm across her to keep her in her seat. With his free hand he scooped up the reins, struggling to order them and control the frightened bays.

The entire episode could only have occupied the

space of thirty seconds before he had the carriage at a standstill, the horses still restless and sweating between the shafts.

Caroline found both her hands were clenched on the carriage side and she could not seem to let go.

Jervais jumped down, looping the reins over the branch of a nearby tree before coming to stand and look up at her. 'You can let go now.' His voice was half-teasing, but Caroline could see the concern in his eyes.

'That is simpler to say than to do,' she said unsteadily, summoning up a smile. Jervais gently prised her fingers free and held out his arms to lift her down.

'Come down and walk a little, it will steady your nerves. Come, Caro, I know you well enough to believe you will not let this overset you.' He took her firmly by the waist and Caroline let herself be lifted down.

As her feet touched the ground, her knees gave way and she sagged slightly in his arms. 'It is not my nerves that need steadying, but my legs,' she jested, not entirely successfully, irritated with herself for behaving so weakly.

Jervais tightened his embrace, holding her close. He was no longer simply supporting her. She became very conscious of the warmth of his closeness and her hands, already resting on his shoulders, tightened of their own accord as her eyes travelled up slowly to meet his. Being in his arms felt natural, right, as did his kiss when it came.

His lips on hers were gentle, almost tentative, as though he expected her to draw back. Instead her mouth softened, yielded to the familiarity of his lips, welcoming the kiss she had been dreaming of for months.

Jervais broke away and looked questioningly at her upturned face. Caroline smiled back, warmed by the tenderness she saw in his expression. She knew she should draw back, rebuke him for taking advantage of her weakness, but instead she caught his hand and raised it to her cheek.

He needed no further invitation, catching her hard against him, crushing her lips under his in an uncompromising kiss which sapped the remaining resistance from her body.

All thoughts of propriety, prudent behaviour or the probable consequences of their actions fled. Caroline kissed him back with an ardour born of all those restless nights when she had thought she would never see him again, yet his face and the memory of his lips had haunted her sleep.

How long they would have stood there locked in each other's arms she did not know—perhaps forever—if a loud voice had not caused them to spring apart.

'You will observe, gentlemen, this fine example of the puff-ball, *Lycoperdon giganteum*, as Lineus would have it.'

Caroline, frantically straightening her veil, caught sight of the expression on Jervais's face and, despite the mortification of her situation, could scarcely suppress a bubble of hysterical laughter.

'This is quite a small specimen: I see your surprise, gentlemen, but the giant puff-ball may reach the size of a man's head.' The speaker emerged from the far side of the thicket, revealing himself to be an elderly clergyman, carrying a wicker basket and leading a small group of soberly dressed young men, obviously undergraduates.

'Sir, madam! Good morning to you! And what a fine morning it is, too!' Undeterred by the frigid politeness of Jervais's bow he turned to his party. 'No doubt we are in the presence of fellow enthusiasts: see, they are admiring a most handsome specimen of the bracket fungus which, gentlemen, as you know, is most commonly to be found on the beech tree.'

'Indeed, yes,' Caroline responded warmly. 'I have rarely seen a finer at this time of year, although I am only a simple amateur.'

The clergyman, encouraged to find a fellow enthusiast, was intent on showing Caroline the contents of his basket containing the spoils of the expedition when Jervais took her firmly by the arm. 'My apologies, sir, but we have a most pressing luncheon engagement. Good day to you.'

As soon as they were out of sight of the fungus foray, Jervais reined in the horses and let out a great shout of laughter. Caroline was laughing, too, the tears running down her face and it was a few moments before they both sobered.

The silence which followed was uneasy. Jervais let the bays walk on before commenting lightly, 'Rarely can a young lady have had a more effective chaperon than a clergyman and three scholars!'

'They should not have been necessary! I cannot believe I permitted...that we could...' Caroline was deeply shaken by what had happened, by the intensity of the feeling his touch had evoked. She could not voice the true fear that shook her: that he would suppose her to remember everything that had passed between them before. Yet if she did not remember then her response to him was even more outrageously forward. She was caught on the horns of a dilemma: all she could do was to express what any well-bred young woman would under the circumstances.

Her colour high, she said stiffly, 'I cannot account for my recent behaviour, sir, other than to say I must have been more shaken by the incident with the horses than I had supposed, but I must tell you that such conduct is very foreign to my nature.' And why should I alone feel so guilty? she thought indignantly, after all, he kissed me first. 'And as to your actions, sir...'

There was a short pause, then Jervais said coldly,

'Entirely inexcusable, Miss Franklin. I can only attribute it to my relief at discovering that you were unharmed.' Caroline could sense that only his good breeding was restraining him from challenging her with the knowledge of what had passed between them in Belgium. More than ever she was convinced that he knew she could remember, but the more intimate their relationship became, perversely the more difficult it was to admit it.

'We will say no more about it,' Caroline declared firmly, turning the conversation to the scenery they were driving through. To her relief Jervais followed her lead but the conversation was still constrained and impersonal when they arrived back at Brook Street. Caroline, despite the calming effects of social conversation, was still overwhelmingly preoccupied with what had passed. Her heart fluttered uncomfortably and she could not bring herself to look at Jervais.

As the alert footman opened the front door, Flora descended the steps. 'My dear, have you had a successful lesson? Thank you, Lord Barnard, for taking such good care of Caroline. I cannot permit you to leave us without refreshment—will you not join us? A light collation awaits in the dining room.'

To Caroline's amazement, Jervais accepted with alacrity. 'Thank you, ma'am, that would be delightful. If your footman would direct me to the stables, I will join you as soon as maybe.'

As he handed her down from the carriage Caroline gave him a reproachful, speaking look, scarcely able to credit that he would wish to join them after what had occurred. To her embarrassment Jervais not only did not take the hint, but challenged her directly.

'Come now, Caroline: if you do not wish to see me again after what has just passed between us, you must say so and that will be an end to it. However, such an action is bound to cause much unwelcome speculation. . .'

Furiously, she whispered, 'If you were a gentle-man...'

'If I were not a gentleman, Caroline, I would take what was offered to me—as well you know.' His voice was harsh, his eyes angry, although his words were too low to reach the ears of Lady Grey waiting at the front door.

'I have no idea what you mean, my lord—and I have no wish to find out!' Caroline turned on her heel and marched angrily into the house, hot colour staining her cheeks.

Flora observed the signs of fury with concern. 'Caroline, have you quarrelled with Lord Barnard? Tell me quickly before he returns from the mews.'

'Yes, I have quarrelled with him! The man is insuf-ferable!' Caroline stripped off her gloves and flung them on the hall table. Knowing she was as much in the wrong as Jervais did nothing to temper her anger, and the thought of taking luncheon with him was almost insupportable.

'What occurred?' Flora was concerned. 'Please tell me, dear; you were so happy when you left here this morning.'

'He...' She could hardly say he had kissed her, and she had liked it, had responded. 'He shouted at me!' She knew she sounded petulant, almost childlike.

'Oh dear, what did you do wrong? Gentlemen do worry so about their horses! I remember Lord Grey became apoplectic if anyone jabbed the mouths of his favourite pair...'

'But, Flora!' Caroline was shocked that her aunt would readily accept such behaviour.

Flora took her by the arm and smoothed her sleeve. 'All men are difficult about something, dear. You are very young. You will discover that there is something about even the most perfect of men to be tolerated. If you and Lord Barnard were to become...that is to say. . .' She became hopelessly entangled in her own explanation and broke off, slightly flushed.

'I should have known you would be on his side, Flora! I am going to my room to wash my hands and brush my hair.'

When Caroline entered the dining room, Jervais was sitting chatting to Flora with every appearance of ease. 'I was just telling Lady Grey of our disturbing incident this morning,' he said smoothly as he stood up.

Caroline was speechless: surely he had not told Flora of the kiss!

'Do sit down, Caroline,' Flora chided, 'do not keep Lord Barnard standing.'

'What has Lord Barnard been telling you?' she finally managed to ask between stiff lips.

'Why, naturally I told Lady Grey about the stag and the horses bolting. I would not wish to conceal anything from her as she has entrusted your safety to me. After all, she may not wish me to take you out again.'

Caroline was mercifully saved from replying by Flora's interjection. 'My dear Lord Barnard, such a thought had not crossed my mind. Such an incident could have happened to anyone. The fact that Caroline is safely home proves you are just the person to take care of her and to teach her to drive.' She looked reprovingly at her niece. 'Caroline, do pass Lord Barnard the cold chicken.'

The meal passed pleasantly enough. Caroline called on all her reserves of social training and courtesy to make tolerable conversation. After a while she relaxed, finding Jervais a warm and witty guest. With Flora as chaperon, Caroline felt safe from the undercurrents that made conversation so dangerous when they were alone.

Jervais was scrupulous in his attention to both ladies, but Caroline felt he was speaking only to her, that he admired her conversation and opinions as much as her looks. When finally he rose to leave she was warmed and flattered and quite off guard.

Flora insisted Caroline see him to the door while she remained in the drawing-room.

Reaching the hall, Caroline found the normally ubiquitous footman was quite absent. Below stairs had quite as good an idea of what was taking place as their masters upstairs and the servants knew when to make themselves scarce.

Caroline clicked her tongue in annoyance and turned to the bell pull, but Jervais caught her hand. 'No, wait. I must talk to you.'

She looked up at him questioningly. 'Indeed, we have not set another time for a lesson: if you are willing to risk your horses once again, that is!' She was still lulled by the mood of the meal, quite unprepared for what he said next.

His fingers tightened on hers, compelling her attention. 'Never mind the lessons, Caroline, there are more important things we have to discuss.'

'I do not understand you, sir.' She was perplexed, but made no attempt to free her hand from his.

'Why do you not trust me, Caroline?' he urged.

'But I do, Jervais,' she replied, puzzled by his intensity. 'If you mean what occurred this morning, why I am at least as much to blame as you and I intend to put it quite from my mind—have I not just said I wish to drive with you again?'

'Caroline, stop! That is not what I mean and you know it! There is that between us that must be spoken of openly.'

Caroline freed her hand abruptly and stepped back from him, suddenly aware of the pit yawning at her feet. He was referring to Belgium; he must be going to make her a declaration because—and only because—of what had happened there.

She did not want him to propose because of that,

simply because he had compromised her and now must do his duty. No, it was his love she wanted because she realised, with a clarity that shocked her, she was in love with Jervais Barnard.

Somehow she must convince him that she had no recollection of their ever having met before Major Gresham had brought him to the house in Brook Street. If he believed that, then she might be sure that he was courting her out of love, not duty.

'I have no idea to what you are referring, Jervais,' she forced herself to meet his eyes and speak lightly. 'I declare you are being quite Gothick with your hints of mystery.'

Jervais watched her between narrowed lids. Then his face relaxed and he shook his head slightly. 'As you will.' When he spoke again, it was almost as if to himself. 'Perhaps I was imagining things. . .'

'You are very mysterious, sir,' Caroline said lightly, almost flirtatiously, prepared to use feminine wiles to her own ends. Inside she felt an enormous tide of relief, so sure was she that she had finally convinced him that she remembered nothing.

He took her hand and kissed her fingertips lightly. 'Until tomorrow at the same time? Shall we say Green Park for your next lesson? We will be safe from both stags and clergymen there.'

CHAPTER SIX

IT MIGHT have been supposed that for a young woman to discover herself to be in love with an eminently eligible man, who in his turn was paying her the most marked attentions, would have been the pinnacle of her happiness.

But it was not so for Caroline, left alone with her thoughts. Major Gresham called to escort Flora to an exhibition at the Royal Academy, but even the promise of a new work by Mr Constable was not enough to tempt her to accompany them. Pleading tiredness after her lesson she took the new volume of Lord Byron's poetry into the small sitting room intending to peruse it.

'This will not do!' she admonished herself out loud, after several minutes had passed without a poem read or a page turned. 'What good will it achieve to sit here moping? It is no use to wish Jervais and I had never met in Belgium: we did and there's an end to it!'

However, such rallying thoughts were of no practical help to Caroline in her dilemma. Surely Jervais had some tender feelings towards her for him to look at her with such warmth in his eyes, to hold her hands in his, to kiss her with a passion which even now made her head spin? But then she remembered the other embraces, the kisses he had pressed on her, and the circumstances in which they had taken place.

There was no question of love and tender feelings then! Why, he had thought her a lightskirt and had been quite prepared to take advantage of the fact. Jervais was a man of the world, of strong passions, who had hazarded his life across Europe. Of a certainty, he had not lived like a monk and was unlikely to behave like one now.

Perhaps in her innocence she was refining too much on the passion of his kiss in Richmond Park. She could hardly ask Flora how a gentleman behaved when alone with his inamorata—her aunt would be deeply shocked to discover that the slightest intimacy had taken place, even though she made no secret of her approval of Jervais as a suitor.

This is getting me no further forward, Caroline scolded herself, forcing herself to consider all the possibilities. At worst Jervais could be nothing but a heartless rake bent on completing the seduction he had begun in Belgium, at best he was in love with her and what had passed between them after Waterloo had no influence on his actions now.

But it was the middle course that seemed most likely: that Jervais found her attractive enough, no more, and it was only his sense of duty that was prompting him to pay court to her. And given that she was in love with Jervais Barnard, this was a most melancholy thought.

By the time Flora and her major had returned, bickering amicably about the differing merits of the paintings they had been to Somerset House to see, Caroline had argued herself into a mood of cheerful determination. Drooping about at home would not solve the riddle of Jervais's true feelings; she was resolved to put all her doubts behind her and enjoy his company. Surely, as she came to know him better, she would learn to read his heart?

'Shall we go to Almack's this evening, Flora?' she asked, as her aunt rang for the butler and they sat to await the tea tray.

'Why yes, although I should prefer to have a gentleman to escort us and you know Vivian finds it such a bore.'

'May I offer my services?' Major Gresham enquired hopefully.

'Why, Anthony, I thought you were on duty tonight.' Flora was almost coy.

'No. Did I not tell you? After today's parade, I am released from duty for an entire week. Seven days which I intend to devote solely to the entertainment of both you ladies.'

But despite his words, it was obvious that Flora's enjoyment was his prime concern. Nor was her aunt unhappy at the prospect: her cheeks were flushed and her downcast eyes were shining. Caroline was suddenly impatient with this staid courtship: why did he not make Flora a declaration and be done with it? It was obvious they were deeply in love and neither had reason to delay the marriage.

Flora's party arrived early at Almack's. The rooms were somewhat thin of company and only one of the patronesses, the formidable Mrs Drummond Burrell, was to be seen.

They had extracted a reluctant promise from Vivian to join them later. 'Now do not forget the doors shut at eleven,' Caroline had reminded him. 'And those pantaloons will not do! Dress uniform or knee breeches or you will be denied admittance.'

'Very well,' he sighed. 'But you know I find the entertainment insipid: the stakes at the tables are so paltry.'

'Chicken stakes, I agree,' his sister commiserated. 'But think of all the delightful young ladies you will meet, Vivian.'

Her teasing was met with a dark glance. 'And all their delightful mamas as well, no doubt.'

As the major had handed the ladies into the carriage to take them the short distance to King Street, Caroline remarked, 'I do wish Vivian would find himself a nice girl—he shows not the slightest inclination to settle down.'

'There's time yet,' the major said tolerantly. 'He is enjoying himself in the army, time enough to settle down.'

Caroline watched the young ladies chatting and deploying their fans as the rooms gradually filled, reflecting that she could think of no one who was ideal for her brother. Now in her third season, she was no longer a debutante, and she was permitted more latitude than the wide-eyed girls, overawed to find themselves in the heart of the *ton*, but with all the tolerance she could muster, they still seemed an insipid group.

So deep was she in thought that when a man spoke low-voiced behind her, she took it to be Major Gresham. 'Why so pensive, Miss Franklin?'

'I suppose I should not worry about Vivian, but none of those girls would make him a suitable wife, you know.'

'Why does your mind run so on nuptials?' It was Lord Barnard at her side, not the Major. Caroline caught her breath at the unexpectedness of it.

'Oh, all sisters matchmake for their brothers, sir!' she responded in rallying tones. 'Do your sisters not do so for you?'

'Unhappily I have none.' He sounded not in the least regretful.

'Nor brothers either?' Caroline turned, giving him her full attention, blue eyes wide on his face.

'No, no brothers.'

'Then you are quite alone? How sad.' She could not imagine being without the warmth of Flora and Vivian around her.

Jervais regarded her solemn face with some amusement at the intensity which brought a slight crease between her dark brows. 'Do not frown so on my account, Miss Franklin, I entreat you! Remember your aunt's warnings about wrinkles.' But even as he teased her he found it hard to imagine anything ever marring the beauty of her creamy skin.

'Why, my lord, you are not at all polite to speak of wrinkles! You remind me I am in my third season and at my last prayers.' A smile tugged at her mouth: they were both quite well aware that she was looking her best that evening, her slender figure set off by a gown of cream net over an under-dress of jonquil yellow silk.

'Indeed, I had no idea you were so decayed! I am surprised you do not take your place on the chaperons' bench. And why do you not wear a cap? Surely such an elderly lady. . .'

'Sir! You are ungallant!'

Jervais smiled back at her mock outrage. 'I protest, I was only deferring to your age, as you make much of it.'

Caroline was caught by his eyes and the warmth of admiration in them. He was still tanned, his face fined by the pain of his wound, and his bearing was military: she was aware of the quickening of her pulse and an unworthy feeling of satisfaction that all the other young ladies in the room were green with envy because she had his attention.

The orchestra struck up a waltz and Jervais held out his hands. 'Will you dance, Caroline?'

His arm was strong around her waist and she was very conscious of the closeness of him. The waltz was so familiar to her that normally she thought nothing of it, but suddenly it was as though this was the first time she had performed the daring dance with a man.

She forced herself to relax and let him guide her confidently through the other couples crowding the floor, but she found it impossible to raise her eyes above the level of his shirt front.

'Have I offended you in some way?' he enquired as her silence stretched on.

'Why, no!' Caroline looked up startled, then found herself unable to look away. If only this dance would go on forever, the circle of his arm isolating her from everyone else, the flame in his eyes warming her. 'No . . .of course not.'

'I could not attribute your silence to concern for your steps: you waltz very well. May I hope you will dance with me again this evening?'

'Yes, of course,' Caroline said, amazed to find herself slightly breathless.

'Are you not going to make even a pretence of consulting your card?' he asked her gravely.

'No.' This was ridiculous! She must find something to say—she was behaving like a gauche schoolroom miss.

Jervais continued to sweep her around the floor, apparently content to leave her to her silence. When the music drew to a conclusion and he handed her to one of the gilt chairs lining the wall, Caroline looked at her card and declared, with a fair assumption of calm, 'There, I was correct—a country dance is free after supper.'

'Ah, but a country dance will not do,' he said, low-voiced. A frisson ran down her back and she forced herself to meet his eyes. 'I will settle for nothing less than another waltz.'

'Then you must be disappointed, my lord!' Caroline rallied slightly. 'I can hardly break engagements I have already made.' Further conversation was thankfully curtailed by the arrival of her partner for the cotillion which was just forming.

When the dance was over the young man escorted her over to where Flora and the major were seated. As they approached, Anthony Gresham sprang to his feet to give Caroline his chair. Caroline curtsied to her partner as he made his apologies and left to collect the next young lady on his card, then sank down beside Flora with a little sigh.

'I declare I have not danced so much for a month.'

Flora regarded her niece's glowing face and sparkling eyes and patted her hand. 'You looked so right dancing with Lord Barnard.'

'Indeed, he is a very good dancer,' Caroline said hastily.

'That is not entirely what I meant,' her aunt replied drily. 'Has he not said anything to you?'

'Why, any amount—and most of it nonsensical this evening!' Caroline said gaily, choosing to misunderstand.

'Lady Brancaster was remarking upon his attentiveness,' Flora pursued relentlessly. 'She is not the only one who expects him to make a declaration before many more days are past.'

'Well, I am sure I have given no one any cause to think I was expecting—or encouraging—such a thing,' Caroline said hotly. The thought that she and Jervais were the object of gossip was deeply distasteful. 'Why, he pays me no attention out of the ordinary—I should be most surprised if he says another word to me all evening!'

'Then I fear you are about to be surprised,' Flora said archly. 'For here comes Lord Barnard now.'

'May I take you in to supper, Miss Franklin?' he enquired smoothly, bowing over her hand. 'I see Major Gresham intends to escort Lady Grey.'

Past his shoulder Caroline could see the Dowager Lady Brancaster regarding them beadily through her lorgnette. The polite refusal died on her lips: the old tabbies could say what they liked, she would go with him.

'It would be a pleasure, sir,' she said demurely, putting her hand in his.

'Which is more than can be said for the repast on

offer in this establishment,' Jervais remarked acidly, surveying the simple fare of cakes and bread and butter laid out before them.

'I always make the point of dining well before coming to Almack's,' Caroline agreed, accepting a glass of lemonade and a slice of sponge cake. 'I am sorry there are no almond macaroons,' she added with a mocking glint in her eyes.

'Are you not going to allow me to forget my greed? I suspect, Miss Franklin, that you are a very unforgiving person.'

Caroline put her cup down with a rattle. There was something pointed in the seemingly light-hearted comment that jarred, spoiling the mood of the evening. Could he be referring obliquely to Belgium, suggesting that she remembered and harboured a resentment about his treatment of her?

She gave herself a little shake, trying to convince herself he was only teasing, unaware that a shadow had taken the sparkle from her eyes.

'Miss Franklin?' Jervais took her hand in his, raising it to his lips for a fleeting moment, ignoring the shocked stares of several dowagers. 'Forgive me, I have put you out of countenance.'

'Well, sir, you succeed in putting me out of countenance every time we meet,' Caroline said with some asperity, freeing her hand. 'I should be used to it by now!'

'I have hopes you will become even more used to me,' he began, soft-voiced, then broke off as Vivian appeared by their side.

'Vivian!' Caroline cried. 'I had quite given you up— surely the clock has already struck eleven?'

'Indeed it has—and I arrived at one minute to the hour! Although why I troubled myself I do not know. Good evening, Barnard.' Vivian bowed to the older man, then swept a disparaging glance over the refreshments. He winced as his eye was caught by a notorious husband-hunting mama. 'Caro, I rely on you to protect me: if Lady Hilton tries once more to entrap me into dancing with that bran-faced daughter of hers, I swear I will return to Belgium forthwith!'

'Have a soothing cup of tea, Franklin,' Jervais suggested drily. 'I think you will be safe from abduction while drinking it.'

Vivian shuddered, then, surveying the other choices, decided that tea was the lesser of the evils on offer. 'I did not look to see you here, my lord,' he observed to Jervais.

'Surely your sister has told you of my addiction to dancing?' Jervais said blandly.

Vivian glanced from Caroline to Lord Barnard. 'That's all a hum if you ask me,' he remarked sceptically. 'Shan't believe that until I see you standing up for a country dance!'

'Do you doubt my word, sir?' Jervais countered lightly.

Vivian grinned. 'Yes, I do! I suspect you are like me, dragooned here by the ladies...oh lord! Here comes Lady Hilton. Excuse me, I am certain I just saw George Tomlinson—got to talk to him about a horse...' He made his escape with the agility of an eel, leaving his unfortunate sister to greet Lady Hilton.

'Oh, dear, I seem to have missed your brother, Miss Franklin.' Her ladyship was a wispy, innocuous-looking woman with a pale complexion and slight frame which belied her implacable will. It was well known she would stop at nothing to secure eligible husbands for her three daughters.

'I am so sorry, Lady Hilton, he cannot have seen you. May I introduce Lord Barnard?'

She observed with hidden amusement the calculating look which entered her ladyship's eyes as she shook hands with Jervais. As she observed later to Flora when they had returned to Brook Street, 'It was almost as if she was measuring him for his wedding clothes!'

'We have not had the pleasure of your company here at Almack's before I think, my lord,' Lady Hilton simpered, making play with her fan.

'This is the first time I have come here for several years.'

'Lord Barnard has been with Wellington's army,' Caroline supplied demurely, enjoying Jervais's efforts to deflect the lady. 'And was most seriously wounded. His friends are glad to see him out and about again, but I was just telling him, he must not overstrain himself by too much dancing. One can never tell. . .' she added darkly.

'Oh, dear,' Lady Hilton's sympathy was very perfunctory and she soon took her leave.

Jervais observed her fluttering retreat with some puzzlement. 'Did I say something to upset her?'

'No, it was my reference to your wounds, I believe. She intends, I understand, to secure only the most robust husbands for her daughters.'

'Good heavens!' Jervais raised his brows. 'Perhaps I should hurry after her and assure her that, despite your improper hints, my wounds are healed and will in no way impede my duties as a husband.'

Caroline was thrown into total confusion by this daring remark. 'Sir!' was all she managed to get out.

'Miss Franklin, you misunderstand me: I merely refer to the probability of my living to a good age. What can I have said to discommode you so?'

Caroline shut her mouth hard, aware she was blushing like a peony. Her mind was full of the memory of being in his still, shuttered bedroom, of his husky voice entreating her to come into his bed, to allow him to pleasure her . .

'Caroline, you are quite flushed. You have been dancing too hard.' It was Flora on the arm of Major

Gresham, Vivian at her side. 'Here, take my fan and cool your face.'

'I have been trying to persuade Miss Franklin to take another glass of lemonade,' Jervais remarked, taking the fan from Flora and deploying it to cool Caroline's burning cheeks.

'So kind, Lord Barnard,' Flora smiled benevolently on them, well satisfied with the way things seemed to be progressing.

'Shall we all sit down?' Jervais gestured towards an alcove near by.

When the party had settled themselves around the circular table and drinks and cake had been fetched, Jervais continued, 'I am glad to have the chance to speak to you all together, for I have a proposition which I hope may be acceptable to you. By mid-December I expect the west wing of Dunharrow, at least, to be habitable and I would be honoured if you would all consent to spend the Christmas season with me there. I intend inviting two of my brother officers who should be returned to England by then, and my cousin Serena to act as my hostess.'

'For myself and Caroline,' Flora said immediately, 'I accept with pleasure. To be in the country at that season sounds delightful and I have never been into Hampshire.' She turned to her nephew. 'Will you be able to be spared, Vivian?'

'I have already spoken to the Colonel,' he replied. 'I had intended that we go to Longford, but this sounds a capital scheme!'

'Gresham?'

'I would be delighted, Barnard; beside the pleasure of such a congenial party, I would be most interested to see the improvements you are making.' He turned to Flora. 'You remember, I was telling you that Barnard had schemes for the improvement of his agricultural land?'

'Excellent!' Jervais seemed delighted by their enthusiasm and seemed not to have noticed Caroline's silence. 'But I give you fair warning, I shall expect you all to work for your suppers: Gresham, I would value your opinion on the better management of the estate. Ladies, the interior of the house has been sadly neglected by my late cousin, your natural taste will be of assistance in suggesting improvements.'

'And what will my task be?' Vivian asked with amusement.

'I am sure you and my gamekeeper will have many interesting conversations! You must see if there is at least one pheasant to be found within my neglected preserves.'

'And your cousin Serena—I do not think I have met her,' Flora said enquiringly, while Caroline sat mute, still somewhat flushed and quite unable to decide whether she was happy or not at the thought of spending so much time in close proximity to Jervais Barnard.

'I very much doubt if you have made her acquaintance. She is Lady Shannon, her husband has estates in Ireland and they rarely come to London. However, Serena has hopes of launching their eldest daughter Julia next year: she intends to come direct to Dunharrow with Julia for Christmas so the girl can experience a few private parties before entering Society.'

'And her husband?'

'The Earl is no lover of Society. He will remain at home very happily with his racehorses!'

The orchestra struck up for a cotillion and Vivian asked his aunt to dance.

'A very dutiful nephew, indeed,' Jervais remarked, as they turned to watch Vivian gracefully handing Flora in the moves of the dance.

'No such thing!' Caroline laughed. 'If he is dancing

with Flora, then he is not standing up with a debutante, which suits him very well: I quite despair of him!'

Major Gresham laughed. 'This fear of entrapment is merely a phase young men go through. He was much in the company of young ladies while we were in Belgium: it is all these matchmaking mamas who have alarmed him. Never fear, he will be settling down and establishing his nursery before you know where you are.' He shot a swift glance at Barnard and Caroline. 'Now, if you will excuse me, I promised Bellamy a hand of whist.'

'That was neatly done,' Jervais remarked.

'What do you mean?' Caroline, feeling abandoned by her supporters, was inclined to be sharp.

'Gresham shows more tact than one would have expected: with his departure we are alone. . .'

'Hardly, my lord. There are at least two dozen people in this room.'

'Indeed, and we are monopolizing this table: let us remove from here and allow that party over there to sit.' He rose and held his chair for a grateful lady.

Caroline permitted herself to be guided from the room, but instead of re-entering the ballroom, Jervais turned left and entered the conservatory. The room was quite deserted, the groups of tall ferns and potted palms creating a sense of intimacy amongst their shadows.

'My lord. . .' Caroline began.

'I thought I had made it plain I do not wish you to address me so when we are alone,' he admonished, his voice huskily intimate.

Alarmed, Caroline moved away across the tiled floor and began to examine a handsome Chinese pot which formed the centre-piece of the room. 'Do you not admire the Chinese style?'

'I do not, and pray do not change the subject.'

'Was there a subject?' She turned to face him, chin raised, suddenly determined to stand her ground.

'I was asking you to use my name.' Jervais took two quick strides towards her across the tiles and Caroline whisked neatly round the Chinese pot away from him.

'But we are not driving now, my lord.' Her heart was fluttering, and she felt light-headed in the heated, earth-scented atmosphere. There was a gleam in Jervais's dark eyes she had seen before and it both alarmed and excited her.

'You are driving me insane,' he said, so softly she thought perhaps she had imagined the words. He almost reached her side before she darted away again to an array of orchids displayed on a tier of shelves to one side.

'I do not believe these are plants at all: look at them, they are like strange small creatures.' As an attempt to distract him it was a singular failure. Jervais ignored the exotic blooms, stretching out a hand to take hers.

Once more Caroline evaded capture, running behind a bank of palms. There was silence, broken only by the tinkle of a wall-fountain and the distant sound of the orchestra. Where was he? Her pulse drummed loudly in her ears as she twisted and turned, trying to descry him in the scented gloom.

Still, there was no sound from Jervais. Perhaps she had annoyed him by her evasions enough to drive him back to the ballroom. 'Oh,' she whispered, deflated, as she tiptoed out from behind the screen of plants.

Yes, the room was deserted, the only sign of movement that of the palm leaves in the Chinese pot, swaying where he had brushed against it.

'Jervais?'

'Yes?' His voice was right in her ear and as he spoke his arms encircled her waist from behind, drawing her back against him.

She stiffened and began to wriggle in his hold, but

Jervais drew her hard against his body until she could feel the warmth of him down the length of her back, his breath stirring the hairs on her nape.

Still holding her tightly, he began to nuzzle her neck along the hairline, trailing kisses up behind her ear until she was shuddering with delight at the sensation. All thought of evading him had quite gone, all reality was centred in the circle of his arms, his heart beating against her shoulder, the sudden catch of his breath as she stirred against him.

After what seemed an age his lips left her skin and he stood holding her, quite still except for the rise and fall of his breathing, saying nothing.

'Jervais?' Her voice sounded very small in the gloom as she twisted in his arms to face him. She looked up, trying to read his face. She was more than ever certain that she loved him, still as uncertain whether he loved her in return or merely desired her.

'You are a very serious temptation, Caro; I have to keep reminding myself that you are a respectable young lady.'

'And this is treating me as a respectable young lady, Jervais?' She intended it lightly, but her voice shook. She was standing so close she could see a nerve jump in his cheek.

'No, it is not, as well you know.' He opened his arms, freeing her, and stepped back deliberately putting a distance between them. 'Caro, there is something I must ask you. . .'

'Yes, Jervais?' Caroline was unconsciously twisting her hands in the fragile fabric of her skirt, hardly able to breathe.

For the first time since she had met him she saw doubt cross his face. 'I. . .no. No, not yet. I do wish, Caro, you would bring yourself to trust me.'

'But I do trust you,' she urged, puzzled by his reticence.

'Do you? I wonder, Caro. I wonder sometimes whether I know you at all.' He turned away and walked across to the orchids, standing looking down at them for a long moment. When he turned back to her he was his usual assured self again. 'I go into Leicestershire tomorrow to join my friends for the hunting. I will be away six weeks.'

'That long?' Try as she might Caroline could not keep the dismay out of her voice.

'I shall go direct to Dunharrow from Leicestershire. I shall return to London in mid-December and we can all travel down together.'

'Oh, that will be nice,' Caroline said inanely. It seemed hard to believe that a moment ago she had been standing in this man's arms, that he had been kissing her neck, holding her tight against him. Surely he could not behave now as though nothing had just occurred? It seemed he could—and there was nothing she could say!

When he said, 'Shall we go into the ballroom, Miss Franklin?' she could only nod.

As she rejoined Flora, her aunt exclaimed in horror, 'Caroline, what have you done to your gown, the front is quite crushed!'

Caroline looked down at the creases she had inflicted on the delicate fabric with her twisting hands. 'Oh. . .I do not know. Flora, may we go home? I have such a headache.'

CHAPTER SEVEN

'HE IS on the point of making you a declaration! I know it, I feel it in my bones!' Flora waved the sheets of hot-pressed notepaper at Caroline across the breakfast table.

'Who can you mean?' Caroline asked casually, pushing the crumbs on her plate about and not meeting her aunt's eye.

'Caroline!' Flora clicked her tongue chidingly. 'You know I refer to Lord Barnard. He writes to say he is now home at Dunharrow and to suggest travelling arrangements for our Christmas visit.' She scanned the sheets covered in Jervais's bold black script once more. 'He apologises for the fact we will all be cheek by jowl in one wing: but I scarcely feel we could complain of that, for the rooms we will occupy with be newly refurbished. . .'

Caroline hardly heard as Flora chattered on, fluttering the pages as she read them. All she could think of was Jervais's face, the tone of his voice, his arms as he held her close in the dark conservatory. A frisson passed down her spine and she shivered visibly.

Flora looked up in alarm. 'My dear, you are not sickening for a chill, are you? I knew I should never have allowed you to go out driving with Vivian in that cold wind yesterday. And you get such a red nose when you have a cold. . .'

'I do not!' Caroline was indignant. 'And thank you for being concerned more for my appearance than my health!'

'We must be practical about these things.' Flora was unabashed. 'A chill is easily got over, the lasting effects on your marriage prospects of being seen at less than your best, however, are more serious.'

'Flora, if he truly loves me—which he does not—he will offer for me, red nose or no. And what woman of spirit would accept a man who would be so easily deflected? Not that he is going to make me a declaration.'

'Really, Caroline, I declare you protest too much.' Flora folded up the letter and passed it across the table. 'Why should he go to so much trouble to furbish up Dunharrow for Christmas when he could easily have a congenial party of his army friends who would not care in the slightest what condition the house was in?'

'He has to undertake the repairs at some time, you heard him tell how badly the estate had been neglected.' Caroline buttered a piece of bread and considered the range of preserves, finally settling on honey.

'But hardly at this time of year: the spring would have been far more sensible,' Flora observed unanswerably.

'I really could not say, I know nothing about these matters.' Caroline was secretly convinced that Flora was indeed correct and that Jervais was about to make a declaration. The more she considered it, the more she was certain he had been on the point of doing so that evening in the conservatory.

His reluctance to come to the point must be because he was only considering it out of a sense of duty. Yet, inexperienced as she was, there was no denying that Jervais desired her; when he held her in his arms and kissed her, the look in his eyes was not that of a man doing his duty! Caroline had had more than a month to resolve the conundrum of whether he loved her—and if he did not, whether she was prepared to accept him if he still proposed to her.

All her thinking had made no difference. The same wearisome doubts circled like the kitchen dog in his treadmill turning the spit, and to rather less effect.

'. . .do you not think so?'

' Oh, I am sorry; Flora, I was not attending. What did you say?'

Flora sighed patiently and repeated herself. 'I think we should take only my dresser, and Vivian and the major will share Anthony's batman in lieu of a valet— I feel we should not inflict too many servants on the household while they are in disarray with building work. Vivian is proposing to drive down in his curricle with Anthony and we can take the travelling carriage. Plumb can travel with us and the batman and the luggage will go in the other carriage.'

Caroline nodded her agreement, glancing at Jervais's letter as she did so. 'I see he proposes to come to London simply to return at once with us to Dunharrow. Surely that is not necessary, for we will have Vivian and the major as escort.'

'I think it shows a degree of sensibility that is most pleasing,' Flora rejoined smugly, pleased to be able to point out yet another virtue. 'And you know full well that your brother will not want to dawdle along at our pace.'

'And I am certain Lord Barnard will not want to be cooped up in a travelling carriage with us for a whole day either,' Caroline riposted.

'No doubt he will ride, the gentlemen usually prefer to do so,' Flora said. 'Now, that is settled. He writes that he hopes we will reach Dunharrow on the twentieth of December, that only leaves us nine days to prepare. Have you any further shopping you need, Caroline dear?'

Caroline needed very little persuasion to embark on yet another shopping expedition. Since Jervais had departed for Leicestershire, Flora had been amazed at her niece's willingness to be fitted for new gowns, to try on new bonnets and to spend hours shopping for fashionable trifles. This behaviour was so uncharacteristic she could only attribute it to Caroline desiring to look her best for Lord Barnard. Caroline, for her part, was simply aware of a need to fill every waking moment with activity.

'Grafton House, Forster,' Caroline directed the coachman as they took their places in the closed carriage. The ladies pulled the fur-lined carriage rug over their knees and watched the damp and foggy streets unroll as they traversed the short distance.

Once under cover they discovered that many other ladies had decided to while away a raw December morning in like fashion.

The ladies purchased a few necessities: tooth-powder, Hungary Water and eau de Cologne, then settled down to some serious frivolity. Over cups of chocolate at Gunter's two hours later they compared their acquisitions.

'See this fan, Flora—such a novel decoration.' Caroline unfurled it, fluttering the fragile arc experimentally. 'I like those stockings, how much were they? Perhaps I should purchase some for myself. . .'

At last they rose to leave. 'Could you bear it if we went to Bond Street now, Flora?' Caroline enquired, slipping her hands into her muff. 'I still have to find a gift for Lord Barnard. I have made all the rest of my Christmas purchases, or else I am making gifts, but I am quite at a loss to know what to give him.'

'It is difficult,' Flora commiserated, giving directions to Forster. 'There are so few things one can, with propriety, give to a gentleman to whom one is not connected, and yet it would be most discourteous to take nothing for your host. I have left it to Anthony to select something on my behalf, but have you no notion of what to give him?'

'I had thought of a book. After all, Lord Barnard can have had little opportunity to buy many volumes whilst on military duty and I believe he said his cousin's library was much decayed, fit only for the bonfire. But other than the fact he despises Lord Byron, I have no notion of his tastes.'

Browsing through the shelves of Caroline's favourite bookshop in Bond Street, the ladies found three volumes for themselves, but nothing for the elusive Christmas gift. Caroline had almost despaired when her eye fell upon Gilbert White's *Natural History and Antiquities of Selborne* lying open on a table.

'Why, this is the very thing! Selborne is in Hampshire and I am sure he would find it of some interest, it is so very well written and observed.'

The next eight days seemed to crawl by, despite all there was to do. Presents had to be completed and wrapped, a final choice made from wardrobes and trunks packed. The ladies' bedrooms were soon a drift of silver paper and ribbons and Vivian began to complain he could find none of his linen because it was either being laundered or had already been packed.

Miss Plumb, Lady Grey's highly superior dresser, was in her element, directing footmen to bring down heavy fitted dressing-cases from the attics and irritating the butler by sending his staff on seemingly endless errands to the jewellers with items to be cleaned.

'I am not one to complain, Miss Plumb, as you know, but how am I supposed to run this household—what with the door to be answered and the trunks moved and all her ladyship's errands to be run—when if I call for William or Peter I find you have sent them round to Gieves and Hawkes?'

'Well, I am glad to hear you do not wish to complain, Mr Dorking,' Miss Plumb responded with asperity, 'for what could be more important than her ladyship presenting her best appearance at such a house-party?'

'Under the circumstances,' Dorking dropped his voice, 'I should say it's more important that a certain other party looks her best—if you follow my drift, Miss Plumb.'

The appearance of a passing parlourmaid prevented the dresser from immediate reply; the speaking glance she gave him, however, conveyed volumes.

Mr Dorking was therefore not surprised, when opening the door at seven o'clock in the evening of the nineteenth, to find Lord Barnard upon the doorstep.

'Good evening; my lord.' Dorking bowed Jervais into the hall, closing the door on the swirls of mist which eddied around their feet. 'A pleasure to see your lordship again, if I may make so bold. I regret to say her ladyship has just left for a supper at the opera: I believe she did not look to see you until tomorrow morning, my lord.'

'Indeed? I am sorry to have missed Lady Grey. Is Miss Franklin at home?'

Dorking hesitated, then appeared to reach a decision. 'Miss Franklin is at home, my lord, I believe she is reading in the small salon. Shall I announce you?'

'No, thank you, Dorking.' Jervais was already shedding his multi-caped driving coat into the waiting arms of a footman. 'I will see myself up.'

Behind Jervais the footman's eyebrows shot up as Mr Dorking permitted this latitude. As his lordship disappeared around the bend in the stairs, the butler turned to his underling. 'Don't you stand there gawping, lad! Take the port and the brandy up to the small salon—in about ten minutes. There is no hurry.' He permitted himself a small smile and made his way magisterially down to the housekeeper's sitting-room to convey this gratifying development to the senior staff.

Caroline had just laid aside her book and was walking across the room to ring for Dorking when she heard the door open behind her.

'Ah, there you are, Dorking,' she said, without turning round. 'I was just about to ring for supper. It is a little early, I know. . .'

'Caro.'

She whirled round, her hand dropping from the bellpull, her cheeks turning quite pale at the surprise of seeing him after so many weeks' absence.

'Jervais. . .Lord Barnard!' She collected herself rapidly and advanced, her hand outstretched to shake his. 'We had not expected to see you until tomorrow morning: did you not believe we would take your instructions to the letter? I assure you we are quite packed and ready to set off at eight o'clock tomorrow morning.'

Jervais took her proffered hand, but instead of shaking it, stood holding it, staring down intently into her face. Caroline, further unnerved, found herself prattling on. 'And you have just missed Flora: she was quite unexpectedly invited out to the opera by the major. . .'

'I know.' Jervais was still holding her hand, all his attention focused on her.

'You know? How could you?' Then she saw the betraying twinkle in his eye and gasped indignantly. 'Why, you put him up to it! Whatever made you do such a thing?'

'Well,' he said reasonably, 'I could hardly do this with Lady Grey present.' And with no more ado he took Caroline firmly in his arms and kissed her with a thoroughness which robbed her of her breath.

When he finally let her go she put her hands to her

burning cheeks and exclaimed, 'Jervais! What are you about?'

'If you do not know, Caroline, I had better do it again.'

This time she was too quick for him, dodging behind a tambour table, panting slightly.

'Let us sit down—look, I will sit here, at a safe distance.' Jervais dropped easily into a bergère armchair, crossing his long legs at the ankle and regarding her benevolently as she sat cautiously, as far away as she could. 'I have missed you, Caro. Have you not missed me? I had rather hoped you had.'

'Well, naturally, from time to time...but we have had much to do.' This was ridiculous! Here she was making conversation with a man who had just had the effrontery to kiss her—in her own home. 'This is most improper. I do not know what Dorking was about, letting you up like this; he knew my aunt was out.'

'I suspect he guesses why I have come.' Jervais got to his feet and strolled across to sit beside her. Caro slid along the sofa away from him, her heart thudding uncomfortably. 'Do you know why I have come?'

'I...my lord...'

The door opened to reveal Peter bearing a tray with decanters. 'Mr Dorking thought you might be desirous of refreshment, my lord.' He set the heavy tray down and bowed himself out, managing with an effort to keep from staring at the startling sight of the young mistress, quite unchaperoned, sitting on a sofa with a man.

'A glass of sherry, Caroline?' Jervais seemed quite unperturbed by the intrusion. He crossed to the tray, poured himself a brandy and brought it and the sherry across to Caroline.

The interruption had given her a moment to gather her wits and to discover she was not a little irritated by Jervais's air of assurance.

'You take a great deal for granted, my lord,' she said frostily when he presented her with the glass.

'Oh, I am sorry. Would you have preferred madeira?'

'That is not what I am referring to, as you know full well.'

He watched her, admiring the fair complexion, heightened by the flush of annoyance in her cheeks. Although she had planned an evening alone, her slim figure was dressed, with the easy elegance he had come to associate with her, in a simple silk gown of a deep cornflower which echoed the blue of her eyes. As she looked up to meet his scrutiny one of the dark curls framing her face tangled in her pearl earring and she gave a little exclamation of annoyance.

Jervais reached out one finger and gently unhooked the fine hair. Caroline froze as the tip of his finger brushed fleetingly against her skin: looking into his eyes she could see them soften.

'Caro, you must know why I am here. . .'

Caroline, quite unable to speak, shook her head slowly, hardly able to believe he was, in truth, about to make her the long awaited declaration.

'Dammit! I had no idea this would be so difficult.' He got to his feet and paced across to the fireplace, uncharacteristically at a loss. He squared his shoulders and turned and she had a sudden glimpse of how he must have looked going into battle. Abruptly formal he knelt beside her and took her hand. 'Miss Franklin. . . Caroline. . . I have the honour to ask if you will be my wife.'

All the weeks of worry and indecision vanished in a rush of love for him that brought tears to her eyes. The fact he had not said he loved her was lost on her in that moment, all that mattered was that he was there beside her, asking her to be his wife.

'Yes. . .oh yes, Jervais.'

He needed no further encouragement to take her in his arms and this time his kiss was a long, sensuous, gentle declaration of mastery. Caroline sensed she was being claimed, owned, yet she did not care, so swept up was she in joy at the thought she was to be Jervais's wife, married to the man she loved.

At length he gathered her up, lifting her onto his knee and holding her tightly against his chest. Caroline, very conscious of his lean body against hers, snuggled her head under his chin and listened to his heart beating rhythmically under her ear.

'This is very improper you know,' she murmured after a while. 'Have you asked Vivian's permission to pay your addresses?'

'Under the circumstances I thought it best to speak to you first,' Jervais muttered, his lips nuzzling gently in her hair.

'Circumstances?' Caroline twisted out of his embrace and sat upright on his knee to stare at him in perplexity. 'What circumstances? Oh, do you mean that Vivian is so much younger than you? I can see it might seem ridiculous, to find yourself, a more senior officer, asking his permission!'

'No,' he said slowly, and apparently with some reluctance. 'I mean the circumstances of our first encounter.'

Caroline felt the blood drain from her face. So, it was true: he had only offered for her because he had compromised her in Belgium. 'Whatever was there in your first visit to Brook Street. . .'

Jervais took her by the shoulders and gave her a little shake. 'Caroline, stop this play-acting! It is no longer necessary—indeed, it never was necessary. You know as well as I that I picked you off the road on the battlefield, that we spent the night together before our return to Brussels, that you ran away from me.'

'You knew I had regained my memory?' she said

very slowly. 'You knew right from the beginning that I remembered all about it?'

'When I walked into this house and saw you, I was too taken aback to consider it rationally. I recognised you at once, but it was obvious you had no wish to acknowledge the fact we had already met. Then you seemed so unconscious of any awkwardness that I concluded that the brain fever, or shock, or whatever had caused your first loss of memory, had also robbed you of your memories of me: that you had, in confusion, wandered from the house and been found by your friends.'

Caroline got to her feet and moved away from him to the fireplace. There was such restraint in the way he was speaking, such reserve that she knew he was controlling some emotion only with difficulty. Jervais stood, too, but made no attempt to approach her. Suddenly she was very cold and she shivered as she held out her hands to the blaze. 'Then what betrayed me? When did you become suspicious?'

'You knew my rank, although I had been introduced as Lord Barnard, and you knew Percy. After that you betrayed yourself to me in so many little ways—although no one else would have guessed.'

'Thank goodness for that,' she said shakily. 'I was in a terror that Vivian or Flora might realise something was amiss: they had accepted my explanation of a fall from my horse and having been taken in by a respectable Belgian family. I could have scarcely told them the truth!'

'Caroline,' Jervais asked patiently, 'why could you not have trusted me, told me that you remembered? I asked you to trust me, do you not recall?'

'How could I trust you on such short acquaintance? When you think of the circumstances under which we were together!' She shuddered and averted her face.

The look of patience vanished from his face to be

replaced by anger. 'So you did not trust my discretion? When I saw you here I never doubted you were exactly who you purported to be: a lady. Do you think so little of me that you fear I would damage your reputation in Society by carelessness or spite?'

'Your delicacy does you credit, my lord!' Caroline flung back at him, goaded by the reproach in his voice. 'What a shame it was not much in evidence when you were trying to inveigle me into your bed!'

'I thought you were one of the muslin company,' he began indignantly. 'You knew that.'

'I did not know who I was! You leapt to the conclusion that I was a loose woman on the flimsiest of evidence—why, it was the merest chance I was not ruined, in fact! And then you ask me to trust you after you took advantage of me in that outrageous manner? Oh, no, my lord, I am not quite so gullible.'

'Leapt to conclusions!' Jervais raked his fingers through his hair in angry exasperation. 'What the hell am I to conclude when I find you in a dress only a courtesan would wear and with paint on your face?'

'You might have given me the benefit of the doubt!' Even as she said it, it sounded weak and improbable: all the evidence had been against her respectability, not least her own ready comprehension of what he had been suggesting.

'What doubt? And to cap it all, you showed a knowledge of things no innocent young lady should have had an inkling about.'

Caroline drew herself up and said icily, 'From your conduct, sir, I should imagine your acquaintanceship with innocent young ladies is somewhat limited!' She had no intention of telling Jervais about her father and his string of mistresses.

'You still have not explained to me what you were doing in that dress,' he persisted.

'Not that I owe you any explanation, Lord Barnard,

but the truth of the matter is that I have no recollection.'

'Truth? I am beginning to doubt you have any conception of the meaning of the word. Your loss of memory is strangely convenient, it seems to me.'

Caroline, goaded beyond prudence, took two jerky steps towards Jervais and slapped him hard across his cheek. He caught her raised hand painfully in his and pulled her against him. 'I ought to turn you across my knee for that!'

'And when Vivian heard of it he would call you out!' she gasped, still too angry to think what she was saying.

'So you have confided all the details of your little adventure to your brother, have you? I had not thought him so complaisant.'

'I tell you I cannot remember. . .'

'Oh, yes, you can, but you dare not admit it. What was it, a dare between you and one of your feather-headed friends that went disastrously wrong? Consider yourself lucky, madam, that it was I who picked you up and not a common foot-soldier: there would be no talk of respectability then.'

Caroline stared agahst as his harsh face. 'You think . . .you believe I would dress up in such an improper garment for a game. . .risk my reputation. . .and at such a time? In the midst of all our worry about Vivian and the battle?'

'What else would you have me believe if you persist in lying to me?' His expression was grim. 'How long were you away from home?'

'From Saturday midday, which was when I rode out to seek advice on whether we should leave Brussels. . .'

'And I found you at midnight on Sunday: thirty-six hours to be accounted for. Can you not think of a convincing explanation?'

'My horse bolted and took me out of the city. I fell off and hit my head!'

'You went riding in the dress I found you in?' He was making no attempt to hide his scorn at her story.

'Why, no, of course I did not—I was wearing a riding habit.'

'Then with whom did you spent those thirty-six hours?' he demanded.

'No one! Or, at least, I cannot remember. . .' Her voice trailed off at the look of disbelief on Jervais's face, then she recovered herself. 'I do not lie! Why did you ask me to marry you if you think such terrible things of me?' Caroline freed her wrist, shaking Jervais off. 'I would not marry you, sir, if you were the last man on earth!'

'I am delighted to hear it, because believe it or not, Caroline, having asked you I would have felt it my duty to honour my offer regardless. Now I can see I have had a fortunate escape.'

'You are no gentleman, my lord!' Caroline could hardly choke the words out past the tears that threatened to overwhelm her.

'If I am no gentleman, then ask yourself what lady would be prepared to ally herself with a man she mistrusted as much as you mistrust me.' He ignored the tears which were running down her cheeks. 'Perhaps you had other reasons: had you made some enquiries into the size of my inheritance? As you are no doubt aware, it is substantial. Or after your little escapade did you think you had better take the first man who offered for fear of scandal?'

'Go!' was all she could manage to say, burying her face in her hands.

'With pleasure, madam,' Jervais replied softly. 'With pleasure.'

It was three hours after the front door had shut behind Jervais that Caroline heard the unmistakable sounds of Flora and the Major returning from their visit to the opera.

During those interminable hours she had passed from sobbing despair to dumb misery. At first she had wanted nothing more than for Flora to return so she could pour out the whole story. Then she realised she could not. Once she learned the truth of what had really happened in Belgium, Flora would insist on telling all to Vivian and he, regardless of how violent the quarrel had been between the couple, would demand that Lord Barnard marry his sister.

And she would never agree to that. Jervais had made it as clear as though he had told her so that he had offered only because he had compromised her. Nor could he love her if he was not prepared to accept her word that her memory had only partially returned, that she still had no recollection of how she had come to be on the battlefield. As to what he believed she had been doing. . . Caroline could hardly bring herself to think about it.

By the time Flora returned, Caroline had decided that all she could do was to tell her aunt that Jervais had proposed, that she had refused him and that it was too embarrassing to expect her to spend Christmas at Dunharrow as his guest.

Flora would be extremely displeased with her, and it would mean the break-up of the party at the last moment, but rack her brain as she might, no other solution offered itself.

Where was her aunt? It must be quite fifteen minutes since Caroline had heard the buzz of arrival in the hall. Perhaps she had gone direct to her chamber, but there had been no sound on the stairs.

Caroline looked at her reflection in the glass and hesitated, then decided that her swollen eyes and pale cheeks could be attributed to maidenly distress at rejecting a suitor. She walked slowly downstairs, finding the hall empty and the house quiet.

Then she saw the study door was ajar, light spilling

out across the marble checkerboard floor. Flora must have decided to take a book up to bed with her, or perhaps she was penning a note.

Caroline pushed open the door, then froze. In a cruel parody of what had passed upstairs only hours before she saw the back of the Major's head as he sat on the chaise longue, Flora in his arms.

'Anthony, my dear, I cannot say when we can be married,' her aunt was saying. 'I must see Caroline settled first. I promised her dear mama I would not leave her until she was married. . .'

Tiptoeing silently out of the study and back upstairs to her room Caroline felt sick at heart. It was a double blow: both to lose the man she loved and, in doing so, deprive Flora of her chance of happiness. She knew her aunt too well to believe she would yield easily to any persuasion either she or the Major might employ. Caroline had turned down the only man she would ever love, condemning both herself and her aunt to unhappiness.

Nor could she tell her aunt she was not going to Dunharrow. To spoil her happiness now would be a cruel blow; somehow she would have to break the news, but not yet, not just before Christmas.

When Jervais arrived tomorrow to collect them—if, indeed, he did—she would have to speak to him and plead with him to betray nothing of what had passed between them that evening.

Then all they had to do was to play act for two interminable weeks; she as though her heart was not broken, he as though he did not hold her in the deepest suspicion and contempt.

CHAPTER EIGHT

THE appointed hour of eight o'clock came and went without sign of Lord Barnard. The entire household was in that state of restlessness consequent upon being fully prepared and having nothing to do but wait. The travelling carriage was packed with all the necessities for a long journey on a cold winter's day and the coach with the trunks had left at dawn.

The dank mists of the past fortnight had been banished overnight and replaced by a sparkling hard frost. Dorking had hot bricks waiting in the bread oven until the last minute before the ladies, well wrapped in fur travelling rugs, stepped into the carriage and he could pack them around their feet.

Vivian and the Major had already left as agreed, Vivian driving the curricle gingerly across the icy cobbles.

Flora, still in a secret, happy daze from last night's agreement with her Major, was doing her best to soothe her agitated niece. Her instincts blunted by her own happiness, she misinterpreted Caroline's unhappy restlessness.

'It is but twenty minutes past the hour,' she said placidly from her seat by the fire. 'There is bound to be some small delay, especially with the weather so icy.'

Jervais was not coming. She must have been mad to think he would after what had passed between them last night. Such bitter words could not easily be unsaid, and they had both uttered accusations which in the cold light of day appalled her.

As the minute hand of the clock crept round and

Flora continued to sit placidly waiting, Caroline steeled herself to tell her aunt the truth—all of it. She could not live with this feeling of guilt for deceiving her: now Jervais was not coming she could pretend no longer. She must persuade Flora that Caroline's mother would never have intended her sister-in-law to sacrifice her own happiness by interpreting her promise so literally, not after Caroline had ruined her own chances of marriage so disastrously.

'Flora. . .'

The sound of the knocker reached them faintly from the floor below. Caroline spun round and craned to see down through the frosted window. But the horse standing by the kerb, its breath making white plumes in the bitter air, was an ordinary hack, not Caesar.

As she watched, a groom emerged and mounted the horse, walking it slowly away down the treacherous road. Shortly afterwards Dorking entered the salon, carrying a silver salver with a note on it. 'Lord Barnard's compliments, my lady.'

Caroline sank down onto the window-seat. She should have said something sooner to Flora; now the shock of discovering Caroline's behaviour and the consequences for her own alliance with the Major, would be all the greater.

As Caroline watched her aunt scanning the note, she saw her brow furrow and she made a soft sound of distress. What could he have said? Caroline's heart contracted as she imagined the contents.

'Oh dear, how distressing for Lord Barnard,' said Flora in a worried tone.

'Distressing! Is that what you call it? I suppose he has told you all. . .'

Caroline broke off at the sight of the perplexed expression on Flora's face. 'What are you talking about, Caroline? Of course Lord Barnard has told me all!'

'All! On one sheet of paper?' Caroline cried.

'My dear, you are not well, you speak so strangely!' She looked at Caroline's strained, pinched face. 'Are you feverish? Oh dear, oh dear, I must send to Lord Barnard immediately—we cannot travel if you are unwell.'

'Travel?' Caroline croaked. 'We are still going to Dunharrow?'

'But, of course, this is only a short delay.' Flora put a cool hand on Caroline's brow. 'You do not seem to have a fever. I know what it must be—you are over-excited, and you did not sleep well last night. I heard you moving about in your chamber.' She looked closely into Caroline's face. 'I do not know how I can have failed to notice it before, but your eyes are quite heavy.'

'I am quite well, but I did not sleep much—it is the thought of the journey, for some reason I found it unsettling.' She could contain herself no longer. 'May I see his lordship's note? How does he account for the delay?'

Flora handed her the missive and she scanned it with anxious eyes. Caesar, it seemed, had slipped on the icy cobbles in the mews and had strained a tendon and there would be some delay whilst another horse was saddled. Jervais would be with them directly.

Relief threatened to overwhelm her and she turned away to hide her face from Flora. He had said nothing of her secret, nor had he withdrawn the invitation to Dunharrow. Caroline knew she should be relieved on her aunt's account, but all that she was conscious of was thankfulness that he had not severed all contact, that she would see him again, however difficult it would be. It seemed you did not stop loving someone just because you discovered they held you in distrust and considered you a liar.

She had scarcely laid the note aside when Jervais

strode into the room, his heavy caped riding coat
brushing the furniture. Without a glance towards
Caroline, he bowed over Flora's hand, his gaze intent
upon her face.

'Why so solemn, my lord?' Flora teased. 'Did you
think you were in for a scold for keeping us waiting? I
can assure you that in this house we are so inured to
Vivian's unpunctuality as to almost expect it of everyone! But I should not joke—how is your poor horse?
Not badly hurt, I trust?'

'You are most forgiving.' Flora saw his face relax
and thought with satisfaction that he must care very
much for Caroline's good opinion if he was so concerned at being late. 'And thank you, but Caesar will
be well enough in a few days.'

Caroline swallowed hard and forced her unwilling
legs to cross the room to him. 'Good morning, my
lord.' She held out her hand, and he took it briefly.
'You will not be hunting him for a while, I imagine.'

She had schooled her face into an expression of cool
politeness and was wounded to see no hint of emotion
of any sort in his.

'If you ladies are ready, shall we set out? We have a
long journey and the weather is against us: the only
consolation is that it is too cold to snow.'

As Plumb helped her into her warm pelisse and
handed her a fur muff, Caroline reflected grimly that if
this cold correctness were to characterise their relations
over the next few weeks, then so be it. She could be as
chillingly punctilious as he.

Once clear of the treacherously slippery streets of
London, the horses were able to increase their speed
more safely on the metalled road. Jervais, mounted on
a black gelding Caroline had not seen before, cantered
beside the carriage, his expression as frozen as the
weather.

Flora talked animatedly as they drove, apparently

unaffected by the bounding of the well-sprung carriage on the frozen surface. Caroline sat abstracted, answering her aunt in monosyllables. Plumb, as was her place, sat jealously guarding her mistress's dressing-case, regarding the frozen countryside with the deep disapproval of the town-bred.

Caroline watched Jervais, telling herself she should be grateful that his correct demeanour would do nothing to raise suspicion that anything untoward had passed between them. But her irrational longing was for him to storm at her, or take her in his arms—anything to show he felt something, that he cared for her.

'Lord Barnard must be frozen,' Flora remarked. 'When we change horses at Guildford, see if you cannot persuade him to ride inside with us, Caroline.'

'He should be warm enough,' said Caroline indifferently, watching the rider as she spoke. He was wearing a heavy caped greatcoat which hung down over the flanks of the gelding and quite covered his riding coat and buckskins. The coat was of military cut and brought back the memory of him in uniform, of sitting up behind him as they rode back to Brussels.

For a fleeting moment she was back in the heat of that June day, remembering again how he had looked after her, protected her despite his wounds, his gentleness and understanding of her fears.

Angry tears pricked at the back of her eyes and she blinked them away. She was angry with herself for still loving him, despite everything; at him for failing to trust her, at the unfairness of life.

It was well after dark when they reached Dunharrow and the clock over the stable block was striking six as the carriage drew up at the front door. Despite Flora's best efforts at persuasion, Jervais had continued to ride and the ladies had long since run out of conversation so it was a cold and weary party, grateful to have reached its destination, which finally shed its coats in the hallway.

'Are the rest of our guests here, Chawton?' Jervais enquired as the butler took his coat.

'The Major and the Lieutenant arrived an hour since and are in the drawing room with Sir Richard and Major Routh, my lord. The heavy luggage is also here and has been taken up.' He turned as a homely woman came in and curtsied to the ladies. 'Mrs Chawton will show the ladies to their chambers.'

Miss Plumb nodded stiffly to the housekeeper, obviously considering such bucolic servants beneath her touch. Caroline and Flora followed her gratefully, wanting nothing more than to change out of their travel-stained clothes, wash and warm themselves by a good fire.

'What a handsome staircase,' Flora remarked as they ascended. 'This part of the house seems of recent construction.'

'Indeed, ma'am, I believe it was built by his late lordship's father some fifty years ago,' the housekeeper replied as they reached the first landing. 'This is your room, my lady, I trust you will be comfortable.'

The chamber she showed them into was spacious and Caroline guessed that in daylight it would afford a fine view down the driveway towards the gate-house.

'And this room is for you, Miss Franklin.' The woman opened the door into the adjoining chamber which must, from the arrangement of its windows on two walls, be on the corner of the new wing. 'There's a handsome prospect of the park from this side,' the housekeeper commented. She ran a critical eye over the arrangements in the room. 'There is hot water coming and the maid will unpack for you if your dresser will direct her. Is there anything else you require, Miss Franklin?'

Before Caroline could reply Flora entered, untying

her bonnet strings as she did so. 'Why, what a beautiful room! His lordship has had it decorated in the most exquisite taste.' Her discerning eye travelled over the delicate cream panelling set off by rich jonquil yellow draperies at the windows and above the four-poster bed. The bed curtains themselves were a froth of fine muslin, swagged and tied with matching yellow ribbons. 'Do you know, this colour scheme puts me in mind of that gown of yours, the one you wore to Almack's the evening Lord Barnard invited us here.'

The housekeeper turned from stirring a bowl of potpourri on the tallboy. 'It was originally going to be a green room, my lady, but his lordship sent orders for it to be changed at almost the last minute—why, I declare the paint is hardly dry!'

Flora shot Caroline a knowing look, amused by the colour which was staining her niece's cheeks. 'Indeed, Mrs Chawton. And are all the refurbished rooms as fine as this one?'

'Well, my lady, they are all very fine and a great improvement on what there was before—his old lordship did neglect things something awful, as everyone does agree—but I think this room is the finest.

'I do wonder whether his lordship intends to make this into the room for the lady of the house. At present, that is the chamber at the back overlooking the Fountain Court, and to be sure Lady Shannon has that as hostess, but he hasn't had it decorated as lovely as this. And this would be as convenient as that is,' she added with a twinkle, 'there being a door through to his dressing room from this one. It is locked, of course, just now.'

'So I should hope,' said Flora firmly, but her tone belied the triumphant light in her eyes. To her, there could not have been a more blatant indication of Jervais's intentions towards Caroline than to install her in the bedroom of the mistress of the house.

Caroline turned away to unbutton her pelisse, almost unable to bear the thought that he had intended all this for her, not just for a short visit, but for the rest of her life as his wife.

The thought was still uppermost in her mind as, changed out of their travel-stained garments, they entered the salon an hour later to join the rest of the party before dinner.

The room seemed full of people and Caroline felt relief that she was not going to be thrown together with Jervais without the company of others.

Tonight he was dressed with severe formality in evening dress, his dark blue tail coat in sharp contrast to the dress uniforms of the male guests, all still serving officers. His expression as he approached the ladies seemed blandly welcoming, but Caroline caught one, brief betraying glance in her direction that hinted at hidden depths to his thoughts.

'Lady Grey, may I introduce you to my cousin, Lady Shannon, who has kindly agreed to act as my hostess. Serena: Lady Grey and her niece, Miss Franklin.'

'How do you do.' Lady Shannon shook hands with them both with a frank, welcoming smile. 'What a terrible journey down you must have had! I do hope you are quite warm and rested now and that you have everything you require. Let me introduce my daughter, Julia, to you.'

As Lady Julia made a rather shy curtsy Caroline saw how like her mother she was. Both were blonde, fine-boned and full-figured. Lady Shannon had a matronly dignity that in time Julia would acquire, but for the moment she was still very obviously just out of the schoolroom with a wide-eyed innocence of expression that was very endearing.

Lady Shannon turned to include the two officers standing by the fireside. 'And may I make known to you Captain Sir Richard Holden—' the tall young man in question bowed politely, the light glinting off red hair which clashed unfortunately with his scarlet jacket '—and Major Simon Routh.'

The Major was older than Sir Richard, a stocky, dark man with a roguish twinkle in his eye as it rested on Caroline. 'Enchanted,' he said.

Flora, observing his ready admiration of her niece, promptly engaged him in conversation, drawing Anthony Gresham into their discussion of the latest news from Europe.

Caroline smiled at Julia who was standing to one side, her eyes cast shyly down. 'I understand you live in Ireland: have you been to England before?'

As Caroline skilfully drew out the debutante, Lady Shannon turned to her cousin. 'So, Jervais,' she remarked in an undertone, 'this is the cause of your sudden desire to entertain! I must congratulate you on your discernment, Miss Franklin appears to be a charming young woman—everything I could have hoped for.'

'I have no notion what you mean, Serena,' he replied lightly. 'You know full well you inveigled me into holding a house-party to help you launch Julia.'

'Nonsense, Jervais. We would have been quite content to spend a few weeks quietly in London attending to Julia's wardrobe! And do not attempt to gull me into believing you have had this wing lavishly redecorated in the depths of the winter merely for the sake of your brother officers. So long as the food and the shooting are good, they would not notice if they were billeted in the barn!'

'You will excuse me, Serena,' Jervais said abruptly. 'I must speak with Chawton about the wine for dinner.'

Lady Shannon watched him move across the room, noticing he did not so much as glance in Miss Franklin's direction. She might be married to a bluff country-loving peer with more regard for his horses than for intellectual pursuits, but she herself was a shrewd observer of people. There was something deeply amiss with her cousin, however well he hid it from his other friends: she knew him too well to be deceived.

Serena looked consideringly at Miss Franklin who had succeeded in drawing out Julia into a laughing conversation. So, she was as kind as she was beautiful, Julia's mother mused, knowing not many young women would have relished the competition afforded by her daughter's burgeoning looks. And they were so different that they made a charming pair, the one so blonde and rounded, the other slender and darkly elegant.

Caroline was dressed with deceptive simplicity in a deep rose gown with a hem quilted in a darker shade and a spider's-web gauze scarf. Lady Shannon commended her taste and resolved to enquire the direction of her dressmaker.

So what was Jervais about? Serena would have expected him to confide his intentions to her, yet he had almost snubbed her just now. He made no attempt to single out Miss Franklin: that might simply have been discretion. . .and yet, it was more than that, she could sense a deep unhappiness in him. And that was most perplexing.

Dinner was a most convivial occasion: even Caroline, miserable as she was, found herself relaxing. The food and wine were excellent, the gentlemen were lively and amusing conversationalists and Lady Shannon had skilfully disposed her guests around the table to overcome the problem of the extra gentleman.

Jervais, at the head of the board, was out of Caroline's line of sight, for she found herself placed near her hostess at the other end of the table between Sir Richard and Major Gresham.

Opposite her, she was amazed to see, Vivian had

struck up an animated conversation with Julia. He seemed to have found just the right note to take with her, for she showed none of her previous shyness and was chatting happily.

Caroline was concentrating on drawing out Sir Richard who, although pleasant, was rather hard going as a dinner companion, being rather serious and high-minded for her taste. She glanced up at one point and met the admiring eye of Major Routh, diagonally opposite. Her immediate impression on meeting him that he was something of a ladies' man was under-scored by the warmth in his face as he raised his glass in a toast to her.

Caroline smiled back, somewhat repressively. He was obviously a rogue, but, in her judgement, a likeable and harmless one.

At the end of the meal Lady Shannon gathered the ladies with a glance and rose, saying with a laugh, 'Well, I suppose we must leave these men to their port and what they will tell us afterwards is a serious discussion of affairs!'

The drawing-room, lit by branches of candles, was cosy, the firelight flickering on its pale oak panelled walls. Flora immediately engaged Lady Julia in conversation, drawing her out about her plans and hopes for the coming Season.

Lady Shannon gestured in a friendly manner to the sofa beside her, 'Do sit by me, Miss Franklin, and tell me your opinion of Jervais. I own I have been a little concerned for his health since he returned from Belgium; his wounds gave us such cause for anxiety when we heard of them. I wrote at once to beg him to join us in Ireland, but he would have none of it. I could not, at the time, imagine why.' The sideways look she gave Caroline was full of meaning.

'Lord Barnard is in the habit of visiting your estates

often, I collect?' Caroline tried to ignore the suggestion implicit in that last remark.

'Well, we are the only family he possesses. Even when his late cousin was still alive, Jervais came more to us than to Dunharrow.'

'I would not want to speak disrespectfully of the late Lord Barnard, but he does seem to have been somewhat. . .eccentric.'

'Eccentric! The man had maggots in his head—did Jervais tell you about his fearful ginger wig?' She lowered her voice and added, 'And there was not a family in the village who would permit one of their daughters to work here. No doubt Jervais and I have several relatives down in Dunharrow Parva!' Seeing the look on Caroline's face, she said immediately, 'Forgive me for putting it so frankly, my dear! I am used to plain talking, and you seem such a poised young woman, I quite forgot you are still single.'

'I have been out for several Seasons,' Caroline replied absently, still meditating on the appalling habits of his late lordship.

'Indeed? And you are not, I believe, engaged to be married?'

'My aunt tells me I am far to nice in my requirements of a husband,' Caroline replied evenly, uncomfortable with the direction the conversation was taking.

So, Lady Shannon mused inwardly, he has done something to upset her, has he! How unexpectedly clumsy of Jervais. 'Julia, my dear,' she called across, much to Caroline's relief, 'did you bring down your pianoforte music? You know Jervais likes to hear you play.' She lowered her voice again. 'He has no more fondness for amateur playing than the next man, but she needs to overcome her nervousness at performing in company.'

As Julia opened the instrument somewhat reluctantly, the men joined them. Major Routh was saying as they entered '...sounds capital! I'm ready for a game; Holden, Gresham, Franklin—will any of you join us to try Barnard's new billiard table? If the ladies will excuse us?'

'Yes, of course,' said Lady Shannon gracefully.

'For myself, I would remain, if the ladies have no objection to my company,' said Vivian, to Caroline's complete amazement. When she saw Julia's flushed cheeks and downcast eyes, she understood what had made him lose interest in masculine company.

'Lady Julia is about to play for us, Vivian,' Caroline informed him slyly, only to be confounded when he leapt to his feet and asked:

'May I turn the music for you, Lady Julia?'

'I do hope you do not object to my brother showing such a marked partiality to Lady Julia,' Caroline murmured as the first chords were struck. 'I am amazed, he normally flees from debutantes!'

Lady Shannon was regarding the young couple indulgently. 'It is early days yet, they have only just met and she is not yet out. I would not want her fixing her interest whilst she is still so young, but it will do her no harm at all to enjoy a light flirtation with a young man such as your brother.'

Caroline rather doubted if a light flirtation was what Vivian had in mind. He was usually so impervious to the charms of young debutantes that she suspected he was falling in love. But there was no need to raise that possibility yet.

'Will you excuse me a moment, ma'am?' she asked, getting to her feet. 'I seem to have left my reticule in the dining-room.'

Having retrieved the little bag which had fallen under her chair, Caroline paused to order her hair in the glass over the mantelpiece. The door behind her closed with a sharp click and in the mirror she saw

Jervais reflected. He crossed the room to her side, showing no surprise at finding her there.

Caroline turned, her heart thumping at the shock of being alone with him, but she believed she had succeeded in keeping her thoughts from her face. 'My lord. . .'

'Miss Franklin. Is anything amiss?' He was closer than was quite comfortable—or quite proper, but with the fire at her back she could not retreat.

'I forgot my reticule.'

'That is not what I meant.' He was looking almost sinisterly saturnine in his dark clothes and the subdued light. His face was expressionless apart from his eyes which showed some emotion she could not interpret.

Caroline opened her mouth to make a light riposte, then found herself unable to maintain the pretence that nothing had happened any longer. 'What could be amiss, my lord? Other, of course, than the fact that you and I are closeted here together for the next two weeks when, after last night, you heartily wish me elsewhere!'

'You seem very certain of my feelings,' he replied evenly.

'How can you pretend it could be otherwise after what passed between us last evening! What do you imagine must be my feelings at having to pretend nothing is amiss? I realise that you could not withdraw the invitation to Dunharrow without reason, without having to explain all to my aunt. . .'

Caroline knew her colour was high, and she could feel her fists clenching at her side. She had known this conversation was bound to occur, but what she had not anticipated was how she would feel. Anger was uppermost, but underneath the anger she wanted to be in his arms and the need made her tremble.

'Perhaps I was afraid your brother would call me out if he knew what had. . .' a fractional pause '. . .passed between us,' he said calmly.

'Sir, you are insufferable!' she cried, goaded.

'And you, Caroline, are a very irritating young woman.'

'Oh!' The attack was so unexpected it took her several seconds to formulate her reply. 'Irritating! No one has ever described me so—how dare you!'

'There are many things I dare do, Caroline,' he said, suddenly husky and before she realised what he was about, she was in his arms being thoroughly kissed.

For perhaps five seconds she stiffened angrily, struggling, then the warm strength of him overcame her and her struggles were only to free her arms to twine them round his neck, to draw him closer.

Drugged by the intensity of her feelings, she clung to him, hope welling up that the harsh and bitter words they had exchanged last night were behind them, that he had come to believe her and was prepared to trust her after all.

It was Jervais who broke the embrace. 'This must stop. I was a fool to let myself be alone with you— I should have learned by now you are a temptation I find it impossible to resist.'

So that was all she was to him: a temptation. No doubt his late, unlamented cousin had found the serving girls an equal temptation!

'I had not observed much attempt at restraint in you, sir,' she began angrily, ashamed that she had gone into his arms so easily.

'Caroline, you wrong me.' There was colour in his face now. 'I assure you I am exercising considerable restraint to prevent myself making what would probably be the biggest mistake of my life.'

'If by that,' she stormed, 'you are inferring that you are restraining yourself from making me another offer, I can assure you that nothing would suit me better! And if you think I would permit you to lay one finger on me again. . .'

There was no question of Jervais hiding his feelings now. He was at least as angry as she as he said icily, 'That, madam, I have no trouble in assuring you! Gratifying as your ready response to my caresses has always been from the moment I picked you up on the battlefield. . .'

Angry tears stung her eyes so that she could not see him clearly. 'Let me past! I hate you. . .'

Jervais stepped aside without a word, making no attempt to restrain her as she ran from the room.

CHAPTER NINE

CAROLINE dashed the angry tears from her eyes and realised she was in a deserted, dimly lit passage in part of the house she had not seen before.

In her flight from Jervais she must have taken a wrong turning, although how many minutes she had spent angrily pacing she could not guess. Not long, she realised after a little thought, for she was still quite warm and the stone-flagged passage was chilly.

Resolutely Caroline turned her thoughts from Jervais and diverted herself to looking about. This had to be one of the older wings of the house, she deduced, wandering further. It did not seem to be the servants' wing for there were some fine, although dirty, portraits on the walls and when she turned a corner her heart leapt in her mouth until she realised the lurking shadow was only a suit of armour.

The sound of voices ahead of her drew her on, although cautiously, for she had no wish to encounter anyone with her cheeks still tear-streaked.

A door was ajar, spilling light onto the flagstones. Caroline tiptoed forward, drawing her skirts tight in her hand to stop them rustling. A sharp click and an exclamation of 'Damn good shot!' made her realise she had inadvertently found the billiard room.

Unable to resist a peek into this male domain, Caroline looked through the crack at the hinge side of the door and found she had a good view of the room and its inhabitants.

Anthony Gresham, jacket discarded, was leaning across the table, lining up a tricky shot. Sir Richard, also in shirt sleeves, was moving the pointer on the score-board whilst Major Routh lounged against the wall, drawing on a cigarillo and squinting through the smoke at the lie of the billiard balls on the baize cloth.

'Come on, Gresham! Hazard the shot, man—I'm growing old while you work out your angles.'

'Typical artillery approach,' Sir Richard drawled. 'Thank goodness he doesn't have to calculate elevation as well, we'd be here all night.'

Ignoring the attempts to distract him, Gresham potted a perfect shot and straightened up, chalking the end of his cue. 'And we all know why you do not want to be here all night, eh, Routh?'

'Why not?' Sir Richard enquired absently, circling the table to set up his own shot.

'Because he's got a little ladybird stashed away down in the village, that's why.'

He had all Holden's attention and Caroline, who had been on the point of tiptoeing away, also stopped to listen. 'I say, old chap, that's a bit much, isn't it—I mean, guest of Barnard's and all that. . .'

'I'm not asking him to feed or house her,' Routh replied breezily. 'And if I left Fanny alone in London, she wouldn't be alone when I got back, if I know her.'

'Even so. . .' Amongst his friends Sir Richard was known as something of a stuffed shirt: one or two had even suggested he was in the wrong profession and was a natural-born bishop.

'Damn it, man,' Routh riposted, grinding out his cigarillo butt. 'If he hadn't got the ladies staying, Barnard would not turn a hair if I had Fanny here. In fact, knowing him, he'd want to know why I hadn't brought her friends.'

'Indeed?' Gresham enquired. 'You do surprise me; I had no idea our host was a womaniser.'

It was no surprise to Caroline, remembering all too vividly his reaction to her in Belgium, the easy way he seemed prepared to take her under his protection. She suppressed an indignant snort and reapplied her eye to the crack. It was totally improper to be eavesdropping at all—her aunt would have the vapours if she knew—and to be listening to such scandalous revelations was quite beyond the pale. But if they were talking about Jervais, she wanted to hear every detail, however shocking.

'Well, to be fair,' Routh remarked, raising an eyebrow as Sir Richard missed his shot by several inches, 'womaniser is not the word I'd use to describe him. One woman at a time, that's his style—and looks after them well at that. Do you remember that little Spanish piece who followed him all over the Peninsula, Holden?'

'Portuguese, I think,' Holden corrected him coldly, the conversation obviously not to his liking.

'Well, whatever.' Routh waved his hand dismissively. 'The point is, he stuck to her right through the campaign and made sure she was well provided for when we crossed the frontier into France.'

A stab of jealousy struck Caroline, much as she tried to tell herself that she could expect nothing more or less from an unmarried fighting man, hundreds of miles from home, never knowing from day to day whether he'd survive to nightfall.

'And just how do you propose visiting your paramour?' Sir Richard enquired. 'Climbing down the wisteria?'

'No need for anything so crude, old chap. I've slipped the butler a few sovereigns and got the backdoor key. Can come and go as I please.'

The clock in the billiard room struck the quarter and Caroline realised with a shock that she had been away a full half hour. What would Lady Shannon be thinking of her? Hastily she tiptoed away, breaking into a run once she was around the corner. In only a short time she found herself opening a door which led into the hall.

She patted her hair into order, brushed a lingering trace of dust from her hem, and wracking her brain for a plausible excuse for her absence, once more entered the drawing-room.

'Oh, there you are, my dear,' said Lady Shannon placidly. 'Jervais explained how you had torn your flounce. I would have sent my maid up to you, but Jervais insisted you had said it would only take a few stitches to catch it up.'

Miffed that his lordship was, as usual, quite in control of the situation, Caroline shot him a far from grateful glance. He was sitting next to Flora, helping her sort coloured silks for her embroidery and managing to look entirely domesticated. Caroline tried to imagine him, battlestained in the Spanish dust, returning to a dark-eyed girl who would soothe away all the horrors of the day and found the resulting vision so disturbing that she turned abruptly to Lady Shannon.

'Are you to take a house in Town for the Season?' she enquired, managing to retain a look of bright interest as her hostess recounted the trials and tribulations of finding suitable rented accommodation.

'Jervais offered us the use of his town house, but to have the house full of chattering debutantes and callow youths would be asking too much of his good nature! After all, if Julia's darling papa cannot face the thought, I really do not think it fair to inflict it upon Jervais.'

Caroline laughed and offered some suggestions as to suitable house agents until Flora began to pack her silks away in their box. 'Thank you, my lord, I find those pale colours so difficult to match in anything but daylight—your eyesight must be excellent! Caroline, my dear, I think we should retire, for it has been a long day.'

'Indeed, yes,' Lady Shannon concurred. 'You must have risen at the crack of dawn.' She looked across to where her daughter was sitting near the piano, turning over sheet music with Vivian, her cheeks pink with animation. 'And you, too, Julia!'

Caroline was woken the next morning by the rattle of curtain rings as the maid pulled back the heavy drapes, letting in the sunlight to fill the room. The light had a cold clarity as it reflected off the hard hoar frost, but the girl had already set a taper to the fire and the room was comfortably warm as Caroline scrambled out of bed, pulling a wrapper around her shoulders.

The windows in the side of her room faced south-east, catching the rising winter sun. Caroline took a cup of steaming chocolate and went to perch on the window-seat to admire the view over the park. The frost-whitened lawns swept down to a ha-ha beyond which the park stretched out with fine stands of trees on the slopes and, in the distance, a herd of fallow deer.

She rested her head against the shutter and drank in the cold tranquility, sipping occasionally at the chocolate. The stillness was broken by two spaniels, ears flopping as they raced across the grass, chasing each other in their exuberance. They were followed by a tall figure clad in a caped greatcoat, a low-crowned hat on his head and suddenly Caro's dreaminess was quite gone.

Caroline knelt up on the seat the better to see him as Jervais whistled at the dogs, bending to pull at their ears as they gambolled round his booted ankles.

As she watched he turned to stand with his back to the house, staring out over the winter landscape. She knew instinctively he was savouring the sense of ownership now this place was his. Without ever having discussed it with him, she knew he would want to return Dunharrow to the beauty it used to have before his cousin's neglect had besmirched it.

Lost in a futile dream of how it would be to help him in this task, Caroline was taken by surprise when he turned to stare up at her window. Across the distance their eyes met and locked: a sudden terrible sense of loss swept through her and she had to turn back into the room, away from him. He was the man she loved, the only man she would ever love, and he was irretrievably lost to her unless he could find it in his heart to trust her unreservedly.

He had made it perfectly plain the evening before that much as he might desire her, he would never ally himself to a woman with a mystery in her past she would not confide in him. And Caroline knew that even if she had that missing piece of knowledge about how she had come to be on the battlefield, she would not tell him now. If he could not trust her unreservedly, she must learn to live without him.

Over breakfast Lady Shannon suggested the ladies might like to accompany her on a walk into the village.

'Not that Harrowbridge is truly a village, like Dunharrow Parva which lies to the west, it is more of a small town. There is really quite a good haber-dasher's shop—you may be able to match that rose pink silk you have been wanting, Lady Grey.'

'That would be very pleasant,' Flora agreed. 'At this time of year it is such a pleasure to be able to take the air, one can never tell when the weather will turn to rain or snow. Will you accompany us, Caroline dear?' It might put a little colour in her cheeks too, Flora thought privately. Those wan looks would not attract his lordship's eye.

Caroline agreed willingly, and Julia, too, was enthusiastic for the expedition.

Sir Richard also offered to join the party, '. . .in case

you have any small purchases you would wish carried, ma'am. Unless you are taking a footman?'

'Oh, I never trouble in the country, Sir Richard. We should be most glad of your escort.'

Vivian also seemed about to make one of the party when Jervais said, 'I've a litter of hound puppies I'd be glad of your opinion on, gentlemen. A little short in the muzzle, I suspect, but I may be wrong.'

Sir Richard was, therefore, the only gentleman to accompany the ladies as they set out, well wrapped up, to Harrowbridge.

'It is less than a mile if we take the path across the park,' Lady Shannon assured them. 'And the ground is so hard, there is no danger of mud.'

Harrowbridge was, indeed, a large village with a straggling high street widening into a green with a frozen duck pond overlooked by a church, some houses and a respectable-looking inn, the Barnard Arms.

Caroline excused herself from the visit to the haberdasher's, explaining that she would like to look around the church. Sir Richard immediately offered to escort her. 'A most interesting example of early Perpendicular, if I am not mistaken,' he said, causing Caroline's heart to sink at the prospect of a prosy lecture.

'Do not get chilled,' Lady Shannon cautioned. 'We will meet you at the Barnard Arms: ask the landlord to bring coffee to the private parlour if you are there before us.'

The party divided. Caroline found to her surprise that, far from being the bore she had expected, Sir Richard was most informative on the subject of church architecture and they spent a pleasant half-hour looking at the church.

As Caroline had expected, the others were not at the inn when they reached it. 'Too much to expect three ladies to have done with silks and ribbons in half an hour, I am afraid, Sir Richard,' she smiled.

'No matter,' he said amiably as the landlord escorted them to a private room with a roaring fire and a commanding view of the green. 'This is most congenial, and if you, my good fellow, will bring us coffee and perhaps some macaroons for the lady, we will be comfortable enough.'

'Thank you for explaining about the wall-paintings,' Caroline said as they took their seats beside the fire. 'I had no idea there was so much symbolism in them—I shall look at such things with new eyes from now on.'

'I have one or two treatises in my library which you might find informative,' Sir Richard was saying when they were interrupted by a soft exclamation from the doorway.

'I beg your pardon, I'm sure,' the young woman standing there said, dropping a slight curtsy. 'I had no idea the parlour was occupied.'

They both turned and looked at her, Sir Richard with a raised brow as he took in the somewhat daring cut of her overtrimmed pink gown that did nothing to disguise the opulent figure it was clothing.

Caroline felt a tremor of familiarity as she looked at the interloper. Like Sir Richard, she recognised a member of the muslin company when she saw one—life with Papa had taught her that much—but unlike him she did not feel a shudder of revulsion. She had always thought such women were as much sinned against as sinning, and her recent experience had taught her just how vulnerable a young woman could be.

'Indeed,' Sir Richard was saying frostily, 'this parlour is taken for a private party.'

Sir Richard's tone appeared to wash over the young woman, for she twinkled pertly at him and said, 'Then I will take myself off, sir, but first I must find my needlework that I left here this morning.' There was a swish of skirts as she came into the room to retrieve the calico bag from the window seat. 'You know what they say about idle hands, don't you, sir? Must keep busy!'

Sir Richard coloured with embarrassment, but Caroline could not suppress a small giggle. The girl—although now Caroline could see her closely she realised she was nearer seven-and-twenty than seventeen—glanced at her again and a look of surprise, swiftly suppressed, crossed her features.

'Thank you kindly, sir, ma'am.' She dropped a slight curtsy again and shut the parlour door behind her.

'Shall I ring for the waiter, Miss Franklin? I cannot imagine what is keeping the fellow.' Sir Richard tugged the bellpull irritably. 'I suppose one should not expect too much from a village inn—not even the privacy of a parlour, it seems.'

Caroline scarcely heard him, although she nodded politely in acknowledgement. Ever since the young woman had come into the room she had been increasingly uneasy, filled with a nagging sense of recognition which was driving everything else from her mind.

Surely she could never have met her before? Even if she were in her late twenties she was still too young to have been one of the late baronet's fancy pieces. And yet. . .and yet the amiable, pert face was one she had encountered before—and not very long ago. The mass of pale blonde hair was not that unusual, but those green eyes, like a cat's, were.

'Ah! Here you are at last.' Sir Richard glared at the waiter who was struggling with a loaded tray and nearly managed to upend the coffee pot and plates in his agitation.

Caroline ignored them, her eyes staring unfocused on the fire. Yes, she had seen those green eyes before, but not in a room. The memory was of them, filled with consternation, staring down at her. And she had been lying down, on something hard and uncomfortable which jolted.

'Miss Franklin!' Sir Richard said, right at her elbow.

'Oh dear! I do apologise, Sir Richard. I have been daydreaming. Yes, that is exactly how I like my coffee. Thank you.'

He put the cup down on a small table beside her and moved to the window. 'I espy the rest of our party. I think I should go and offer my arm to the ladies, for the street is really very treacherous underfoot. Will you be comfortable here alone for a few moments, Miss Franklin?'

'Indeed, yes, please do not trouble about me,' she assured him hastily. 'It would be dreadful if Lady Shannon or my aunt fell on this ice.'

As he left the room she began racking her brain again in pursuit of that elusive memory. Then her head had been hurting...and she had been wet...and mud was oozing between her fingers as she had tried to sit up...and the reins had broken, her horse halfway to Brussels...

'Of course!' Caroline exclaimed aloud as the last piece of the puzzle clicked into place. That was how she had come to be on the battlefield...

'Has he gone?' She jerked round at the sound of the whisper. It was the young woman. What was her name? Sarah? No Sally...no...

'Fanny!' Caroline exclaimed, starting to her feet. 'I could not remember, but now I see you again, it all comes back.'

'It would be surprising if you could remember your own name,' Fanny remarked, coming fully into the room. 'What with the bump on the head you got falling off that horse.' She peeped out of the window. 'We can't talk now, that stuck-up cove's coming back, but don't you worry, I won't say nothing about you being with us girls. But what happened to you? I've been that worried. . .'

'It will take too long,' Caroline said urgently. 'May we meet somewhere and talk at length? I am staying at Dunharrow.'

'That's a laugh! Up at the big house? Along of Simon Routh?'

'Major Routh?' Caroline was surprised. 'Do you know him?'

Fanny patted a rather flashy enamelled necklace which curved over her ample bosom. 'Oh, I know the gallant major. Who do you think is paying my shot here? Listen, here they come and you can't afford to be seen talking to the likes of me. . .'

'But I must talk to you,' Caroline protested. 'Can I come back this evening? Or meet you somewhere?'

'Too cold outside. Look, come back to the inn after dinner. Simon never turns up before two. He likes his cake and eating it, does the major. He won't miss his dinner and billiards to come hurrying down to me—he knows I'll wait up.' She began to slip out of the door.

Caroline seized her arm, 'Wait! Where will you be?'

'In here. There's no other guests.'

Fanny had hardly vanished up the stairs before Flora, Lady Shannon and Julia came in through the door, laughing and shaking the frost off their hems. Sir Richard, handicapped by a bandbox, a parcel tied in brown paper and string and two umbrellas, followed the ladies.

'My dear Captain, I must apologise for burdening you with our purchases,' Lady Shannon said. 'I really should have brought a footman! Let us leave the box and parcel with the landlord and I will send down for them later.'

'Did you have an interesting visit to the church, Caroline?' Flora enquired. 'A cup of coffee—the very thing, I do declare my lips are blue with cold.' She peeled off her gloves and sat down, accepting a cup from her niece.

Caroline pushed all thoughts of Fanny swiftly to the back of her mind. 'Sir Richard made it most interesting, thank you. Did you find the silks you were seeking, Flora?' She passed the macaroons to Lady Shannon and managed to look interested while the other recounted the results of their shopping expedition.

Lady Shannon took them back to Dunharrow by a different route, one which brought them up the drive towards the house. 'I often think this is the best view,' she remarked to Flora. 'I prefer the new wing in the classical style myself, although there are those with a taste for the Gothick who prefer the older wings.'

'Parts of the house are very much older, then?' Caroline enquired as they paused to admire the vista with the house set off on its slight rise by well placed clumps of trees. 'I must agree with you that in this light the classical formality of that front is quite magnificent.'

'Well, the oldest surviving part is the Elizabethan wing which is in a state of some disrepair. Unfortunately, that is where the kitchens are. It is joined to the modern part by a rather undistinguished section built in 1701 by the then Lord Barnard who had the thought to complete the other three sides of the square. Fortunately, he was killed in a hunting accident before he could do more.'

'Mama!' Julia protested. 'You cannot be glad the poor man was killed?'

'Nonsense. Anyone with taste would rejoice he met a timely end. Mind you, my dear,' she said, turning confidentially to Caroline, 'nothing would induce me to visit the old wing after dark.'

'Why not?' Caroline was enjoying the rather irreverent Lady Shannon. 'Is it haunted?'

'By a headless monk!' Lady Shannon announced dramatically.

Lady Julia was forced to protest again. 'Mama! How could it be a monk if the wing is Elizabethan?'

'There! You see the inadvisability of educating girls,' announced her fond mama. 'I warn you, Julia, take care not to contradict gentlemen in that manner—they do not appreciate it!'

Julia pouted at the reproof, but was unexpectedly championed by Sir Richard. 'On this occasion, Lady Shannon, I must support Lady Julia, for it cannot be a headless monk unless, of course, it is a revenant from a monastery slighted at the time of the abolition of the monasteries.'

Further argument was curtailed by the sound of hooves approaching. The party turned to see Jervais cantering up the drive behind them, a pair of hounds following close on his heels. As he drew up to greet his guests, Vivian also appeared from the woods, riding a particularly handsome grey which Caroline did not recognise.

The riders dismounted and walked alongside the others, Caroline dropping back a little to admire her brother's mount. 'It's a very nice goer,' he confided. 'I offered to buy it, but Jervais won't sell: he's intending to hunt it later in the season.'

As if hearing his name, Jervais stopped and waited for them to catch up to him. 'Serena tells me you are interested in the Elizabethan wing, Miss Franklin. Would you like to see over it?'

'I. . .I would not want to put you to any trouble, my lord,' she said uncertainly, not wanting to be alone with him after their encounter the previous evening.

'It is no trouble, I can assure you. I am still exploring the property myself: perhaps you will see possibilities for improvement in the older wing which have escaped my eye.'

Caroline was startled that he should still show any interest in her opinion, and annoyed with Flora for the knowing look she sent her.

'Perhaps you would care to go after luncheon,' Jervais continued. 'In the safety of daylight,' he added.

'Is it really haunted, then?' Caroline asked lightly, trying to hide her feeling that to be anywhere alone with Jervais was hardly safe.

'Haunted?' He looked startled. 'Oh, Serena has been indulging in her taste for the Gothick, has she?'

'Mama says there is a headless monk, but that is not true, is it, Cousin Jervais?' Julia demanded.

'Good heavens, no! I have told you countless times, Serena, it is not a monk but a nun, walled up alive in what are now the cellars. She committed a nameless crime.' Mischief danced in his dark eyes as Julia gave a small squeak of alarm. 'The monk is only seen on Shrove Tuesday...'

Having reduced Julia to wide-eyed dismay, Jervais swung easily back into the saddle, slipped his booted feet back into the stirrups as the horse fidgeted uneasily. 'The horses are getting chilled. I will see you all at luncheon.' He touched his hat to the ladies. 'And afterwards in the small salon, Miss Franklin?' He did not wait for her answer but cantered off across the frosted grass towards the stable wing, Vivian close behind.

Caroline went directly to the small salon after luncheon and found the room empty. She wandered around uncertainly, picking up some of the small carved ivory pieces which decorated the side tables, then putting them down again with scarcely a glance.

They had eaten early, keeping country hours, and the clock on the mantel was striking half past one when Jervais joined her.

'You are admirably prompt, Miss Franklin,' he

observed. 'I would suggest a warm shawl at the very least, that part of the house is unheated.'

'I have one here,' Caroline rejoined, wrapping it round the shoulders of her garnet-red wool dress as she spoke. 'I thought it sensible to put on stout shoes as well in case the floors were dusty.'

As they went out into the hall, Jervais picked up a lantern and tinder box. 'It is the shortest day today, we cannot rely on the light lasting for more than an hour in those rooms, the casements are so small.'

Caroline followed his broad back down the stone-flagged passage she had paced in her agitation the night before. He paused outside the billiard room and threw open the door. 'If you lose any of the gentlemen in the evening, no doubt this is where they will be found.' Caroline coloured slightly, feeling guilty about her eavesdropping the night before, but Jervais was already moving on.

The old wing, when they emerged into what have been the Great Hall, was indeed already deep in gloom, but Caroline could see it had once been magnificent.

'Oh, how fine!' she exclaimed, touching the intricate carving on the staircase, then recoiling as her hand came away covered in sticky dust.

'And how dirty,' Jervais added drily. 'I something think the simplest thing would be to set a taper to the whole thing.'

'How could you think of such a thing? I would not have thought you so easily discouraged!' she said indignantly. 'All it requires is some resolution, hard work and a good housekeeper. Just think how fine this panelling would look with the application of elbow grease and beeswax.' Enthusiasm overwhelming her awkwardness at being alone with him, she walked rapidly into the centre of the room.

'Caroline! Have a care!' But almost as Jervais called

out and began to move towards her there was a crack
and her right foot went through the floor board as
though it were made of kindling.

She gave a sharp cry of pain and stood still, too
frightened to move in case more of the floor should
give way. Jervais was at her side in an instant, his
fingers strong on her ankle as he freed her foot.

As soon as it was disentangled from the splintered
wood, he lifted her in his arms and carried her to the
foot of the stairs. Unceremoniously he deposited her
on the fourth step, ignoring the puffs of dust that
eddied round her skirts.

'Jervais! I mean. . .my lord!' Caroline gasped as he
lifted her hem and gently explored her ankle and foot
with strong fingers. 'Ouch!' she protested, torn between
shock at his intimate action, the pain of her wrenched
ankle and a guilty pleasure at the closeness of him.

'Be still!' he commanded sharply. 'Now is no time
for propriety and, after all, I have seen rather more
than your ankles before.'

Caroline was still simmering at such a tactless
remark when he got to his feet and pronounced,
'Nothing broken, not even a graze, but it is bruised: I
think you will find it a little sore tomorrow. I will ask
my housekeeper to bring you some witch hazel.'

He put out a hand and pulled her gently to her feet.
Caroline found herself standing on the bottom stair
which brought her eyes to a level with his mouth.

She stared at the firm, moulded lips, remembering
the sensation of his mouth on hers, the pleasure it
evoked and the anger with which he had kissed her
last night. She shivered.

'Can you walk or shall I carry you?' He was already
reaching for her. Caroline swayed towards him,
seduced by his assumption of mastery, her own yearn-
ing to be held close against him. At the last moment
she realised what she was doing and stiffened.

'No! No... I am quite capable of walking alone, thank you.' Suddenly she needed to be away from him, away from the danger that she might blurt out her feelings or fall into his arms.

Wincing as her injured foot met the ground, Caroline gathered up her skirts and walked as briskly as she could back to the safe warmth and companionship of the new wing.

CHAPTER TEN

'Now, my friends,' Lady Shannon announced, clapping her hands lightly together to gain the attention of everyone gathered in the drawing room after dinner. 'I am not going to permit you to become indolent during these long winter evenings! I have a scheme which I trust will find favour with you all.'

Heads turned as she made her announcement, faces showing reactions ranging from the alert interest on Flora's to the apprehension on Vivian's.

'What do you have in mind, Mama?' asked Julia from her seat beside Vivian on the sofa where they had been poring over an album of prints. 'Mama has the must amusing schemes,' she added enthusiastically as the other gentlemen broke off their discussion of the arrangements for the Boxing Day meet of the local hunt and came across to listen to their hostess.

'Allow me to hazard a guess, Serena,' said Jervais with the hint of a laugh in his voice. 'You are about to propose a theatrical entertainment?'

'Is there a group of players in the district, then?' enquired Flora.

'I rather fear, if I am correct about Serena's scheme, that we will form the company,' said Jervais drily.

'Oh, do not discourage the others before I have explained all,' protested his cousin. 'We often perform such entertainments at home in Ireland, and it proves a most delightful diversion, does it not, my dear?' she appealed to her daughter.

Julia clapped her hands together in pleasure. 'Indeed!' She turned to the others, her eyes sparkling.

'But we rarely have such a large party. Why, we can mount a fine production.'

Flora looked a little doubtful. 'Theatricals, Lady Shannon? Do you consider it quite proper for young ladies to appear on the stage?'

'Not in the ordinary course of things, but this would be quite privately, my dear Lady Grey, merely for our own entertainment, and perhaps that of some friends,' Lady Shannon assured her.

'Then we will have no audience for our efforts?' asked Major Routh.

'I had intended asking some of our neighbours to a small party for New Year's Eve,' Jervais remarked. 'They can form our audience. What is your opinion, Miss Franklin? Will you agree to be one of the company?'

Caroline felt herself flush at being singled out so. Why did he persist in asking her opinion on every topic? It only added fuel to Flora's expectations of an early declaration. And yet, his manner was so cool and correct she felt quite chilled by it. It was as though, having been forced to maintain the invitation to Dunharrow despite everything, he was determined to treat her correctly.

'It sounds most diverting.' She addressed herself directly to Lady Shannon. 'Did you have any particular play in mind?'

A general discussion immediately ensued, with Lady Shannon proposing scenes from Shakespeare; Julia, supported by Vivian, suggesting they write their own one-act play and Sir Richard offering to scour the library for some suitable works of drama. Flora was still inclined to be dubious and put forward the idea of readings from poetry, a suggestion which met little support.

Conversation was still animated when the footman

brought in the tea-tray. As he was leaving, Caroline heard Jervais call him over.

'Richards, will you ask Chawton to make certain the doors are all double locked and the bolts secure. And remind him to ensure the shutters are firmly latched.' He was speaking low-voiced, and Caroline realised he did not wish to alarm his guests, but she caught a little of what he added, *sotto voce*, to the Major. 'I heard from the head keeper that Pendleton Manor was broken into last night and some plate stolen. I see no cause for concern, but there is no need to take risks.'

Caroline thought, with well-concealed amusement, that the improved security would put a spoke in Major Routh's wheel, then realised that she too would be locked in. How was she to reach the inn and talk to Fanny?

The problem exercised her so much that she hardly took any part in the decision that they should perform a work of their own devising. However, her brother volunteering to assist Lady Julia in penning it startled her back into the conversation.

'Are you certain, Vivian?' she asked in amazement, knowing he never willingly set pen to paper and had to be badgered into responding to invitations.

'Come, Caro,' he protested, looking hurt at her imputation. 'You have no need to make it sound as though I can scarcely write my own name!' He turned to the rest of the group. 'Now, we must agree upon a theme.'

Later, as the party broke up and Flora and Caroline were ascending the staircase to their chambers, Flora confided, 'I do not know what has come over Vivian. I would have thought him as likely to take up *petit point* as play writing!'

'Really, Flora, cannot you see he is besotted with Lady Julia!' Caroline was tart. 'You know what will happen: Julia will write some piece of amusing nonsense and

Vivian will moon around the library gazing at her and sharpening her quills!'

'You do not sound very pleased at the prospect.' Flora halted at the threshold of her room and regarded her niece in perplexity. 'I thought you were eager for him to settle down with a suitable wife.'

'I would not call a child not yet out a suitable wife for Vivian,' Caroline rejoined as she kissed her aunt goodnight.

A few moments later, alone in her chamber, she wondered at herself for being so tart. Why should not Vivian be happy with Julia? She seemed a charming, well-brought up and intelligent girl, just what Vivian needed, in fact. And perhaps having a very young and inexperienced bride to look after would give Vivian an anchor of responsibility. Always at the back of Caroline's mind was the fear that Vivian, so like her father in looks with his height and blue eyes, would turn to his irresponsible ways.

No, her lack of enthusiasm for her brother's budding tendresse stemmed more from her own unhappiness over Jervais. She felt ashamed of the jealousy which made her feel so grudging. Whatever happened, she and Jervais would never share that first tentative, shy courtship. With a heavy sigh she sat down in the window-seat, turning her mind to the more immediate problem of getting out of the house to meet Fanny.

As the ladies had retired, the men had strolled off towards the billiards room, with Vivian making rather wild wagers on the outcome of a match he proposed with Simon Routh. It seemed certain that the gentlemen would be safely occupied for some time to come.

Caroline remembered the gnarled branches of ivy which covered the wall at the corner of the house. Lady Shannon had remarked upon the shrouding climber as they had walked up the drive, observing that Jervais must have it attended to or it would damage the stonework.

She opened the doors onto her balcony, shivering as the bitter cold cut through her silk gown. By leaning over the balustrade she was able to test the size of the stems, finding them as thick as a man's arm. As she looked down on the branches she could see that many of them grew horizontally, providing what appeared to be a secure stepladder.

If she hurried down now before Chawton made his rounds, she could leave through the front door and return this way and no one would be any the wiser.

Caroline pulled off her evening dress and rapidly donned her warmest gown and thick stockings. She winced as she laced up her stout walking shoes over the purpling bruise on her foot, but pushed the discomfort out of her mind as she searched for warm gloves.

She drifted downstairs, hugging the shadows as she crossed the hall, pulling the hood of her fur-lined cloak over her face as she did so. The door was on the latch and opened with a well-oiled silence as she slipped into the frosty night.

Everything seemed to conspire with her in her escape—even the moon was full, reflecting off the frosty ground with a light which made walking easy. Caroline set off down the drive at a brisk pace, half expecting a shout from the house as someone saw her, but none came.

She climbed over the gate at the lodge, not daring to risk the wicket squeaking, but there was no light showing at the windows and she passed on unseen.

Getting away undetected had occupied Caroline's mind, but now she was abroad on the highway she began to feel uneasy. The woods on either side of the road were full of dark shadows and furtive noises. Branches cracked, dead leaves rustled and her own footsteps sounded loud on the frost-hardened road.

Caroline had to speak firmly to herself to quell her fears and had succeeded quite well when the night was rent by an unearthly shriek. She broke into a run and did not stop until she arrived at the first cottage on the outskirts of the village, where she stopped, her heart banging against her ribs.

Fool! she rebuked herself. How many times had she heard the cry of a vixen before? To be panicked into headlong flight was thoroughly foolish—and had done her sore foot no good into the bargain.

If her need to speak to Fanny and reassure herself that now she truly did recall everything that had happened to her on the battlefield had not been so great she would have turned tail and gone back to Dunharrow without delay. The prospect of scaling the ivy ladder now seemed foolhardy in the extreme.

The inn looked warm and welcoming and the noise of raised voices and laughter rose from the back of the building. There was light between the drawn curtains in the window of the private parlour. She tapped discreetly on the pane, keeping back in the shadows. The curtain was moved so quickly Fanny must have been waiting for her signal: in response to her gesture Caroline hurried to the front door which was swiftly and silently opened.

'You must be freezing, miss,' Fanny declared, urging her into the parlour. 'Sit by the fire and have some punch. I ordered it earlier—we don't want to risk anyone seeing you here with me.'

Caroline sipped the pungent liquor gratefully, wrinkling her nose in distaste at the unfamiliar smell of rum but welcoming the warmth it spread through her chilled body.

'Take off your cloak and gloves, miss, or you won't feel the benefit when you go out again,' Fanny chided, bustling round. When Caroline was settled she sat down opposite her and regarded her with shrewd eyes.

'So what's the story, miss? Why are you so hot to find out what happened?'

'Why, anyone would be concerned,' Caroline protested. The green eyes assessed her, then Fanny shook her head.

'No, there's more than that. There's a man in this somewhere, I'll be bound.'

Caroline found she could not meet the woman's gaze and dropped her own eyes. 'Well, yes, there is—the man who found me on the battlefield. But never mind him now—I need to know if what I recollect is what truly happened. For if there is anything, anything else at all, I must know. My memory has been returning, but only in fits and starts.' She laughed shakily. 'I do not believe I can stand any more surprises!'

'You tell me what you think happened,' said Fanny, refilling her own—and Caroline's—glass and settling back in her chair, 'and I'll tell you if you go wrong.'

'Well, I was riding through Brussels to find someone to advise us on whether we should leave the city. All the rumours were that Napoleon was on his way and his troops would take it by nightfall. I had not ridden for days and my horse was over-fresh.' She sipped the warming punch, then continued. 'There was such a hubbub in the streets, so many people pushing and clamouring I could hardly hold him. . .' In her mind she was back in the mêlée, broken carts, screaming children being tugged by their mothers through the crush of bodies. . .

'I became quite lost. By the time the crowd thinned enough for me to descry my surroundings, I was almost on the outskirts of the city. At least the crowds were less—everyone was going in the opposite direction, of course.' She grimaced ruefully. 'I should have realised then I was totally out of my way. But I had no time to think—a column of infantry was going past and a musket was discharged accidentally. The wretched animal took off like a bullet himself and the next thing I knew, we were galloping towards the sound of the fighting, across fields.'

'It's a wonder you stuck on so long,' Fanny said. 'I never could get the knack of this horse-riding lark myself.'

'Well, I came off soon enough—right over the top of Gypsy's head and into a puddle.'

'And that's where we found you,' Fanny chimed in. 'Do you remember that?'

'Very well—I was never so glad to see anything in my life as I was to see your wagon,' Caroline said with feeling.

'You did look a sight, sitting there in the mud,' Fanny chuckled. 'Oh, sorry, miss, it's wrong to laugh, but I tell you, we was glad of the diversion. All of us were worried about our boys: we knew Nosey had ordered an all-out attack. And then we'd been bundled into that filthy old wagon, all anyhow—and half our nice things left behind for those filthy Frenchies to steal. Some of the girls were having a good cry, so you were a godsend to take our minds off our troubles.'

'You were all very kind,' Caroline said warmly.

'And so were you,' Fanny responded roundly. 'No side to you, treated us just like we was ladies, not working girls at all. A nicely brought-up girl like you should have had the vapours at being picked up by the likes of us.'

'A nicely brought-up girl would not recognise your profession,' Caroline responded with a flash of humour. 'But then life with my late papa gave me an early acquaintanceship with all manner of things I should not know!'

'I do not know when I've been so uncomfortable as on that journey,' said Fanny reminiscently. 'What with the state that wagon was in, and that old fool of a driver with his endless moaning. . .'

'And the poor horse,' Caroline recalled. 'It did hate the thunderstorms so.'

'Well, so did I, but you'd have thought it would have been glad to get to its stable in Brussels instead of sticking its hooves in and refusing to move.'

'We couldn't have gone on in such a storm,' Caroline said reasonably. 'That lightning!'

'I suppose you're right,' conceded Fanny. 'And it did give us a chance to get you out of those mud-soaked clothes and get you washed up a bit.'

'I am afraid I have lost your dress, the pretty red silk one you lent me. And the slippers.'

'It doesn't matter,' said Fanny smugly. 'I got a whole new wardrobe from Simon: if we had more time I'd show you.' She gave Caro a wink. 'Very generous gentleman is the gallant Major.'

'I imagine he is.' Caroline thought of the frank warmth in Major Routh's eyes when they had been introduced. She shook her head ruefully. 'That dress, though, it caused a dreadful misunderstanding.'

Fanny grimaced. 'No, I 'spose it wasn't the best of choices, not for a lady of quality like you to wear. And the face paint can't have helped.' She shook her head. 'We only put it on because you looked so white, even after you'd had something to eat.'

'It was amusing,' Caroline reassured her. 'It was something I would never have dared do and I must admit, I enjoyed seeing what a little rouge and eye black could do for my looks.' Fanny was still looking doubtful, so she added, 'It passed the time until we could set out again, and none of us could have guessed I would not have the chance to wash it off again.'

'We all felt so badly about that! Looking back, I suppose one of us should have stayed awake, but we was all too tired by the time we set off again. And in the dark we didn't know the old fool had taken the wrong road!' Fanny threw up her eyes to the ceiling.

'Miles out he was come Sunday morning. I know it was dark, but how do you miss a place the size of Brussels, for heaven's sake!'

'So that was why I was so confused,' Caroline exclaimed. 'I had thought it was the bang on the head, but I could not make any sense of the landscape when daylight came.'

'But what happened to you?' demanded Fanny. 'One minute we were all there, and the next, when we woke up, there you was gone!'

'I fell asleep as well. I was sitting right by the tailgate—do you remember? I was woken by a terrible lurching of the cart and the next thing I knew, I had tumbled out. For the second time in a day I was sitting on the muddy ground.'

'Why didn't you get back in?'

'I was winded and it was dark and raining. By the time I had got to my feet I could see nothing—not even a track. I think the driver must have lost the road completely by then.'

'You poor lamb.' Fanny was all sympathy. 'What did you do?'

'I was cold and wet, but most of all I was frightened of coming across troops—theirs or ours! I found a spinney with a hollow oak in it and spent the rest of the night there. When daylight came I started to walk, but there was no sun to guide me with all that drizzle and for all I knew I was walking away from the city.'

She rubbed her forehead, shivering at the unpleasantness of the memory. 'I could hear fighting, but it seemed to come from all directions. I was getting hungry and I was more frightened than I had ever been in my life before—or ever want to be again!'

'But you got back to Brussels?'

'No. I found a track at last, but it was getting darker. I can remember feeling faint and dizzy, then nothing. . . I must have fainted.'

'And then?' Fanny's eyes were bright with excitement, she was almost on the edge of her chair.

'I woke up in a barn. With a dog, a horse—and a man.'

'Oh, er!' Fanny was wide eyed. 'What sort of a man?'

'A gentleman—of sorts,' said Caroline bitterly.

'Lawks! Did he. . .er, I mean. . .?'

'Very nearly.' Caroline made no pretence of misunderstanding the other woman's drift. 'He was too badly wounded, however. He assumed I was one of your profession, and because my memory had completely deserted me—so did I, for two days.'

Fanny's face showed complete comprehension. 'Well, he would, wouldn't he? What other women would be on the battlefield, and with you dressed like that, with a painted face. . .' She eyed Caroline shrewdly. 'This gentleman, he got you home safely, then? And no one any the wiser?'

'He offered me his protection.' Caro fell silent, recalling vividly how that protection had felt, how safe, yet how vulnerable Jervais had made her feel. 'My friends think I was taken in by a respectable Belgian family. No one other than the man, myself and you know the whole truth.'

'Well, you need not worry that I'll let on to anyone,' said Fanny roundly. 'We girls need to stick together. After all, you can only trust a man as long as your looks last, but your girlfriends stick by you.'

'Let me at least give you something for the dress and the shoes,' Caroline offered.

'That'd be very civil of you, miss.' Fanny, no blackmailer, was obviously used to taking whatever benefits came her way.

'Call me Caroline,' Caro urged, pressing a folded banknote into the young woman's hand.

'Thank you kindly, Caroline! Now, you'd better be on your way or you'll be running into Simon Routh.'

'Oh, I should have told you,' Caroline said as she got to her feet. 'He may not be able to come down this evening—the doors are all being double-locked because there are housebreakers at large.'

'That's nice,' Fanny commented. 'The bed to myself for a night. Men are all right, but they do snore... Here, where does that leave you? How are you going to get back in?'

'Up the ivy,' said Caroline grimly as she drew on her gloves.

'You're a game one,' Fanny said admiringly. She drew back the curtain and peeped out. 'Here, look, it's started to snow! Have another noggin before you go, keep the cold out.' She pressed the mug into Caroline's hand.

Caroline, her mind on the journey back to Dunharrow, swigged back the punch without thinking, squeezed Fanny's hand with gratitude and hurried out into the snowy night.

The snow was lying light and powdery, already obscuring the road surface. Caroline shivered and pulled her heavy cloak closer round her shoulders. Her bruised foot was throbbing, her head was muzzy from the punch and the cold hurt her throat. The journey back seemed endless and somehow she did not seem entirely in control of her feet.

'I'm tipsy!' she exclaimed to the dark night in horror. That punch must have been stronger than she had realised: certainly far stronger than the genteel fruit cups she was used to. Fuzzily she recalled Vivian remarking on one occasion that cold made the effects of drink worse. That was all it was...once she was in the warmth of her room, she would feel quite herself again.

The house was in darkness when she finally reached

the end of the drive. Unaware of the footprints she was leaving in the snow she trudged across the lawn looking for the root of the ivy. Really, this cold was so extreme it was now affecting her eyesight: there seemed now to be two main streams growing up, one each side of the corner.

It seemed very amusing all of a sudden. Caroline stood swaying slightly. 'Eeny meany... This one, I think.' The right hand one was the thicker and stronger.

Really, it was surprisingly easy and she was not frightened at all. Her foot slipped and she giggled, but kept on climbing. The edge of the balustrade presented a hurdle, but with a lurch she was over it and safe on the balcony, albeit sitting in the snow.

'Whoops!' Another giggle escaped her, then remembering she might be overheard by Flora, she whispered 'Sshh!' and gently pushed the French doors opens.

Caroline swayed towards the dark bulk of the bed, shedding clothes as she went. Now where was her nightgown? Lighting a candle seemed far too much trouble and the room was beginning to swim in a most disconcerting manner. By the glow of the embers of the fire she could see something white at the foot of the bed. Ah, there it was!

She reached out a hand towards it, missed and fell headlong onto the bed. Oh well, now she was here...

Everything that followed happened very swiftly. The bed next to her came alive. A large form heaved itself up, throwing bedcovers all over her, smothering her startled scream. As she struggled to free herself from the folds a hand slammed down on her throat, almost choking her. 'One move and I'll break your damned neck!' Jervais's voice snarled.

Jervais! 'Aargh!' Caroline managed before the hand relaxed its grip. Seconds later the light of a candle flickered.

'Come out of there and make no false move, my friend, I have a pistol trained on you.' There was a soft click as a hammer was cocked: this was no bluff, he thought she was a housebreaker.

Caroline peeped gingerly over the blankets and found herself staring down the single black eye of a pistol. Jervais, wearing only a nightshirt, was standing beside the bed, one knee on the edge.

'Caroline! What the hell are you doing?'

She struggled up in the bed with some difficulty. The straps of her shift were sliding dangerously down her shoulders and she hitched them up with great dignity, enunciating carefully.

'Why are you in my bedchamber, Lord Barnard? And kindly do not point that thing at me!'

'Your bedchamber? This is my room, Miss Franklin!' He put the pistol aside, regarding her quizzically, then leant towards her and sniffed delicately. 'Rum! I do believe you are drunk, Caroline! How? Where the devil have you been to get spirits?' He seemed amused rather than annoyed.

'Merely a glass of punch. . .or two. Hic!' Incorrigibly truthful, Caroline corrected herself. 'Or perhaps three?'

Jervais, hands on hips, his lips twitching with laughter, enquired, 'But where? And, judging by the state of you, I would hazard four glasses at least.'

'It is a secret,' Caroline responded with dignity. 'And it is a well-known fact that cold makes the effect of strong drink worse.' Unfortunately another hiccough escaped her. Irritably she pushed at the heavy covers. 'Don't just stand there! If this is your bedchamber I must leave—help me!'

Jervais obligingly tossed aside the bedclothes and took her hands in his. 'Upsadaisy.' He was humouring her, she could tell. 'Time you were in your own bed. . .'

She offered no resistance. His strength pulled her

into his embrace with more force than he had perhaps
intended. Shift and hair awry, Caroline found herself
chest to chest with him, only the thin fabric of two
garments separating their bare skin. The tolerant
amusement ebbed out of his face. In the flickering
candlelight his eyes went very dark.

Jervais bent his head and kissed her hard. Caroline,
all inhibitions gone, returned the embrace with ardour.
Her shaky legs lost what little strength they had and
she overbalanced, falling back onto the bed, taking
Jervais with her.

For a hectic moment their bodies intertwined on the
rumpled bedding, then Jervais exclaimed, 'My God!'
He freed his mouth and stared down at her. 'Your feet
are frozen! Where have you been?'

'Mmm,' Caroline murmured, snaking her arms
around his neck to draw him close again.

'Oh, what the hell. . .' Jervais seemed to have
reached a decision. With one hand he pulled her close
against him, with the other he dragged the covers over
both of them.

Jervais held her tight, wrapping his warmth around
her, but making no attempt to kiss or caress her.
Caroline wriggled, confused and disappointed by his
lack of ardour. The unfamiliar weight of him against
her, the strength of his arms, the heat of his body were
terrifyingly, wonderfully new.

'Stop squirming, Caro! You are testing my will-
power to the utmost. You should not be here, I should
not be holding you like this—and as soon as you are
warm, and sober enough not to rouse the household,
you are going straight back to your own bed.'

'Jervais. . .' she pleaded softly against the satiny
smoothness of his neck.

'Caroline. . .stop it!' The words came out between
gritted teeth. 'You are going to feel sorry enough for

yourself in the morning as it is—do not add to that something you will regret for the rest of your life.'

Foggily Caroline knew he was right. She should not be doing this, should not be there with him. She... they...were behaving scandalously, but the warmth and strength of him were too much for her will-power. There was nowhere else she wanted to be, ever, and she could trust Jervais. Slowly the warmth of his body overcame the chill of hers and the rum was making her drowsy: her eyelids drooped and with a little sigh of content she gave herself up to sleep.

CHAPTER ELEVEN

THE door crashed open with a sound like artillery firing and the room was suddenly lit by flickering candlelight.

'God! Sorry, old chap. . .bit unsteady, been drinking with Routh. Here, Barnard—you asleep? If you are I'll go 'way, but had to tell you. . .lost that bet you made on me! Rolled up, beaten hollow—damned good game you missed.' A loud hiccough echoed round the silent room.

Caroline, waking with a start to the sound of her brother's voice, half-rose from the pillow only to be unceremoniously shoved back under the covers by a ruthless hand.

'Hell's teeth, Franklin, I thought you were a gang of housebreakers!' Jervais sat up in bed, achieving, to Caroline's frantic hearing, a credible note of amused tolerance. 'What time is it, man? You're as drunk as an owl—get to your bed, we'll talk about it in the morning.'

'No, you're a good chap and I'm determined to explain how I came to lose your guineas.' Vivian waved a finger in the air, lurching towards the bed.

'Go to your chamber, Vivian,' Jervais said evenly.

The younger man gazed at him, looking very like the owl he had compared him to and lurched again.

'Watch those candles, man!'

'Sorry. . .put them down here.' Caroline heard the bump as a candelabra was set down on the night-table beside the bed. 'There we are. . . Think I'm drunk, old man—damn good port, by the by—I'll just sit down here while I explain about the game.'

There was a jolt, then the mattress next to Caroline sank as her brother's weight landed on it. With a loud 'Whoops!' he lolled back, hitting Caroline's head with one arm. Even through the blankets it was a painful—and unexpected—blow.

Without thinking, before she could stop herself, Caroline protested, 'Vivian!'

A dreadful silence followed that none of them seemed capable of breaking. Eventually, unable to bear the stifling darkness, Caroline peered over the top of the blankets at the two men.

Jervais, sitting up against the pillows, had his eyes closed, a look of utter resignation on his features. Vivian, mouth agape, eyes popping, was gazing in stunned horror at the sight of his sister revealed, scarcely clad, in his host's bed.

Vivian leapt from the bed, suddenly sobered by the implications of what he was seeing. 'Sir!' he thundered. 'How dare you!' His young face darkened. 'Name your friends, sir—my seconds will wait on them tomorrow. Caroline—' he turned stern features on his sister '—Caroline, go and pack your bags and wake your aunt. We leave this house immediately!'

'Vivian.' Caroline also was horribly sober and awake. 'It is not what it seems!' It sounded feeble even to her own ears.

Beside her Jervais stirred at last. 'Caroline, please be quiet, leave this to me.' He swung his legs out of bed, reaching for his brocaded dressing-gown and shrugging it on. 'Come and sit down, Franklin—I cannot believe you wish to involve the household in this matter.' He guided Vivian's still unsteady feet to the fireside and pushed him into a chair, taking the one opposite.

'Now look here,' Vivian persevered. 'You need not think to fob me off, my lord! I am not so much in my cups as to forget what I have seen tonight, or my challenge.'

Jervais sighed deeply. 'I have no intention of avoiding my obligations to your sister, Vivian. It would be quite ineligible of me to fight my future brother-in-law, would it not?'

'You are intending to marry her, then?' Vivian demanded. He was increasingly rational as they spoke, his words sharper and more coherent.

'Of course I am. Why the devil do you think I invited you all down here? Your aunt realised, even if you did not.'

'But Flora would not permit this any more than I will,' Vivian said icily.

'Well, of course Lady Grey would not!' Jervais snapped, then reverted to a calmer voice. 'Listen to me, Franklin. I have every intention of marrying your sister, I have always intended to marry your sister. It is unfortunate that you have discovered us, but you cannot be so naïve as to believe that such an anticipation of the ceremony does not go on in polite society!'

Vivian regarded the older man through narrowed eyes for a moment, then relaxed. 'Well, of course I know such things go on; it is just somewhat of a shock when it is your own sister involved! I will not deny it is a good match and if you intend to do your duty by her — and, of course, I accept your word as a gentleman that you will — I withdraw my challenge. You have my consent to the union.'

Caroline had been listening with increasing embarrassment and anger. How could they discuss her as if she were a piece of livestock to be disposed of at will! Why, it was as though she were not even in the room. . .

'But not necessarily mine,' she interrupted icily.

Both men turned to look at her in surprise. 'What did you say?' demanded her brother.

'I said, you do not have my consent to the match,' she repeated, struggling out of bed and pulling the coverlet around her chemise for decency.

Vivian was outraged. 'You stand there in your shift, in a man's bedchamber and tell me you will not marry him?'

Caroline's chin came up. To be lectured by her young brother as if he were her grandfather was insupportable, but the anger kept at bay the dreadful embarrassment of being found by him like this. 'It would be nice to be asked.'

Vivian looked enquiringly at Jervais who got to his feet, strode over to her side, went on one knee and took her hand in his. 'Madam, I have the honour to request that you be my wife.'

She looked down at his head, bent as he kissed her hand. She had no choice but to agree. It was what she wanted above all things. . .'But not like this,' she murmured desperately. Jervais must have heard her for his head came up and he looked her in the eye.

'We have no choice,' he murmured back, so low-voiced it could not have reached Vivian. Then he stood and led her over to her brother. 'We will speak in the morning. Go back to your room, you will be getting cold.'

At her doorway she whispered to Vivian, 'Do not tell Flora any of this!'

'Of course I will not—how could I? Really, Caroline, I must tell you I am very disappointed in your behaviour.'

'Oh, don't be such a prig, Vivian!' she hissed back, suddenly furious with him and every other man in the world. When she had closed the door on his disapproving face, she leaned back against the heavy panels, sick with reaction and the effects of the rum. Her head throbbed and she felt queasy. And so thirsty.

Caroline poured herself a glass of cordial from the

flask on the night table and crossed to the uncurtained window, trailing Jervais's coverlet behind her. The snow was lying thickly now, blanketing the park in silence under the moonlight. It was so beautiful, so tranquil and she was so utterly confused and miserable.

She was going to marry Jervais, the man she loved— but for all the wrong reasons. When they had met again in London she had pretended not to know him so that he would have no compulsion to offer for her. When he had made a declaration she had believed it was because he loved her, only to have that belief dashed when he showed he did not trust her. Even that was better than the prospect that faced her now: the knowledge that unwittingly she had trapped Jervais into marriage.

Getting out of bed the next morning with the worst headache she had ever had in her life was an act of sheer will and determination. Caroline sat on the edge of the bed, attempting to master her rebellious stomach, marvelling that men were prepared to tolerate the after-effects of strong drink on a regular basis.

The maid came in with hot water, full of excited chatter about the thick snow that had fallen during the night. 'And they do say the village is quite cut off, miss. . .'

Caroline flapped a limp hand. 'Oh please, Katy, do not prattle so, I have such a headache I can scarcely think!'

'You shouldn't be out of bed, miss.' Katy looked concerned as she dragged the heavy drapes back from the window. Caroline winced and shut her eyes against the clear white light that flooded the room. 'It's early yet, miss, why not lie down again and I'll ask Cook to make you a soothing tisane.' She regarded her mistress, taking in the pale, pinched features and the shadowed eyes.

The temptation was almost overwhelming, but Caroline fought against it. No, she must speak with Jervais before Vivian had the opportunity to tell the entire house-party of his sister's good news.

Seated before the looking glass, she reflected that at least Vivian also must feel somewhat fragile this morning and if luck were with her would keep to his chamber for a while yet. 'Something very simple, Katy, if you please!' she exclaimed as the maid approached with hairpins and brush to arrange her black curls. 'Leave it loose, simply brush out the tangles.'

Food was set out in the breakfast room but as Caroline had hoped, no one of the party was yet at table. She was hesitating, wondering if she dared go to Jervais's bedchamber to talk to him, when she heard the sound of the library door shutting: no one but the master of the house was likely to be about in there at this hour.

Jervais was standing before the cold fireplace, one booted foot resting on the fender. He was dressed for riding, but seemed in no hurry to be out, for he was gazing pensively into the glass above the mantelshelf, drumming his fingers slowly on the marble.

Their eyes met in the reflected image: his dark and unreadable, hers shadowed and anxious.

'Jervais, I looked to find you alone. . .' she began, moving across the room towards him.

He turned, but made no move to meet her. Instead he looked hard at her face before announcing abruptly, 'You look ghastly.'

'Thank you, my lord!' Caroline snapped. 'You may be assured I feel it.'

'That is not to be wondered at, considering the state you were in last night. You need the hair of the dog.' As he spoke he was already pouring a small tot of brandy from the decanter. 'Here, drink it.'

'Oh, no!' she said in revulsion. 'I shall be sick!'

'No, you won't,' he said grimly. 'Knock it straight back.'

Caroline did as she was told, closing her eyes with a shudder as the spirit burned the back of her throat. For one frightful moment her stomach rose in revolt, then she opened startled eyes. 'Oh! That is better.' She set the glass down and smiled shakily at him. 'I cannot conceive how you gentlemen drink for pleasure if that is how you feel every morning.'

'From that, may I deduce that my affianced bride is not in the habit of imbibing rum toddies nightly?' The words were said humorously, but there was little humour evident in the saturnine face.

'Of course not, do not be so absurd! But never mind that now—we must agree what to do before Vivian starts spreading news of our engagement.'

'Do? What is there for us to do?' He put his hands behind his back and rocked slightly on his heels as he watched her. 'I had assumed that Lady Grey would be placing a notice in *The Times* and that she and you would be buying your bride clothes once you return to Town. Of course, if you wish to discuss which church we are to be married in, or what arrangements you wish to make for the domestic staff at the town house, I am at your disposal. But after breakfast, surely, is soon enough?'

He offered her his arm as if to take her into breakfast. 'Jervais!' Caroline protested. 'That is not what I...'

'Expected?' he finished for her. 'Forgive me, Caroline. You must think me most undemonstrative, unloverlike. But I hesitated to press my attentions on you, looking as frail as you do. However...'

He took the hand he had tucked under his elbow and raised it to his lips, pulling her close against him as he did so. Caroline gazed up, mesmerised, into his intent face. She felt her lips part involuntarily and drew in a shuddering breath before his mouth came down on hers.

His mouth was hard and demanding, almost cruel in its insistence that she yield to him and Caroline felt her few defences crumble. His tongue touching hers caused a shock that thrilled through her; she moulded herself more closely against his body, all her determination to reject him melting in the heat of his embrace.

Jervais stooped to cradle and lift her in his arms, carrying her languid and unprotesting to the chaise longue. He sank down slowly, taking Caroline with him to nestle on his lap: not once had he freed her mouth and she was scarcely conscious that she was no longer standing, so swept up was she by the feelings he was arousing.

He bent his head to trail kisses across the gentle swell of her breasts where they rose from the confining lace of her bodice. A shudder convulsed her; when he glanced up enquiringly she locked her fingers in his chestnut hair to impel him to continue.

Instead he laughed huskily, sitting up straighter and pulling her back to rest against his shoulder. 'Enough of this, my little wanton! I am beginning to think that what I said about anticipating the wedding ceremony has some merit.'

The words were enough to recall her to her senses. 'But that is what I came to talk to you about, Jervais.'

'Anticipating the ceremony?' he queried.

'No! Cancelling it—and as soon as possible, before Vivian tells anyone. Why else do you think I am here so early?'

His face hardened. As swiftly as she had found herself on his knees she found herself seated upon the chaise longue beside him. 'Do I understand you aright, Miss Franklin? After what has just passed between us, after having been discovered drunk in my bed by your own brother, you tell me you do not wish to marry me?'

'Yes,' she stated baldly, tugging the lace up over her heated bosom.

'And precisely what do you think you were about just now?' His voice was calm, interrogative, but with an underlying danger in it which she chose not to heed.

'Well, you kissed me. You took me by surprise.' Caroline got to her feet, smoothing down the tell-tale creases in her muslin gown where it had been crushed against his thighs.

Jervais was on his feet too, very close beside her, but not touching her. 'I begin to wonder if you can be as innocent of the effect your actions have upon a man as you would have me believe.'

'Sir!' But her outrage did not quite ring true. Caroline was burningly aware that Jervais only had to kiss her to incite her own ready need for him. 'Stop it, Jervais—you are distracting me.' She ignored the incredulous expression that crossed his face and pressed on. 'I mean, we must discuss this before we are joined by the others. I cannot marry you.'

'There would appear to be only one explanation for your refusal,' he remarked. 'If, of course, one discounts the notion that you intend to remain unmarried for the rest of your days. And forgive me, Miss Franklin, if I find that hard to believe, judging by your responses to me.'

Caroline felt hot colour suffusing her face at his unseemly implication. 'Sir! You are no gentleman!'

'Madam,' he replied evenly, 'in my arms, I find you no lady.'

Caroline clenched her fists as if to strike the sardonic face, but he easily encircled both wrists with one hand and held he away from him.

'Let us stop beating about the bush, Caroline. Who is he?'

'Who?' She wriggled ineffectively in his grasp. 'You are hurting me!'

'Only when you struggle. Keep still. I refer to the man you were with last night, the man you had your clandestine meeting with. Is he the same man you were seeking on the battlefield when we first met?'

Caroline was utterly speechless. 'Or is this somebody else who has caught your fancy?' he added, raising an interrogative eyebrow.

She found her voice, although it emerged as an outraged squawk. 'How many men do you think I am entangled with, for heaven's sake?'

He released her hands and shrugged dismissively. 'I would not like to hazard a guess.'

Caroline controlled herself with difficulty. Eventually she said, with deceptive calm, 'I was on that battlefield for a perfectly innocent reason and if you cannot trust me enough to believe that, then I have no intention of furnishing you with an explanation!'

'So you no longer maintain you have lost your memory?' He folded his arms across his chest and leaned against the mantelshelf.

'I did lose my memory and now I have regained it— but not all of it. . .until last night.' As soon as the words were uttered she could have bitten her tongue, for his eyes narrowed.

'I had not considered the liberal application of rum to be a memory reviver.'

'Oh, never mind the rum! And what I was doing last night is none of your concern. You are neither my father, my brother nor my husband—and never will be! Jervais, will you please believe I do not wish to marry you!'

She was flushed and panting with emotion and the desperate need to convince him—and herself—that it was so.

Jervais looked down into her eyes and said softly, 'Yes, I believe you.'

Caroline closed her eyes with a sigh of relief. Then the feeling was swept away, overwhelmed by regret. She could not marry Jervais knowing he neither loved nor trusted her: but, oh, how it hurt to do the right thing and set him free, loving him as she did!

'Caroline, dear.' It was her aunt, a note of indulgent chiding in her voice as she entered the room to find her niece unchaperoned with Lord Barnard.

'Flora!' Caroline jumped, startled out of her intense preoccupation where only she and Jervais existed.

'You really should have waited to come down to breakfast with me, Caroline,' Flora admonished her niece fondly, while sending Jervais a look which implied that her protest was merely a matter of form, that she trusted him implicitly.

'Yes, Flora, I am sorry.' Caroline took a step towards her, but was halted in her tracks by Jervais's hand on her arm.

'My dear, allow me to tell your aunt of our happiness. Lady Grey, yesterday I asked Sir Vivian for the honour of addressing Miss Franklin, and I am overjoyed to tell you she has accepted my proposal.'

Caroline's gasp of shock and horror was lost in her aunt's fervent embrace and shower of kisses. It was impossible to get a word in as Flora, bubbling over with excitement, gave vent to her feelings.

Finally she ran out of breath, gave Jervais a resounding kiss on the cheek which took them both by surprise, and fluttered out, calling over her shoulder, 'I must tell Anthony. . . I mean, Major Gresham. . .'

'Jervais! Have you lost your mind?' Caroline exploded the moment her aunt was out of sight. 'You have just released me from the engagement. . .'

'I told you that I believed you when you said you did not wish to marry me.'

'Well, then?' Caroline stamped her foot in fury. She wanted to strike his complacent face, drive that superior, knowing expression from his features.

'What you want, Caroline, is not of first consequence here: there are greater considerations at stake.'

'I fail to understand what other consideration there can be beyond my. . .our feelings.'

'Our feelings are not at issue—and I was not aware that we had discussed mine in any case. No, your reputation and my honour, these are of paramount importance.'

'I only want to do the right thing,' she burst out, tears stinging the back of her throat. 'And all you do, you self-righteous. . .prig, is prate about reputation and honour. If you had kept quiet, then neither would be at risk!' Almost blindly she stumbled to a chair and sat, her face averted. Surely her expression would betray how she felt, how much she loved him, her turmoil at having her sacrifice thrown back at her. . .

A long silence ensued. At length Caroline ventured a surreptitious peep through wet lashes at his calm, patient face. She was searching for some vestige of emotion, some sign of his true feelings, the slightest hint that he wished to marry her for herself, not for honour or duty. . . She opened her mouth, the words 'But do you love me?' trembling on her lips.

Their eyes locked, he took a step towards her and the words were almost out when there was a rustle of gowns, an excited chattering and the library was suddenly filled with people.

Lady Shannon was kissing Caroline; Major Gresham was shaking hands with Jervais, whilst Sir Richard and Major Routh added their congratulations and Vivian, with Julia at his side, had the proprietorial expression of a man who has just seen his sister make a most eligible match.

It was almost a relief. Caroline found she was not

required to do anything except smile and nod and accept graciously the good wishes which showered upon her.

Serena Shannon, noticing Caroline's damp lashes, stroked her arm maternally. 'You are quite overset, my dear—tell me, when did my cousin propose?'

Caroline shot Jervais a glance inviting him to answer this pertinent question. Vivian, suddenly overcome by confusion, opened his mouth to speak but Jervais cut in urbanely.

'Oh, very early this morning.' He tucked Caroline's hand firmly under his arm, ignoring her startled look. 'We both found ourselves up—' he paused '—and about at an unconscionable hour—I seized the moment, and to my great joy Caroline accepted me.'

Caroline, nettled by his ready manipulation of the facts, looked up at him and found herself transfixed and rattled by the intensity of his expression as he looked at her.

They could have been alone. Their eyes locked and held for what seemed like for ever. She seemed to see a reflection of their past embraces in his eyes; his mouth curved, conjuring up the memory of its pressure on her own, the answering ardour of her response.

Caroline drew breath sharply. He was an excellent actor, there could be no doubt of that, but equally there could be no doubting his desire for her. And mine for him, she thought dumbly.

Breakfast seemed to have taken on the air of a betrothal party. Caroline was aware of a procession of servants sneaking glances round the screen which shielded the entrance to the butler's pantry and twice as many people than were necessary were serving, considering that the table and buffet were already laid for guests to help themselves.

Jervais held out a chair for her, enquiring solicitously what she would eat.

'Oh, nothing. . .perhaps a little bread and butter and some tea. . .'

When she looked at the plate he put before her she found it quite full with shaved ham, omelette and slices of warm bread. 'I cannot eat all this,' she protested.

Flora, overhearing, leaned across. 'Now do eat up, my dear Caroline. I think you look quite pale this morning. The excitement, I expect,' she added smugly to Lady Shannon who nodded in agreement.

Jervais spoke low into her ear, his breath stirring her hair. 'The after-effects of the rum more like,' he murmured.

'I declare, I will never touch alcohol again,' she murmured back, shuddering delicately. 'And, just at this moment, I do not believe I will ever eat again either!'

In response Jervais cut off a morsel of the omelette and held it to her lips. 'Eat it, trust me, if only in this.'

Her startled eyes flew to his face, but there was nothing sardonic there. He smiled, coaxingly and she opend her mouth.

The food was warming and savoury and surprisingly good. 'Oh, that is better!'

Caroline was aware of a sudden silence in the room and looked up to find most of the others gazing at the affianced couple with expressions of indulgent approval. Only Major Routh, not a man to neglect his food for the sake of sentiment, was addressing himself to a large sirloin.

Embarrassed and irked, Caroline spoke so that only Jervais could hear. 'I have no trouble in trusting you in matters concerning the after-effects of strong drink, sir!'

'There are many things of which I have more experience than you, Caroline,' he responded huskily. 'It will be my pleasure to be your tutor.'

Flora, observing, but not able to overhear this

byplay, saw the hectic flush rise to her niece's cheeks and intervened. 'What a beautiful crisp day it is,' she announced brightly. 'But the snow is too deep, I hear, for us to venture outside. What shall we do today, my dear Lady Shannon?'

'I shall be occupied all day with domestic tasks, I am afraid, Lady Grey—I must review the menus with Cook in case we are snowbound for long and cannot get fresh supplies from the village. And I must speak with Mrs Chawton: if the weather breaks sufficient for our guests to come for our New Year's Eve party, we must have rooms prepared in case they cannot return that night.' She looked enquiringly at her guest. 'Would you perhaps care to accompany me? Jervais has had one of the new cast iron ovens installed—you may be interested. . .'

'Indeed, yes!' Flora was all enthusiasm. 'I have read of them, and I did think of having one put in at Brook Street, but our cook is sadly hidebound in her views and does not think it would be an improvement.'

Vivian, overhearing, laughed. 'What she actually said, Lady Shannon, was that it was flying in the face of nature, would blow up, burn us all in our beds and she would never be able to make a decent egg custard again.'

The whole party laughed at Vivian's lively imitation of Cook's outraged Essex accents. Caroline, relieved to be no longer the centre of attraction, concentrated on finishing her breakfast.

'Is there anything I can do to assist you, Mama?' Lady Julia enquired. 'Because if not. . .'

'I know,' her mother said indulgently. 'You wish to continue with your play. Well, I see no objections unless Lady Grey has any little tasks she would like you to perform.'

Flora caught Vivian's eye and smiled. 'No, you go

and enjoy yourself, my dear. Vivian, how do you intend to occupy yourself?'

Vivian looked somewhat self-conscious, but replied easily enough. 'If Lady Julia would care for my assistance, I would be happy to join her.'

'Oh, please do,' Lady Julia was positively glowing. 'You are such a help!'

Caroline, reaching for the honey, stopped, arrested by the unlikely vision of her brother as literary muse. 'Just how do you help, Vivian?' she enquired innocently.

Julia answered for him, all girlish enthusiasm. 'He sharpens my quills for me, and stands by with Dr Johnson's *Dictionary* should I be at a loss for a word. And he is very encouraging when I read a scene to him. He always laughs at my jests.'

Caroline managed to get her twitching lips under control and turned back to her breakfast, only to find that Jervais was cutting her honey soldiers from brown bread.

'I am not an invalid!' she said sharply as he handed her the plate.

'You must allow me the pleasure of looking after you, Caroline,' he said mildly. 'I intend to start as I mean to go on.'

The look in her eyes was bleak as she said softly, 'There is no escape now, is there?'

Equally quietly, he responded, 'No, none at all for either of us.' And his voice was grim.

CHAPTER TWELVE

The two days before Christmas passed swiftly. Caroline moved as if in a dream, unable to believe the rapid changes that had occurred in such a short space of time. She was affianced to Jervais, mistress-to-be of Dunharrow and treated with due deference by the servants; and, embarrassingly, Lady Shannon showed the greatest alacrity in consulting her at every turn on household matters.

Caroline was used to managing her father's household when he was alive—both the town house and the country seat, Longford—but neither were on the scale of Dunharrow.

Indeed, the most modern wing where they were living presently, and where all the renovation had been done, was almost as large as Longford. On Christmas Eve, as she stood in the interior courtyard with her hostess gazing round, she marvelled out loud at the work still to be done.

'I quite agree, it will be many years before it will be complete. The old wing will be very fine once restored, but as to this—' Serena Shannon gestured at the dismal facade of the central, linking wing '—the sooner Jervais's plan to demolish it is put in hand the better. It has neither architectural merit nor domestic convenience.'

'How difficult it will be to manage whilst that work is being done,' Caroline mused. 'The kitchens are, after all, in the old wing!'

'I see you are already applying your thoughts to the matter,' Lady Shannon remarked approvingly.

The remark brought home to Caroline her own

involvement in Dunharrow. All that had occupied her
since Jervais had announced their engagement was her
feelings for him. But his cousin was forcing her to see
that in a few weeks she would be the mistress of this
estate with all that that entailed. She shivered, pulling
her cloak more closely round her shoulders.

'Forgive me, my dear Caroline,' Lady Shannon said
with a concerned glance. 'With my enthusiasm for
architecture I have kept you out in the cold for an
unconscionable time. Let us go back inside, there is
something I particularly wanted to show you.'

They hurried back into the house, their footsteps
crunching loudly on the crisp snow. Still, foggy weather
had set in after the snowstorm: Dunharrow seemed
isolated in a silent white landscape, but the roads were
passable and, provided no thaw set in to mire the roads
with mud, the party was still expected for New Year's
Eve.

Lady Shannon shook the snow off her hem and led
Caroline up the great oak staircase.

'Is the floor safe?' Caroline asked anxiously, remembering her own accident in the Great Hall.

'The upper floors are still secure, and, of course, the
kitchen and ground floor passages are all stone flagged.
It is only the Great Hall floor which has dry rot. That
will cost a pretty penny to put right,' she added.

'Yes, indeed,' Caroline said, with more meaning in
her voice than she had intended.

She had been wondering for some time about the
amount of money Jervais had obviously already spent
on the house. The restrained opulence and good taste
evident in every one of the restored rooms spoke of
lavish resources: in the small hours of the morning the
unworthy thought had crossed her mind that Jervais's
insistence on marrying her despite all obstacles and her
own resistance might be due to his need to marry an
heiress.

Lady Shannon looked at her sharply. 'You need have no fear Jervais is marrying you for your money, my dear. Cousin Humphrey was always known to be a very warm man, but when he died the size of his fortune came as a surprise to us all. Besides,' she added, patting Caroline on the cheek, 'you only have to look at Jervais to see he is deeply in love with you.'

Oh, no, he is not! Caroline thought bitterly, just a consummate actor. But she hastened to respond, 'Oh, Lady Shannon, forgive me—I had no intention of implying that Jervais was a fortune hunter...'

Her confused apology was cut short by her hostess throwing open the door into a darkened room. She gathered up her skirts from the dust with a moue of distaste and crossed to the window, throwing open the shutters to let in the bright snow-reflected light. Even under the patina of dirt and shrouding cobwebs, it was evident that the room had been a nursery.

'Cousin Humphrey was a man who believed in procreation outside wedlock,' Serena observed tartly, finding a rag and flapping dust off a charming carved cradle, 'and therefore never had need for this room. Which, when one thinks of it, was a most fortunate circumstance for you and Jervais! I am sure it will not be long before this pretty cradle will be filled.'

Caroline, who had been amusing herself pushing a wooden baby walker across the floor, looked up, shocked. Her face flamed as she took in the thought of being the mother of Jervais's children. 'I never thought...' Her voice trailed off.

Serena was indulgent. 'Well, you may be sure your husband-to-be will have considered the matter! It is about time Jervais was setting up his nursery...'

She was prevented from elaborating further by a voice called along the corridor. 'My lady! My lady!'

Lady Shannon bustled onto the landing. 'What is it?'

At the bottom of the staircase a scrawny lad in a

baize apron stood panting. 'Cook says, can you come quick, my lady! The copper has burst all over the scullery and flooded the floor and Mrs Chawton says she don't know how she's going to get the washing done...'

'Oh dear, I suppose I had better see what can be done!' She turned to Caroline. 'Excuse me, my dear, if I leave you: if it isn't one thing it's another in a house this size, as you will soon discover!'

Caroline wandered back into the nursery, attempting to come to terms with the thought of motherhood. She stood, one finger gently rocking the cradle, trying to imagine what her children would look like. Would they favour her or Jervais?

'What a charming sight you make,' Jervais remarked from the doorway.

Caroline whipped round, her heart thudding with the shock of seeing him.

'What have I said to make you colour up so?' he asked in an amused tone, strolling into the room. He was dressed for riding in buckskins and top boots, his greatcoat unbuttoned, his gloves still in his hands. It seemed he had newly returned from riding, for the cold had raised the colour in his cheeks and his eyes were sparkling.

Caroline looked at him, suddenly helpless in her love for him. The harsh cold light reflected off his hair and sharpened the bones of his face and she wanted nothing more than to throw herself into his embrace and kiss the snow-chill off his skin. She took an involuntary step towards him, then checked herself.

'Lady Shannon was showing me around...but she has had to go to the kitchens, there has been some crisis with the copper...'

'Tell me why you are blushing.' He caught her confused glance at the cradle and laughed. 'Ah, I understand, Serena has been talking of nurseries in her

forthright way. And that alarms you?' The question
was not a simple one to answer, involving as it did
emotions she did not really wish to examine. Jervais
was watching her carefully, but to her surprise made
no move to touch her.

'No. . .not alarm. Of course I want children. . .'

'But not mine.' The statement was hard and flat.

Tears stung the back of her eyes. Caroline felt
trapped, aware she had hurt him, but unable to make
things right. She gathered up her skirts and, before he
could stop her, ran from the room, down the stairs and
along the cold corridors back to the others in the new
wing.

Caroline took care not to be alone with Jervais for
the rest of the day, firmly putting all thoughts of babies
out of her mind. In the event, this proved easier than
she might have hoped for the household was in turmoil
with preparations for the Christmas meal.

The disaster with the copper had not affected Cook's
ability to produce a magnificent repast and the table
was groaning with delicious accompaniments to the
goose, a noble bird borne in with much ceremony by
Chawton. Jervais sent for Cook, who arrived red-faced
and resplendent in her best apron to receive the congratulations of the party.

'Your very good health, Mrs Burke. Chawton, take
six of the best burgundy and see that the staff sit down
to their own dinner now.' He turned to Caroline,
seated at his right hand. 'I trust you do not disapprove
of our family tradition of serving ourselves at our
Christmas table?'

'Of course not,' she said warmly. 'It has always
seemed to me unjust that the servants should have to
wait until they return from church. Will you carve the
goose, my lord?'

After the meal was consumed they exchanged gifts

with much laughter and exclamations, leaving a sea of silver paper and abandoned ribbons.

Caroline's gift of *The Natural History of Selborne* was a great success and she glowed as Jervais passed it round the table for all to admire. 'You must inscribe it,' he insisted, once it was back in his hands.

She had finished opening all the packages before her, smiling and thanking her friends for their gifts. But there was nothing from Jervais: surely he would not have forgotten her when he had made presents to everyone else?

Serena Shannon was regarding them both with an arch smile, which turned to one of satisfaction when she saw the blue Morocco case Jervais lifted from the sideboard.

'This was my mother's, Caroline, I would like you to have it now,' he said gravely, placing the large flat case before her.

Hesitantly she opened the catch and put back the lid. A gasp escaped her lips as a blaze of white fire dazzled her eyes. A parure of diamonds lay on a bed of blue velvet, their myriad fires dancing in the candlelight.

'Oh, but I cannot wear these!' she gasped.

'Magnificent!' Flora declared, coming round from her seat to admire the jewels. 'But, yes, you can wear them. Coloured stones, of course, would be quite ineligible until you were married, but diamonds, especially now you are betrothed, are most suitable.'

Caroline stared dumbly into the box, at the tiara, necklace, earrings, bracelets and pins, which sparkled back at her. She had never seen anything so fine, but it was not the splendour and the worth of the gift that had overwhelmed her. These were Jervais's mother's jewels, the mark of how her life was about to be turned upside down within a few weeks. They were the jewels of Lady Barnard, not of Miss Franklin.

'Will you permit me, Caroline?' Jervais asked softly and before she could respond he was unfastening the modest pearl necklace at her throat and clasping the cold diamonds in their place. His fingers were warm at her nape as he disentangled a few fine hairs from the setting and she shivered responsively. His hands settled possessively on her bare shoulders as he bent to kiss her cheek. On impulse Caroline turned her face to him and his lips met hers.

The caress could only have lasted a few brief seconds, but everyone watched them silently until Sir Richard broke the mood by clearing his throat noisily.

Flora, whose cheeks were quite pink, turned to her hostess. 'Should we not get our cloaks and prayer-books? I think the clock just struck the hour.'

The party broke up, to reassemble on the steps where the carriages were already drawn up to take them to the parish church. Jervais, Serena, Julia, Caroline, Flora and Vivian travelled together in the large carriage while Sir Richard and Major Routh followed in a curricle.

'Do you intend to have the chapel at Dunharrow put into repair for your wedding, Jervais?' Serena asked her cousin as the carriage made its cautious way down the drive.

'It will take too long: I swear every woodworm in Hampshire has taken up residence there. Besides, I have not yet discussed with Caroline where she wishes to be married.'

'Well, properly I suppose it should be from Longford,' said Flora dubiously when Caroline made no reply.

'Lord, no!' Vivian groaned. 'Not with that prosy bore of a parson. I want to enjoy the wedding, not spend two hours listening to a bad sermon.'

'Well, dear, your father installed him in the living, so presumably you can dismiss him,' Flora remarked. 'But

I have to agree, the man is a complete bore.' She turned to Lady Shannon. 'A good sermon I do enjoy, but Mr Colwell. . .'

Jervais spoke low to Caroline in the gloom. 'Well, your family has made their feelings plain—but what do you want?'

'You know what I want!' she hissed back vehemently. 'I do not want this marriage to take place at all!'

'But given that it will, do you have any preference?' His gloved hand closed over the fine kid of her own and he began rubbing one finger gently down the back of her hand. Her breath tightened in her throat and she could hardly speak, the diamond necklace cold and heavy round her neck.

'I do not care. . .' she began as the carriage drew up at the lych gate and they entered the parish church, thus ending all conversation.

They arrived back at the house soon after midnight with the sound of the church bells still echoing across the frosty valley. Glad to be back inside, they shed their cloaks before entering the drawing room for a glass of warming punch.

'That was a splendid sermon,' Flora observed. 'And such an attractive church. Much nicer than St Godric's at Longford. Why not hold the wedding here?'

'Have you settled on a date yet?' Serena asked.

'Not yet,' Caroline, compelled by a direct question, replied. 'But surely there is no need for haste? Let us consider it after the Christmas season.'

'There is no need for haste, indeed,' Flora agreed, 'but equally there is no cause for delay.'

'Quite,' observed Major Gresham, *sotto voce*, with a speaking glance at his beloved, who blushed rosily. Caroline caught the exchange and reproached herself for her selfishness. Flora had sacrificed much to provide a home for her orphaned nephew and niece and every

day Caroline postponed her own wedding put off
Flora's own match with her patient major.

Her glance fell on her brother as he sat shoulder to
shoulder with Lady Julia, turning over an album of
prints she had given him, their two heads dark and
blonde almost touching. It was early days yet, but
Caroline sensed that they could make a match of it,
and her position as Jervais's wife would help the
courtship along, making it more acceptable to the Earl
of Shannon.

Lady Shannon, perhaps feeling that this public
debate was a little unseemly, rose, saying to her daughter, 'Come, Julia, it is time we were both to bed. My
friends, the season's blessings on you! Good night.'

The departure of their hostess signalled a general
retirement, although Major Routh attempted to press
the men to a game of billiards. Caroline had just set
foot on the bottom stair when Jervais reached her side.
He caught up her hand, detaining her as the others
mounted the staircase.

'I will have a decision before the week is out,' he
said softly, his head bent over the hand he held.
Caroline gasped as his lips grazed the sensitive skin of
the inside of her wrist in a possessive caress: her other
hand closed over his trapping it as if she wanted the
kiss to last for ever. Perhaps, she thought shakily, he
really does love me.

'I. . . I. . . Jervais, all I want. . .'

'And all I want, madam,' he said, looking up with
hard, dark eyes, 'is to get you respectably married. I
warned you before, I will not be fobbed off: I expect a
date from you by the end of this week.'

Caroline, who had been on the verge of telling him
she loved him, snatched back her hand as if stung and
ran upstairs, sick with reaction. She flung herself down
on the bed and pummelled the defenceless pillow. He
did not love her, that was abundantly clear: and how

humiliating it would be if he guessed her own feelings for him!

This evening had proved to her the futility of trying to escape this marriage. Too many people knew of it and too many people had a stake in it: Flora and Anthony Gresham, Julia and Vivian—and Jervais himself, with his wretched concepts of honour and duty.

Caroline undressed slowly, her mind twisting and turning futilely. Very well, then, tomorrow—no, today, for the clock was chiming one o'clock—she would tell Jervais to have the banns read. Today was Monday, so it would be almost a week before the first banns were called, with another two weeks' grace after that: it would be almost the end of January before any ceremony could take place.

Christmas Day dawned crisp and sunny and Jervais took Caroline to matins in his curricle. As they passed between the snowy hedgerows with the barouche following more sedately behind, Caroline found her spirits rising in the frosty, invigorating air.

Jervais glanced sideways at her. 'Are you warm enough? It is good to see the colour back in your cheeks—you have been too pale of late.'

She bit back the retort that had risen to her lips that he was the cause of her pallor. She was going to marry this man, the man she loved when all was said and done, and nothing was to be gained by endless bickering and sparring. It was a beautiful morning, everyone else was happy; she was determined, suddenly, to make the best of things.

Caroline twisted on the seat to look at him better and smiled, her face alive and vital. 'Oh yes, I am quite warm enough! This is such a beautiful day after all that lowering fog. Can we not drive on a little after church?' She saw the fleeting look of surprise on his face and dropped her eyes. 'There is something I wish to discuss with you.'

'Very well,' Jervais agreed, as they drew up at the church. The groom who had ridden with the barouche jumped down to take the horses' heads and the whole party entered the church.

Caroline tried hard to keep her thoughts from wandering during the service, but felt guiltily that her Christmas devotions had been somewhat distracted. Lady Shannon, on hearing of their plans, said, 'A good idea, we are all fusty from so much time indoors. What do you think, Lady Grey? Shall we take a turn around the park before returning?'

It was agreed and Jervais reined back his team until he saw what direction the coachman was taking, then turned their heads down the opposite road. They drove in silence for a space, then Jervais drew up on top of a slight rise with a view over a fine burst of country below. The sun was red and low in the sky casting a roseate glow over the snow-clad fields.

'Do you hunt?' he asked.

'Always, at Longford,' Caroline replied. 'I have missed it in London.'

'Will you come out for the Boxing Day meet?'

'I would if I had my mare with me, but she is at Longford,' Caroline said absently, her eyes assessing the fine hunting terrain with the clipped hedges and neat banks.

'You must let me mount you, there is a bay gelding in my stables which would just suit you.'

'Then I will hunt, with pleasure,' she agreed.

Silence fell between them again. Jervais seemed content to survey his land, but Caroline struggled to find the words to introduce the subject of their wedding day.

'Jervais. . .' she began, just as he said,

'There was something you wished to say to me. . .'

They both broke off, then he prompted, 'Go on.'

'Our wedding date—let us have the banns called soon. Next Sunday, if you wish, then we can be married on, say, the twentieth of next month.'

'As you wish,' he said with cool politeness. 'But what of your bride clothes? Does that allow you sufficient time to order them up?'

'Oh, that is not important!' Really, he was the most exasperating man! Here she was, finally agreeing a date with him and all he could do was demur about bride clothes. . .

'Not important?' He raised an amused eyebrow. 'Why, I thought the bride clothes were an overriding consideration in a bride's mind—in the ordinary scheme of things.'

'Well, this is not the ordinary scheme of things, is it?' Caroline responded tartly, then remembered her resolution to remain pleasant and not spoil the day. 'Fortunately, my wardrobe is well furnished at present,' she added in a more conciliatory tone.

'You are being surprisingly matter of fact about this, all at once, Caroline,' Jervais remarked, eyeing her closely. 'Why?'

The directness of his question startled the truth out of her. 'As you yourself pointed out to me, there is no escape from this marriage, so I have resolved to shift as best I can. And it occurs to me I am being selfish to those I love best.'

'What do you mean by that?' he demanded.

'I overheard Flora tell Major Gresham she could not marry him until I was safely settled: now they can be married. And Vivian is showing a marked partiality for Lady Julia. . .if I am married to you, perhaps the earl will look more favourably on his suit.'

'How very flattering,' Jervais said frostily. 'I had no idea you were of such a romantic disposition: how noble of you to force yourself to marry me for their sake! I trust they will be grateful for your sacrifice.'

'Oh, get down from your high horse, my lord!' Caroline said, half laughing at the thought he might be wounded by her words. 'You know you are forcing me to marry you—would you have me be such a hypocrite as pretend I am marrying you for any other reason?'

There was a pregnant pause. Caroline stole a sideways glance at his set profile, wondering if she had perhaps gone a little too far this time. But when Jervais finally spoke there was no trace of the chagrin she thought she had detected.

'I commend your honesty. Between ourselves then, let us not pretend we are marrying for any other reason save necessity. But that should not preclude us behaving civilly each to the other, I trust?'

'Indeed not,' Caroline agreed warmly. 'After all, marriages of convenience have existed for centuries: I am sure we can reach an accommodation and learn to deal agreeably together.'

The horses shifted uneasily as though his hands had tightened on the reins. 'Your horses are becoming restive in the cold,' Caroline observed.

'Indeed.' He shook the reins and the team walked on. 'Would you care to expand a little on what you mean by "an accommodation"?'

'Surely you do not imagine I am consenting to anything other than a marriage of convenience?' she stammered. 'There is no question of. . .'

'Let me assure you, Caroline, that there is every question that I require an heir,' he declared bluntly.

'Oh!' Caroline reddened. 'But that means you. . . I mean, I must. . .oh, dear!'

'You must have realised what it would entail.' His irritation seemed to be dissolving into amusement.

'But you are only marrying me because you have to,' she wailed.

'And I fully intend making the best of it! Come now, Caroline, nothing in our past dealings has led me to believe you would find our lovemaking so repugnant.'

Even the memory of the encounters between them made her tingle from top to toe, but she could not, would not, give herself to a man who did not love her! Unable to answer him, she averted her burning face, biting her lip as she stared unseeingly at a cock pheasant stalking over the nearby field.

'Are you frightened?' he asked, his voice suddenly gentle. 'There is no need, you know—I will be very gentle.' Receiving only a muffled sound in response, he added, 'You should speak to your aunt, she will set your mind at rest.'

Still, she could not look at him, only shake her head mutely. She felt the cool soft leather of his gloved finger tracing down the line of her cheekbone. 'We will say no more of this now, Caro. Come, luncheon will be awaiting us.'

The rest of the day passed quietly. Caroline felt chilled and could not get warm, although Flora, noticing her shivering, insisted she sat by the fire, and scolded Jervais roundly for keeping her out in the cold.

When bedtime came at last, Caroline was still feeling very subdued. As her maid unpinned her hair and unfastened her dress, Caroline's eyes fastened on the big bed. She had pushed to the back of her mind the outcome of accepting Jervais as her husband. She knew he only had to touch her for her senses to be on fire, but she had thought little beyond kisses and caresses since that moment when she had almost gone to his bed in Belgium.

Of course she knew what marriage entailed—in theory! But the practice was shadowy and not something it had occurred to her—until now—to fear.

Flora came in with a warming cup of chocolate and,

when the maid had gone and Caroline was sitting against the pillows sipping it, said, 'What is wrong, my dear? You have been very subdued ever since you returned from your drive this morning.'

Caroline blushed rosily. 'It is nothing, Flora. Jervais. . . I mean, he. . .' Her voice trailed away.

'Ah,' said Flora knowingly, settling herself on the edge of the bed. 'So Jervais has been making love to you and it has alarmed you. You must make allowance for the ardour gentlemen feel on these occasions. I am sure he would not have overstepped the mark.'

It was almost a question and Caroline said feebly, 'No, no, of course not.'

'Then what is it, Caro? You can talk to me, my dear, I have been a married woman!'

'It is just that I had not considered. . .' Caroline searched for the words '. . .the wedding night.'

'Well, that is something a young lady has no need to consider,' Flora said briskly, then relenting, added, 'It will be all right, my dear, especially after the first time.' Rather pink herself after that pronouncement, she gathered up her skirts and hurried out. 'Good night, dear Caro. Sleep well.'

Sleep well! After that helpful intervention, she doubted she could sleep at all! As she pulled the sheets up around her shoulders, Caroline found herself viewing quite starkly the intimacy that marriage would entail. How would she ever conceal from Jervais that she loved him? And when he found out, how would he react? Which would be worse—that he pity her or that he despise her?

CHAPTER THIRTEEN

ONLY Flora remained behind the next morning as the party set off for the first meet on the village green in Harrowbridge.

Julia and Lady Shannon had their own horses with them, fine Irish hunters, which showed off both ladies as accomplished horsewomen. Julia looked particularly fetching in a bronze-green habit which moulded itself to her slender figure and, to Caroline's hidden amusement, Vivian could hardly take his eyes off her.

Caroline was well satisfied with the bay gelding Jervais had ordered saddled for her. Although it was several months since she had last been in the saddle, she was pleased to find herself coping easily with the fresh young animal's playful cavortings. She was heavy eyed after a restless night but, somehow, in this morning's sunlight and crisp air, her fears of yesterday seemed exaggerated.

She glanced over at Jervais, caught his eye, and they both smiled spontaneously. Caroline was delighted to see that Caesar, now recovered from his injury, had been hacked down from London by a groom and was now jumping out of his skin with fitness and oats.

Jervais, immaculately dressed, seemed to control the big horse by the pressure of his thighs alone, one hand only holding the reins lightly as the cavalry charger tossed his head and mumbled the bit impatiently. Seeing him brought back all her memories of Jervais in uniform astride Caesar on the battlefield, of herself sitting up behind him as they rode back to Brussels, the feel of his muscular torso under her encircling arms. . .

'A penny for your thoughts?' Jervais asked, riding close beside her.

'I was thinking of Belgium,' she replied honestly. 'Seeing Caesar called it all to mind again: the battlefield, riding back to Brussels. . .'

There was a slight pause while Jervais smiled reminiscently. 'I must say, Caroline, you are more suitably dressed for riding than you were on that occasion.'

That remark was too near the knuckle for comfort: Caroline was not going to dwell on what had passed between them then and had no intention of allowing him to do so either.

'So you approve of my new riding habit?' Caroline enquired lightly, gesturing at the garment which was in the very height of fashion.

Garnet red cloth had been tailored in a dashing military cut. Black frogging laced the close-fitting jacket and reached from the cuffs to the elbow. The skirts, in contrast, flowed lavishly from the tight waist to show the occasional glimpse of matching half-boots and the entire ensemble was crowned by a black veiled hat tilted pertly over one eye.

'Very fetching, Caroline, but then, I have always thought red becomes you.' The words were cool, but the look in his eyes scorched her, leaving her in no doubt that his thoughts were of removing the outfit rather than admiring it!

She was saved from having to reply by their arrival at the village green where the Master, a local squire by the name of Stacpoole, was shouting at the hunt servants who were unleashing the hounds.

'My lord!' He hailed Jervais bluffly, riding across to be introduced to the house party. 'It is good to see a Barnard hunting with us once more. May we hope to meet at Dunharrow again as my father told me we used to?'

'Next year, perhaps,' Jervais agreed, bending to

accept a stirrup cup from one of the waiters scurrying to and from the inn with loaded trays.

The entire gentry of the surrounding areas seemed to have converged on the meet. Caroline was introduced to local farmers, clergymen astride cobs, young ladies showing off new habits under the doting eye of approving papas and a host of people who Jervais told her would be among the guests at the New Year party.

The hounds wove in and out of the horses, sterns waving in excitement as they stole as many of the savory pasties as the waiters let drop in the crush.

At last the Master gestured to the whippers-in, the hunting horns blew and the entire hunt streamed off the green and down the lane towards the first covert.

Caroline's horse kept trying to break into a canter and she was forced to rein it in. The side-saddle was either new or very well polished and she found it took all her skill to keep her seat.

'Is he too fresh for you?' Jervais enquired, coming up beside her, and bringing Caesar close, protectively.

Caroline laughed. 'No, indeed not! He is full of the fidgets, but as soon as we draw this covert and I can let him have his head, he will calm down.'

'Yes, you are right, the snow will make heavy going,' Jervais agreed.

The field reined in at the first covert and stood around in small knots exchanging gossip and news. A tenant farmer stopped to ask Jervais's opinion of the wisdom of diverting a small stream and he listened with half an ear, his attention on Caroline.

Seeing him engaged, she walked the bay over to talk to Major Routh and Sir Richard. Jervais's eyes followed her intently. He had never seen her looking so beautiful and vital, glowing in the red habit against the snowy backdrop.

Nor had he ever found her so mystifying. Yesterday, she had seemed apprehensive, as though he were a

stranger to her, not a man who had held her quivering
with passion in his arms. And she was capable of great
passion, of that he had no doubt. Despite the angry
accusations he had made he had never really doubted
that she was a virgin, yet there was that secret she
would not reveal even though they were about to be
man and wife.

He shook his head at the turn his thoughts were
taking and the tenant farmer, misinterpreting the gesture, said in a disappointed tone, 'I am sorry you feel
like that, my lord, but, of course, if you do not wish
it. . .'

'Forgive me, Johnson, I was wool-gathering. It
sounds a capital scheme: come up to the house the day
after next when Hambledon will be going over the
leases with me.'

'Very well, my lord. I will attend you and your
steward as you suggest.' The man tipped his hat and
moved aside as the hounds gave tongue and the field
swung round to see the flash of russet as the fox broke
cover and ran for the distant woods.

Horns were sounding the 'gone away' and the riders
fell in behind the Master as he began the pursuit. The
snow cloaked the fields, making it difficult to dis-
tinguish stubble from plough and at first the riders
were cautious.

At the first hedge they were still bunched close
together and there was much jostling and milling
around as the more confident took the jump whilst the
more prudent went through the gate or crashed
through gaps in the quickthorn.

Caroline used the gate, nodding her thanks to the
curate, who was holding it open with the handle of his
riding crop. Once through, she let the gelding have its
head and found herself towards the front of the field,
now strung out across the white downland.

At first she was too concerned with controlling the

strange horse to notice where Jervais was. Her eyes were stinging in the cold as the air whipped past her face, her ears were full of the drum of hooves on the hard ground and the snorting breath of her mount.

Then, after a few minutes, she began to feel more confident. Her horse settled into his stride and responded to her signals and Caroline glanced round to see where everyone else was. In front, the Master and hunt servants led the field, the pack well in sight. The young bloods in the party were also in front of her. 'view hallooing' with noisy enthusiasm and she saw that the curate on a particularly fine hunter was up with them.

Lady Shannon was a hundred yards to her right, in her element, the raw-boned Irish hunter well in hand. Julia and Vivian must be somewhere behind and she was just wondering where Jervais had got to when Caesar came up on her off side.

'I thought you must have fallen off!' she shouted, her words snatched by the breeze.

There was a flash of white teeth as Jervais laughed at her jibe. Caroline thought how brown his face still was, in contrast to the white faces of the other gentlemen, and what a raffish air it lent him. She laughed back at him, totally at ease, as though nothing existed except the excitement of this moment and the pleasure of being together.

'I didn't fall,' he shouted back, 'but you did well to take the gate back there: the ditch on the far side of the hedge caught several people by surprise—I think Caesar thought himself back in a cavalry charge!'

A flock of sheep which had been sheltering in the lee of a hedge now scattered in bleating panic at the approach of the horses. Before she had time to think the bay had taken the scrubby hedge, soaring over the dense thorn and easily clearing the ditch beyond. Her blood sang in her veins with the exhilaration of it all, the speed, the stinging air, her rapport with her mount and Jervais's presence by her side.

'This way!' he shouted, pulling Caesar to the right, up the slope and towards a patch of woodland. 'We can cut through here.'

The horses dropped to a trot as they wove through the trees. Caroline realised Jervais was following the contour round at a higher level than the fox, and its pursuers, had taken. After a few moments they reached the edge of the woodland again, emerging to look down on the slope of the valley.

'Lost the scent, by the look of it,' Jervais observed, gesturing with his whip at the pack which was milling round, casting for the scent. The Master and the whippers-in were shouting encouragement to the hounds and the front of the field was reining in to allow them to work.

'Look,' Jervais pointed again, and Caroline saw a flash of red beyond a frozen pond. 'Reynard's got the best of us this time.' The fox trotted off almost contemptuously, ignoring the tumult behind it.

'He's outwitted the Master—who does not seem best pleased!' Caroline observed. Even at a distance the rubicund face of Squire Stacpoole glowed like a beacon. 'What will he do now?'

'Curse and swear for a while, then draw Hangman's Covert, I would guess,' Jervais answered almost lazily. His eyes were no longer on the Squire and the hounds. Caesar had dropped his head and cocked one hoof in the attitude of a horse which had learned to take a rest when one was offered, and Caroline's bay moved closer to the big grey in a companionable manner.

Finding herself almost knee to knee with Jervais, Caroline was very aware of him, and of how she must look, flushed and panting in the clinging habit. Her bosom was rising and falling, constrained by the close fitting garnet cloth, and underneath the veil her eyes sparkled.

'Caroline.' It was all he said before he reached out and with one arm pulled her against him. The horses stood like statues and Caroline found herself supported by her one foot in the stirrup, the rest of her weight held easily against Jervais's hard body.

'My lord!' she managed to squeak, knowing she should resist and equally knowing she could not. His mouth came down on hers through the coarse veiling. She gave a little gasp at the strangeness of the sensation, then yielded to the heat and urgency of the kiss. She dropped the reins to encircle his neck and he lifted her bodily onto the saddle in front of him.

The bay snorted and moved aside, but the two of them were oblivious, locked together. Jervais's gloved hands were cold where they touched her body at waist and throat, his cheek against hers was cold also, but his lips were burning on her chilled skin. His heart beat against her breast, he was holding her so tightly, and Caroline was startlingly aware that the two of them were on equal terms in their mutual desire.

This man was going to be her husband very soon and all the fears she had been experiencing the previous day had evaporated in the heat of their embrace. She wanted him. . .now. If he pulled her to the frozen earth, claimed her as his wife now, she would offer no resistance, would go to him eagerly.

Caesar proved an unexpected chaperon. Growing bored with the inexplicable behaviour of his master, he lifted his head and began to amble forwards to where the bay was cropping a bedraggled patch of grass.

Jervais swore under his breath, snatched up the reins one-handed and snarled, 'Stand!' Caesar obeyed immediately.

'My lord. . . Jervais. . .we should not. . .' Caroline stammered. Through the pounding of her pulse she was conscious that her hat was awry, her stock almost under one ear and a mere hundred yards away the entire hunt were gathered. '...not here,' she added, then blushed furiously, scarcely crediting she could have said anything so bold.

'You are quite right,' Jervais said huskily, gently letting her slide to the ground before dismounting himself. He caught the bay's reins over his arm and lifted her, hands firm at her waist, into the saddle.

He swung back onto Caesar, and turned the horse around. 'This is not the place. Come back with me to Dunharrow: I want you...now.'

Caroline stared at him, her lips parted to protest, but no words came.

'And you want me,' he stated. 'Come.'

She gathered up the reins and kicked the bay to follow Caesar. It was outrageous, it was shocking and given the depths of misunderstanding between them, it was unwise, but she did not care. She loved him, she wanted to be with him, part of him—and when she was in his bed, in his arms, she could at last show him that love and he would know he could trust her.

They took the most direct route back to the house, cantering across the fields wordlessly, oblivious to the fading clamour of the hunt behind them as the hounds picked up the scent once more. At the outskirts of Harrowbridge they reined in and looked at each other. Jervais's lips twitched. 'I think you should do something about your hat and your stock, or onlookers will believe you have fallen from your horse.'

'And you, too,' Caroline murmured with a sideways glance. 'You are uncharacteristically dishevelled, my lord.'

He straightened his stock and tugged at his jacket. 'Not as dishevelled as I intend to be shortly, madam,' he remarked, casting her into total confusion.

They rode sedately along the village street, outwardly composed. Caroline could hardly believe she was doing such a thing, going unmarried to a man's bed, even if he were her affianced and the man she loved.

'Lord Barnard! A word if I may!' It was the rector, striding down the churchyard path.

Jervais reined in with a glance at Caroline. 'I had better see what he wants. Ride ahead and I will catch up with you.'

'Will he not think me rude?'

'Not at all, and you are a little discomposed, you know. We would not have him wondering at the cause. . .'

Indeed not! Caroline waved to the rector and urged the bay on down the street. As she passed the inn a voice called, 'Miss. . .miss!' and Fanny came out, almost tumbling in her haste, pulling on a cloak.

'How are you? Did you get back home safe the other night?' The young woman stood with one hand on the horse's neck looking up, real concern on her pretty face. 'Oh, I have been all agog to know how things go—but I can't ask Simon—Major Routh, I should say.'

'I got back safely,' Caroline assured her. 'But what an adventure! I was quite tiddly with that punch, you know, it led me into a terrible scrape!'

Fanny's eyes shone with glee. 'Ooh, er! But everything is right and tight now, isn't it?' she asked shrewdly, nodding to herself at Caroline's ready blush. 'That's the party all the excitement's about, isn't it?' she asked, nodding towards Jervais, who was still being detained by the rector.

'Well, yes,' Caroline admitted. 'Lord Barnard and I are to be married.'

'Well, if that don't beat all,' Fanny exclaimed delightedly. 'A big London wedding?'

'No, that is, it is not yet decided,' Caroline began,

then glancing down the street, added quickly, 'You had better go, here he comes!'

Fanny whisked inside. For a moment Caroline believed Jervais had seen nothing, but as he reached her side she saw his eyes were narrowed and his expression far from pleased.

'You should not be seen talking to persons of that kind,' he said firmly.

'What kind?' Caroline asked innocently, although her heart was thudding.

Jervais was not deceived. 'You know perfectly well what kind, madam!'

'No, I do not,' she said stubbornly.

'One of the muslin company, if I am not mistaken.'

'Well, you would know better than I if that were the case, sir.' Her cheeks were red, her temper rising.

'And just what do you mean by that?' he enquired dangerously.

'You leapt to that conclusion very readily, Jervais,' Caroline riposted. 'Did you not make the same judgement of me when we first met?'

Jervais laughed without humour. 'It is the normal conclusion one reaches when confronted by a young woman in an indecent gown and with paint on her face.'

'There is nothing indecent about Fanny's gown!'

There was a long silence. 'So you are on first name terms with that little ladybird? Tell me, just how do you come to know Major Routh's whore so well?'

Caroline drew breath sharply. 'How dare you use such language to me! Sir, you are offensive and you have no right to speak of Fanny so...'

'I have every right to guard my wife against unsuitable company.'

'I am not your wife yet, sir, and you have no rights over me that I do not chose to give you!'

He leaned over and snatched her rein from her hand,

pulling both horses to a standstill. The bay snorted and tossed its head in alarm.

'Have a care, Jervais!' Caroline cried, afraid she was about to be unseated.

'No, you have a care, Caroline. You are going to be my wife—perhaps sooner than you think—and that gives me every right I choose to claim! I insist you tell me what you are about with that woman.'

'Or what?' Caroline glared back at him. 'What sanctions do you threaten me with? Do you intend to beat your disobedient wife? Confine me to my room, perhaps?' He made an exclamation of impatience, but she pressed on. 'If you cannot decide, perhaps you should yield to the inevitable: we can always say we have decided we do not suit.'

'You will marry me, Caroline.' His voice was harsh, commanding. 'You will receive no help from me in whatever tarradiddle you choose to peddle to your friends: I will merely say you are suffering from pre-wedding nerves. No one will pay you any attention.'

For the first time that day she used her blunted spur on the gelding, sending the startled animal galloping up the drive towards the big house, Caesar thundering behind them.

At the front steps she reined in hard and slid hastily from the plunging animal. As Jervais reached her side, she threw the reins to him, forcing him to control both horses while she ran into the house.

Caroline flung the front door open in the startled face of the butler, who jumped backwards in alarm. 'Miss Franklin! I beg your pardon, I was not expecting...'

'No, indeed, Chawton, I beg your pardon for startling you so.' Caroline tried to calm her breathing. She peeled off her gloves and smoothed down the jacket of her riding habit, forcing a smile to her lips. It would never do to give Jervais's servants cause to gossip

about their master. She walked briskly across the hallway to the stairs, her hearing straining to catch any
sound of Jervais beyond the heavy door.

'Shall I send your maid up, Miss Franklin?' the
butler asked, hurrying in her wake.

'No, no, thank you, Chawton. I have had rather a
tiring ride and I am going to lie down. Please say I am
not to be disturbed.'

Caroline gained the passage outside her room, surprised there was no sound of footsteps in pursuit. She
glanced nervously over her shoulder as she put her
hand on the doorknob, but there was no sign of Jervais.

Safely inside she leaned back against the panelling
and closed her eyes with a sigh. Her heart was still
thudding in her chest, but it was nothing to do with her
flight from Jervais. No, her agitation stemmed from his
words, and the way he had looked at her as he had
declared his intention to marry her and do as he
wished, come what may.

A frisson of apprehension tinged with excitement
ran through her. Had she not encountered Fanny she
would even now be in his bed, irrevocably bound to
him. But that meeting in the village had once more
demonstrated the vast gulf of misunderstanding and
distrust that lay at the heart of their relations.

A faint click from the other side of the room made
her open her eyes. Jervais stood in the doorway of her
dressing room.

'Jervais! How did you. . .?' The housekeeper had
assured her that the connecting door between her
dressing room and the master dressing-room was
always locked.

He smiled lazily and held up the key. 'No doors are
locked to me in my own house.' The smile was deceptive: as he strolled towards her, she realised that it
masked a tightly reined anger. 'You are provocative,
rebellious, devious and difficult, Caroline. I have

decided that the sooner you are my wife, the sooner I can curb these unfortunate tendencies in you.'

Caroline's sharp intake of breath was clearly audible. 'This is not the Middle Ages, my lord! You cannot coerce me into marriage and you can control neither my behaviour nor my thoughts!'

'Coerce is an unfortunate word,' he said silkily. 'However, I do hold all the cards in this game. Your aunt earnestly desires this match—not only for your sake, but for hers also. Your brother knows you are so compromised he has no choice but to insist that you marry me. And, of course, you realise that if you make a scandal, any chance he has of an alliance with Julia is at an end.'

Caroline stared at him as he stood before her, implacable. 'All you give me, Jervais, is a catalogue of reasons why I cannot escape marriage to you. Now, give me a reason why I should want to marry you.' Her chin came up and she met his hard gaze defiantly, willing him to speak of love.

'Considerations of your honour and mine. . .'

'To hell with honour!' she retorted angrily. 'My own is my concern, and as to yours, I suggest it would be better served by not forcing an unwilling woman into marriage.'

'Unwilling?' he murmured softly, moving towards her. 'Oh, I think not. And if you are asking me for a reason why you should want to marry me, I will give you this one. . .' He reached out a hand and gently trailed his fingers down the line of her cheek, down her throat, across the swell of her breast.

Caroline gasped, unable to conceal her response to the thrill of his touch, even through the fabric. She grasped his hand to remove it, but instead her betraying body pressed more insistently against the warmth of his palm.

'Well?' he enquired huskily. 'There is your reason for you.'

'It's. . .it is not enough,' she managed to say in a scarcely audible whisper. 'I cannot give myself in marriage where there is not love.'

She saw his face darken and she was suddenly afraid. Mercifully, there was a tap on the panels at her back and Flora's voice came clearly. 'Caroline, my dear! May I come in?'

Jervais gave her an unfathomable look and stalked back across the room, pulling the dressing-room door shut softly behind him. Caroline stood looking after him until Flora called again, more insistently this time. 'Caroline! Are you unwell?'

Caroline reached behind her and turned the knob, stepping aside to admit her aunt. Flora bustled in, peering anxiously at her niece. 'Chawton informs me that you appeared somewhat discommoded when you returned from the hunt, and that you came back alone. Is anything wrong?' Her eyes surveyed the subtle disorder of Caroline's habit. 'Have you had a fall?'

'I cannot marry him!' Caroline burst out, ignoring Flora's questions. She moved agitatedly to stare out over the snowy park. 'I cannot—I will not—do it!'

Flora bit back a sharp response with an effort, telling herself this was only pre-wedding nerves. 'Now then, Caroline, do not be gooseish! It is natural that you should feel some apprehension, but this is mere foolishness. Why cannot you marry Lord Barnard?'

'He does not love me!'

'Young women of our class do not expect to marry for love,' said Flora firmly. 'There are higher considerations: family, propriety, the alliance of equals to continue family lineage. . .'

'You are marrying Anthony for love!' Caroline burst out rebelliously.

'I am a widow. Anthony is my choice.' She flushed.

'Lord Grey was my father's choice, and a most suitable one, of course. Naturally, he knew what was best for me. . .'

'Oh, I see. I must marry Jervais and hope to be widowed so I may find a second husband who will love me!' Seeing the shock and pain on her aunt's face, she instantly regretted her bitter words. 'Oh, I am sorry, Flora, I did not mean that. . . I know you would never have thought like that when you were married. . .'

But she had gone too far for Flora's patience and forbearance. 'You are beside yourself, Caroline,' she said icily. 'What do you want? You have a man who is eligible, intelligent, handsome to a fault. He is indulgent towards you, totally acceptable to your friends. . . You will never receive a comparable offer. If you were much younger, just out, I could understand these vapours, but I remind you, you have been out some time. If you cannot consider your own best interests, then think of others—your brother, for example.'

Looking at her aunt's angry face, Caroline knew she deserved the tirade. Upbringing and duty to her family must make this match acceptable to her. Even if she explained everything that had happened in Belgium to Flora, that would only serve to add greater weight to the need to marry Jervais. Love was something women of her class found as a happy accident, not something she had any right or expectation of finding in marriage.

'I suggest you stay in your room until you have regained your composure and have come to your senses,' Flora continued, her tone frigid.

Caroline sighed, turning her eyes once more to the frosty landscape. 'I have come to my senses. I will marry Lord Barnard: do not concern yourself, aunt, there will be no further scenes.'

'I sincerely hope not,' Flora remarked, gathering up her skirts. 'I will have some luncheon sent up. You should rest until this evening, by which time you might have regained your composure.'

Caroline spent the afternoon in intense thought, scarcely noticing the short day swiftly drawing into darkness. Too intelligent to suppose she had any realistic alternative now but to marry Jervais, she resolved to make the best of it. And she did love him.

Balancing the scales, that love weighed heavily. Added to it were the happiness of both her brother and her aunt. On the other side of the balance was the knowledge that Jervais did not love her, although undoubtedly he desired her passionately. Nor did he trust her. Well, she must live with that, hope that with marriage the trust would grow.

When Katy came to dress her for dinner she found her mistress composed and cheerful. To her own surprise, Caroline found that now she had made her decision a great weight had lifted from her. She knew what she faced and what she had to do. She must make Jervais trust her first, unconditionally: then would be the time for explanations. To tell him all, to set his suspicions to rest, would only serve until the next time they had a misunderstanding and they could not build love on such shaky foundations.

Jervais was crossing the hall as she began to descend the staircase for dinner. He glanced up at the sound of her skirts, then stopped, his eyes following her every step. He took in the frosty drift of silver spider gauze over aquamarine silk, the burnished sheen of her hair confined in a silver filet and the ice fire of his diamonds at her throat and on her arms.

'Caroline.' He looked at her, unsmiling, and she braced herself to meet coldness. 'You look ravishing: an ice princess.'

It seemed she was forgiven. Letting her relief show in the warmth of her smile she responded, 'I would rather be a baroness, my lord.'

There was no mistaking the pleasure that lit his face as he handed her down the last two steps. 'You are reconciled then, to our marriage?'

'Perfectly,' she said, demurely, fighting down all her fears as she spoke.

'You make me very happy,' he replied. The calm formality of his words were belied by the heat of his kiss as he brushed her fingertips with his lips. 'Shall we join our guests?'

CHAPTER FOURTEEN

THE weather broke overnight. The twenty-seventh of December dawned sodden and dank, depressing everyone's spirits at breakfast that morning.

'Well, that puts paid to hunting today,' Major Routh remarked, regarding the slushy lake which had been the front lawn. 'The scent will never hold up even if I was prepared to take my animals out in this heavy going. Which I am not,' he added, sitting down to a plate of kedgeree.

'We must find some other occupation,' Lady Shannon remarked bracingly.

'But, Mama, what of the play?' Julia broke in earnestly. 'We only have four days to learn our parts and rehearse if we are to perform it on New Year's Eve for Jervais's guests.'

'You have finished writing it, then?' Lady Shannon queried, slicing a little thin bread and butter. 'I must confess I thought you would tire of it before it was complete.'

Julia looked shyly across at Vivian. 'Sir Vivian was such a help, Mama.'

'I'll be bound,' Major Routh muttered into his coffee.

'I think it is a splendid idea,' Caroline encouraged. 'It will keep us from getting dull until we can venture out again. I do not know the weather in Hampshire, but at Longford we have found that once a thaw sets in at this time of year it will be days before the weather lifts.'

Flora smiled round the table, seeing nods and looks of interest from the assembled party. 'Shall we all meet

473

in the library after breakfast? We can decide the parts.'
She looked at her beloved Major Gresham with sparkling eyes, 'I will confess I did not quite approve at first,
but now I find I am quite excited.'

'For myself, I consider play-acting, within reason, a
most rational entertainment,' Sir Richard declared.

Caroline caught Jervais's eye and smothered her
smile with her napkin. Jervais obviously found Sir
Richard as pompous as she did on occasion.

In the library they found Julia fussing over piles of
paper. 'I have written out all the parts,' she explained.
'Now, we must decide who will take which rôle.'

Caroline could see that once Julia grew out of her
girlish uncertainties she had the potential to be as
decisive as her mama. Just what Vivian needed, in fact!

'We need a heroine, a hero, a villain, a heartless
father, a clergyman, a faithful retainer and a lady's
maid,' Julia explained shyly. 'There is a part for everyone except, of course, Mama and Lady Grey, who said
they did not wish to act.'

'I will take charge of the costumes,' Flora offered.

'And I will be prompter,' added Serena.

'I think Julia should be the heroine,' Vivian
announced, his eyes warm on her blushing face.

'Then you must be the hero Sir Ambrose,' she
responded.

'I think not,' Serena said firmly. 'It would be more
seemly if Caroline were to act the heroine's part.'

There was general agreement and Caroline found
herself cast as Rosalyne, an innocent heiress.

'May I be the villain? It really is a capital part!'
Major Routh looked up from his reading of the script.
He twirled his moustache and read, in throbbing tones,
'There is no escape from me now, my proud beauty!'

'I shall take the part of the clergyman, if you all
agree,' Sir Richard announced. This seemed so appro-
priate, there was no dissent.

'That would seem to leave you and I with the faithful old retainer or the harsh father,' Major Gresham remarked to Jervais. 'I think I can dodder better than I can rant, so if you are agreeable, old chap, that leaves you as Papa.'

Jervais grinned. 'I shall just have to remember how I dealt with headstrong subalterns and act accordingly! Julia, does that leave you a part?'

'Only that of Dorcas, the maidservant,' Julia said primly, managing to look both noble and disappointed simultaneously.

'But you have a truly dramatic speech in the second scene when you throw yourself at the feet of the cruel father, pleading for your mistress,' Vivian said consolingly.

Jervais's eyebrows shot up. 'Good grief! What have I taken on? I shall go and look out a horse whip and start practising at once.'

There was general laughter and even Julia smiled. Serena bent towards Flora as they sat together on the sofa and murmured, 'I really do not feel it suitable that Julia and Vivian should be seen swooning in each other's arms, do you, Flora? At least, not until they are officially engaged to be married.'

'You would have no objection to an engagement, then?' Flora queried, low-voiced.

'Indeed not. A most eligible young man, and so kind and charming. I know the Earl would concur. But they are young yet: I would wish Julia to have her first Season before anything is said.'

'I do so agree with you, Serena.' Flora clapped her hands to gather the attention of the players. 'If I am to be in charge of costumes, I must know when the play is set. Julia dear, does it take place in this day and age, or is it an historical play?'

The author of the piece appeared unsure and a general debate broke out. Sir Richard wanted to perform the play in Roman togas but was voted down on the grounds of unseemliness and warmth. Major Routh urged Elizabethan dress, apparently feeling he would appear to best advantage in a ruff, but Sir Anthony drew the line at wearing tights.

At length Jervais held up a hand to still the hubbub. 'I believe there are several trunks of old clothes and hangings—silks and brocades—in the attics. Could not something of no particular period be contrived from those?' He looked round for agreement. 'Good, then I will order them fetched down for Lady Grey's approval. You must summon us for costume fittings, ma'am, when you are ready.'

The cast took their scripts and dispersed to con their lines, each in their own way. Major Routh rendered the breakfast room uninhabitable by striding about it, twirling his moustache and declaiming loudly. Sir Richard took to his room, requesting that he was not disturbed while he thought himself into his character; Major Gresham reduced Flora to fits of giggles by doddering in the drawing room, and despite Lady Shannon's best intentions, Julia and Vivian sat, heads together, helping each other with their lines.

Later that afternoon, Caroline found herself a quiet, book-lined alcove in the library and tried to memorise her first speech. This was an uncomforable experience as most of her lines called for her to protest against a marriage of convenience.

'No, no, Papa!' she declaimed. 'Although I am a dutiful daughter, you cannot ask this of me! To marry a man against my heart. . .'

From behind her, Jervais said softly, 'I see the part has been written for you.'

Caroline jumped, then felt the hot colour flood her cheeks. This was a little too near the mark for comfort. 'I did not hear you come in. . . I thought I was alone.'

'I am sorry I startled you. It occurred to me you

might like someone to read through your lines with—
but I can go away if you prefer.' Jervais turned on his
heel.

Caroline reached out and touched his sleeve. 'No,
Jervais, please do not go. I would like someone... I
would like you to help me learn my part.' She stood
up and tentatively kissed his cheek. 'The theme of the
play is unfortunate, but I hope we can put that to one
side, now you and I have reached an agreement.' She
looked up into his unreadable face and her heart
contracted with love for him. Taking a deep breath she
plucked up all her courage. She would tell him how
she felt, however unwise that was. 'Jervais, I. . .'

'You are quite right,' he said pleasantly. 'We must
not be over-sensitive and spoil the others' pleasure in
the entertainment. Now, shall we read through the
scenes we play together or would you prefer to read
all of your part and I will listen?'

'I. . . I will read mine through.' Caroline managed to
disguise her disappointment; perhaps, after all, he had
saved her from making a very unwise declaration.

By the twenty-ninth the party were almost fluent in
their parts. The continuing wet weather was ignored by
all, so absorbed were they in Julia's melodrama. Small
groups could be found in every room holding spon-
taneous rehearsals, much to the well-hidden annoyance
of the servants hampered in their household duties.

In the kitchen Mrs Chawton grumbled to Cook. 'I
don't know what they think they're about, spanielling
all over my nice clean carpets with those filthy old
trunks. They fetched so much dust and cobwebs down,
I'll have to get the girl to go over the floor with damp
tea-leaves after!'

'And no interest in their food, do what I may,' Cook
opined. 'Mr Chawton tells me they spend so much time
talking they're letting it go cold! I just hope my lady

comes down to talk to me about the big party on New Year's Day: we've got to get the poultry soon and I still don't know how many we're expecting.'

The two women fell silent, musing on the strange ways of the gentry. Then Lady Shannon appeared as if she had been summoned by their complaints and paused inside the kitchen door regarding the long faces. 'Now then, Mrs Chawton, Cook—why so gloomy? We have no time to mope about! There is much to do. Now, as to the poultry. . .' The two women exchanged speaking glances before listening attentively to their mistress.

Upstairs Jervais and Caroline had commandeered the hall to rehearse their big scene. Caroline cowered on her knees, hands raised imploringly while Jervais struck an attitude of implacable sternness.

'Father, do not cast me out, I implore you! It is snowing!'

'Thankless child! Ingrate! Will you obey me, then?'

'Never! I will die in the snow sooner than marry that monster!'

'To your room, then! You shall have bread and water until you submit to my will!' He broke off with a snort of laughter. 'I swear that Julia has used every old chestnut from every ghastly novel she has ever read. I am not sure how the bishop will react.'

'Is he to be amongst the guests, then?' Caroline sat back on her heels and looked up at him. Once she had got over the unfortunate subject matter, she had started to enjoy the play-acting. Or rather, if she was honest with herself, she was enjoying being with Jervais when he was in such a light-hearted mood.

'Yes, along with all my neighbours! I must have been mad to agree to make such an exhibition of myself.' He reached down a hand to help her to her feet. 'Come, it must be nearly time for luncheon. Let us find the others.'

He tucked her hand snugly under his arm and they strolled companionably into the library together. The well-oiled door opened soundlessly and they stood on the threshold without Julia and Vivian realising they were there. The young lovers were sitting close on a window-seat, gazing deeply into each other's eyes. Vivian was holding Julia's hand and was obviously in the act of raising it to his lips.

Caroline tugged Jervais's sleeve gently and they backed out unseen. Closing the door with care, she said, 'I am so thankful Vivian has found a girl like Julia. They are deeply in love: I am so pleased for him.'

Jervais was silent, although she felt the muscles of his arm tense under her hand. 'I had feared that what he encountered under my father's roof would make him hard and cynical about marriage,' she continued.

'You never speak of your father. Why not?'

Caroline hesitated, then said frankly, 'I should not say such things of a parent, I know, but after the death of my mother he knew no restraint. He drank too much, kept a string of mistresses. . .'

'My God, Caroline! I had no idea! And this happened when you were at home?'

'Oh, yes. It was not so much the mistresses in London who were such a trial, although, of course, they were very expensive. No, it was rather the occasional young women who turned up on our doorstep. What you would call "bits of muslin", no doubt.'

'But you would have had nothing to do with them!' There was shock in Jervais's tone.

'I had to buy one of them off, once. Poor thing, he was very thoughtless and, after all, it is men like him who make women like that what they are. I could not see her suffer by his negligence.'

A short silence ensued, then Jervais exclaimed, 'So

that is how you come to be acquainted with Major Routh's. . .er, friend!'

Caroline recognised the relief in his voice at having found an acceptable reason for her scandalous acquaintance. It would have been very easy to allow him to continue thinking that, but she would not lie to him. 'No. To my knowledge she had no dealings with my father, although she is very much in his style.' She met his eyes frankly, unprepared to elaborate further, challenging him to persist in his questioning.

For a second, she thought Jervais was going to demand she tell him about Fanny, but the moment passed, leaving a feeling of constraint between them. Caroline was painfully aware that the feeling of trust had vanished.

New Year's Eve being a Sunday, the normal revels were to be held on New Year's Day, but despite attendance at church, morning and afternoon, the house-party and the servants all found themselves busier than usual for a Sabbath.

Flora was being driven almost to distraction by Major Routh's inability to stand still while she finished his costume. As the villain, Earl Dastardly, he was suitably sinister in his own dark coat and breeches, but Flora had decided to put the finishing touch with a swirling black cloak fashioned out of some old velvet curtains. She had persuaded the Major to stand on the library steps whilst she pinned up the hem, but compelling him to stop posturing was quite beyond her powers.

Sir Richard found her gazing despairingly up at Simon Routh, her mouth full of pins, and took charge. 'Stand still, man!' he barked. 'Cannot you see her ladyship is in difficulties!'

He earned a feeling look of gratitude from Flora,

and startled obedience from the Major who goggled at his friend's costume.

'By jove, old chap, the clerical get up becomes you well!' Simon Routh said somewhat slyly. 'Didn't realise you carried a dog collar and gaiters around in your luggage. . .?'

'I borrowed them from the rector,' Sir Richard replied loftily. 'Fortunately, he has no conscientious objection to play-acting and being much of my size was able to oblige me.'

Meanwhile, Caroline was practising controlling her long skirts in the passage outside her room. Flora had found a heavy silk gown of the fashion of perhaps forty years before and had removed the heavy petticoats. It now flowed and swept around Caroline's feet producing a most Romantic effect, but used as she was to the shorter, slimmer skirts of the day she was finding it difficult to manage without tripping.

Jervais's door opened as she passed and he stepped out, stopping immediately at the sight of her. Caroline struck an attitude, one hand pressed to her forehead, the other resting on the swell of her breast exposed by the *décolleté* of the gown. 'Oh, Papa!' she quavered, 'Do not send me to the nunnery!'

Jervais caught both her hands in his and stared down at her. 'When I see you like this, the last thing I feel is paternal!' he said huskily.

'You like my costume?' she enquired, her voice not quite steady.

He stepped back regarding her, still with her hands trapped in his. 'You look ravishing. There is something not quite right, however. . . I know!' He released her hands and began to unpin her hair, freeing the black curls from their confining ribbon and fanning the soft hair with his fingers until it stood out like a halo around her face.

Caroline shivered with pleasure as his cool fingers

ran through her hair, closing her eyes in anticipation of the kiss that must surely follow as Jervais's hands dropped to her shoulders, pulling her tight into his embrace.

A discreet cough broke the moment and Caroline stepped back hastily, patting her hair into some sort of order. Jervais turned to face his cousin and said drily, 'Your sense of timing, Serena, is, as always, superb.'

'It needs to be, cousin,' Lady Shannon retorted with good humour. 'You two may be engaged, Jervais, but Caroline still requires chaperonage.'

'But not for long,' Jervais remarked, with a glance at Caroline.

'Ah, yes, I was going to enquire about that.' Serena took Caroline's arm and steered her towards the head of the stairs. 'Let us go down to tea, my dear. No, never mind the dress, it will be good practice in managing those skirts. Now, Jervais, the wedding. We must make some arrangements; I was saying as much to Lady Grey only this morning.'

'I had assumed we would call the banns next Sunday,' Caroline said. 'Then we would be married at the end of the month. That is what we agreed, is it not, Jervais?'

'I was not aware that we had come to an agreement on that,' Jervais said smoothly, holding out his hand to steady her as she gathered up her long skirts. 'We will not have banns called: I prefer to be married by licence. We will speak to the bishop tomorrow.'

They were entering the library as he spoke. Lady Grey waited until the footman who had just brought in the tea tray left before adding her approval to the scheme. 'Are you discussing marriage by licence rather than by banns? I do so agree, it seems so much more discreet than having one's affairs bruited about in public.'

Caroline was beginning to feel that events were

sweeping her along. 'But. . .when do you intend us to be married then, my lord?'

'Why, next Saturday, to be sure.' Jervais seemed surprised at her confusion.

'Next Saturday!' Caroline was aghast. With all her heart and body she yearned to be his wife, yet her mind was still not accustomed to the idea, to the reality of tying herself to a man from whom she still had secrets, a man who did not love her or completely trust her.

'You had not intended to invite a larger party than are already gathered here, had you?' Lady Shannon asked gently as she began to pour the tea. 'And you and Lady Grey agreed it was unnecessary for you to return to London to obtain bride clothes before the ceremony. And the weather, of course, you must allow to be a consideration. For the party to disperse, only to reassemble at the end of the month would be quite impractical.'

Jervais, seeing Caroline's agitation, secured two cups of tea and steered her towards a window-seat at the far end of the room. Serena and Flora, already settled to a comfortable discussion of wedding breakfasts, and the difficulty of decorating the church at this time of year, scarcely noticed their absence.

'Do you regret your decision, then, Caroline?' he asked her gently.

'I. . .no. . .no, of course not! It is just so soon. . .'

'Yes, I imagine the prospect and the actuality of marriage are somewhat different things,' Jervais said drily, causing her to blush deeply. 'I do not wish to frighten you, Caroline. And I do not believe you are frightened of me and of what marriage will entail— when I hold you in my arms you respond to me so warmly. . .'

'Oh, hush!' Caroline pleaded, glancing nervously down the room towards the tea party. 'It is not that I am afraid of you or of. . .what marriage will bring. It is just. . .' She broke off, her hands trembling so much she had to put her cup down.

'Then what is it? Caroline, you must tell me!'

'I cannot convince myself that marriage without love is right!' she burst out in a desperate whisper.

Before he could respond she jumped to her feet and hurried down the room to sit beside Flora, who gave her a warm smile and drew her into the discussion of wedding preparations.

Caroline could only regret her outburst, but as she had no occasion to be alone with Jervais for the remainder of that day, or the next morning, she had no opportunity to set things right.

The entire household was a hive of activity the next morning. Servants Caroline had not set eyes on before were to be seen scurrying up and down the staircases and in and out of rooms, and most of the village women appeared to have been pressed into service in the kitchen and scullery.

Julia was in a high state of nerves about her play and drove Chawton almost to distraction by redirecting the footmen from their duties about the house in order to rearrange the library furniture and the makeshift stage at what seemed like hourly intervals. Even Lady Shannon was relieved when Vivian persuaded her to leave well enough alone and help him polish his lines in the small parlour.

On the occasions when Caroline came across Jervais, he seemed quite as normal and made no reference to her outburst the day before. If she could have been alone with him, Caroline would have tried to explain, but there was never a suitable moment and as time passed it seemed more and more difficult to say anything.

The guests began to arrive in the early afternoon

while there was still some light remaining. The front hall grew quite chilly as the front doors were opened and closed incessantly, and Caroline struggled to remember names as Jervais introduced her to one party of neighbours after another.

It was obvious that the reopening of the refurbished Dunharrow and the opportunity to meet the future Lady Barnard had overcome any qualms about making a journey on such a drear winter's day and the gathering seemed set to become the social event of the local season.

The bishop arrived with his wife and an attendant curate just as the daylight was finally fading. He greeted Jervais warmly, then turned to Caroline with evident approval. 'My dear! Let me join my congratulations to those of your friends on this most happy occasion! Mrs Browning!' His wife, a rather sharp-nosed, mousy woman, scurried obediently to his side. 'This is Miss Franklin, who is shortly to become Lady Barnard.'

Caroline curtsied to the Bishop's wife and thanked his lordship for his good wishes with suitable modesty. He seemed most taken with her and demanded of Jervais who would be conducting the ceremony.

'Our rector, Mr Colwell.'

'Indeed? Excuse me a moment, Barnard.' The bishop, his ecclesiastical purple a startling patch of colour amongst the more soberly clad male guests, forged across the room to where his curate and Sir Richard were deep in conversation with the rector.

When he returned he had the rector, looking somewhat bemused by this descent of authority, in tow. 'Well, Barnard, that is decided. I will personally perform the ceremony with the able assistance of Colwell here. No, no,' he dismissed Jervais's thanks with a wave of his hand. 'It is the least I can do. And it is many years since I conducted a wedding in a parish church.'

Caroline guided him towards the cold collation, encouraging him to reminisce about his earlier career and the many marriages he had presided over in the past.

As the hour struck she noticed Chawton move discreetly to Julia's side and address her low voiced. In turn she went to speak to her mother, than began to circulate amongst the rest of the cast, reminding them it was time to change into costume.

'My lord!' Lady Shannon's voice rang out over the babble of conversation. 'Ladies and gentlemen! Members of the house-party have prepared a light entertainment for your amusement: I crave your indulgence if they leave you to ready themselves.'

'Are you participating in this mysterious diversion, my dear?' the bishop asked Caroline.

'Indeed, my lord. It is nothing but a short and very frivolous play, but one which we hope you will find amusing.'

The Bishop's wife gave a disapproving sniff, but her husband hurried to disagree with her unspoken views. 'Now, now, Mrs Browning. It is not the Sabbath, and this is a private party. I am sure Lady Shannon would permit nothing unseemly. . .'

Caroline slipped away while he was still debating the point. The rest of the cast were already in the hall. The ladies were to change in the Blue Parlour, the gentlemen in a rather draughty anteroom.

Sir Richard, looking uncommonly pale, was being chafed by Major Routh. 'I do declare you are nervous, old chap! Come, come, you know your lines better than all of us!'

'I have to confess I find the idea of playing a clergyman in front of the bishop somewhat daunting.'

'Nonsense! Get a grip, man! It's not as if you have

to perform a ceremony. . .' The door closed cutting off the remainder of the Major's attempts at reassurance.

Caroline was surprised to discover that she, too, was suffering from nerves, but forgot her own feelings when she saw Julia's white face. 'There is nothing to worry about,' she began as their maids helped them out of their dresses.

'When it was just for us, it was such fun,' Julia wailed, her voice muffled by the plain skirts of the maid's costume which were being lowered over her head. 'But all these guests. . .and I wrote it. . .' Her face emerged, looking more worried than ever.

'Nonsense!' Caroline declared in tones as bracing as she could manage, considering the tight lacing her gown necessitated. 'Just think how proud Vivian will be of you. . .' She was interrupted by a small sob and added rashly, 'Come, come. Is this any way for the future wife of a soldier to behave?'

That did the trick. Julia regarded her wide-eyed with hope. 'You would not object? Oh, if only Papa and Mama will agree. . .'

'I will be delighted to have you as my sister, and to see Vivian so happy,' Caroline assured her warmly. 'And you may rely on Lady Shannon to persuade your papa, I am sure of it. Now, no more vapours, you are first on the stage!'

An hour later, sweeping a curtsy at the end of the performance, Caroline could not believe how well it had gone or how much she had enjoyed it. And there was no doubt the audience had enjoyed it, too: they had laughed in all the right places, had booed the villain roundly and there had even been a stifled sob at the end when father and daughter were reconciled.

The cast spilled out into the hall, glowing with excitement. Caroline picked up her flowing skirts and ran lightly up the staircase to her room to change. The sooner she got out of the terrible tight-lacing of her bodice, the better. She could scarcely breathe! As she opened the door her maid scurried past her, dropped a small curtsy and was gone.

'Katy? Come back. . .'

'I told her to go,' a low, husky voice spoke from the shadowed corner.

'Jervais!' Caroline protested as he strode across to close the door firmly behind her. 'But I need her. . .my hair. . .'

'I like your hair as it is.' He ran his fingertips through it, fanning it into even greater disarray. 'I told you before, Caroline, acting those scenes with you makes me feel anything but paternal.' He did not wait for any response, drawing her hard into his embrace, kissing her ruthlessly, making no effort to disguise his desire.

His mouth was hot and hard, sealing over hers, his tongue invading and claiming. Unaware of her tight lacing, Jervais held her closer, his arms bending her back into his embrace.

All Caroline was conscious of was a total inability to breathe, an overwhelming feeling of panic that she must surely suffocate in the intensity of his embrace. She struggled to free herself, desperate for air and, in doing so, fetched him a sharp blow across the ear with her flailing hand.

He released her instantly, his face suffused with anger. 'There is no need to box my ears, madam! If my attentions are so repugnant to you, you merely have to say so.'

Caroline, appalled, and with an apology forming on her lips, gasped at the injustice of his anger. 'How dare you! You force your way into my chamber, dismiss my maid, maul me. . .'

'Maul you! I would have you know I have never in my life mauled a woman! Do you think me some yokel, forcing my attentions on a milkmaid?'

Caroline was suddenly as angry as he. 'If the cap fits,

wear it, my lord! I am sure the many women you have bought—your "bits of muslin"—always bent to your will. But I give you notice now: I have no intention of doing the same!'

Jervais smiled thinly. 'You may think so, madam. But as my wife you will do as you are told. Now, make haste and change; our guests are waiting.' And he was gone.

CHAPTER FIFTEEN

How Caroline endured the rest of that evening she would never know. Somehow she managed to show a pleasant face to the guests, play-acting the part of the radiant bride-to-be. Jervais, to her eye, appeared constrained, but nobody else seemed to notice anything amiss.

When they found themselves alone briefly in the hall at one point, Caroline forced herself to ask, 'When do you intend announcing that our engagement is broken?'

'Broken?' He raised an interrogative brow. 'I have not broken the engagement: nothing has changed. We will be married as planned in a week's time. Now, come into dinner, our guests will be waiting.'

She was still perplexed, and still angry with him, when Flora came into her chamber to bid her goodnight. Caroline sat up against her pillows and patted the edge of the bed. 'Flora, may I ask you something? You have more experience than I in the way men's minds work.'

Flora looked at her knowingly and sat down. 'I thought so—you and Jervais have had a tiff.'

'A tiff! A pretty understatement! He kissed me— very passionately—while I was wearing my costume for the play. I was laced so tightly I could not breathe, and when I tried to free myself and accidently hit him . . .he became most angry.'

'Hit him?' Flora's eyebrows nearly disappeared. 'My dear Caroline, what unladylike behaviour!'

'What should I have done,' her indignant niece demanded. 'Faint?'

'That would certainly have answered the purpose. Now listen to me, Caroline, men do not like to feel rejected, it hurts their pride. And for a man in love it would be particularly galling.'

Flora looked severe. Caroline almost blurted out the truth, then recollected herself. This was not the time to tell her aunt she was marrying a man who did not love her.

A short silence followed, then Flora, obviously picking her words with care, said, 'The, er. . .physical side of marriage is always a shock. But you will become accustomed and after you have presented your lord with an heir, you will find his attentions will be less pressing.'

'Because he has taken them elsewhere, presumably!' Caroline riposted sharply, thinking of Fanny, of her father's dalliances.

'A well-bred wife does not think of such things, let alone speak of them,' Flora reproved, equally sharp. 'I think you are overtired, Caroline. You will feel better in the morning, with all the preparations to be made. Goodnight, dear,' she added more gently, dropping a light kiss on Caroline's head.

The sun came out from behind scudding grey clouds to greet Lord and Lady Barnard as they emerged from the church porch six days later. Caroline blinked in amazement at the crowd of villagers who had gathered to wish them well; she had hardly spared a thought for the other changes that marriage would bring. Now she was lady of the manor, mistress to all these people who had become her responsibility the moment she had said 'I do.'

Caroline and Jervais walked slowly down the church-yard path, stopping frequently to exchange a few words with well-wishers, and she strove hard to remember names and faces.

As they reached the lych gate a woman pushed forward a shy little girl. Her face, emerging from a thick wool shawl, glowed from a recent scrubbing as she struggled to recall the words her mother had spent all morning teaching her. The child's memory failed her at the sight of such a beautiful lady and, speechlessly, she thrust a tiny fistful of snowdrops and ivy trails at Caroline.

'For me?' Caroline bent down and stroked the child's soft cheek with her gloved finger. 'Thank you very much! Did you pick them yourself?'

The child, now totally overcome, hid her face in her mother's skirts. Caroline smiled at the woman and caught a look of satisfaction on Jervais's face. At least he seemed to be pleased with his new wife's demeanour with the tenants of Dunharrow.

She gathered up her skirts carefully, although the dry weather and strong wind of the past day and night had done much to dry paths and steps. The carriage awaited them at the lych gate and Caroline noticed for the first time how beautifully turned out were the team of horses. Truth to tell, on the way to the church with Vivian and Flora, she had been so nervous she would not have noticed if the horses had been winged.

Jervais took her hand to help her into the carriage and she felt the strength of him, even through the fine kid of her gloves. The fog which had seemed to swirl through her mind for the past week was clearing, leaving her acutely aware of the man sitting beside her—her husband.

A little shiver ran through her, although wrapped as she was in a blue velvet cloak she was snug enough against outside chills.

'Caroline, you are cold, here, let me. . .' He pulled a fur rug from the opposite seat and tucked it carefully around her. 'There should be some hot bricks under the seat.'

As he bent, Caroline touched his arm, 'No, no. I am quite warm enough, thank you, Jervais.'

'If you say so.' He looked doubtfully at the ivory silk of her gown peeping over the wide collar of the cloak. 'That gown is very beautiful, but I fear it is inappropriate for the season.'

That exchange appeared to have exhausted conversation between husband and wife. After a tentative glance at Jervais's calm profile, Caroline turned to the window just in time to catch sight of Fanny waving from the steps of the inn.

Mercifully Jervais had not seen the other woman, but the shock jolted Caroline into speech. 'How fortunate, my lord, it did not snow again last night.'

The feebleness of the words fell into the silence, then Jervais said, almost conversationally, 'Never mind the weather, that bonnet is damnably in the way.' His fingers were already working on the ribbons under her chin; seconds later, her fine velvet hat was tossed carelessly aside and Jervais was kissing her with a conviction and thoroughness that brought home to her more forcibly than any wedding ceremony that they were indeed married!

Caroline swayed closer into his embrace, clutching his lapels as the coach swung between the gateposts of Dunharrow. Faintly in her ears came the muted cheers of the ground staff and keepers gathered round the lodge, but Caroline felt no embarrassment that the servants should see them embracing.

As the coach slowed Jervais released her, picked up her hat and gently placed it back on her head. His gloveless fingers worked deftly to retie the ribbons, then just as the coach came to a halt he touched and traced the delicate curve of her upper lip with a warm finger. 'You are so very beautiful, Caroline,' he murmured huskily.

Stepping down onto the gravel, Caroline felt a surge

of hope that it was going to be all right, that Jervais had put behind him all their previous misunderstandings, the suspicions, now they were indeed married.

But there was no time for further reflection, for Chawton and Mrs Chawton were leading out the entire domestic staff to line the steps, the menservants on one side in their best livery, the maids on the other with new ribbons in their caps.

As the carriages conveying the guests drew up behind, Caroline walked slowly up the steps while Jervais formally introduced her to the staff as the new mistress of Dunharrow.

After a period of confusion, whilst fifty or so guests shed pelisses and top coats, ladies were shown to bedchambers to tidy their hair and gentlemen warmed their coat tails before blazing fires, Chawton managed to seat everyone in the dining room.

The long table, augmented by all of its four extensions, was further enlarged by two end tables set crosswise. Caroline and Jervais sat at the centre, presiding over a quite magnificent wedding breakfast.

Caroline swallowed a moment of panic and realised that the bishop, seated on her right hand, was speaking to her. '. . .a most sumptuous collation. You are to be congratulated, my dear Lady Barnard, on such an achievement, especially considering the difficulties of the season.'

'Oh, I can take no credit, my lord,' Caroline demurred. 'My aunt and Lady Shannon arranged all.' As the servants began to pour wine and the gentlemen to carve the various dishes set before them, Caroline glanced round, seeking out the familiar faces of her friends amongst the throng.

Vivian was opposite her with Julia on his left hand. Beside Julia, Sir James Porteous, a neighbour she scarcely knew, was engaging Flora in conversation, apparently to the disapproval of his very plain wife seated further down the table.

Serena was out of sight beyond the bishop's wife on Jervais's left hand, but Caroline could hear her robust tones discussing the difficulties of obtaining pineapples in January.

A partnership further down the board caught Caroline's fancy and she put her head close to Jervais and said in low tones, 'See Major Routh! I fear Serena's stratagem to separate him from the prettier guests has misfired.'

Lady Shannon, having taken Simon Routh's measure early in their acquaintance, had intended to give him no opportunity for flirtation and so had seated him between a rather deaf dowager in her eighties and the bishop's drab little mouse of a daughter.

The Major, always one to relish a challenge, had evidently set out to fascinate Miss Lavinia, whose sallow cheeks were becomingly flushed as a result of his badinage.

Jervais laughed. 'Simon is incorrigible,' he responded softly. 'I just hope he does not break her heart.'

'She has more sense than that, I am sure. But a flirtation will give her some confidence—perhaps enough to discharge her dressmaker!'

They exchanged warm, intimate glances and Caroline felt her heart skip a beat. With an effort she turned from her husband and began to make conversation with her immediate neighbours.

Outside the light was dying as the afternoon wore on and the meal progressed. At last the servants brought in the sweetmeats and fruit, people were pushing back their chairs a little and several portly gentlemen looked as though they wished they could unbutton their waistcoats.

With a glance at Jervais, Vivian rose to commence the speechmaking, to be followed by the bridegroom himself. Sir Richard, who had acted as Jervais's supporter at the church, rose finally to deliver a charming and surprisingly witty address of thanks to the bridesmaids and to Lady Shannon for the magnificence of the wedding breakfast.

At last, Caroline, in her new role of lady of the house, rose, caught the eye of the other ladies present and bore them off to the various upstairs chambers set aside for their convenience.

She and Lady Shannon met on the landing after all the female guests had been accommodated. Serena smiled warmly at her new cousin. 'Welcome to the family, my dear. I am so pleased Jervais has found a bride like you. No, no false modesty,' she insisted as Caroline blushingly protested. 'You have the style and presence Jervais needs in a wife but, more importantly, the spirit and intelligence to keep him interested! I speak frankly, I hope I do not give you offence, but he sets standards which are too high, both for himself and for others. You will be more than a match for him!'

Having succeeded in casting Caroline into considerable confusion, Serena swept off to her own chamber. Downstairs the servants cleared away the remnants of the feast and set out card tables in the small salons. Chawton surveyed the ballroom and noted with satisfaction that the hothouse flowers were at their peak, scenting the warm air. Musicians arrived and began to set up their scores and tune their instruments for the evening's dancing and in every bedchamber in the house guests loosened stays, unbuttoned waistcoats, eased off shoes and rested until ready to begin again.

In her chamber, Caroline was helped out of her wedding gown and into a loose wrapper by Katy, almost beside herself with the excitement of the day and the heady realisation that now, as the lady's maid to the mistress of the house, she had achieved a position in the household second only to that of Mrs Chawton.

'Shall I redress your hair now, my lady?'

Caroline, still accustoming herself to being addressed thus, looked at her flushed face in the glass before her and thought how unchanged she looked from the unmarried girl of the morning. Perhaps she would look different tomorrow morning...but the implications of that thought were too agitating to dwell on.

'No, just unpin it and brush it out, please, Katy. I will wait until I am ready to go down before we redress it. You may go now, I think I will lie down for a while.'

Caroline had realised she was weary after the day's excitements, but she had not expected to fall so quickly into a light doze. She awakened with a start to the sound of a light knock on the dressing-room door. The room was in shadows: all but one branch of candles had gone out and the chamber was lit by the flickering fire.

The door swung open to reveal Jervais in shirtsleeves and breeches, his shirt open at the neck. 'Did I wake you? May I come in?'

'Of course you may.' Caroline sat up hurriedly against the pillows, running her hands through her disordered hair. Somehow she had not expected him to come to her like this before the night and her heart was beating wildly.

Jervais crossed the room and settled himself at the foot of the bed. She had grown used to him, to the urbane and well-groomed Lord Barnard, but half-dressed in the flickering firelight he was once again the dangerous saturnine stranger of the battlefield.

Seeing her eyes widen, he asked her softly, 'What are you thinking of?'

'Of the first time I met you...of waking up in the barn beside you.'

'But now you have your memory back,' he observed

gently. 'You know who you are, and who I am.' His fingers ran lightly over the arch of her bare foot and Caroline started, but did not draw away.

'My husband,' she replied, her eyes steady on his face as his fingers strayed higher, caressing her ankle.

'You must not be afraid, Caroline. I am not the ogre you sometimes believe me to be. No, let me speak,' he insisted as she opened her mouth to protest. 'I will not do anything to alarm you, you have my word as a gentleman.'

Caroline wanted to cry out that nothing he could do would alarm her, that she welcomed his embraces and what would follow, but she still could not be absolutely open and trusting with him while he did not trust her. He was a man on his wedding day; he might well be putting to one side all the doubts and suspicions which he had of her, but they would surface again when this night was over.

Jervais watched the play of emotions on her face, marvelling that someone seemingly so open, so guileless, still held back secrets from him.

To her surprise he stood up. 'I can see you still doubt me: but I promise you, Caroline, you will believe me tonight.' Before she could reply he was gone, the door closing softly behind him.

Caroline danced the evening away in a dream, unable to concentrate on anything but Jervais's words to her, the way he had looked, the thought of the night to come.

She did her best to be a good hostess, but was unaware of the indulgent smiles of the guests who, noticing her high colour and abstracted manner, forgave it easily as only to be expected of a new bride.

As the clock struck ten, Jervais, who was waltzing with Caroline, manoeuvred her neatly out of the door into the hall. 'Come, Caroline,' he said, holding out his hand and leading her up the staircase.

Caroline felt her knees weakening until she feared they would hardly support her as the sound of the music diminished behind them. She was conscious of the swish of her gown on the wooden treads, of their shadows thrown on the walls by the sconces of candles as they passed, of the warmth and sureness of his hand as he led her inexorably towards her bedchamber door.

She was conscious of a slight feeling of surprise. She had not expected to slip off with him this way, had assumed they would retire at the same time as the guests and that he would come to her room later. And why, if they were retiring together now, why did they not go to the master bedchamber?

To her surprise Jervais turned not to the big, waiting bed, but to the chairs by the fireside. He seated her firmly in one and took the other, remaining at a distance. For a long moment he said nothing, his expression serious as he regarded her. Caroline thought she saw a nervous jump in his cheek, but perhaps it was only the firelight dancing on the planes of his face.

The silence was almost tangible. Caroline felt the pleasurable frisson of apprehension that had filled her since Jervais had taken her away from the celebrations become a leaden foreboding.

'Caroline. . .I have been giving much thought to what you have said. . .of love in marriage. I know it is not expected that people of our rank and station will necessarily make a love match, but I understand now how much it means to you. I am sorry I cannot give you that.'

It was as though he had struck her to the heart: all her hopes that he might love her died. Caroline fought the pain with all her pride and training, masking it behind a façade of cold composure. Only her hands, tightly clasped in her lap, betrayed her, but Jervais's eyes were fixed implacably on her face.

'Under these circumstances,' he continued relentlessly, 'you need have no fear I shall force my attentions upon you.' He stood up. 'I will leave you now, you must be fatigued. Goodnight, Caroline.'

For several minutes after the door clicked shut behind him, Caroline sat unmoving, gazing into the fire. The flames were blurred before her eyes as the tears coursed silently down her cheeks.

There could be no doubt he did not love her. Surely if he had any tender feelings towards her he would have coaxed her, wooed her into the marriage bed? She was not so innocent as to believe a man needed to be in love before he bedded a woman, especially his wife. But this cold formality could only mean he distrusted her so deeply that he could not bring himself to lie with her. The angry accusations he had thrown at her, his obduracy in refusing to believe there might be an innocent explanation for her presence on the battlefield meant he could not bring himself to trust her.

Eventually, overcome by emotion and exhaustion, she fell into a deep sleep in the chair.

She woke as dawn broke, stiff and cold before the ashes of the dead fire. For a moment she was confused, then it all came flooding back.

Katy must not see her like this! Caroline cringed at the thought of the gossip which would spread like wildfire below stairs if she were to be discovered still in her gown of the evening before on the morning after her wedding night.

She struggled out of her gown, dropping it and her stockings onto the chair. Her hair was already so tumbled that it only needed her to pull out the remaining pins for it all to come down. Crossing swiftly to the foot of the bed she pulled on her nightgown, leaving the ties at the neck undone.

Caroline scrambled into bed, disordering the pillows and covers on both sides. It was humiliating to have to undertake such a deception, but the alternative—having everyone know that the marriage had not been consummated—was worse!

She was only just in time; no sooner had she wriggled down under the covers than a soft knock heralded the arrival of Katy with her morning cup of hot chocolate.

Caroline feigned sleep whilst the maidservant cautiously approached the bed and set the cup down. 'My lady?'

'Oh. . . Katy. Good morning.' She sat up with a show of reluctance, rubbing her eyes.

'Good morning, my lady. Miss. . .madam, I should say, you're still wearing your earrings.'

Caroline's hands flew to her ears. 'How careless of me,' she said lightly. 'It is fortunate they did not catch in the lace.' She knew she was blushing, but realised that, above everything, confirmed the picture of a new bride.

Despising herself for the deception, Caroline took up the hot chocolate and began to sip it while Katy gathered up her discarded garments. The girl was obviously agog but Caroline was not going to give her any encouragement to chatter.

Caroline dressed with care. When the maid had gone she crossed to the glass and schooled her face into an expression of calm serenity, far from what she felt inside.

When she reached the small salon Jervais was already breaking his fast, alone. 'Oh, my lord. . .where are the other guests?' she stammered. She had been hoping for the protection of company.

'Good morning. You have just missed your brother

who has gone out riding with some of the other men. I believe the ladies have had trays sent to their rooms.'

Caroline sat at the opposite end of the table feeling gauche and awkward. 'May I pour you coffee, my lord?'

'Thank you, I have some.' Jervais paused, then said with a touch of impatience, 'I thought I had made myself plain last night: there is no need for you to be so stiff in my company, I shall not force myself upon you. But,' he added drily, 'I am afraid you will have to accustom yourself to being alone with me from time to time.'

Caroline rallied. 'I understand that. However, you must agree that not everything was said last night that needed to be said!'

'Very well. When you have finished your breakfast perhaps we can meet in the study.' Jervais pushed back his chair, made his wife a slight bow, and left.

Caroline toyed with a piece of bread and butter, then, realising she had no appetite, rose and followed him.

Jervais was sitting at his desk, but rose immediately she entered the room. Once again he led her to a chair by the fire, but this time he remained standing, one foot on the fender while he waited for her to speak.

Caroline took a deep breath. 'Jervais, why did you marry me?'

'Because I had compromised you, of course.' His brows drew together as he looked at her. 'We have been into this before—I had compromised you, not once, but twice. We might have escaped the consequences of your battlefield escapade, but once your brother had discovered you in my bed, there was no alternative.' She made an abrupt gesture with her hands which he interpreted as impatience. 'You have no heed for your reputation, madam, but as a gentleman, I must.' His voice was as hard as she had ever heard it.

'And as a gentleman, you will not force yourself upon me,' she observed, equally cold. He nodded curtly. 'But do you not expect an heir as part of the bargain? I can assure you the world will expect one.'

Jervais removed his foot from the fender and faced her. 'You are very frank, madam!'

'I am a married woman now—at least, in name.'

Jervais appeared to choose his words with care. 'In a few months, when we are more accustomed to one another, we will speak of this again. There is no need for you to concern yourself with it now.'

If she had thought that by speaking so frankly she would pierce his armour, glimpse his true feelings, she was sorely disappointed. This morning her husband's cold implacability seemed impenetrable. Caroline stood, swept him a curtsy and left the study. She was mistress of Dunharrow now, with duties to perform and servants to order. Swallowing her pain and her anger, Caroline resolved to throw herself into her new rôle. At least she understood it, which was more than she did her husband.

Three nights later, Simon Routh pulled off his boots, unbuttoned his waistcoat and cast himself down on a low chair in front of the blazing fire in Fanny's bed-chamber at the inn.

'By God, that's better! You know how to make a man comfortable, Fan, my girl.' He reached out a hand and pulled her down to sit on his lap.

Fanny, snuggling down accommodatingly, remarked, 'Not comfortable up at the big house, then?'

Simon took a deep draught of the hot punch Fanny had prepared before replying. 'Oh, comfortable enough—as far as that goes. No, it's something else... the feel of the place. There's something very much amiss with our newly-weds: I tell you, Fan, if things don't cheer up soon, we're back to Town!'

Fanny sat up, her face concerned. 'What's amiss, then?'

'No good asking me, I'm not a married man, so I don't understand wives. But, I tell you, if that marriage has been consummated, then I'm a Dutchman.'

'But she is crazy in love with him!'

'And I would have said that if there was ever a man in love it was Jervais Barnard,' Simon added grimly. 'But there is something between them...if I didn't know better,' he brooded, 'I'd say he was a man who had discovered some dark secret about his new wife, but was having to make the best of the bargain. But that must be nonsense, Caroline's a real lady if ever I... Here, Fan! Where are you going?'

Fanny had jumped off his lap and was pulling her cloak from its peg. 'Come on, get your boots on. You are going to take me up to the house now: I'm going to talk to his lordship, whether he wants to hear me or not. Men!'

At about the time that Fanny had been pushing the cloves into an orange to make Simon's mulled wine, Caroline had been sitting before her chamber fire, deep in meditation.

After three miserable days, and even more miserable, lonely, nights, she had come to the conclusion that if anything were to change, then she must initiate it. What was the point of having her pride intact, in insisting on some ideal relationship where Jervais trusted her implicitly, when her heart was breaking? What had she to look forward to, but years of loneliness with the occasional cold coupling when dynastic considerations demanded it? Perhaps she would find comfort in her children, but they seemed very remote now.

The clock struck midnight and she reached a decision. Testing his trust no longer seemed of any importance:

she needed Jervais. If he knew her presence on the battlefield and those indecent and compromising clothes had all been an innocent accident of fate, then at least he could trust her and might show her affection. She would have to settle for that.

The connecting door between her room and his dressing-room was locked, and had been since their wedding night. Caroline did not even trouble to try it. She pulled on her thin wrapper and emerged gingerly into the corridor outside her room. To reach Jervais's door she had to creep along one passage and round a corner and she had no intention of being discovered. The house was very silent; all she could hear was the blood pounding in her ears as she tiptoed over the boards and eased open his door.

The room was empty, lit only by a branch of candles on the dresser. Jervais had been there: his jacket and neckcloth lay discarded. Puzzled, Caroline looked round the room and saw a splash of red cast across the bed.

Her hand flew to her throat. Blood! Then she realised it was not blood, but vivid cloth. The carmine dress she had last seen in Belgium lay on the covers, startling, incongruous in this masculine room. As if drawn to it, Caroline crossed the room and picked it up, feeling the flimsy silk, remembering how it felt to wear it, remembering Jervais's face as he looked at her dressed in it.

A latch clicked and she looked up, unconsciously holding the dress to her bosom, as Jervais walked in from his dressing-room.

'You kept it,' she whispered.

'Of course. It was all I had of you,' he replied as directly. 'When you ran away in Brussels, I had to have something to remind me of you.'

'But why did it matter?' But, looking into his face,

she thought she knew—if only she dared believe it. 'You thought I was a. . .'

'I was a fool. I am a fool.' He walked slowly across the room towards her. 'I told myself I was right to marry you because I had compromised you. But then I realised how you felt, and that it would be wrong to ask for more when you did not love me. But I don't care. I love you, Caroline, and I will make you love me if you will only give me the chance.'

Caroline was struck speechless, her throat tight with tears of happiness. Jervais took her by the shoulders, looking down into her face with eyes dark with passion and tenderness. 'I know you do not love me, Caroline, but I also know you are not indifferent to me. Trust me, let me show you how much I love you, my darling. . .'

The kiss he claimed was dizzying in its intensity. For a moment, Caroline was so stunned by all that she had seen in his face she did not respond, then she was kissing him in return with equal passion, her arms twining round his body, seeking to lose herself, melt into him.

He released her, gazing down in disbelief. 'Caroline, do you. . .?'

'Yes, I love you, Jervais! I loved you from the beginning, even when I did not know who I was, I loved you. But I thought you did not trust me, and I did not think there was any future for us if you could not trust me.'

He kissed her again, then asked, 'Then what are you doing here?'

'I could not bear it any longer. I had to tell you I loved you, tell you what had happened. Even if I would never know if you trusted me, at least I knew I was keeping no secrets from you. But where were you?'

'On the same errand. I had to tell you that I did not care why you were on the battlefield wearing this—' he touched the dress '—that I loved you, and we had to make a fresh start together.'

At that moment the door opened without a knock and Fanny marched in, followed by a protesting Major Routh.

'Damn it all, Fanny, you can't walk into a man's bedchamber in the middle of the night!' He caught sight of Caroline and stopped dead, his face crimson with embarrassment. 'Oh, my God! My apologies, ma'am! Fan, get out of there!'

'No, I will not, not until I've said my piece! Now look here, my lord, I know you're a gentleman and I'm just a working girl, but I'm an honest girl and I stand by my friends. And I won't see you make Caroline unhappy, just because of some silly accident!' She wagged a warning finger at Jervais. 'Now don't you go interrupting me now!'

He leaned back against the bedpost, one arm still round Caroline. 'I would not dream of it, my dear lady,' he said solemnly.

'Good! She was looking for her brother after the battle and she took a tumble off her horse and banged her head. We—the girls and I in our wagon—we picked her up and lent her a dress 'cause hers was all muddy. Well, we couldn't leave her there, could we, with those nasty Frenchies about? We shouldn't have painted her face like that, but it passed the time and she looked so pale. Then we all fell asleep and she must have tumbled out when the wagon went over a bump. That's when she hit her head again and you found her. And all I can say is, if you think the worse of such a nice young lady just because of a bit of face paint and a skirt—well, you're not fit to be her husband!'

Fanny, having run out of breath and indignation, came to a full stop. Simon Routh had dropped into a chair, his head in his hands and was moaning gently.

Caroline crossed to the girl and gave her a big hug. 'It is all right, Fanny. He does trust me, and he loves me and everything is going to be wonderful. But it was so brave of you to come to my rescue. Thank you.'

'You sure?' Fanny shot Jervais a dubious glance.

'She can be quite sure, miss. . .?' Jervais was holding out his hand.

'Masterman,' said Fanny stoutly, taking it. 'Well, you look after her—she deserves it. Come along, Simon.'

Jervais's straight face lasted until a spluttering Major Routh was bundled firmly out by Fanny. Then he turned the key in the lock and gave a great shout of laughter.

Caroline found herself caught up in his arms and whirled round. Jervais deposited her on the bed, caught her against his chest and bent to kiss her.

'Oh, Jervais, I am so sorry! Poor Major Routh! But was Fanny not magnificent? We must do something for her. . .a little shop, perhaps?'

'Not now, Caroline.' Jervais slowly, and with infinite promise, began to trail kisses down her throat, and across the swell of her breast. He tugged gently at the ties of her nightgown and Caroline caught her breath in a little gasp of anticipation. 'We have more important things to do tonight. I have waited quite long enough to show you that you are indeed my much loved wife.'

'And you are my much loved husband,' she murmured as she drew his head down to her breast again.

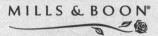

MILLS & BOON®

*M*akes
any time
special

Copyright © Harlequin Enterprises Limited 1997
All rights reserved

Enjoy a romantic novel from
Mills & Boon®

Presents...™   *Enchanted*™   TEMPTATION.

Historical Romance™   **MEDICAL**
ROMANCE™

THE

Regency

COLLECTION

Where rogues find romance

Look out for the eighth volume in this limited collection of Regency Romances from Mills & Boon® in December.

Featuring:

Fair Juno
by Stephanie Laurens

and

Serafina
by Sylvia Andrew

Still only £4.99

MILLS & BOON®

Makes any time special™

Available at most branches of WH Smith, Tesco, Martins, Borders, Easons, Volume One / James Thin and most good paperback bookshops

MILLS & BOON®

Historical Romance™

MISFIT MAID
by Elizabeth Bailey
A Regency delight!

Lady Mary Hope refused to be pushed into marriage
with a man she disliked. So she presented herself to
Laurie, Viscount Delagarde, and asked him to sponsor
her for a Season! Laurie was flabbergasted—he was the
least suitable person for such a task!

JACK CHILTERN'S WIFE
by Mary Nichols
A Regency delight!

Kitty Harston runs away to find her brother in France, and
Jack, Viscount Chiltern, can't leave her to fend for herself.
They pretend to be husband and wife, but to avoid scandal,
they ***must*** marry…for real.

On sale from 5th November 1999

*Available at most branches of WH Smith, Tesco,
Martins, Borders, Easons, Volume One/James Thin
and most good paperback bookshops*

MILLS & BOON®

Historical Romance™

THE MASTER OF MOOR HOUSE
by Anne Ashley

The dawn of a new century…

For Megan Drew, the arrival of 1800 brought back
Christian Blackmore into her life. Both of them had
changed immeasurably, but if Megan were truthful, *one*
thing had never changed—her feelings for the man she
loved beyond words.

THE QUIET MAN
by Paula Marshall

The dawn of a new century…

For Allen Marriott, 1899 was proving to be a tumultuous
time. Not wishing to reveal his connection to his employer,
Gerard Schuyler, he was forced to involve Trish Courtney
in his secret, heightening the thrill of their illicit meetings…

On sale from 3rd December 1999

*Available at most branches of WH Smith, Tesco,
Martins, Borders, Easons, Volume One/James Thin
and most good paperback bookshops*